WHAT THE HEART
REMEMBERS
MOST

Praise for M. Ullrich

Pretending in Paradise

"*Pretending in Paradise* has real depth while still maintaining the lightness and sexiness of a true romance novel and it is this unique mix that really makes M. Ullrich's books the ones to look out for when you're on the search for the next steamy romance read."—*Curve*

Against All Odds

"*Against All Odds* by Kris Bryant, Maggie Cummings, and M. Ullrich is an emotional and captivating story about being able to face a tragedy head-on and move on with your life, learning to appreciate the simple things we take for granted and finding love where you least expect it."—*The Lesbian Review*

"I started reading the book trying to dissect the writing and ended up forgetting all about the fact that three people were involved in writing it because the story just grabbed me by the ears and dragged me along for the ride…[A] really great romantic suspense that manages both parts of the equation perfectly. This is a book you won't be able to put down."
—*C-Spot Reviews*

Love at Last Call

Love at Last Call is "a very well written slow-burn romance. Another great book by M. Ullrich."—*LezReviewBooks*

"[I]f you enjoy opposites attract romances—especially ones set in bars—you'll love this book! I'll definitely be looking up the rest of the author's work!"—*Llama Reads Books*

Love at Last Call is "exciting, addictive (I was up all night reading it) and still gave me all the major swoon moments

I've come to love from this author. Can I give it more than five stars?"—*Les Rêveur*

"This book was like a well-crafted cocktail—not too sweet, not too bitter, and left me with a warm feeling in my body."—*Love in Panels*

"*Love at Last Call* is M. Ullrich's fifth full-length novel and it's truly excellent. The writing is smooth and engaging, with perfect pacing and a plot that's sure to please fans of contemporary romance. If you're looking for a book to sink into, have some fun, and get away from it all, you'll want to pick this one up."—*Lambda Literary*

Against All Odds

"*Against All Odds* by Kris Bryant, Maggie Cummings, and M. Ullrich is an emotional and captivating story about being able to face a tragedy head-on and move on with your life, learning to appreciate the simple things we take for granted and finding love where you least expect it."—*The Lesbian Review*

Time Will Tell

"I adored the romance in this. I got emotional at times and felt like they fit together very well. They really brought out the best in each other and they had a lot of chemistry. I really did care whether or not they were together in the end…It was a very enjoyable read and definitely one I'd recommend."—*Cats and Paperbacks*

"M. Ullrich just keeps knocking them out of the park and I think she's currently the one to watch in lesbian romantic fiction."—*Les Rêveur*

"*Time Will Tell* is not your run of the mill romance. I found it dark, intense, unexpected. It is also beautifully romantic and sexy and tells of a love that is for all time. I really enjoyed it."—*Kitty Kat's Book Review Blog*

Fake It till You Make It

"M. Ullrich's books have a uniqueness that we don't always see in this particular genre. Her stories go a bit outside the box and they do it in the best possible way. *Fake It till You Make It* is no exception."—*The Romantic Reader Blog*

"M. Ullrich's *Fake It till You Make It* just clarifies why she is one of my favorite authors. The storyline was tight, the characters brought emotion and made me feel like I was living the story with them, and best of all, I had fun reading every word."—*Les Rêveur*

Life in Death

"M. Ullrich sent me on a emotional roller coaster…But most of all I felt absolute joy knowing that in times of darkness you can still love the one you're meant to be with. It was a story of hope, tragedy, and above all, love."—*Les Rêveur*

Life in Death "is a well written book, the characters have depth and are complex, they become friends and you cannot help but hope that Marty and Suzanne can find a way back to each other. There aren't many books that I know from one read that I will want to read time and time again, but this is one of them."—*Sapphic Reviews*

Fortunate Sum

"M. Ullrich has written one book. That one book is *Fortunate Sum*. For this to be Ullrich's first book, well, that is just stunning. Stunning in the fact that this book is so very good, it was a fantastic read."—*The Romantic Reader Blog*

By the Author

Fortunate Sum

Life in Death

Fake It till You Make It

Time Will Tell

Love at Last Call

Pretending in Paradise

Top of Her Game

What the Heart Remembers Most

Against All Odds
(with Kris Bryant and Maggie Cummings)

The Boss of Her: Office Romance Novellas
(with Julie Cannon and Aurora Rey)

Visit us at www.boldstrokesbooks.com

WHAT THE HEART REMEMBERS MOST

by

M. Ullrich

2020

WHAT THE HEART REMEMBERS MOST

ISBN 13: 978-1-63555-401-4

THIS TRADE PAPERBACK ORIGINAL IS PUBLISHED BY
BOLD STROKES BOOKS, INC.
P.O. BOX 249
VALLEY FALLS, NY 12185

FIRST EDITION: APRIL 2020

CREDITS
EDITORS: JERRY L. WHEELER AND RUTH STERNGLANTZ
PRODUCTION DESIGN: STACIA SEAMAN
COVER DESIGN BY JEANINE HENNING

Acknowledgments

This book…

If you were one of the few I leaned on during the process of developing and writing this book, I am forever grateful. From concept to final product, this was a long and bumpy road. But I am proud of the story that came from such a challenge, and I think the journey is fitting for this book. Life is unexpected and beautiful and hard sometimes, but love is what keeps us going. Love is what makes this world a beautiful place. Love is the reason why.

I'm thankful for my supportive family at Bold Strokes Books, from Radclyffe to Sandy, my editor, Jerry, and everyone else who helps me along the way. You're all seen and appreciated more than I can say on this page.

I love my homeslices: Maggie, Kris, Erin, Aurora, and every single sprint participant who cheered me on when I needed it most. Heather, your support has held me up more than you know, and I appreciate how you were on board even when I wanted to kill every character… especially that one…the eulogy would've been so good.

To Heather,
My heart's favorite memory

CHAPTER ONE

2 hours, 9 minutes, 52 seconds

Jax hated being a light sleeper. Anything could wake her up, from a loud cricket to the incessant buzzing of a phone. She turned over and burrowed into the warm body beside her. Soft naked skin was the kind of wake-up call she wouldn't get mad about. The buzzing started again, and Jax flopped on her back with a huff. She grabbed her phone from the nightstand and looked at the screen with one eye open. An unknown number. She checked the time and knew no good phone calls came after eleven at night. Her heart hammered in her throat.

"Hello?"

"Is this Jacqueline Levine?"

"Jax…yes, this is she. Who is this?" Jax sat up and wiped the sleep from her eyes.

"I'm Dr. Hudgens from South Shore Community Medical Center."

Jax's mind kicked into overdrive, trying to fill in every blank before the doctor even continued. Her panic made it hard for her to concentrate on his next words.

"You're listed as the emergency contact for Gretchen Mills. She was in an accident earlier this evening—"

She stood and started getting dressed. "What kind of accident?"

"It appears she fell down some icy steps and suffered a severe head injury."

"Where is she? Is she…" Jax couldn't finish the sentence.

"She's being airlifted to the trauma center at Jersey Shore Medical. They're the best equipped for this kind of head injury. They should land in thirteen minutes."

"Thank you." Jax hung up and tossed her phone on the bed. She grabbed her sneakers and socks and pulled them on.

"What's going on?"

Jax froze. She had completely forgotten about Meredith. "Gretchen's in the hospital. I have to go."

Meredith sat up. Her blond hair was tousled and her face heavy with concern. She held the sheets around her bare chest. "What happened?"

"She fell or something. Listen, you can stay if you want. Just lock the door in the morning when you leave."

"I can come with you."

"No." She took a deep breath, knowing she was being a little harsh. But this was no place for Meredith. "I appreciate it, though." Jax put on her thickest sweater and grabbed her leather jacket from the back of her bedroom door. She crawled across her king-sized bed and gave Meredith a quick kiss. "I'll talk to you later." She grabbed her phone from the bed and started out.

"I'm surprised she still has you as her emergency contact." Meredith's simple words stopped her in the doorway.

Jax thought of the past few years and everything she and Gretchen had been through. Every fight and hurtful word. "So am I," she said, turning back to Meredith one last time. "I guess she missed that when she filed for divorce." Jax felt the familiar flare of anger in her chest. On her way out the door, she dialed Amanda. Ever vigilant, Amanda picked up on the first ring.

"Jax? What the hell?" Amanda's voice was deep and froggy, but mostly filled with confusion.

"Gretchen fell and is being airlifted to Jersey Shore. I'm heading there now." Jax climbed into her pickup and started the ignition. She blasted the heat, trying her best to cut the January chill from the space around her. But her shivering had very little to do with the brutal winter.

"Is she okay?" Amanda's voice was muffled by a shuffling sound. "I mean, obviously she's not okay but...is she okay?"

"All I know is she suffered a head injury. They didn't give me any more details."

"Well, did you think to ask any questions?"

"No, I didn't." Jax tightened her grip on the steering wheel and pulled out onto the highway. She tried her best to drive calmly, knowing the phone was already enough of a distraction. "I was more concerned with getting to the hospital."

"I should be there."

"Will you just stay with Caleb?" Just mentioning her four-year-old's name hit her with a fresh wave of panic. What would happen if Gretchen...? "I'll talk to the doctors when I get there and get all the information. I don't want to scare him."

Amanda stayed silent for a minute. "Fine. But I swear to God, Jax, if anything happens to my sister, and I'm not there because you don't keep me in the loop—"

"I will. I promise."

"Fine." Amanda disconnected the call.

Jax spent the remainder of the twenty-five-minute drive stewing in silence. She imagined every horrific outcome. She pictured their son standing at his mother's grave, not understanding what was happening. Christmases without Gretchen, Caleb's fifth birthday, his high school graduation...

A car horn blared, and Jax jumped in her seat. She had been sitting at a green light for who knew how long. She accelerated quickly, screeching her tires. She hit the next three red lights, and she started to think about karma by the fourth. A potent mixture of relief and fear hit just as she pulled into the hospital parking lot. She took the first spot she could find, not caring about fines or towing.

Jax ran to the front door of the Emergency Room and argued with the automatic revolving door. It wasn't moving fast enough. She squeezed her body through the small opening as soon as she could and stumbled to the front desk.

"I'm looking for Gretchen Mills? She was airlifted from..." She racked her brain. "South Shore! She should be here." The desk clerk started typing. Jax watched through the double doors as doctors rushed about. Very few people occupied the waiting room, and she didn't understand why she was still waiting. "Where is she?"

"I need a photo ID for all visitors."

Jax wanted to scream at the miserable old man. "Is she here?"

"Proper identification, name, and relation, please."

Jax breathed in deeply through her nose. She forced herself to understand this idiotic man was just doing his job. She pulled her wallet from her pocket and took out her driver's license. She dropped it on the counter in front of him. "Jax Levine. I'm her wife."

He looked at her over his reading glasses. Without another word, he copied her license and printed out a visitor's pass. "She's back with the doctors now. Have a seat in the waiting room. Hang on to that pass. It's only good for twenty-four hours."

She sat in the nearest chair, bouncing her leg to release some of her anxious energy. She had to believe she wasn't allowed to see Gretchen for a good reason. She had seen enough medical dramas to know the trauma center was no place for a visitor. She looked around at her company.

A young woman sat against the far wall and thumbed through a *People* magazine. Her face was passive, not concerned or panicked. Down at the far end of Jax's row of chairs was an older gentleman twiddling his thumbs. Seated directly across from Jax was a woman who couldn't be much older than her. She looked more worried than the rest combined. She held a child against her. Jax assumed they were mother and daughter.

Again, Jax thought of Caleb. She didn't know whether bringing him to the hospital would do more harm than good. Maybe she should ask her partner in suffering. Were they there for the kid's other parent or for themselves? Jax scanned each face again, and the discomfort of being in a hospital started to fully set in. She stood and started to pace. Jax wanted to leave the waiting area, but she was afraid to go too far. She turned at the sound of the double doors opening. She stared at the young doctor expectantly.

"For Evan Riley?"

Jax sighed in disappointment. She dropped her tense shoulders and continued pacing. The woman and child stood and followed the young doctor through the doors.

"For Gretchen Mills?"

Jax spun around so quickly she felt dizzy. She raised her hand and walked directly to the doctor. "I'm her wife," Jax said right away, wanting to avoid any legality dance. "How is she?"

The doctor looked at the chart in her hands. She flipped the papers. "Jacqueline Levine?"

"Jax, please."

"I see Dr. Hudgens contacted you. I'm Dr. Melendez, the chief of neurology here." She reached out to shake Jax's hand.

Jax shook Dr. Melendez's hand and said, "How is she?"

"Gretchen is mostly stable."

Jax's stomach dropped. "What do you mean *mostly?*"

"She's going through a few tests and scans right now. She'll be put in a room right after. I'll catch you up on everything while I take you there." Dr. Melendez scanned her ID to open the double doors.

Jax dodged a nurse as she followed Dr. Melendez. "Did they tell you exactly what happened?"

"It looks like she fell down some icy steps at her office building. She had mild hypothermia when EMS got to her, so she could've been lying there for over an hour. Does your wife make it a habit of working late and alone?" Dr. Melendez pressed the elevator button, and the door opened.

Jax stepped on, thinking of the many, many fights she'd had with Gretchen. "She does."

"She hasn't regained consciousness, and from the physical signs of her injury I'm not surprised. She lost a lot of blood. We had to stitch up a significant laceration on the back of her head and clean out some scrapes on her face. She has a few bruised ribs, and her shoulder was dislocated."

"Jesus." Jax fought against a wave of nausea.

They stepped off the elevator together, and Dr. Melendez directed Jax to a wing of private rooms. She put her arm out, letting Jax enter the room first.

Jax looked at the room number: 815. She let out a sad laugh at the irony. Their wedding anniversary was August fifteenth. "How long before she's settled?"

"About an hour. I'd recommend taking that time to get anything you need to get settled because once she's back in this room, all we can do is wait."

"Dr. Melendez," she said earnestly, stopping the doctor from leaving. She tried to read her face but couldn't. "What's her prognosis?"

"It's hard to say."

"Just give me an idea. No promises. I understand that."

Dr. Melendez stared at the paperwork in her hands for a moment before dropping her hands to her sides and looking at Jax with sympathetic eyes. "I can't know anything without the results of her head CT, but I've seen injuries like this before, and the human body is capable of a lot of things. However, if I were you, I'd call her family and ask for all the prayers you can get."

Jax fell into one of three chairs in the room, unable to form words. She nodded to Dr. Melendez, who left her alone. The sounds of chatter from the hallway faded, a singular feeling of fear engulfing Jax. She stared straight ahead at the empty hospital bed. The sheets were a crisp, pristine white. She needed to call Amanda, but she couldn't move.

She barely blinked as a series of memories shuffled through her mind, the final one being the day she left with two suitcases and a duffel bag. Gretchen's eyes were red from crying, and Caleb sat in the living room playing on his mother's phone. Seventeen years together weren't supposed to end like that.

She pulled her phone from her pocket and dialed Amanda's number, listening to it ring. Amanda picked up and asked what the doctors said.

Jax couldn't look away from the bed. She was scared of seeing Gretchen, battered and bruised and unconscious.

"Jax?"

Jax's chin started to quiver. She bit her lip and clenched her jaw against the swell of hysterics and tears. She cleared her throat and tried her best to regain her composure. "You're going to want to come here. As soon as possible. And bring Caleb."

She ended the phone call before Amanda could ask any questions. A sob escaped her, and the steady walls of strength she had put in place over the years fell away one by one. Jax dropped her phone to the ground and cried into her hands.

Seventeen years together weren't supposed to end like this.

CHAPTER TWO

13 hours, 23 minutes, 42 seconds

"After relieving the pressure in her skull, her vitals stabilized. We're keeping her in a medically induced coma for now," a resident said. Jax didn't get his name during introductions because she was busy keeping an eye on her antsy son. "This will give her brain time to heal without the worry of added injury."

Amanda crossed her arms. "I thought the idea was to get her to wake up."

Jax held Caleb by his shoulders to keep him from going to play in the bathroom. Again. "I'm with Amanda. How will we know if Gretchen will wake up if we don't let her?"

The young doctor looked nervous. "This is the best chance we have of getting the swelling down. This actually increases her chances of waking up."

Jax was skeptical to say the least. "I guess we just have to trust you."

"Trust Dr. Melendez. She's the best."

"Then why haven't we seen her all day?" Amanda said firmly.

"Thank you, Doctor," Jax said. She wanted to laugh as he practically ran from the room, but she couldn't find much humor with the hiss of Gretchen's ventilator in the background.

Caleb slapped Jax's hand. "Is Mommy better?"

Jax looked at Amanda before she dared to meet Caleb's large, curious eyes. He resembled Gretchen so much it was scary. "Not yet, Cricket."

"What did your boss say when you called him this morning?" Amanda said.

"He didn't really care. He told me to take whatever time I needed as long as I didn't slack on my accounts." She pulled a coloring book out of the bag Amanda was smart enough to pack and opened it to a blank picture. "I kind of want him to fire me. I'd be able to collect unemployment until I find a job I don't hate. Like these," she said, holding up the coloring book. She smiled at Caleb. "Would you like it if Bug made coloring books?"

Caleb's eyes lit up, and he nodded enthusiastically.

Amanda sat in the chair right next to Gretchen's bed. She held her hand delicately. "You can't go from graphic designer to coloring book designer."

"Bug can do anything," Caleb said as he climbed on Jax.

She smiled at Caleb. If it wasn't for him, she'd be a complete wreck by now. Any strength Jax had was coming from the squirming boy on her lap. "Yeah, Aunt Amanda, I can do anything."

Amanda opened her mouth, but a knock at the door stopped the conversation. She placed Gretchen's hand back on the bed and opened the door. It was Jax's best friend, Wyatt, holding a comically large bouquet of flowers. He looked completely harried and greeted Amanda with a worried smile.

"I'm so sorry I couldn't get here sooner." He handed the flowers to Amanda and rushed over to Jax. "Hey, buddy," he said to Caleb. Wyatt extended his hand and went through a lengthy series of high fives with Caleb.

Jax set Caleb down and stood up to greet Wyatt. Facing Amanda was tough, but looking at Wyatt? Jax felt her defenses start to crumble. She wrapped her arms around him and didn't let go until she had to. Jax took a deep breath to push down her rising tears and stepped back.

"Thank you so much for coming."

"Carly wanted to come, but she's having a tough third trimester. Swelling, pain, poor balance—the whole nine yards." Wyatt scratched his beard and approached the hospital bed. He removed the knit beanie from his buzzed head and held it to his flannel-clad chest. When he turned back to Jax, his eyes were misty. "What the hell happened?"

Jax looked at Caleb, who had started coloring again. "Amanda, would you mind if we ran downstairs for coffee? I'll be gone for no more than twenty minutes."

Amanda waved her off. "Do a few laps. I'll go for a walk once you're back."

"Text me if anything changes. Hey, bud?" Jax waited for Caleb to look at her. "Are you hungry? Do you want a cookie and some milk?"

"Yes!"

"It's not even ten in the morning."

She shot Amanda a look. "Be good for your aunt, and I'll bring you one."

She walked next to Wyatt through the hospital. They stood together in the elevator and Jax stared at the digital display, not knowing where to start. "Icy steps."

"What?"

"Icy steps," she said again, looking at him this time. "From what they can tell, she slipped on some ice and fell down the stairs at her office." The doors opened, and they stepped out into the bustling main floor of the hospital. Jax followed the signs to the café, not yet sure of the hospital's layout. She paused at the café's doorway. The line for coffee was twenty deep.

Wyatt put his hand on her shoulder. "That's fucking crazy. Just another reason to hate winter. I can't wait to move to Florida."

"You're not going anywhere!" Jax started to panic. "You have to stay here and help me because—"

"Stop," Wyatt said, placing his other hand on Jax's shoulder. "I know where your mind is heading right now, and you need to stop." He shook Jax until she looked up. "You know I'm not going anywhere, and you know I say weird shit when I'm nervous."

Jax took a deep breath. "I know."

Wyatt ruffled her hair. "Let's get some coffee, and we'll talk this through."

They fought the line of patrons and snagged two cups of fresh coffee before the carafe ran out. Jax sat on a small ledge by the hospital's large windows instead of at one of the small café tables. She needed to look out at the sunny day, even if every tree on the property looked dead.

"They can't tell you anything else?"

Jax stirred her coffee and watched the tiny whirlpool and spinning bubbles. "No. I expected...I don't know what I expected. It's been less than twelve hours—you'd think they'd still be *doing* something."

"I guess not doing something is technically doing something."

Jax placed the lid back on her coffee and took a sip. She didn't want coffee. She didn't want anything. She wanted Gretchen to wake up. "They did at least a hundred scans and emergency surgery to relieve the pressure by drilling into her skull." Wyatt puffed out his cheeks and blew. Jax could tell she was making him queasy. "And then I'm sitting there bickering with Amanda like nothing's wrong. Like her sister isn't lying lifeless…"

"Hey, everyone copes differently. You do what you have to do to keep your head on straight."

"To keep myself from thinking about being a single mother."

"That's not going to happen."

"I appreciate your positivity, but did you see Gretchen? A machine is breathing for her. She's black and blue and has a hole in her skull."

"She's a fighter."

Jax looked at Wyatt. Her heart tried hard to be hopeful, but her brain whirred with statistics and worst-case scenarios. "I don't know if this is a fight she can win."

Wyatt nodded sullenly. He looked out the window and squinted at the bright light that illuminated his brown eyes. "Remember when we were sophomores and Gretchen broke her left hand? She had so many finals and projects lined up, and her dominant hand was out of commission. She had to teach herself how to function all over again."

Jax started to smile. "Our sex life got wild."

Wyatt held up his hand. "I'll take your word for it."

"Oh yeah." Jax wiggled her eyebrows for good measure.

"The point I'm trying to make is Gretchen knows how to adapt and tackle challenges. She knows how to fight and win. She aced every single final with zero help."

Jax scrunched her face up. "I helped." Her shoulders fell when Wyatt looked at her incredulously. "Well, I refilled the paper in the printer a million times."

"I know things haven't been great."

"Filing for divorce is a little beyond not great. Just yesterday morning we fought over whether Caleb should bring carrots or apples to preschool. I accused her of not caring about him the way she cares about her clients. Over snacks!" Shame overwhelmed and choked her. "That was the last thing I said to her."

"It'll be okay."

"I shouldn't even be here. We're barely in each other's lives, and we wouldn't be at all if it wasn't for Caleb."

"You're here because she's still the woman you've loved since your freshman year of college. It's been, what? Sixteen years?"

"Seventeen." Jax looked at the shiny floor in thought. "Fourteen were happy, but the last three have felt like walking through the darkest valleys of hell."

Wyatt chuckled. "It couldn't have been all that bad."

"It was."

Wyatt looked at her like he was seeing her for the first time. "How did I not know?"

"I didn't want to burden you. You and Carly are in such a good place. I didn't want to scare you away from the altar with my marriage woes."

"What happened?"

She blew out a long breath and looked around at the strange faces passing her. Where should she start? "We fought a lot and never really healed after—" She stopped herself from saying more and pressed her fingertips to the glass. "The worst part was how she was never around to even try. Her work came first. Always. I hated seeing Caleb come in second, and I couldn't handle being in third place. I didn't even want to talk to her when she eventually came home."

"I'm so sorry, bud." Wyatt placed his hand on Jax's shoulder.

Jax waved off his caring expression and the tears that traveled down her cheeks. "Enough about me and my soon-to-be ex-wife who may or may not live to sign the divorce papers." Jax felt detached from reality as she laid her situation out in one sentence. "How's Carly feeling?"

Wyatt shifted, clearly skeptical of the sudden mood and subject change. "She's ready to not be pregnant anymore, but we still have about five weeks to go."

"I'm really excited for you two." Jax really was, but she could barely muster up a smile. "Speaking of kids, I should probably get mine that cookie I promised." Jax started to get up, but Wyatt stopped her.

"I hope we're good parents."

Jax let out a small, sad laugh. The idea that Wyatt wouldn't be a good father was ludicrous. "You will be."

"I see how you are with Caleb, how Gretchen was—is." He cleared his throat. "I want to be *that* good."

Jax finally stood. She took Wyatt's empty coffee cup and tossed it out along with her full cup. She patted his shoulder. "You got this."

They walked through the small café one last time to grab Caleb's snack and started back toward Gretchen's room. Just outside the door, Jax paused and looked at Wyatt.

"Don't put your kid down. Let them dream as big as they want and teach them everything you wish someone would've taught you as a kid. Remember those things, and you'll be great."

"What are you teaching Caleb that you wish someone had taught you?"

Jax looked at Caleb, who was flipping through a coloring book with Amanda and making her laugh. He was clearly being a goofball. She thought of the homes she was bounced between as a foster kid and the happiness she felt once someone finally believed she was worth keeping around. Jax turned to Wyatt and his big, curious eyes. "I'm teaching him to be himself."

Chapter Three

8 days, 2 hours, 9 minutes

The hospital room was full of Gatorade and apple juice, but not one bottle of water. Jax dropped the shopping bag on the nearest chair and huffed. Amanda was supposed to stop by to relieve her, but she was running behind. They'd agreed to switch on and off for mornings and evenings, managing some semblance of normalcy and routine. Not that watching Gretchen's freakishly still eyelids would ever feel normal.

"Good morning, Jax," Dr. Melendez said too cheerfully as she entered the room. "I know a resident was in earlier to take vitals, but I wanted to check in on you to see if you have any questions or concerns." She rubbed her hands together after dispensing a small bit of hand sanitizer into her palm.

Jax was momentarily surprised into silence. She hadn't seen Dr. Melendez more than three or four times since Gretchen's accident over a week ago. "I don't really have anything." She tried to rack her brain for anything Amanda would ask. She was always better in these situations. She was known for her million-questions mind. "Nothing's changed."

"That's not entirely true. Gretchen is stable, which is good news. Her latest scans do show some healing, but it's just not progressing as quickly as we'd like. We'll continue to keep an eye on her vitals and her brain. We won't keep her like this any longer than necessary."

"And then what?"

"Then we stop the medication and wait for her to wake up."

"Do you think she will?" Jax said earnestly.

Dr. Melendez had very kind dark eyes. They brimmed with sympathy as she looked at Jax. "I can't say for sure, but we're doing everything we can."

"What about us? What can we do?"

Dr. Melendez smiled. "Just keep showing up. Talk to her, make sure your son does, too. Surround her with all the reasons why she needs to wake up. There's no medical proof, but I believe human connection can be the biggest key to surviving. Some patients read to their loved ones, while others talk about their day like they were sitting at the dinner table. Find what works for you."

Jax nodded, not fully believing a conversation could save Gretchen's life, but she didn't want to be rude and blow off the advice. "Okay, I think we can do that. I can bring Caleb back after he gets out of preschool. Lord knows he always has plenty to say then." She forced a smile Dr. Melendez quickly mirrored.

"Very good. I'll be back in tomorrow if there are no sudden changes."

Jax watched her leave and stood in the center of the quiet room. She checked the time and sat beside Gretchen's bed. After a deep breath, she looked at Gretchen's profile. She took in Gretchen's long eyelashes and healing bruises. Jax checked the doorway quickly to make sure no one was watching her.

"It's Thursday," she said. "Today was Caleb's first day back to school. I wanted to keep him home another day, but he insisted. I've never met a kid who loves school as much as he does. He must get that from you." Jax let out an airy laugh. Gretchen's ventilator hissed back. "This is stupid. What good will this do? Hearing my voice is probably the last thing you want or need. You didn't want to hear it when we were together—why would you want to hear it now?"

"Sorry I'm late."

Jax jumped up at Amanda's sudden intrusion. "You just missed Dr. Melendez."

"What did she say?" Amanda tossed her heavy down jacket on the foot of Gretchen's bed, treating the room like her home. "Anything new?"

"No," Jax said, her tone heavy with disappointment. "She did recommend something crazy."

"What's that?"

"She said we should talk to her, to Gretchen, because hearing us could be the push she needs to pull through." Jax analyzed the way Amanda looked at Gretchen with the softest, most hopeful gaze. "I know it sounds ridiculous—"

"I talk to her every minute I'm alone with her."

"You do?"

"You don't?"

Jax shook her head. "I just didn't think of it."

Amanda rolled her eyes and went about setting up for the day. She always brought a knitted blanket, an e-reader, and her own tea bags. "I read to her when I run out of things to talk about. One time I even read the ingredients off a pack of crackers. I want her to know I'm here."

"Maybe I don't want her to know I'm here," Jax said quietly, more to herself than to Amanda. "She won't wake up then."

"Oh, cut the pity-party bullshit."

Jax looked at Amanda in shock. "What?"

"This isn't about you, Jax. I know you believe everything is, but not this. This is about Gretchen and Caleb. Not you."

"I do not—"

Amanda raised her hand. "Don't even. Since day one, you've made sure your relationship was about you. Gretchen gets a new job, you talk about how it affects you. When she was pregnant, you talked about her symptoms like they were your own. Now this? Step back and realize who this is really about. For once."

"Wow." Jax paced in front of the door. "Tell me how you really feel, Amanda. Was my selfishness what killed my marriage, too?"

"Gretchen wasn't a saint."

"You're goddamn right she wasn't." Jax looked at Gretchen's still body with guilt.

"But she's the one in a coma, and we need to figure this out together, with Caleb in mind."

"I haven't stopped thinking about Caleb since I got the call," she said vehemently. "I'm getting out of here. I'll bring Caleb by after dinner. Text me if you need anything." Jax grabbed her jacket and marched out the door. Her footsteps were heavy and angry. She didn't stop walking until she stepped out into the frigid fresh air. The sun was hidden behind thick gray clouds, and the winter felt like the longest in history.

Jax tugged her leather jacket around her body and walked against the wind. The parking garage was too far away. By the time she made it to her pickup truck, her hands were numb and her cheeks were on fire. She didn't even have music on in the car, a rarity for her.

She pulled into her designated spot and looked out the window at her apartment building. Her bones ached at the thought of another stroll in the biting wind. She prepared herself and dashed from the car. The heat in her apartment was welcome, first penetrating her bare skin and finally her clothing. She tossed her jacket on the couch and went to her bathroom. Toothpaste, shampoo, floss, and hair products were strewn about her small vanity. A damp towel sat in her sink.

Her entire routine had been thrown off since she was spending most of her days in the hospital. Jax felt her anxious energy building up and longed to exhaust it at the gym, but she knew she didn't have time for that. If it wasn't so cold, she could go for a quick run, but she wasn't going outside voluntarily.

Jax stripped away her layers and stood in her sports bra and boxer briefs. She stared at her reflection in the mirror on her rickety old medicine cabinet. Her eyes were dull and underlined by heavy bags. She opened the cabinet and started to put away the toiletries scattered about. Showering seemed like a daunting task, and Jax knew she was procrastinating with fake tidiness. She was so tired. Jax spun the toothpaste tube between her fingertips. She was thinking of herself and Amanda's unkind but not untrue words. Jax slammed the cabinet door shut with such force the mirror broke. Shards of glass fell on the counter and shattered.

"Great," Jax muttered, not at all fazed. "Let's add seven more years to my bad luck." She picked up pieces of glass and winced when one pierced her skin. "Son of a bitch!" She held her finger up and watched as the blood formed a trail down to her palm. She wrapped it loosely with toilet paper and finished cleaning up by brushing the debris into the trash. The blood between her fingers turned sticky. Jax got in the shower.

She couldn't remember when she had showered last. She let the hot water loosen her tense shoulders and neck, and she massaged her body wash into the fatigued muscles of her lower back. She slowly uncoiled and relaxed. When she stepped out of the shower, she felt a bit lighter, but in desperate need of a nap, regardless. She dried as she walked to her bedroom and grabbed some sweats. When she tossed her towel on the bed, she noticed a bloodstain on the cloth. She grimaced at the still-bleeding wound on her hand. She got dressed and walked back to the bathroom in search of a Band-Aid, growing frustrated after looking through every cabinet and drawer. She knew she had bandages somewhere.

She remembered seeing a box while packing up her things, and she suddenly remembered. She'd never unpacked the boxes from her art studio, and that's where a small first-aid kit was. She had too many accidents in the name of art.

The small second bedroom served as storage for Jax. She couldn't fit all her stuff into her apartment, and she figured it'd be safer to keep it packed. She started sorting through boxes, annoyed by the wad of toilet paper she had around her finger to stop the bleeding. Three boxes and a dozen curse words later, Jax finally found the first-aid kit as well as something she had forgotten all about, a beaten and worn shoebox she hadn't opened in years.

The kit fell to the floor with a loud clatter. She grabbed the box and took a deep breath before opening it. Nothing in Jax's life was as organized as this box. Every letter was perfectly folded and filed chronologically. She ran her fingertips over the letters, pulling out the first one in the box, the last letter Gretchen ever wrote her. The date was over four years ago, but Jax clearly remembered reading it for the first time.

> *Jax,*
>
> *I know we just spent the day celebrating our pregnancy with everyone we know, but I never want to stop celebrating this next step with you. I think about raising a kid, and it scares me so much, until I picture you with our child. You are extraordinary and when you love someone, you love them BIG. I'll admit I'm feeling a little selfish and jealous. I'm afraid all that big love will be spent on our little one, and you won't have any left for me. But then you hold me and touch me, then you look in my eyes. Me and this baby are so lucky to be loved by you, forever.*
>
> *With so much love,*
> *Gretchen*

Jax folded the paper once and then twice. She tucked it back into the envelope and put it right in its place in the shoebox. It had taken her a while, but she was able to see some of the positive, instead of constantly focusing on the failure of their marriage. They had many good years together, more than many people were blessed with. Every memory tucked away in the box was a good one, and there were dozens. An idea hit Jax. She grabbed a handful of letters, beginning to hope that maybe, just maybe, she would be able to play a part in Gretchen's recovery.

CHAPTER FOUR

11 days, 22 hours, 4 minutes

Jax's patience was starting to wane. A group of overtly judgmental occupational therapists from Gretchen's office stopped by to visit and treated Jax like a reject, and now Caleb just would not calm down. He was jumping on chairs, trying to climb on a tray table, and running back and forth from window to door and back again. Jax was about to lose it.

"Caleb," Jax said sternly, "I need you to sit down and calm down."

Caleb looked back at her and his lip started to quiver. "I'm sorry."

"He's probably tired of being cooped up in this room all the time." Amanda opened her arms and waited for Caleb to come running to her. Jax frowned. "If it was nice out, we could play outside."

"Well, it's not nice out, and none of us are happy about being cooped up." She shifted around in her chair. She was about twenty minutes away from asking a nurse to check her for bedsores. "I should just call Meredith to come get you."

Amanda visibly stiffened at the name. "Where he *should* be is with his mothers."

Jax pointed at herself and raised her eyebrows. "He's going to drive this mother crazy."

"I said sorry," Caleb said, his voice high with the start of a wailing cry.

Amanda released Caleb and stood. "I'll take him home with me."

Jax felt terrible. "You don't have to go. I'm sorry I'm in such a mood. Gretchen's friends from work really pissed me off."

"You barely know them—why let them bother you so much?"

She rolled the question around in her mind as Amanda pulled on her coat. "I don't know," she lied. She didn't know what they had been told about their breakup, and she hated knowing those men and women heard only Gretchen's side of the story. She couldn't bear being a villain in strangers' eyes—she wanted to be liked by everyone. Jax picked Caleb up and squeezed him. "I'm sorry for being so grumpy, Cricket. I love you."

"I love you too, Bug."

Jax buried her nose in Caleb's black hair. She smiled and cherished the smell of baby shampoo. "Be good for your aunt."

"He always is," Amanda said.

"I always am!"

"I know you are." Jax bundled Caleb up and kissed his forehead. "Say good-bye to Mama." She picked him up to sit on the edge of Gretchen's bed. The way he innocently looked at his broken mother made Jax's heart ache.

"Good night, Mama. See you tomorrow."

Jax fought back her tears and held him tightly as he reached to kiss Gretchen's forehead exactly the way Jax kissed his.

"With kisses like those, she'll get better in no time," she said with more confidence than she felt, needing to be a beacon of hope for their son. She shared a look of understanding with Amanda.

She said good-bye and sat next to Gretchen's bed. She had learned to tune out the chatter of people in the hallway and the sounds of machinery. The silence was overwhelming. "He really is a great kid, but damn, his energy wears me out." She chuckled hollowly. "I can't remember ever being that energetic." Jax swore she heard Gretchen's voice. "I know—that's because I'm old. But if I'm old, you must be ancient." She hadn't referenced their one-month age difference in such a long time. "Maybe this year for your birthday I'll get you a walker." Jax smacked her forehead the moment the snarky comment left her mouth. "I'm obviously not very good at this. Maybe I should just stick to a script."

Jax reached into the inside pocket of her jacket hanging on the chair. She pulled out a letter and unfolded it slowly. "Remember our first vacation together? We had no money but figured we could still have a good time in Wildwood. We weren't wrong, but it wasn't the best idea either." Jax smiled at the memory. "I got so sunburned and you got sick from a gas station hot dog. We didn't want to tell anyone how much of a disaster the trip was when we got home, but all of our friends were asking." She traced the feminine loops of Gretchen's handwriting and marveled at how it had never changed. Jax cleared her throat and began reading.

"*Thank you for the weekend away. Our trip was far from perfect, but every mishap led me to one conclusion: you are perfect.*" Jax paused and rubbed her sternum. She kept her hand over her heart. "*You took care of me even when you could barely move and that meant a lot to someone who has always depended on themselves. No one has ever taken care of me that way. If I didn't love you so damn much already, I'd certainly love you more now.*"

Jax reached out and carefully covered Gretchen's hand with hers. Even with their marriage coming to an end, she still felt the instinct to care for her. She placed the letter on her lap and rested her head back.

"It was easy caring for you," she said, no longer needing the letter. "Back then, before the baby and all the grossness that came along with him, I'd usually run for the hills if someone was sick around me, but all I wanted was for you to feel better. Maybe I was just being selfish and wanted to get you back in your bikini as soon as possible." She flashed Gretchen's motionless body a smile. She took out another letter and began reading before checking the date.

"*I love you,*" Jax nearly stumbled over the blunt and lovely opening. "*There's no reason for this letter other than needing you to know and needing it to be in print. I love you, Jacqueline Shay Levine. Even the act of writing the words fills my stomach with butterflies and makes my heart beat so fast.*" Jax clenched her jaw against a rush of anger and sorrow. She knew the butterflies would eventually die, but goddamn, why did their love have to die, too?

"This is stupid," Jax said, throwing the letter on Gretchen. "You need to wake up, do you hear me? I can't do this without you. Caleb needs you, and even though we're getting divorced, I need you, too." Jax realized the tight grip she had on Gretchen's hand and pulled back.

"Amanda definitely needs you." Jax drummed her fingers on the bedding, not really knowing what to do with her hands. "Your work seems to miss you a lot," she said begrudgingly. "And I bet, even as you lie there, you can't wait to get back to it." A soft knock at the door jarred her.

"I'm sorry if I scared you," a nurse said. He didn't look much older than Jax's own thirty-seven, but she was also terrible at guessing people's ages. "I'm just making my rounds." He looked at her meekly. "Visiting hours are just about over."

Jax checked the time on her phone and couldn't believe how late it had gotten. She also had three messages from Meredith. She looked from the nurse to Gretchen and back again.

"I'll give you a minute," he said kindly, stepping out in the hallway.

She shook her head. "I guess that's my cue to say good night." She stood, pulled on her jacket, and grabbed her messenger bag. But she couldn't leave. Not yet. She just had to do one more thing. Jax leaned over the bed and kissed Gretchen's forehead. She lingered, feeling her warmth and softness. She pulled back and said, "I'll see you tomorrow." She said good-bye to the nurse on her way out.

❖

Jax was surprised to see Meredith waiting in the lobby of her apartment building. Her cheery smile brightened Jax's spirits a bit, but she couldn't shake her gloom.

"Hey there," Meredith said as she approached her and kissed Jax on the cheek.

"Hey. What are you doing here?" They waited for the elevator.

"You weren't answering my messages, and I wanted to see if you were okay. I don't have to stay."

She took Meredith's hand, feeling bad. "No, I mean yes, stay."

When they got up to Jax's apartment, Meredith commented on the state of the place. Jax waved it off. "Do you want a beer or anything to drink?"

"Did you eat anything today?"

"I had a bagel and some chips at the hospital."

Meredith took the bottle from her hand and popped the cap off with an opener she must've grabbed when Jax wasn't looking. Meredith handed it back to her with a smirk. "Why don't you change into something comfortable, drink that, and I'll cook you something."

Jax was too tired from her emotional up and down to protest anything. "I'm not in the best mood."

"You think I've only seen you in your best moods?" Meredith took her shoulders and turned her toward the bedroom. "Go, change, drink." She swatted Jax's butt.

Jax smiled and started for the bedroom. She thought back to the letter and how she had taken care of Gretchen. Maybe she'd be able to let Meredith take care of her now.

"You have no food," Meredith called out from the kitchen.

She laughed against the mouth of her beer bottle. "Check the drawer next to the sink. All the takeout menus are in there."

Meredith popped her head into the bedroom a minute later, a

dramatic pout weighing down her gorgeous face. "But I wanted to cook for you."

"You can order for me—does that work? Anything you want."

"Anything?" Meredith looked devilish.

"Anything but seafood."

Meredith bounced from the room.

By the time Jax cleaned herself up and changed, Meredith had set the table and their mystery meal was on its way. Jax sat in one of her simple wooden kitchen chairs and sighed. "So, what are we having?"

Meredith sat on Jax's lap facing her, a serene expression on her face as she ran her fingers through Jax's short hair and massaged her scalp. The tender, therapeutic touch traveled to Jax's tense neck and shoulders next. Meredith didn't stop until Jax let out a soft moan.

"You like that?" Meredith purred.

Her eyes were closed. "You know I do."

"I'm sorry you're going through such shitty stuff right now. Please don't forget I'm here to help you through it."

Jax felt no malice directed at her, just sympathy. "I'm—"

Meredith pressed her finger to Jax's lips. "Do not apologize. Just remember, you're not alone."

Jax knew she wasn't. She had Wyatt and Amanda, but in that moment, she wanted to be selfish and soak up the presence of this one person who was there solely for her. She wrapped her arms around Meredith's waist and pulled their bodies together. "I'm happy you're here."

"You are?"

"I am." Jax buried her face into Meredith's neck. "I got tired of seeing doctors and nurses all day. I missed your friendly face." She punctuated her words with a nip to Meredith's skin.

"No pretty nurses are keeping you entertained?" Meredith's tone wasn't all light and teasing.

Jax didn't mind the thought of Meredith being a little jealous. "No, no pretty nurses. But Gretchen's doctor is pretty smokin'. Like a librarian played by Salma Hayek." She laughed when Meredith pinched her. The buzzer sounded, letting them know their food had arrived.

Meredith jumped up from Jax's lap. "I'll get it. You just sit there and relax." Meredith grabbed her wallet from her purse and walked out the door.

Jax dropped her head back and closed her eyes again. She'd felt guilty when she first started seeing Meredith. Even though she was formally separated from Gretchen, it still felt wrong. But the longer she was with Meredith, the more she grew to accept that she, too, was allowed to be happy.

Meredith reentered the apartment, all smiles and holding a stuffed paper bag. "I hope you're hungry."

Jax's stomach growled. "I didn't think I was, but now I'm worried you didn't get enough food."

"Trust me, I got enough." Meredith giggled adorably. She pushed her blond hair over her shoulder and started unpacking the bag. "I got two paninis, two salads, garlic knots, and a calzone because I know you regret it every time you don't order one."

She studied the way Meredith set out the food with such serious concentration on her face. Her light blue sweater hugged her torso, drawing attention to her breasts and the curve of her waist. Jax stepped up to Meredith, who looked at her curiously. She cupped Meredith's cheek gently and kissed her. Her lips were warm and so soft. She weaved her fingers into Meredith's thick tresses and deepened the kiss. Jax was addicted to the power she felt when she kissed Meredith, and the way Meredith responded to Jax's every touch. Any lingering guilt fell away.

She was allowed this happiness. Gretchen was her past and Meredith was her future.

Chapter Five

13 days, 13 hours, 6 minutes

Jax hated going back to work. Not because she couldn't be at the hospital constantly or there for Caleb, but because her job made her more miserable than anything. She hated her boss, Randy, and couldn't stand any of the other people working in the office. She'd promised herself five years ago when she took the job that it was temporary. She needed something to help pay the bills, and graphic design allowed her to apply her art degree and experience to a steady career with benefits, much more than she got as a freelance artist trying to make a name for herself in New Jersey.

"The pizzeria and the boutique are taken care of. I'll have the menus and flyers ready to go by the end of the week." Jax stared her boss in the eye and imagined how great it would feel to strangle him. "I've been working on them from home and haven't lost a minute."

"That's good. The last thing I needed was for you to flake on me."

Jax knew her boss was a dick, but could he possibly be that heartless, too? "I promise I won't *flake* on you. Not even when my wife is in a coma," she said flatly.

"Great. I'll see you at our four o'clock meeting." His eyes were on his phone. He was clearly done with her.

Jax tugged at the collar of her gingham button-up as she left his office. She planned on finding a new job as soon as things with her family got back to normal, and even though she'd made the promise to herself every day, this time she meant it. This job with these people was bad for her health.

Fatigue settled in, weighty and strong. She walked straight to the break room and prayed there was still coffee left. She would even drink a cup of instant if they had it. Jax tried her best to sleep, and Meredith was a blessing with all the ways she tried to help relax her, but the nights were still mostly sleepless. Gretchen's lifeless body haunted her mind. She made a quick cup of coffee and pulled her phone from her pocket the moment she sat down and started typing a message to Amanda.

How are things?

Jax brought up her latest accounts and tried to focus on work, but she was much more concerned about Gretchen and the meeting she wanted no part of. Meetings at Shoreline Design often dragged and included only three members of the ten-person staff. She didn't have time to sit and play spectator. Her phone buzzed.

They took her back for another scan.

Jax read and reread the message. She knew Amanda wasn't her number one fan, but communicating more wouldn't kill her.

Did the doctor say anything?

I'm waiting for them to come back in the room.

Jax rubbed a firm circle in the center of her forehead and turned back to her work. She fiddled with a design, shifting images and changing text over and over, but nothing looked right. Nothing felt right. Jax's gut twisted with an odd unease she had never felt before. The fine hairs on the back of her neck stood at attention. Her palms began to sweat, and her chest felt heavy. What was wrong with her?

She started at her phone's vibration. She stared at it, foreboding bubbling up through her stomach into her throat. Jax was afraid to read Amanda's message. Her heart pounded as she unlocked her screen.

They're stopping the pentobarbital.

Jax remembered the name from their early days in the hospital, but she could not remember what stopping the drug would do or why they would want to.

What does this mean? She shot the message to Amanda and stared, unwavering, at her screen. Anything less than an immediate response was unacceptable. *Do they think she'll wake up?*

I don't know.

Jax frowned. *What did the scan show?*

I don't know.

What do you— She stilled her thumbs. Fighting with Amanda wasn't going to solve anything, give her answers, or get her to the hospital any faster. She deleted the words and typed again. *I'll be right there.*

Jax grabbed her scarf and jacket. She popped her head into Randy's office and said, "I have to go to the hospital. Send me an email with anything important from the meeting." She didn't give him a second to answer before running out the door. She really did not care if Randy fired her.

Her jacket was only halfway on when she climbed into her truck and started the ignition. With midafternoon traffic, it should only take twenty-seven minutes to get to the hospital. Jax hoped the cops had better places to be than Route 18.

She pulled into the parking garage in just under twenty-two minutes. Her moves were graceless as she stumbled to her feet and rushed to the entrance. Sweat was beading her upper lip by the time she turned the corner to Gretchen's room. Amanda greeted her arrival with wide eyes. Caleb looked just as alarmed.

"Hey," Jax said breathlessly. She heaved air in and out while gripping her side to alleviate a very painful cramp. She really, really needed to get back to the gym. "Did they stop the meds? What's going on?"

"Yes, you maniac. Please sit down before you scare people into thinking you should be admitted." Amanda offered her a drink and Jax waved her off. "And they're weaning her from the ventilator."

"Now what?"

"We wait."

"All we've been doing is waiting!" Jax's voice carried and Caleb flinched. She collected herself and took a deep breath. "Sorry."

Amanda narrowed her eyes at Jax, but after a moment her hard expression softened. "She's still unconscious, but now we can hope she wakes up soon."

Jax looked at Caleb, who was playing with plastic dinosaurs. "Is there a chance?"

"Dr. Melendez seemed hopeful."

"Hopeful." Jax smiled at Caleb's small giggle. A triceratops fell to the ground after an intense battle. "I'll take hopeful."

Hopeful filled Jax's tank for only eighteen hours, when she started to grow impatient at the start of visiting hours the next day. She watched Gretchen's face closely until Amanda told her to back away. She paced and huffed and complained. The whole drive to and from Caleb's preschool served to fill her mind with more questions and annoyances.

"Oh my God!" Apparently, Amanda had had enough. "Sit down and shut up. You're driving me crazy."

"I'm not as good at sitting around and doing nothing as you are."

Her retort was met with a death stare. She regretted her words instantly and started to wish she could disappear.

Amanda stood from her chair, the one she had rarely left for the past fourteen days, and stepped up to Jax. "What did you just say?"

She swallowed hard. Amanda's dark, hard eyes reminded Jax of her mother-in-law, a woman she was wholly terrified of. "I didn't mean it like that."

"*Sitting around and doing nothing*," Amanda mimicked. Anyone overhearing would've thought they were sisters by blood, if not for their vastly different appearances. Amanda's mahogany skin didn't mask her face, red with anger. "How exactly did I misinterpret that?"

"I'm not saying you misinterpreted. I think I could've said it better."

"How about you try again?" Amanda crossed her arms over her chest.

She searched her rattled brain for the most diplomatic phrasing she could come up with. "I'm not okay with waiting. It makes me nervous and anxious, and I don't have the patience you do."

"You think I'm okay? You don't think I'm anxious or nervous while I sit and do nothing? I'm waiting for my baby sister to prove she can take a breath on her own, and you think I'm *okay*?"

Jax shook her head and readied herself for one last try. "Look, Gretchen has been a part of my life for almost half of it. I know how this feels for me, and I can't even begin to imagine what it's like for you. I meant no offense." She rolled up the sleeves of her sweater, trying to ward off the anxious hot flash creeping up her neck. She knew she was beet red. "You have been at her side and taking care of Caleb—she's lucky to have you."

Amanda's jaw flexed, and her eyes started to well with heavy tears. "You don't even—" She stopped to collect herself, barely having any control over her emotions. Her words sounded thick. "You stopped loving her and you left her. I hate you for that."

Jax felt blindsided by this characterization of their split. "*She* asked for the divorce."

"But *you* left. You wanted that divorce but were too much of a coward to be the bad guy. Why? Did you not want Caleb to resent you?"

Jax shook her head forcefully. "No."

"Then why?"

"Because I thought she'd come begging for me to come back!"

Jax's confession echoed in the room. Her ears were ringing with heat and embarrassment. "She pushed and she pushed, and she *pushed.* Finally, I got tired of feeling like a single mom in a shared house and acting like everything was normal."

Jax didn't bother trying to fight back her tears. She hadn't told anyone the truth, not even Wyatt, and it felt cleansing as she did so now. "So I walked away. I thought if my wife loved me and still believed in our marriage, she'd come and get me. Well, guess what, Amanda? She never came. The phone would ring, and I'd pick it up like a hopeless fool thinking she'd be on the other end asking me to come home." Jax laughed at her own naivety. "She was only calling about Caleb, or to tell me she saw a lawyer."

Amanda dropped her head and shook it. "Gretchen is stubborn. You know that as well as I do. She didn't want you to leave."

"But she let me go. And none of that really matters now."

Amanda was shocked. She looked at Jax like she was bananas. "Of course it matters. You can't give up on your marriage."

"Our marriage..." Jax looked at the door when a strange sound caught her attention. Hospitals were never truly quiet. "It's over. It's been over. Right now we're fighting to keep our attention on Caleb and be as civil as possible."

"You should tell her. When she wakes up."

"Tell her what? That I tried to manipulate her into proving to me that I mattered? That *we* mattered. Nuh-uh. That stays between us." Jax noticed Amanda shift uncomfortably. "Amanda, you have to promise me. You can't tell Gretchen. We've both been through a lot, and we need to keep our focus on Caleb. I don't have any fight left, and neither does she." Jax glanced at Gretchen. She imagined her soon-to-be ex-wife nodding in agreement.

"Is this because of Meredith?"

Jax's shoulders went slack with sudden exhaustion. She laughed. "No. This has nothing to do with Meredith."

"I just want my sister to be happy."

"Trust me," Jax said with sadness in her heart, "she will be happy without me."

Jax and Amanda heard a noise and turned to the windows. They couldn't place it. It wasn't thunder or wind. This sounded strangled and...human.

Gretchen struggled to take a breath.

CHAPTER SIX

14 days, 15 hours, 3 minutes

"We heard it. We both heard it."

Dr. Melendez moved her stethoscope around Gretchen's chest and listened intently. When she stepped back, she released a long breath. She unplugged her ears and wrapped her stethoscope around the back of her neck. Gretchen was breathing on her own, but not much else appeared to change.

"Coming out of a medically induced coma isn't easy," Dr. Melendez said somberly. "There's fluid in her lungs which we will treat and monitor, but her pupils are responsive. This is very good news."

Jax felt her breath come easier but worry still nagged her. "What other risks and side effects are we looking at?"

"Medically induced comas are basically a heavy dose of anesthesia. Some individuals have a hard time reaching consciousness after a three-hour surgery. Gretchen has been under for two weeks." Dr. Melendez made a few notes for herself in her notepad and adjusted a few monitors. "Some patients report feeling sick and sluggish for days to weeks after waking up, and some experience vivid nightmares. The time it takes to shake the symptoms is different for everyone."

Jax widened her eyes. "Vivid nightmares?"

"The mind is an amazing and crazy thing," Dr. Melendez said offhandedly. "I'm going to have a nurse come in for checkups every hour now. If you notice anything change, and I do mean anything, please call someone and have them page me. I think we're going to see Gretchen really soon." Before Dr. Melendez could leave, Jax stopped her.

"How much experience do you have with medically induced comas?"

Dr. Melendez's smile was pleasant. "I see it often but not every day."

Jax opened her mouth to ask another question, but Amanda elbowed her. "Ow."

"Thank you, Doctor," Amanda said. "We'll let you know if we notice anything, and we'll keep the nurses updated as well."

Dr. Melendez winked at Amanda and left the room.

"Did she just wink at you? Why did she wink at you?" Jax's paranoia set in. "Do you guys talk about me when I'm not here?"

"She winked at me because you're a handful, and I just saved her from you. Now sit down." Amanda pointed to a chair. "Do you want to pick up Caleb today, or do you want me to go?"

Jax sat on the edge of the chair. "I asked Wyatt to get him and take him out for an early dinner. I didn't know what to expect here."

"He's already seen so much."

"I know." Jax tried to see everything through a four-year-old's eyes every day, but she would never really know how Caleb felt. "It scares me to think about something happening to Gretchen and him not having that last good night or good morning." She flexed her hands and ran her thumb along her bare ring finger. "You know how Gretchen felt."

"She hadn't spoken to our mother in over a year before she died."

"The situations aren't the same, I know, but I can't imagine carrying that kind of feeling with me for the rest of my life. You know how I am about family, after Michael took me in and we had so little time together." Jax saw the look on Amanda's face. "You think I'm making this about me again."

Amanda shook her head. "No, for once I don't." She smiled. "I think you're a good parent who really cares about their child's future."

"Shouldn't all parents?"

Amanda looked sad as she relaxed back into the chair she had claimed as her own over the past two weeks. "Our father didn't when he left, and our mother…"

"She cared. In her own way."

"That's what I keep telling myself, too."

Jax stared at Gretchen's toes buried deeply beneath layers of scratchy hospital blankets and sheets. "Remember the first family dinner I came to?"

Amanda cackled. "I'll never forget it."

"I haven't been able to eat roast beef since without flashbacks."

"Good ol' Rochelle spent hours in the kitchen preparing the perfect meal, her *best* meal, just because she was hoping it'd be your last."

"She accused me of having a fetish for black women," Jax said, recalling the conversation so easily. "And when that didn't stick, she then wondered if I was after your family money, money I knew nothing about."

"And she noticed your ears perk up. I almost choked on my peas."

"I always wanted to be good enough in her eyes. Maybe so much so that I became blind."

"Blind to what?"

"Being good enough in Gretchen's eyes."

"Jax…"

"I'm sorry," Jax said loudly. She stood and paced. "I really am trying here. I'm not the selfish prick you think I am."

Amanda reached out and grabbed Jax's hand. "I know you're not. I was so unfair to you during that dinner, too. I was jealous of everything Gretchen had and all she had done, like leaving the nest."

She gave Amanda's hand a squeeze and felt oddly calm and comforted then. And hungry. "I'm going to run to the vending machine for something chocolate, preferably covered in more chocolate. Can I get you anything?"

"No, thank you."

Jax walked the familiar halls on autopilot. She had eaten many meals from the same vending machine. She even knew the treasure she was hunting now could be acquired with two dollar bills and pushing D3 on the worn keypad. She dug into her jeans pocket and pulled out a long thread and a five. She let out a deep chuckle. *I'll eat good today.*

She had already eaten half of her first candy bar on the way back to Gretchen's room. A cute nurse winked at her as they passed one another in the hall. Jax could barely contain the extra skip in her step as she entered the room. She burst in and was about to announce that women still winked at her, that she still had some mojo left at her age, but the room was empty save for its constant occupant.

"She's probably tired of listening to me," Jax said. She had grown more comfortable talking to an unconscious Gretchen as the days went on and on. She tossed her spare snack on the bed next to Gretchen's feet. "I bet you wish you could run away from me, too."

❖

My head hurts. Where am I? Jax, yes. I hear you. I'm running away—no. I'm running toward you. Keep talking, keep leading me because I can't see anything in this darkness. One foot in front of the other. Is that you? Are you waiting for me in the light? I'm coming, Jax, I'm running to you. Never away.

CHAPTER SEVEN

14 days, 15 hours, 37 minutes

Jax could swear Gretchen's foot moved. She blinked and rubbed her eyes. This wouldn't be the first time her mind was playing tricks. During the first week, she had seen various parts of Gretchen shift, only to be disappointed.

Jax stared intently. She'd give herself the same fifteen seconds of hope she always did, and then laugh at herself. Fifteen seconds and another bubble burst.

Jax went back to her chair, but she turned around when she heard the sound of her candy bar hitting the floor. She picked it up and put it back on the bed, jumping when Gretchen's foot moved toward her hand. "Oh my God." Jax looked around frantically. She dropped her chocolate and ran for the door. "Hey!" she shouted. "Hey, I need someone! Hello?"

Amanda almost collided with Jax. "She's moving."

"Her foot moved," she said at the same time. Jax shook her head, not fully understanding what was happening.

"Dr. Melendez is on her way. Gretchen's fingers twitched a minute after you left, and I went to get her." Amanda spoke so quickly and with tears in her eyes. "I can't believe this."

"I didn't expect…not so soon." Jax walked back into the room and stood beside Amanda next to Gretchen's bed. They both hovered over her, watching for more.

Gretchen's eyes shifted behind her eyelids, and ever so slowly, one eye started to peek open. Amanda stepped back with an elated smile. Gretchen opened her eyes just a slit, but it was enough for Jax to look into them. The corner of Gretchen's mouth turned up very slightly.

Jax's heart started to pound.

"I hear we have some action in here," Dr. Melendez said as she rushed into the room. She scanned Gretchen's monitors and grabbed a penlight from the pocket of her navy-blue scrubs. "Gretchen? Are you with us, Gretchen?" She pulled back Gretchen's eyelids for a quick check of her pupils. She adjusted Gretchen's bed to bring it upright a bit. "Gretchen, my name is Dr. Paula Melendez. If you can hear me, give me a nod or squeeze my fingers." She placed her hand into Gretchen's palm. Gretchen squeezed.

Jax let out a heavy sigh of relief and brought her clasped hands up to her mouth. She couldn't believe the weak nod Gretchen offered Dr. Melendez.

"You had an accident and are in the hospital. Do you remember what happened?" The monitors started to go crazy. "It's okay, it's okay," Dr. Melendez soothed. "If you're tired, just go back to sleep." She placed her hand on Gretchen's shoulder and looked back at a nurse. "Her heart rate is rising."

"What's going on?" Jax tried to step closer but another nurse entered the room and blocked her. Jax overheard Dr. Melendez direct a nurse to give Gretchen a sedative. "What are you doing? I thought the goal was to have her wake up."

"And she did. She responded and reacted to me. These are very good things." Dr. Melendez's face did not reflect the positivity of her words.

"But…?"

"But she started to panic, which is completely normal for someone who just woke up in the hospital. For Gretchen, however, it's less than ideal." Dr. Melendez offered a quick thank-you to the nurses as they left the room. "We still don't know the extent of her brain injuries. We know what the scans have told us, but we don't know if she has been affected in any other way. Until we do, we have to be careful."

"Careful of what?" Amanda said, stealing the question from Jax.

"A multitude of things, but I'm concerned with causing any further injury. It's not uncommon for a brain injury to result in stress-triggered seizures after the fact. I'd rather she take a little more time coming to full consciousness than risk more damage."

Jax started to get pissed at this constant push and pull with medical jargon. "Why the hell didn't you tell us about this before?"

Dr. Melendez smiled softly. She exuded the kind of calm that must come from years of dealing with patients and their families. "One of my goals as a doctor is to never give someone false hope, and to take one day at a time. I encourage the patient's loved ones to do the same. I wasn't going to add to your list of worries when we weren't sure we'd even get to this point. Believe me, Jax, I am doing what's best for Gretchen, and right now I'm celebrating this milestone. Be happy because we can finally start looking forward to tomorrow." She shot Amanda a smile and another wink as she left.

"She really needs to stop with the winking. I'm getting a complex," Jax grumbled.

"You already have a complex."

"Maybe she likes you."

Amanda snorted. "Good deflection." Amanda sat down and took Gretchen's hand. She patted it gently. "Maybe the next time you wake up, we can talk about how annoying this one is."

"She already knows." Jax picked up the candy bar she'd dropped and threw it in the garbage. "When do you think she'll wake up?"

"I have no clue."

"Do you think soon?"

"A few weeks ago, before all of this, I was watching Caleb for Gretchen because she had a late appointment—"

"Shocker," Jax said drolly.

"He kept asking me questions. Not silly questions either, thoughtful ones. About how I was cutting my vegetables, how vegetables grow, and about farming. I knew some answers but not all. I wondered where this kid got his curiosity from."

"You're talking about me, aren't you?"

"Yes."

"Well, at least he got something good from me, and at least I know he'll drive you crazy for me once I'm not..." Jax stopped talking. She couldn't even think about the divorce at the moment. She forced a stiff smile and opened her second candy bar instead of talking.

CHAPTER EIGHT

14 days, 21 hours, 9 minutes

"I can't thank you enough, Wyatt." Jax held Caleb, who hugged her like he'd never let go.

"You know I love hanging out with my buddy, and Carly thinks it's great practice." Wyatt ruffled Caleb's hair.

"Please," she said with a grunt as she set Caleb down. "You're a natural. You were comfortable with this kid before I was." Jax shook a giggling Caleb's shoulders. "Now go home to your pregnant wife. Please. I'm starting to feel guilty."

"Keep me updated if *you know what* happens again," Wyatt said with wide eyes and raised brows. Jax had sent him a text with strict instructions to not talk about it in front of Caleb.

She nodded. "Of course."

Caleb tugged at Jax's sweatshirt. "Dinosaur." He said it like *dine-sore*.

Wyatt's smile was large. "Because that's pretty big news."

"*Dinosaur.*"

"It is. We're happy to finally see some improvements."

Caleb tugged her hand. "*Dinosaur!*"

"What are you screaming about, Cricket? You want to play dinosaurs?"

"No! I forgot my T. rex in Uncle Wy's car." Caleb's voice wavered and bordered on a screech, the exact pitch that preceded a full-blown meltdown. "Need my T. rex!" He stomped his foot.

"Let's go get him." Wyatt reached for Caleb's hand, but Jax stopped him.

"I don't think that's a good idea. I'll take him. He's about to blow at any second."

"Stay here," Wyatt said firmly. "This is good practice, remember?" He smirked and took Caleb's hand.

Jax heard Caleb's footsteps slamming down the hallway. "God bless that man." Jax reclaimed her seat and started a game of Yahtzee on her phone. Amanda was halfway through a paperback. "You can go home if you want."

Amanda didn't look up from her book. "Nah. It's less lonely here. Don't tell anyone I said that."

Jax chuckled and played a full house. "Your secret is safe with me."

"Ja—"

"What?" Amanda and Jax said at the same time.

"Oh, I thought you were saying my name. I'm hearing things now. Great."

"I heard it, too."

Jax sat straight up. "Gretchen?"

"Ha…"

Jax rushed to Gretchen's bedside, elated to see her opening her eyes. She was struggling, but she was opening them. "Hey."

Gretchen fixed her unfocused gaze on Jax and smiled weakly. She lifted her hand, shakily reaching toward Jax.

Jax took Gretchen's hand. It felt thinner than before. "Do you remember talking to the doctor earlier?" Jax hoped she did, because she didn't want to be the one to break the news to her. Again.

Gretchen clamped her eyes shut and shook her head gently. Pain was obvious on her face.

Amanda stepped up and touched Gretchen's shoulder. "You had a bit of a fall at work. You're in the hospital, but you're getting better every day. Your doctor is wonderful and gets as annoyed by Jax as I do."

Jax's appreciation for Amanda grew in that moment. Gretchen remained calm and Jax was sure it had more to do with familiar faces than the drugs she was on. Gretchen winked at her, and Jax finally felt a hint of happiness.

Gretchen pulled her hand away and touched Jax's forearm. "I…" Gretchen started coughing, clenching her body in pain.

"Can she have water?" Jax raced around the room to get her water bottle. "She needs a straw." She spun the top off so frantically, it flew up into the air and landed on the floor.

Gretchen raised her hand and waved off Jax's concern and water.

Her coughing fit was over, and she was smiling again, even with red and watery eyes. She held Jax's hand again. Amanda left the room in search of a straw.

Jax was so content seeing her alive, she didn't care how awkwardly she had to twist her body so Gretchen could hold her right hand. She held her breath the moment she felt three little squeezes. She searched Gretchen's face for more, but she saw nothing in Gretchen's heavy eyes.

Gretchen's eyes suddenly flew open, and she started looking around the room. She tried to sit up and whimpered in pain.

"Whoa, whoa, slow down," Jax said, encouraging Gretchen to lie back and relax again. "What's wrong?" Jax read Gretchen's full, dry lips as she mouthed a name. "Caleb is with Wyatt."

Gretchen looked at her skeptically.

Jax considered the expression a gift. "It's fine. Carly said it's good practice."

"Car—" She started coughing again, but this time she caught her breath more quickly.

"Carly is smart, I know."

"They should be back any minute," Amanda said, reentering the room with a hospital cup filled with ice and water, and a straw. "Here you go." She sat on the other side of Gretchen's bed and held the cup to Gretchen's lips. Gretchen drank slowly, one sip at a time, and smiled serenely when she was done.

Jax knew Gretchen was probably going crazy with questions, or maybe she knew she had been near death and didn't care about the details. "We should probably call Dr. Melendez in." She tried to stand up, but Gretchen wouldn't let her go. She held up two fingers, and Jax assumed she was asking for two more minutes. "We shouldn't wait."

Gretchen touched Jax's face. She ran her fingers into her hair as Jax looked at Amanda from the corner of her eye.

"I'll get Dr. Melendez." Amanda left the room.

"I think Dr. Melendez has a crush on your sister," Jax whispered. She shifted uncomfortably as Gretchen continued to trace her cheekbones and nose and then the faint dimple of her chin. "I know Amanda isn't interested or even into women, but I think she should go for it anyway. When will she ever get a chance with a doctor again?" Jax knew she was rambling, but Gretchen's reaction was the last thing she expected. She didn't think she'd feel her touch ever again. "Even your mother would push her—"

Gretchen placed her finger against Jax's chattering lips. The current that traveled between them felt like old times.

Gretchen wrapped her hand around the back of Jax's neck and pulled her down so their foreheads could touch. She held Jax's face in both hands the best she could, considering the IVs and monitor leads.

Jax couldn't keep her emotions in check much longer. No matter what had happened between her and Gretchen, Jax was grateful she was alive and coherent. Gretchen seemed like she would be okay. Caleb would still have the mother he knew and loved, and that meant the world to Jax. Maybe the accident would even repair a bit of their rift, and they could co-parent happily and easily. She could only hope. Her moment of peace was shattered when Gretchen leaned up and kissed her. She sat back quickly and widened her eyes.

"What—why…?" She reminded herself not to upset Gretchen. Keeping her calm was important for her healing. "I know things will be different now, but we can't." Jax let out her best fake laugh. "You're probably high as a kite right now, so I'll let this slide."

Gretchen shook her head. She tried to sit up but sucked in a breath and fell back against the pillow. "What…" she said deeply, her voice so gravelly the word sounded like a growl, "are…you talking about?"

"Hello again, Gretchen." Dr. Melendez was all smiles as she entered the room with Amanda. "I wasn't expecting to be back so soon, but this is a wonderful surprise. And I hear you're alert and trying to talk."

Gretchen's eyes were wet, never leaving Jax as she nodded at the doctor's question.

"Your throat is probably very sore from the intubation, but I need you to do the best you can to talk, okay?"

"She coughs every time she tries."

"Just do the best you can." Dr. Melendez grabbed Gretchen's toes. "Wiggle for me?"

Gretchen followed the command.

"Do you remember meeting me earlier?" Dr. Melendez said.

Gretchen stared at Jax and stayed silent.

"I don't think she does," Jax said.

"I really need Gretchen to answer."

Jax stepped back, properly scolded, and listened as Gretchen croaked out her own negative answer.

"Can you tell me your full name?"

Gretchen's voice crackled and strained, but she said, quietly, "Gretchen…Rebecca Mills."

"Very good. Does it hurt when you take a deep breath?"

Gretchen took in a breath and coughed. She nodded.

"On a scale of one to ten, how badly does it hurt?"

"Seven."

"Does it hurt here?" Dr. Melendez felt along Gretchen's ribs. Jax watched anxiously as she neared one of her injuries. "What about here?"

Jax winced when Gretchen did. "Why are you hurting her?"

"I'm not," Dr. Melendez said calmly. She had Gretchen move her arms in various directions. "What is your birth date?"

"November twenty-third, year withheld." Gretchen smirked. Her breathing was labored, the vigorous wakeup clearly beginning to take its toll.

"What's the last thing you remember?"

"Working and rushing to get home." She started coughing and reached for the water. After two sips, she sat back. She looked so tired. Jax wanted to stop the interrogation.

Jax spoke up. "Maybe we should let her sleep."

"I didn't want to be late for the barbecue."

Everyone in the room froze. Jax looked at Amanda, who wouldn't stop staring at Gretchen. Dr. Melendez took a pad out of her pocket and started scribbling.

"What barbecue was that?"

Gretchen's face was pure bliss. "Fourth of July, Caleb's first. I'm sorry I missed it, baby. I hope you still had it. You were so excited to show him fireworks."

Jax's stomach dropped. Her face heated up, and her hands started to shake. She felt like she was going to throw up.

"Who is in the room with us right now, Gretchen?"

"The gorgeous one behind you is my wife, and the worried one next to me is my sister." Gretchen cleared her throat roughly. "I'm surprised Mom's not here telling me what I did wrong."

Amanda grabbed her hand tightly. "Gretchen—"

"Oh my God, Gretchen!" Wyatt's voice boomed in the room.

"Mama!" Caleb got away from Wyatt and dashed to Gretchen's beside. Jax was too slow to stop him.

Gretchen stared at Caleb in a panic. She backed away from his tiny hands as he reached for her and tried to climb on her bed. "I don't—who?"

"Hey, Cricket, come over here by Bug for a bit. Mama's still a little tired."

"That's not Caleb," Gretchen said softly.

"It's me, Mama."

"No...Caleb is a baby."

"I'm your baby!"

"You're not my baby."

"Come on." Jax forcibly pulled Caleb from Gretchen's bed and held him. He started to cry instantly and slammed his little fists into Jax's shoulders. "It's okay, Caleb."

"Mama's being mean."

"No, no." Jax rubbed calming circles on Caleb's back to little success. "She's just a little confused after getting hurt."

"I'm not confused. I know my son. I know my wife. What is going on? What have you done to me?" Gretchen's voice cracked as she struggled to yell at Dr. Melendez.

"Gretchen, I need you to calm down." Dr. Melendez tried to grab Gretchen's hand, only to be swatted away.

"*You* calm down."

"You suffered a head injury," Dr. Melendez said. "Your memories are a bit mixed up. Are you sure that was the last thing you remember? Try again."

Gretchen watched Jax rubbing Caleb's back. "Where is your ring? Why aren't—" Gretchen's expression went blank.

"Gretchen?" Jax started toward the bed.

Gretchen's eyes rolled back, and she started thrashing.

"She's seizing. I need a nurse in here!" Dr. Melendez moved Gretchen onto her side.

Jax turned Caleb away and stepped out of the room. She looked on as medical personnel worked on Gretchen. She held Caleb tightly, absorbing his shrill cries with her body. She wanted to erase it all. She wanted to make it go away.

❖

Peace. Finally, some peace. I can still hear Jax's voice somewhere in the distance, through all the fog. I need to follow it. I need to find her. I can feel the safety of her in my chest, blossoming as warmth. The more

I focus on finding her, the brighter the glow surrounding me becomes. I have to find her and Caleb. I know my life with them. Where are they? I can't see anything, but I can hear them. Focus, Gretchen, and think. Find a way back to them, to the life I know, the life I love...

Chapter Nine

14 days, 23 hours, 46 minutes

Gretchen tried to stretch her arms above her head but could barely move. Her body felt as if it was suspended in rubber cement. She struggled to open her eyes, but every time she almost did, her body would force them shut.

I hate falling asleep with the light on. Jesus, what kind of bulbs did Jax get from the store. This is a bedroom, not the lighting section at the Home Depot. I can't even open my eyes. It's too bright and I'm too tired. She had zero control over her physical self. Her brain screamed to move, but her limbs and face would remain motionless. She lay still and listened instead.

Footsteps shuffled and unfamiliar voices carried. Unpleasant and sterile smells hit her all at once. Muffled conversations became more clear, and finally, cutting through everything, came the one voice Gretchen needed to help direct her.

Jax. Jax is here. I found her.

Gretchen flexed her throat and strained to part her lips. They felt welded shut with dryness. Panic started to set in. She started to breathe heavily. A constant, rapid beeping filled the space around her. She needed to open her eyes, or she felt like they might never open again.

Move, dammit! Open your eyes and find Jax. She'll make this better. She'll fix this.

Gretchen shifted her eyes back and forth as quickly as she could, treating them like a windup toy getting ready for release. With every ounce of strength, she broke her lips apart and cracked her eyes open.

"He—" Her throat hurt too much to force a word, but her eyes were finally cooperating. She looked around and saw Jax at the edge of the room. The room wasn't familiar, but the setting was otherwise unmistakable.

She blinked hard to clear her vision. Jax was talking to another woman wearing a white lab coat, presumably a doctor. Pain radiated from various parts of her body. Although she knew she was in the hospital, she didn't know why. With a deep breath, she mustered up the energy to make a fist and knock on the bed rail.

All she wanted to do was smile when she saw Jax, but she was still too weak. She grew stronger with each passing second. With each step Jax took toward her bed, Gretchen felt a bit of life seep back into her aching body.

"You're awake," Jax said, touching her forehead gently. "You gave us quite a scare."

Gretchen's eyes involuntarily closed at the contact. She clung to the image of Jax. She was okay now. The unbearable heat turned into comforting warmth, and drowsiness started to overtake her.

"Gretchen? Can you hear me? It's me, Dr. Melendez."

She opened her eyes and vaguely recalled the attractive woman standing over her, shining a light in her eyes. It was uncomfortable and hurt her head. She tried to turn away from it.

"Do you remember me, Gretchen?"

She tried to look at Dr. Melendez again, this time through the dancing spots in her vision. Yes, she did remember her, but she couldn't say the words no matter how hard she tried. She knew the word. Gretchen even spelled it in her head. But she couldn't say it. She nodded.

"Do you know where you are?"

Gretchen managed the most incredulous look she could. It didn't take a rocket scientist to recognize a hospital room. She could also easily decipher the concerned look on Dr. Melendez's face.

"Can you talk?" Dr. Melendez said.

Gretchen looked from Dr. Melendez to Jax, who looked sad and tired, her normally bright and bold demeanor now dull. How long had she been in the hospital?

Jax took her hand. "Can you answer the doctor? One word, that's all we need."

Gretchen's eyes burned, and she flinched against prickly tears. She wanted to yell and scream, but all she could do was open her mouth.

Dr. Melendez backed away from Gretchen and motioned for Jax to join her. Gretchen stared at them as they talked. She hated the way Jax looked back at her with pity. She might be the patient, but she wasn't helpless. They should be including her in the conversation. She needed to know what was happening and what was wrong with her.

Gretchen tried to get their attention by knocking again, but neither of them budged. She slapped the mattress as firmly as she could, but it made no difference. She tried to whistle, but nothing more than a gust of air came out between her curled, dry lips. She could feel her face getting red and hot with anger. She did not handle being ignored very well.

She pushed her bedside cart and tried to speak one more time. "Hey!" The one word echoed in the room. She fought to catch her breath from the exertion.

Jax was the first to turn back to her. Jax's smile should not have been so big after being yelled at, but she grinned, regardless.

"It's not much," Dr. Melendez said, typing on an iPad, "but I'll take it as her first word."

Gretchen reached for Jax again, hungry for her comfort and their connection. She was much less scared when Jax was near. It had always been that way. She held Jax's hand with the tightest grip she could manage and gave it three quick squeezes. She guessed it was too firm by the strange look on Jax's face.

Dr. Melendez started to make her exit. "I encourage you to rest some more. Sleep is the best medicine for a healing brain. I'll be back in in the morning to check on you and ask some questions to figure out your progress." She looked between them. "But for now, I'll let you relax and enjoy the rest of visiting hours." Dr. Melendez left the room, and an odd silence fell.

Gretchen was tired, but she felt like she had been sleeping for years. She had so many questions, and no ability to ask them. She found solace in knowing Jax was there. A thought hit her.

"Caleb," she whispered. The sound of whirring machines almost drowned out the name. She knew Caleb was safe, but a nagging image and memory kept bothering her. Caleb was a baby…but was he *still* a baby? Gretchen jolted at the loud, intrusive memory of a screeching toddler with hair like hers. He had Caleb's eyes but… She looked at Jax.

Jax looked around sadly. "You don't remember, do you?"

She took a deep, calming breath and released it shakily. She tried not to cry when Jax pulled her hand back. "Not…" Gretchen growled in frustration. Words were easy, and she hated how hard it was to just spit them out. She pressed her lips together to sound out a *B*. "B-baby?"

Jax rubbed her face and stood. She walked to the window. Darkness surrounded the hospital, but there was no indication of the time. "Caleb is four." Jax's tone was hard and cold, and she sounded like a stranger.

Gretchen clamped her eyes shut and shook her head gently. The boy in her mind, wild and loud with eyes like honey. Was that her son? She took another deep breath. Her mind was scrambled, playing like a static-filled television. Her eyes pinched together as she fought through the fog to remember something, anything that told her to believe she had a child who was four years old. All she had was one split second of him screaming.

"He wants to have a bowling party for his birthday, and just last week you and I were fighting about him going to kindergarten." Jax turned back to face Gretchen, but she didn't look at her. She crossed her arms over her chest and sighed. Gretchen didn't recognize the fuchsia sweatshirt Jax was wearing. "His preschool teacher recommended keeping him back because he has a hard time concentrating. I was willing to hear her out, but you cried. You insisted he was just energetic, and that there's nothing wrong with that. He needs to adapt. We shouldn't cater to the whims of the school."

How could she not remember any of this? Caleb was old enough to be in school and was having difficulty learning, but she had zero recollection. She touched her hand to her face and winced.

"I wouldn't do that if I were you," Jax said, rushing to the bed to pull Gretchen's hand away from her wounds. "The stitches are out, but it's still pretty fresh." Jax dropped Gretchen's hand and stepped back. She shuffled about awkwardly before standing against the far wall. She shoved her hands into her pockets. "They don't expect any crazy scarring or anything."

Gretchen didn't care about her face nearly as much as she cared about Jax and her odd behavior—acting hot and cold, seemingly concerned one moment and then distant the next. She thought about what it must be like for Jax. Gretchen couldn't imagine what she would do if Jax was hurt badly, never mind nearly losing her. Jax was Gretchen's everything.

She beckoned for Jax to come close again, exhausting the last of her energy as she patted the bed beside her. Jax looked scared as she approached.

Jax sat carefully and stared at a spot beside Gretchen's head. "Did you know Caleb's four?" she said. Jax's shoulder's slumped when Gretchen shook her head. "I have to get Dr. Melendez."

"W-wait," Gretchen said, pain radiating through her throat. She gripped Jax's thigh and felt rejected when Jax jumped slightly. The next word came out no louder than a breath of air. "Stay." Gretchen closed her eyes once Jax covered her hand with hers.

Minutes passed in silence, and she started to slip into a peaceful slumber. The shifting of the mattress awoke Gretchen, but she didn't open her eyes, wanting desperately to hold on to sleep. She heard Jax say that visiting hours were over and she had to leave. She listened to Jax's footsteps, and the sound of her slipping on her jacket was like a lullaby. She started to dream of their mornings together, when Jax would be rushing out the door on Gretchen's day off. Jax would never want to go because leaving her beautiful wife in bed alone was a sin— at least that was what she'd say.

"It's not fair, you know?" Jax's voice cut through the silence, but she was speaking so quietly, like she didn't really want to be heard.

Gretchen kept her eyes closed.

Jax sighed heavily. "You better remember, because I can't be the only one who does." Jax's words were nearly silent, but their bite was painful. The next sound was the door opening and closing.

Gretchen opened her eyes and stared at the ceiling. Whatever Jax was talking about left a weight of foreboding in her gut. She shifted in the hospital bed, and the first moment she had to herself filled her with fear. Every twinge of pain was stronger. She could only handle concentrating for so long before she closed her eyes and willed herself to focus on sleeping. She'd get answers in the morning.

Chapter Ten

15 days, 12 hours, 12 minutes

Gretchen was sitting up a little by the time Dr. Melendez entered her room. She managed enough words to get an update on her injuries and what procedures had been done. The idea of a small hole being drilled into her skull freaked her out for a good fifteen minutes, but she declined a dose of sedatives. Talking to Jax was next on her list. Gretchen had high hopes for visiting hours, and when her door opened, she expected to see Jax. Her disappointment must've been apparent when Amanda walked into the room.

"Well, good morning to you, too." Amanda placed a large shopping bag on the chair and took off her heavy coat. "I wanted to come last night when you woke up, but visiting hours were almost over. How are you?"

Gretchen eyed Amanda. Her hair was shorter and darker than Gretchen remembered. She leaned forward in bed as far as she could without pain to look at the door.

"She'll be here a little later. She had to drop Caleb off at school and then head to the office for a bit. That douchey boss of hers insisted she be present at a meeting." She unpacked the bag. "I brought some rice and beans for you, if you're feeling up to it."

Gretchen tapped the bed to get Amanda's attention. "Mom?"

Amanda froze. "Holy shit. Jax wasn't fucking with me." She wiped her forehead and took a seat. She took Gretchen's hand in a firm hold. Very sweetly she said, "I'm sorry, sis, Mom died two years ago." Amanda's face was pure sadness.

The news settled oddly in Gretchen's chest. She started laughing and let go of Amanda's hand to hold her aching side. She couldn't stop, and tamping down the cackles only served to heighten her giggles. She put her hands up and started to control herself.

"Sorry," she said. Her inability to say full sentences without pain or confusion frustrated her, but she was able to put together a few words and understand them. "How?"

"Heart attack. I found her," Amanda said firmly. "So this little stunt you pulled was totally uncool."

Gretchen felt like an asshole. She grabbed Amanda's hand again and rested it on her lap. She lay back and closed her eyes. She wasn't entirely sure how to process her mother's death for the second time two years later. How did it affect her the first time? She dug deeply into her mind, trying desperately to remember something, anything that would point to grief or relief. As terrible as it seemed, she felt more relief than anything.

"You didn't come to the funeral."

Gretchen raised her eyebrows. She supposed that answered her question. Not going to your parent's funeral was pretty telling. "Sorry."

"I know you are." Amanda looked her over before turning away to her purse. "Let's talk about happier things." Amanda pulled out a tube of lipstick and started applying a coat to Gretchen's dry lips. "That's better."

Gretchen didn't mind. Actually, she enjoyed Amanda's caregiving side. There had always been an odd rift between them. Gretchen hated how unsure she was of their relationship now, how the death of their mother changed them, and whether Amanda had found happiness. "Wish...could talk."

Amanda sighed and sat back. "I'm sorry, sis." Amanda's eyes lit up, and she reached back into her purse. She pulled out a pen and a small notepad. "Maybe you can write?"

She stared at the objects in fear. She was already struggling with her impaired speech. What if she couldn't write, either? She knew those skills could be regained through therapy, but months with a therapist wouldn't help her understand what was happening with Jax right now. She took the pen and pad in her trembling hands.

She took a deep breath in and out, and then she pressed the tip of the pen to the paper and willed her muscle memory and brain to take over. After only a few seconds, Gretchen had a sentence written, and she was certain it made sense. She showed the paper to Amanda, who scowled. Gretchen started to panic.

"I don't understand the question, that's all," Amanda said. "What do you mean, *What about us?*"

Gretchen fought back tears of relief. She could communicate. She wrote again. *You and me.*

Amanda watched Gretchen this time and started nodding. "After Mom died, we did start talking more. I watch Caleb a lot for you when you work late. We're not perfect, but we're getting there."

Gretchen worked Amanda's answer over in her head a few times before coming up with her next question. She wanted to ask about Jax, but going straight to the source was better. She'd have to be patient. Gretchen tapped the pen twice before writing. *Your personal life?*

Amanda laughed instantly. "I am single but have been on a few dates." Gretchen mimicked wearing a stethoscope and wiggled her eyebrows. "Your doctor cares about *you*, not me."

"Jax…"

"Is a troublemaker and a gossip queen. Plus, we know she's not my type because she's a she."

Gretchen wrote the word *doctor* and underlined it several times.

"I know, I know," Amanda said.

Gretchen turned the notepad in her hands. Every time she thought of a question, another one would pop into her head. She had no idea how to organize the words that would help her understand her own life.

"How are you?" Amanda asked.

Gretchen pointed to her ribs and made a pained face.

"No, I'm not talking about physically." Amanda didn't need to be specific. Everything beyond physical feelings was the giant question mark.

Gretchen shook her head. She put the pen to paper but froze. She was feeling a million things. She jotted the one word to sum it all up— *scared*. She showed Amanda and started to cry.

"I know you're scared." Amanda rubbed soothing circles on Gretchen's leg. "But we'll work through this. I'm here for you, no matter what."

"Oh, shit," Jax said from the doorway. She started to turn away.

"Come in," Amanda said to Jax. Gretchen wiped away her tears. "She's been looking for you since I got here." Amanda and Jax shared a look that made Gretchen uneasy.

Jax played with her car keys a moment. She pointed to the door and said, "I'm not staying long. I'm on my way to the office, and I just wanted to stop by to see if anyone needed anything. Has Dr. Melendez been in yet?"

Gretchen hated how Jax refused to look at her. She listened as Amanda filled Jax in on the very little that had happened. Gretchen wrote out a note and lifted it high enough so Jax couldn't ignore it. *We were just talking about you.*

"You can write!" Jax's surprised smile disappeared once she read Gretchen's words. She turned to Amanda. "Why were you talking about me?"

Gretchen tapped the notepad. This conversation was between them, not between Jax and Amanda. She wrote a few more words. *Doctor's crush.*

Jax squinted as she read. "Oh! Dr. Melendez definitely has a thing for your sister."

Amanda rolled her eyes and stood. "I'm going to get coffee." She left Gretchen alone with Jax.

She regarded Jax for a long while. Jax still had a hint of a smile on her lips. Her lavender hair was styled haphazardly, but it still looked nice. Gretchen didn't want to lose the lightness of the moment, but she couldn't stop conversing, otherwise they'd get nowhere. She wrote and kept the topic light. *Nice hair.*

"Thank you. I just got it dyed," Jax said, running her fingers through her short hair. "No matter how many colors I try, I always come back to blond or purple."

Gretchen motioned for Jax to sit with her, and when Jax did, she just wanted to keep crying. She wanted to touch the ring finger of Jax's left hand, to trace the bare skin and ask a million times why. Or maybe she just wanted to know how. But Jax's discomfort was palpable, and Gretchen needed to be able to really talk.

Jax shifted. "What else did Dr. Melendez have to say?"

Gretchen picked up the pen again. She spelled out a few words, but her attention was more on the way Jax followed her movements. *Drilled a hole!* She tilted the pad and pointed to her head.

"Yeah," Jax said with a chuckle. "I freaked out a bit when I heard they'd drilled into your skull, too, but your vitals improved immediately after. So as scary as it was…" Jax took the notepad from Gretchen and started flipping through the pages.

Gretchen felt like Jax was trying to snoop into her earlier conversations with Amanda. But her anxiety disappeared when Jax smiled and handed her notebook back.

"I'll stop at the store and get you another pad or two and some better pens. I know how you prefer gel over ballpoint." Jax started to leave.

"So soon?" she said, her lips feeling foreign as they worked slowly.

"I'm needed in the office today, but I'll be back later with Caleb, if you're feeling up to it."

She nodded, even as fear rose in her chest at the thought of the screaming toddler she hardly recognized. She wrote quickly, the words looking more like a scribble than anything else. But she had no doubt that Jax would be able to decipher it. She smiled sweetly as she turned the paper for Jax to read. *Did you send me flowers?*

Jax tilted her head. "You already have flowers, plenty of them from everyone."

Gretchen shook her head and pointed at Jax. She had looked at every card on every bouquet, and one name was noticeably missing.

They stared at one another, and it felt like more of a standoff than a simple moment of understanding. Jax didn't say a word, and Gretchen wondered just how bad things were between them. Her heart ached, but she tried her best to keep things light. This time, she used her voice and not the pen.

"Cactus?"

Jax was still for a second before a deep, loud laugh bubbled out of her.

"I'm happy to hear some laughter coming from here," Dr. Melendez said as she entered the room. "Good morning, Jax."

"Good morning, Doc."

"Today will be a busy, tiring, and eventful day for Gretchen." Gretchen perked up, and Jax did, too. "I'm pleased with your progress in the last thirty-six hours, Gretchen. You're out of the ICU, following conversation, and your personality appears to be consistent with how everyone knows you."

"But she doesn't remember a thing." Jax's words went unacknowledged.

Amanda rushed into the room with two muffins and a coffee in hand. "Did I miss anything?"

"No, you're right on time." Dr. Melendez winked at Amanda.

Gretchen widened her eyes and looked at Jax, whose face said *I told you so.* She started giggling.

"First, I'd like to get you moving today. Any little bit, but ideally a lap of the floor. I'd like to see if there's been any more physical damage, and I'd also like to avoid any muscle atrophy."

Gretchen was ecstatic to hear the plan. She felt helpless and weak in the big hospital bed and wanted nothing more than to jump out and start running. She started to pull the covers back and move, but her legs felt two steps behind and fifty pounds heavier than she remembered.

"Whoa, now," Dr. Melendez said with a hand on Gretchen's leg. "Let's wait for a nurse and the physical therapist. They'll get here in about an hour."

"Do you think the damage to her brain could've affected her body, too?" Jax stood with her arms across her chest. She appeared so casual, but Gretchen knew her better.

"I'm not overly concerned, but she needs to be evaluated, regardless."

"She's writing," Amanda said excitedly. "Every word is clear, and her handwriting is exactly how it always was."

Jax nodded. "Exactly the same."

She eyed Jax curiously. Something in the way Jax shifted, and the way she stared at the floor with wide, blank eyes, told her Jax was thinking about something else.

"That's very good." Dr. Melendez made a note. "Later this afternoon, I'd like to do a thorough evaluation to determine what we're dealing with in terms of her amnesia."

"So you do think she has amnesia?"

Dr. Melendez looked at Jax like she just asked if she thought the sky was blue. "That much is obvious."

"What does the evaluation entail? Will it hurt her?" Amanda's concern was sweet, if completely foreign to Gretchen.

"It will be tiring and, most likely, frustrating, but all I will do is ask a series of questions to determine her memories and mental state. I will need you both to be present."

"Why?" Jax said loudly, her tone sounding defensive.

"How else will I know if her answers are correct?" Dr. Melendez's response was so no-nonsense that Gretchen wanted to high-five her. Jax nodded meekly. "Can you both be back here around four?" Jax and Amanda looked at one another and shrugged. They both agreed to the time. "Great. I'll see you all then."

Gretchen hated the dismay Jax wore so plainly on her face. "Great," she said in a scratchy whisper.

CHAPTER ELEVEN

15 days, 20 hours, 10 minutes

Gretchen held her new notebook tightly. She was nervous for her evaluation, but what made her feel worse was how tired she was. Her physical therapist was more like a drill sergeant, and the nurses were his minions tasked with pushing her to her limits.

"Are you ready, Gretchen?" Dr. Melendez held her iPad and sat at Gretchen's bedside. "Try to answer verbally as much as you can. I know you're having difficulty, but the more you try, the better."

She nodded, but Dr. Melendez continued to look at her expectantly. Gretchen licked her lips. "Okay," she said, her voice steadier than it had been that morning.

"What is your full name?"

"Gretchen Rebecca Mills." Her words were slow but clear.

"Date of birth?"

"November twenty-third." Gretchen cringed at how hard she worked for simple words.

"Year?"

"Eighty-three."

"Do you know where you are?"

She moved around on the mattress a bit, trying to buy herself a second or two to collect all the words together and feel confident she could make the sounds with her lips. "Jersey Shore Med Center."

"Do you know how you got here?"

She knew the answer immediately but still gave herself a moment to think. "No."

"What is the last thing you remember before being here in the hospital?"

Gretchen leaned her head back and closed her eyes. After pushing herself for an hour to walk around, she was tired, cranky, and hungry. Her ribs ached, and her shoulder was screaming for her to relax. But she had no choice. She had to get through this evaluation.

Jax pushed off from where she was leaning against the wall and sat on the ledge in front of the window. "You already asked her this."

"Gretchen, do you remember me asking you this?"

Gretchen looked at Jax. She had the faintest, foggiest memory, but she wasn't sure about anything anymore. "Kind of."

"What's the last thing you remember before being in the hospital?"

Gretchen closed her eyes again and searched her brain for the very last memory she had before waking up in this nightmare. Her steam was dissipating, and she surrendered to her notepad for this answer. *I told Omar I moved my last appointment up because I promised Jax I'd be home for the barbecue.* She handed the pad to Jax.

Jax read it aloud.

"What's the date of this memory?"

"July Fourth," Gretchen said.

"Did you make it home in time?"

Gretchen stared at Dr. Melendez blankly before looking at Jax. "I…No. I'm here."

"You were thirty minutes later than you said you would be, but we still had plenty of time to eat before we went to see the fireworks."

She remembered a little more. "Caleb's first."

Dr. Melendez wore a soft smile when she asked her next question. "Can you tell me about your son?"

"Caleb Michael Levine," Gretchen said proudly. "We got his middle name from Jax's foster father." She took a deep breath and cleared her throat gently, careful not to agitate her ribs. "He died two years ago."

"Six years ago," Jax corrected.

Gretchen flared her nostrils in frustration. How could so much time just go missing from her mind? "I don't like this," she said with tears in her eyes. "I don't know." She pulled at the sheets around her. "What's happening?"

"I know this is upsetting. We're almost done, and I need you to focus for a little bit longer—then we'll get you something to eat and leave you to rest. Can you do that for me, Gretchen?"

She let out a long breath and smiled weakly when Amanda took her hand. "Okay."

"How old is Caleb?"

Gretchen reached for the notepad, waving for Jax to give it to her. She scribbled quickly and handed it back. *I know he's over four now, but I only remember him as a baby. He was almost one on the Fourth. Where is Caleb? I thought you were bringing him back with you.*

"He's with Meredith. I didn't think a jumping bean would help the evaluation go smoothly."

She understood what Jax said, but something didn't make sense. "Who's Meredith?" No one spoke right away.

Jax cleared her throat and tugged at the sleeves of her sweater. "She's my—"

"Nanny," Amanda said quickly. "She's Caleb's nanny."

"Great. Someone else I'll have to get to know again." Gretchen didn't want to sound like a brat, but the prospect of learning so much of her everyday life again had started to weigh on her.

"Let's keep going," Jax said, directing Dr. Melendez to continue. That was odd.

"Where do you live?"

"Manahawkin, New Jersey."

"Home address?"

"Sixteen fifty Pine Crest Lane. It's a beautiful home." Gretchen wanted to write out the rest. She could've kept her answer simple, but she loved her house. She grinned as she wrote the description. *A small ranch with a covered front porch. Large yard that gets just the right amount of sun to let the flowers grow.*

Jax read it aloud but shook her head when Dr. Melendez looked at her for confirmation. "We added a second floor just after Caleb's first birthday."

"Smart. I guess," Gretchen said. Even her memory of her house was wrong.

This evaluation seemed ridiculously simple, but she still feared answering wrong. So many scary outcomes were on the other side of a list of questions. She sighed when Jax nodded.

"When did you move there?"

Gretchen did a quick calculation in her head. "Nine years ago."

"Thirteen," Jax said quietly. "Your mother got the house almost thirteen years ago."

Dr. Melendez made notes on her iPad. "What day of the week is it?"

"Monday. I think. It's hard to keep track in here."

"What time is it?"

Gretchen looked around for the time. She needed her phone. Why hadn't anyone brought her phone in yet? "Not five. My phone?"

Jax scrunched up her face. "It broke in the fall. I guess you had it in your hand."

She huffed at yet another thing broken in this stupid accident. She needed a favor from Jax. *Pick up a new phone for me?*

Jax wiped her palms on her jeans after reading. "You'll have to order it online."

"Why?"

"We're not on the same account anymore. I don't think they'll allow me to do anything in your name."

Gretchen's gut twisted, and her throat tightened as she prepared herself to ask the one question that scared her the most. "Are we divorced?"

Jax kept her head down. "I don't think this is the time or place—"

"Answer me!" Gretchen's ribs felt like they were ready to break. "I've answered every question," she said forcefully. The sluggishness of her mouth made her angrier. "And now I think I deserve answers." She refused to look away from Jax, even as she listened to Amanda and Dr. Melendez shift around. Jax worked her jaw.

"No. Not yet," Jax said, shaking her head. "We filed, and the papers came in right before all this happened."

Gretchen wasn't sure if this news was better or worse. She finally allowed a few tears to escape, no longer having the strength to hold them in. Her head started to pound, and she felt nauseous from the pain. "You didn't correct me when I gave my address."

Jax's eyes were full of sadness, but Gretchen started to doubt even that. "That's your house. I moved out six months ago." That was the final kick to Gretchen's stamina.

Gretchen sank into the bedding, and she went completely limp. She was tired of listening, of answering questions, of looking into sympathetic eyes, and most of all she was tired of finding out her life sucked now.

"I'm tired," Gretchen said flatly. "Are we done?"

Dr. Melendez stood. "Yes. I have more than enough information. I'll tell the nurse to bring you some food."

"Don't bother." Gretchen covered her bare forearms to warm up. "I'd like something for the pain. Something that'll help me sleep."

"Okay. When you're feeling up to it, we'll have to discuss our next steps. I'd like to have you back at home next week."

She opened her eyes and stared at the ceiling.

"So soon?" Amanda said, concern making her voice too loud for Gretchen's tired head.

"Yes. There may be some planning involved. The most important things will be comfort and familiarity, and she'll need someone with her around the clock at first. She won't be able to drive for six months at the very least."

Gretchen felt detached as she listened to other people talk about her and make plans for her like she wasn't even there.

Dr. Melendez kept talking, even after Gretchen thought she made her desire to be left alone clear. "Going home will be a shock to Gretchen. Although we've discussed what her life is like now, she still only remembers four years ago. You will both be responsible for making the transition into present-day as smooth as possible. Help her remain calm. Help her relearn everyday routines. Help her with Caleb."

"I don't think I should be so involved," Jax said quietly. If she was trying to keep Gretchen from hearing her, she'd failed.

A tear ran down the side of Gretchen's face. "Please leave. All of you."

Amanda touched Gretchen's shoulder. "Are you sure?"

Gretchen nodded.

"I can come back later?"

"No. Let me sleep."

Amanda gave her shoulder a squeeze and stepped away. Even the sound of Jax and Amanda getting their coats on and things together was too loud for Gretchen to handle. She took a shaky breath to help deal with the pain in her skull. She didn't look away from the ceiling until the door shut and she was surrounded by quiet. She saw the three of them outside the small window in the door. Jax and Amanda continued to talk to Dr. Melendez. Gretchen didn't even care what was being said. She was no longer her own person. What was worse was having to strong-arm the woman who was supposed to be by her side in sickness and in health into caring about her.

She looked at the flowers lining her room. Gretchen had many people in her life who cared, but the new addition to the collection stood out. Jax had honored her request and brought back a small flower arrangement. The collection of daisies was bright and too cheery given the circumstances, but she had always loved daisies when she was feeling down.

A folded piece of paper on the floor caught her eye. It sat under the unused chair in the corner of the room, by the windowsill. Gretchen almost called for a nurse to grab it, but then she remembered she was allowed to walk. She waited for Amanda and Jax to leave before sliding out of bed gently. She placed her nonskid socks against the linoleum and walked over to the corner.

Walking was one adventure, and now bending over was going to be a challenge. She sat on the chair and twisted awkwardly so she didn't hurt her ribs any more, and her head ached slightly. She used her foot to grab the paper and slide it closer to her. She knelt on the floor and picked it up. Standing took longer than expected, and she winced when every joint ached with the movement. By the time Gretchen was back in bed, she was winded and sweating.

Her hands were shaking as she unfolded the paper. She started to cry the moment she recognized the opening line.

> *Hey you. I can't believe we're getting married tomorrow. I feel like we just met! I can still smell the books in the library and feel your stare from across the reference section. You were so cute with your floppy brown hair and baggy cargo shorts. I have to admit, I'm glad your style improved over the years! You're going to look stunning tomorrow. I can't wait to see you, to touch you, to promise you forever. I am so lucky to be loved by you.*
>
> *One day away from forever yours,*
> *Gretchen*

A tear fell from Gretchen's nose onto the paper. What was this letter doing here? Why could she hear Jax's voice in her head while reading it? Gretchen held the letter to her chest and lay back. If Jax had brought it to the hospital, she'd had a reason. Gretchen cherished every letter she had written and received, and she had no idea when she had stopped. Gretchen looked at the blank notepad next to her and wondered how many other things had also stopped.

CHAPTER TWELVE

21 days, 15 hours, 31 minutes

The next six days of hospital living were rigorous for Gretchen. She'd wake up in the morning and hardly have a moment to herself after a breakfast of mediocre French toast or pancakes. The nurses had her up and walking, showering herself, and getting set up for her meetings with a speech therapist. Those meetings always left Gretchen feeling positive, yet even more confused. As a therapist herself, she understood how unpredictable healing and recovery could be, but if one more person told her how crazy the brain was, she was going to leave her bed and admit herself to the psychiatric ward. When she returned to her room after the meeting, she was greeted by the unpleasant sight of Jax and Amanda arguing in the hallway. She rolled her eyes at them and went straight to her bed.

Amanda was the first to follow her. "How was therapy?"

"Fine," Gretchen said in a huff. "I'm still expected to make a full recovery." Her speech was surer, and her words came a little faster.

"That's great. You sound great."

"I have to bring Caleb by," Jax said as she entered the room with heavy footsteps. "You can't keep avoiding him. I'm running out of excuses."

"I'm not avoiding him." She felt ashamed to lie and hated how those words came easily when asking for potato chips was still a struggle.

"Yes, you are, and as much as I hate that you're doing it, I do understand it's scary. The kid is loud and in your face, but God, he misses his mother and is so worried about you." Jax looked at her with wide, pleading eyes.

Gretchen's heart started to ache. She thought of their baby, the infant she had in her mind whose eyes mirrored her own. "Okay. Bring him by after dinner."

Jax eyed her skeptically. "Won't you be tired? You get cranky when you're tired."

Amanda snorted.

"I feel pretty cranky right now," she replied sharply. She was proud of how she sounded like her old self.

"How about I go get Caleb now, and we bring you some rocky road from the place across town, not the one right around the corner whose chocolate ice cream tastes like white?"

"It does taste like white." Gretchen crossed her arms over her chest and felt every bit like a child throwing a tantrum. But ice cream did sound good. "A large cup with—"

"Extra sprinkles." Jax smiled at her. They had softened around each other considerably over the past week, but the ice was still there. Gretchen was unsure if she'd ever thaw. Jax grabbed her jacket and left.

"I'm fine. No ice cream for me, thank you," Amanda called out to Jax. "Gotta watch the waistline."

"If I had my phone, I'd be able to text her your order."

"That reminds me." Amanda reached into her bag that seemed to grow a size every day. "This came today. I stopped by the Verizon store and very kindly explained the situation. They helped me restore everything."

Gretchen snatched the box from Amanda's hands and hugged it. "You're a saint. An absolute saint."

Amanda bowed slightly. "For many reasons, but you don't have to bother listing them now."

Gretchen unboxed the phone and grew antsy as she powered it on. The small screen flashed with a bombardment of messages, alerts, and notifications. She deleted the meaningless ones first and then opened her messages. Everything else pending could wait. Amanda deserved any and all ice cream her heart desired.

"What would you like? My treat." She opened a text window to Jax and swallowed hard when their full message string popped up. For all the blessings technology gave, Gretchen felt cursed. She read through each exchange, one more curt and hurtful than the next. She barely recognized herself in the words. "Was this really us?"

"What?" Amanda asked offhandedly, her nose busy in her own phone.

"Jax and me." She tilted the screen for Amanda to read.

"Oh, shit. I shouldn't have had them restore messages."

"Yes, you should have. I want to know everything. It's bad enough my brain has been erased—at least I have this to fill in some blanks." She kept scrolling back as far as she could. Two months of back-and-forth that would read like hatred to anyone else. But Gretchen knew better, didn't she? "I can't believe this is us now."

"It doesn't have to be, does it?"

Gretchen read a message aloud. "*I don't care what you do, just show up and get Caleb on time. I wish I didn't even have to depend on you at all.*" She looked at Amanda, feeling sick with sadness and regret, but mostly denial. "This can't be me. How could I have become this monster?"

"You're not a monster."

"Amanda, I told my wife I don't care about her. The woman I will love until my dying day." The sentiment of her words wasn't lost as she lay back in her hospital bed.

"You've both been through a lot. You both changed. I'm sure Jax has said some pretty ugly things, too."

"What happened between us? Do you know?"

Amanda hesitated before answering. "I don't know specifics. You and I were just starting to get close, and I don't think you felt like you could confide in me. Or maybe you just didn't want to."

"See! That right there. Why wouldn't I want to confide in my sister? What did I do to make you think I wouldn't?" Gretchen took consecutive deep breaths. She had been working on calming techniques since Dr. Melendez stressed the importance of not getting overly upset. But deep breathing didn't stop her tears. "I stopped being a good wife, and I never even tried to be a good sister. I have no memories, but I am surrounded by the smoking wreckage of my life. God, what kind of mother am I?"

Amanda grabbed her hand and rubbed it between hers. "You are an incredible mother. Caleb absolutely adores you. Maybe this is your second chance to make everything else better."

"I don't think there's a way to make things better with Jax."

"You may not be able to repair your marriage, but you can become better people together."

"I love her so much, and it hurts me every time she's here because I know she's counting the minutes until she can leave."

"That's not true."

"We have—" Gretchen stopped herself and bit the inside of her cheek, trying to control her emotions. "We *had* the kind of love you really believe in, you know?"

Amanda's grip on Gretchen's hand tightened. "I know."

"We fell in love in college, for Christ's sake. How do you make it this far and then suddenly just walk away? What are our lives like now? Where is she living? Has she already moved on?"

"I wish I had more answers for you."

She studied Amanda's face. They might not have been close, but there had always been a bond. Amanda knew something she wasn't sharing. "I know you've gotten close to Jax since the accident."

Amanda chuckled. "I wouldn't say that."

"I'm not asking you to betray her trust."

"It has nothing to do with betraying Jax, and more about you and her talking openly. If you want to learn about her life, ask her."

Gretchen wanted to laugh. "She won't answer me. Every time I try to scratch the surface with her, she shuts down."

Amanda was grinning.

"Why are you smiling like a maniac?"

"Your speech is incredible."

Gretchen hadn't even realized how little she had struggled through her last few sentences. "I guess I really earned my ice cream, then."

"Did someone say ice cream?" Wyatt walked into the room, excitement lighting up his eyes.

"We don't get ice cream. Only Gretchen does," Amanda said with a pout.

"I'm having flashbacks to senior year." Wyatt leaned over the bed to kiss Gretchen's cheek. "Hey, babe."

"Wyatt." Gretchen warmed at his familiar face. She had seen him once since she was fully conscious, but it was only for a quick visit to catch up. "How's Carly?"

"Ready to pop," he said, motioning to his own belly.

"I still can't believe she's pregnant. Hell, I still can't believe you two are married." Gretchen laughed along with Wyatt.

"That's almost exactly what you said when I proposed."

"How did you two end up together, again? Last I remember, you were not that into Carly."

Wyatt pulled off his knit hat and took a seat. "I was not, but we reconnected a couple years ago. It was actually at Mike Pearson's Christmas party."

"Mike throws great parties," she said to Amanda. "Were we there? Did I get to watch the sparks fly?"

Wyatt shook his head. "You guys were invited, but a work thing came up and you canceled at the last minute."

"Really? I've never known Jax to pick work over a party."

"It was a work thing for you. Jax stayed home with Caleb."

"Oh."

"Anyway, Carly was there, and we fell easily into a groove. It was like no time passed at all. We spent most of the night catching up, and that led to a date. Turns out you were right all along, and she was perfect for me."

Gretchen smiled warmly and looked at Amanda. "Maybe they know someone I can set you up with," she said with a poke to Amanda's arm.

"I'll check my Rolodex when I get home," Wyatt said. "Hey, Jax told me your speech has improved. She wasn't kidding."

"Every day is a little better. Hopefully, I'll be back to my old self soon."

"You already sound like her."

"That's not true." At least she sincerely hoped it wasn't true. Her old self, the self she failed to remember, was meaner. "I hit some hiccups and sometimes I'm unsure of a word, but my speech therapist made me put away the notebook and is forcing me to talk."

"Meanwhile, at one time, we had to force you to shut up."

"Says the chattiest guy in every room."

Amanda raised her hand and said, "Even I agree with that."

She felt a fraction better in that moment. Wyatt was always a positive presence, and having a regular conversation felt good. She didn't feel pressured to remember any of the missing details of Wyatt's life. They continued chatting casually about Wyatt's impending fatherhood, Carly's wildest cravings, and how Amanda knew where to find the best kebabs in central Jersey. Over an hour had passed when someone questioned Jax's absence.

"Is Jax freezing the cream herself?" Wyatt stood and pulled on his coat. "Let her know I stopped by."

"I can't believe she's taking this long," Amanda said, checking her watch.

"You know how Caleb can be," Wyatt said. "You tell him to get his shoes, and he comes back with a dinosaur." Wyatt and Amanda laughed.

Gretchen felt left out of the joke. Like she wasn't even part of her own child's life. "Is he really that much of a handful?"

Wyatt's face fell, and Gretchen could see the wheels turning as he processed just how much she didn't remember. "No. He's great, like, *really* great."

"He is the perfect balance of sugar and spice," Amanda explained, "but the sugar has made him very hyper."

Wyatt pointed at Amanda. "What she said. It was great seeing and talking with you. You look terrific." Wyatt gave Gretchen another quick kiss and turned to Amanda. "Make sure you give Jax shit for missing me."

"I will," Amanda said, laughing softly. "Especially if she was with her little girl—" Amanda's eyes flew wide. "Especially if she was with her boss. He probably called her in." Amanda and Wyatt stood awkwardly and stared at one another.

Gretchen knew her ears did not deceive her. "Were you going to say girlfriend?"

Wyatt bowed. "I'm out. See you soon."

"Jax has a girlfriend?"

Amanda turned to Gretchen slowly. She clasped her hands together, white-knuckled, and closed her eyes. "This is none of my business."

"You opened the can of worms, Amanda—now tell me."

"It's not my business to tell, and I don't know everything."

Her heart was pounding. "Is this girl the reason why she asked for a divorce?"

"You have to talk to Jax about this, not me."

Then, Jax walked into the room with Caleb at her side. "Go say hi to Mama."

Caleb's eyes were so bright with happiness, Gretchen momentarily forgot her anger. He ran to her bedside and didn't hesitate to climb up to sit with her.

Every second of fear and discontent melted away once Caleb burrowed into her side. She pressed her nose into his unruly hair and recognized his scent, even if she didn't recognize him. She pulled Caleb into a tight hug that made her feel a little more whole and a little less like her whole world was spiraling out of her control.

"Not too tight, Cricket," Jax said. "Mama's still healing."

"She's the one crushing me," Caleb mumbled from against Gretchen's chest.

Gretchen laughed and released Caleb from her grip. She swatted at the tears on her cheek. "I'm sorry, Caleb. I'm just really happy to see you."

"And we're really happy to have ice cream." Jax raised a white bag in the air. Her eyes were misty and her smile bright. "I can't imagine a better way to celebrate this reunion." Jax unpacked the bag, handing a small cup to Caleb along with a pile of napkins just for him. She handed Gretchen her rocky road and a spoon and pulled out another cup for Amanda.

"I know you like strawberry."

Amanda was very obviously touched. "Thank you."

Gretchen didn't open her ice cream. Instead she watched as Jax sat back and enjoyed her own treat. Jax seemed blissful with each taste. She watched Jax's mouth and her strong hands. She thought about Jax with another woman and the image made her mad.

"Did they not give you enough sprinkles? I asked for double extra." Jax looked at Gretchen in concern.

Gretchen turned to Amanda, then the ice cream in her hands, and finally back to Jax. "Did you cheat on me?"

The plastic spoon hung from Jax's mouth as she gawked at Gretchen. "Not now."

"Did you?"

"No. I didn't."

"So, did you just start seeing your girlfriend?"

"Let's just enjoy our ice cream. We can talk about this another time when you-know-who isn't present."

Gretchen knew Jax was right. Caleb looked so happy, smeared in cotton candy ice cream and dancing as he ate. His happiness meant more to her than getting answers, but once she got Jax alone, she would find out everything she was dying to know.

"Fine," Gretchen said harshly. She popped the clear lid off her ice cream and frowned. It was half melted, but she knew her favorite flavor would taste better than hospital dessert, regardless.

CHAPTER THIRTEEN

22 days, 14 hours, 2 minutes

Gretchen sent Jax a dozen messages and even tried to call her, but Jax was blatantly ignoring her. They were set to have a meeting with Dr. Melendez, and both Amanda and Jax were running late. Gretchen knew they'd be discussing her release and future care, which should have made her feel good, but she couldn't have cared less about her own well-being since the girlfriend bomb was dropped. She checked her phone again. Amanda said she was parking, but Jax was still MIA.

"Un-fucking-believable." She opened her email and scrolled through a bunch of junk. She had a few work emails to answer, but she'd promised herself she'd wait until she was home before worrying about work. If she could even focus on anything other than her missing wife.

"I'm so sorry I'm late," Amanda said as she rushed into the room. She pulled off her scarf and jacket in a hurry. "Did Dr. Melendez come in yet?"

"No, but we're getting started as soon as she does. I'm not waiting for Jax."

"She still hasn't answered you?"

"No." Gretchen regarded Amanda. "Are you wearing lipstick?" She leaned closer. "Is that eyeshadow?"

Amanda covered her face self-consciously. "I always wear a little makeup."

"This is more than a little. Do you have a date today? Or is this all for a certain MD?"

"For the last time, I'm not interested in Dr. Melendez like that." Amanda checked the door. "But that doesn't mean I don't enjoy the attention."

"Your cleavage is distracting."

Amanda adjusted her shirt just as Dr. Melendez entered the room.

"Good morning, ladies." Dr. Melendez looked at Amanda's chest for a split second before her attention was solely on Gretchen. "Who's ready to go home tomorrow?"

"Tomorrow?" she said hopefully. "You really think I'm ready?"

"I do. Your speech bounced back more quickly than we expected, your body is healing and moving well, and you're acclimating to your meds with no issues." Dr. Melendez looked around the room. "Should I wait to continue? Jax may want to hear some of this."

"Jax is choosing not to be here."

Dr. Melendez's mouth formed a small O. "Your scans look good. Everything looks good. Do you feel ready to go home?"

Gretchen answered quickly, "I do. I may not remember much, but I'm sure I still love my own bed better than this hospital one." She gripped the rail for emphasis.

Dr. Melendez excused herself as she stepped between Amanda and Gretchen's bedside. She started examining Gretchen's shoulder and ribs. "How has your pain been?"

"Getting better day by day."

"I want you to take over-the-counter meds like Tylenol or Advil instead of continuing with the narcotics. If you feel like they aren't doing the trick, call me and I'll prescribe something stronger."

"I'll be okay."

Amanda chimed in and said, "She's always had a high tolerance for pain. Not like me, I'm a baby."

"I find that very hard to believe," Dr. Melendez said. Her eyes stayed on Gretchen the whole time.

Gretchen couldn't see Amanda's face, but she was sure she swooned. "When can I go back to work?"

Gretchen winced as Dr. Melendez tilted her head to evaluate her wound. The bump on the back of her skull might have been shrinking, but it was still tender to the touch. "I'd like you to wait at least another two weeks, at which time you'll come in to see me for a follow-up and an MRI."

The thought of two weeks at home with no work as a distraction worried Gretchen. But she had a four-year-old to keep her busy.

Jax barged into the room. "What did I miss?" Her face was hard, and she didn't even cast a glance at Gretchen.

They were all silent. Dr. Melendez coughed.

"Gretchen is being discharged tomorrow," Amanda said. "No pain meds."

Dr. Melendez tapped the screen of her iPad. "You will have your antiseizure medication. It's very important you follow the instructions and take those on schedule. Avoid physical exertion, high-stress situations. Just take it easy. Once I see you in two weeks, we'll know what the next step is."

"No driving?"

"Absolutely no driving."

"Can I run? I used to jog every day."

Jax snickered. "You may want to take it easy with that. I don't think you've been running in over a year."

That was impossible. Jax was crazy or messing with her. "Every morning I get up at six, run for a half hour, and then get ready for my day."

"That's what you *used to* do. Now you have to be at work at seven thirty. You stopped running and opted to get a stationary bike, but it's just collecting dust."

"I don't recall that." Gretchen used to love her morning runs, and she couldn't believe she'd give them up so quickly. She had started almost every day with a jog to awaken her body, mind, and senses. She even got Jax to join her most days. She almost proposed they run together again, but Jax's back was to her. Their connection, their togetherness no longer existed.

Dr. Melendez pursed her lips and looked like she was waiting for her turn to speak. "If exercising is something you'd like to do, I encourage it. It's good for mind and body—just be careful not to overdo it. Same goes for other physical activities." Dr. Melendez's tone dripped with suggestion.

Gretchen gaped, then collected herself. "Oh. No. That's not a problem." She pulled at the collar of her pajama shirt. "I will be jogging, though."

"Okay, then. Someone needs to be with you around the clock until we know you're less of a seizure risk."

"When will we know that?" Amanda asked.

Dr. Melendez's face scrunched up like she was working out an actual word problem. "Probably close to the three-month mark, but this is why the follow-up appointments are important. I'll keep checking her progress and her brain. She may be in the clear sooner."

"Three months is a long time," Jax said.

"And during the first two to three weeks, she needs as much familiarity as possible." Dr. Melendez finally addressed Gretchen directly. "Daily routines that feel good, not foreign. What's a typical day for you?"

After over two weeks of doubting everything that was once normal, Gretchen felt blindsided by the question. "Um, a morning run, usually with Jax. A shower and a light breakfast. I don't like to eat a lot first thing. An early lunch, and then a second late lunch." Gretchen smiled at the way Amanda laughed at her. "I go to work, then come home to Jax in the kitchen," she said, finally looking at Jax, her heart forlorn and aching. "I offer to help, but she tells me to sit and have some wine."

"That was before Caleb." Jax's point was made sharply.

"Once Caleb was born, I would get home and nurse him. Instead of telling me to have wine, you'd pour me a Sprite and add a dash of grenadine. I remember all of that, too."

"I can stay with you, but I can't promise my cooking is as good as Jax's." Amanda's tone and stance screamed awkwardness.

"After dinner, I'd do the dishes and tell you to go relax." Gretchen ignored Amanda's offer and carried on with her normal-day narrative. A normal day married to Jax. "Then we'd sit on the couch watching HGTV while Caleb screamed, never really knowing whose arms he wanted to be in. But he always ultimately chose you. We'd go to bed, and I'd fall asleep with a smile because I was so happy knowing I'd get up and get to do it all over again." The room grew eerily silent once Gretchen stopped talking.

Dr. Melendez closed the cover to her iPad. The slapping sound was loud in the tense space. "I recommend whatever can be done to make you comfortable. It's important for you to avoid anything that could potentially trigger a seizure. So if a jog and a Sprite will do it, do it. You'll have to accommodate for Caleb, but I think your son will only add to your happiness and recovery." Dr. Melendez started to make her exit, but Gretchen stopped her.

"Can I ask you something?"

"Absolutely."

"Do you think I'll regain my memories? Just your opinion." Gretchen waited with bated breath for the answer.

Dr. Melendez shook her head and considered the question. "The thing I like most about neurology is how incredible the brain is. It's the most powerful organ, and the one we understand the least about. When it comes to retrograde amnesia, there's never any guarantee, which means I don't have an answer for you. What I can tell you is your recovery is miraculous. Your life now should be cherished and lived, regardless of what you're missing from your past."

Gretchen knew she was right, but Dr. Melendez didn't know what living with a blank space in her head was like. "Thank you."

"You all take care, and I'll see you in the morning when we cut this one loose." Dr. Melendez gave Amanda's forearm a gentle touch as she passed by.

Jax pointed to Amanda's arm. "How are you not going to date her after this?"

"I'm not into women, Jax—get over it."

Gretchen didn't care about Amanda's dating life at the moment. "So, what are we going to do? What's the plan? I'm sure the two of you have been conspiring behind my back ever since Dr. Melendez mentioned my impending dependency a week ago."

"We have not," Amanda said.

She waved off what was sure to be an elaborate story to dance around what she knew was true. "I've seen the hushed conversations and fights." She pointed to Jax. "You don't want to be around me, and even though Amanda is eager to help, that probably makes you feel guilty."

"That's not—"

Gretchen wasn't done. "Don't feel guilty. I don't want you around if you don't want to be there. Yes, you may be the familiarity I need, but this person you are now is not the familiar person I know or want. So I won't burden you." Gretchen fell back against her pillow and crossed her arms over her chest. Getting the words out made her feel better for a fraction of a minute, until Jax left the room without a word. Amanda followed her, and Gretchen turned her head to watch them talk just outside the doorway.

She could hear her name from time to time but couldn't muster up the energy to care anymore. Jax was gone. Their marriage was over. Why prolong the inevitable and force Jax into something she clearly wanted to avoid? Gretchen could find comfort in her new normal. She had to.

Jax was the first to walk back into the room. "Gretchen, listen, about this morning and everything—"

"Save it." Gretchen hated the way her heart betrayed her and skipped a beat after just one glance at Jax. "It's okay, really, just go. You want to, and I don't want to force you into anything. We're basically divorced, right? So any obligation you feel is gone. Just help me out with Caleb—that's all I ask."

"After talking to Amanda, I think it'll be smartest for me to move back until Dr. Melendez gives you the all clear."

"I don't want you to." Gretchen meant it.

"I don't really want to either, but you're going to need constant help with Caleb in the beginning. How am I supposed to do that from my apartment? Amanda is great with him, but I'm his other parent."

Gretchen shook her head slightly. "I don't want your pity."

"This isn't about you," Jax said, sounding annoyed, "and I was just reminded it's not about me, either. It's about Cricket. You need to be the best version of yourself every day for him, and so do I. It'll make things easier for everyone because he won't be bounced back and forth."

"Did Amanda put you up to this?"

Jax stared at her with wide eyes. "No."

Gretchen shot her a look.

"Well, she pointed out a few things, but mostly how the familiarity of all of us being together could help your memory. Who knows, maybe one day of arguing over what to have for dinner will bring it all back for you."

Gretchen was afraid to feel hopeful. "Are you sure?"

Jax nodded. "Amanda will come over while I'm at work or if I just need a break."

"Or if Gretchen needs a break from you," Amanda said, rejoining them.

"I'm not saying it'll be easy or ideal, but it's for the best."

She chose to ignore the insincerity in Jax's eyes. Jax didn't believe a word she was saying, but Gretchen would believe enough for both of them.

Chapter Fourteen

23 days, 14 hours, 2 minutes

The cold air was biting but fresh. Gretchen inhaled as deeply as she could, to cleanse the hospital from her lungs. The sun was shining, and even though it wasn't the summer she remembered, she was happy to be outside. She sat back in the wheelchair and waited for Amanda to come around with her car.

"Remember, take it easy," the nurse who escorted her outside said. "If you have any questions or concerns, you have Dr. Melendez's number. She can be reached for emergencies. Otherwise, call her office, and they'll help you."

"Got it."

"I think this is your ride." The nurse put the brakes on and offered her hand for assistance.

Gretchen insisted on doing it herself. Her body got tired quickly and she was far from in shape, but her body felt better than her mind. She was anxious to get home but worried about being there. "You've all been so wonderful."

"It's easy when the patient is as kind as you. Get better, Gretchen."

Amanda rushed around her car to grab Gretchen's bag and open the door, then waited until she was seated to slam it shut and offer the nurse a polite good-bye. When Amanda got back in the car, she said, "She was one of the nicest nurses I've ever met."

"I can't remember her name for the life of me." Gretchen squinted out the window.

Amanda didn't drive. "Do you think that's your memory?"

"No," Gretchen said confidently. "I think I was here too long and met too many people."

They laughed, and then Amanda said, "That's fair. Do you need me to stop anywhere for you on the way home?"

"If I need anything later, I'll make a list. Right now I just want to be home."

Amanda pulled away from the hospital into late morning traffic.

The trip took longer than it should have thanks to Amanda's overly cautious driving, so Gretchen was bouncing her leg with impatience by the time they entered her neighborhood.

"Whose car is in the driveway?"

"The truck? That's Jax's."

"No. I'd recognize that monster anywhere. The other one."

"That's your car."

"Huh." She scoped out the silver BMW as Amanda parked. She got out of the car and touched the cold exterior. "When did I get this?"

"Last year. Your lease was up, and you wanted to get something fancy. Reward yourself for all your hard work."

"Nice…" She must've had a lot of changes at work if this was the kind of treat she got for herself.

"Go inside," Amanda demanded. "You're going to freeze out here. I'll bring in your bag."

She took each step up to the front porch hesitantly. She held the rail with a tight grip, haunted by her accident. She couldn't remember falling, but her body must. She opened the front door and started to cry the moment recognizable scents hit her.

Their home. *Her* home. This was the first time Gretchen felt like herself, like her life wasn't just a story being told by others.

"Mama!" Caleb ran toward her, Jax hot on his heels.

"Careful, Cricket. Remember what I told you."

Caleb listened and slowed down to a turtle's pace before wrapping his arms around Gretchen's legs. "Me and Bug will make you better."

Gretchen hugged Caleb. They stood in the doorway, swaying slightly, and she believed him. "I've been meaning to ask…Bug and Cricket?" She shot Jax a curious glance and walked into the house.

Jax shrugged. "He'd rub his legs together as he fell asleep. I called him Cricket, then you said it's not very nice and asked if I'd like to be called a bug. It all kinda stuck after that."

"I think this is everything." Amanda placed Gretchen's bag on the couch just inside the front door. "I'll leave you all to get settled. Text me a list for the store later, okay?"

Gretchen hugged Amanda tightly before letting her leave. She'd be lost without Amanda. "I'll talk to you later."

The front door shut behind her, and silence fell in the house. A television played in the distance. She noticed small differences: the decor was a little darker, the pictures were new, and the wall separating the kitchen and living room was gone. The space felt so much bigger.

"Once Caleb came along, we wanted to be able to watch him at all times, but we wanted to stay firm on not eating in the living room."

"I love it."

"You were so happy with the result." Jax picked up her bag and started toward the back of the house. "I'll bring this to your room."

"Same room?"

"Yeah," Jax said over her shoulder. "We moved my office upstairs so the nursery would be next to us, and there's a spare bedroom up there, too. That'll be my room."

Gretchen knew it was coming, but that didn't make it any easier to handle. Jax would be sleeping in a different room. Great. She walked past Caleb's room and stopped. Gone were the elephants and giraffes and other stuffed animals crowding a rocking chair. Now the walls were covered with clouds and airplanes, and his crib had been replaced by a racer bed. Her baby was gone.

"I think the cruelest part of all this is not remembering my son growing up." Her eyes burned with sadness. "What was his first word?"

Jax swallowed hard. She was just as emotional as Gretchen. "Dada, believe it or not."

She laughed through her tears. "Get out."

"I think it's just a sound babies make, and people think they mean their father. At least that's what we told ourselves. Mama was next."

"Are there any videos?"

"I'm sure we have a ton saved on the Mac. Once you're settled, you can go through everything." Jax placed the bag on the bed and left the room without another word.

Gretchen took off her jacket and opened the closet to her left. Every hanger was taken up with drab work clothes—blouses, dress pants, skirts—each duller than the last. She used to hang her jackets in there. She tried the other closet across the room and frowned. What used to be Jax's closet now held her outerwear and shoes. Reality sucked.

Caleb came bouncing into the room. "I colored for you. It's a frog."

She smiled. "I can't wait to see it. Go help Bug with whatever she's doing, and I'll be right out, okay?" She thought he was going to argue by the way he stared her down, but he smiled and bounced out of the room. She sighed in relief and sat on her bed. The bed used to be against the opposite wall, and the comforter was new, but the room still felt like home.

She needed a shower and sweats. The warmest sweats she had. Gretchen went through her dresser drawers, which were also completely mixed up. Her patience started to wane, but she eventually found sweatpants, a worn T-shirt, and a plush sweatshirt. Her underwear and socks were in the same place. She stepped into the connected bathroom and flicked on the light. Nothing about the small bathroom had changed.

She placed her clothes on the vanity and started undressing. This was the first time she'd really be able to see her body. She stripped away her sweater and undershirt slowly. She gasped at the fading bruises on her skin. Both of her sides were marked, and her shoulder still held a hint of purple. She examined the scrapes along her face, now just patches of lighter skin. She pulled off her jeans and looked at the faint bruising on her hips and healing cuts on her knees. It was a wonder her injuries weren't more serious.

She jumped when Jax knocked at the door. "Yeah?"

"Are you okay in there?"

"I'm fine. Just checking out my battle wounds."

"I've started lunch. It'll be ready by the time you get out."

"What are we having?"

Jax didn't answer for a beat. "Lipton noodle soup. I know it seems boring, but I couldn't imagine eating anything else after being in the hospital."

"It sounds perfect. I'll be out in fifteen minutes."

"Take your time."

Gretchen turned on the water and searched the narrow linen closet for a towel and shower cap, in no mood to aggravate the painful bump on her head. She stepped under the hot water and felt more relaxed than she had since waking up that dreadful night.

Gretchen welcomed the comfort of her cocoa butter body wash and exfoliating loofah. After scrubbing her face, taking a pumice stone to her feet, and shaving the important areas, Gretchen started to feel brand new. She dried off quickly and wrapped herself in her thick terry robe. She pulled off her shower cap and pulled on her slippers before leaving the bathroom. She nearly ran into Jax right outside the door.

"I'm sorry." Jax held up her hands. "I was about to check on you."

Gretchen gripped her chest. Her heart was racing. "I'm okay. I promise. You don't have to check on me constantly."

"It's going to take me a while to believe that." Jax looked down at Gretchen's chest. She went back to the kitchen.

Gretchen wondered if they'd ever be normal around each other again.

After getting dressed, she joined Caleb and Jax in the kitchen. Caleb was already halfway through his bowl of soup. He chewed at a piece of buttered roll as he colored.

"He seems to really like coloring."

Jax spun around at her voice. "Yeah. He has about a hundred different books. It's good for us because it keeps him in one place." Jax checked on Caleb before turning back to Gretchen and mouthing *and quiet*.

The dinosaur Caleb was working on had many colors, all inside the lines. "He must take after you," Gretchen said as she sat. The soup smelled wonderful and the golden brown rolls called her name. "I shouldn't eat all these carbs, but I think I deserve them."

"I think you should worry about getting better, not what you eat." Jax filled her own spoon with noodles and ate with enthusiasm.

Dinner progressed with little excitement, for the adults at least. Caleb had all kinds of stories to tell from preschool, and he showed Gretchen the frog he'd colored for her. He was so proud that Gretchen couldn't help but grin right along with him.

"Two artists in one family, and I can barely draw a stick figure. I'm going to get an inferiority complex."

"You would color with him a lot. Hey, Cricket, why don't you grab that picture of the octopus you drew with Mama?"

Caleb jumped off his chair and ran to his room.

"You weren't kidding when you said he was a jumping bean," Gretchen said with a laugh.

"He's always going, always talking, always asking about something we know very little about."

Gretchen knew so little and wanted to learn everything. "Has he been checked?"

Jax stopped collecting the dishes, her mouth agape. "Checked?"

"Yeah. Checked. For ADHD or anything like that."

Jax placed the bowls in the sink loudly and turned on the water full force. "I wish Dr. Melendez had prescribed *me* something for pain."

"Look, I know it's not easy to talk about, but it is something that needs to be considered." Gretchen stood next to Jax and lowered her voice. "It's not uncommon, and it doesn't mean there's anything wrong with him."

"I know," Jax said more loudly than necessary. "That's exactly what you told me the first time we fought about it."

"I didn't know—"

"He does, by the way, have ADHD. You were right then, and you're right now."

"Jax," she said, touching Jax's shoulder gently, "I didn't mean anything by it. I was curious."

Jax stared at her hand like the touch was so odd. Gretchen pulled back. "We agreed to forgo medication until he was a little older."

"Did the doctor suggest that?"

"Jesus Christ. If I have to relive every fight over again, I'm going to lose my fucking mind." Jax scrubbed the dishes forcefully.

"How do you think I feel?" Gretchen's ire rose. "You don't want to repeat a few fights? Well, I don't want to have to relearn my son's entire life!"

Jax's hands stilled in the sink. "I'm sorry."

"Whatever. I'm asking you simple questions, and all I need are simple answers. If you can't *handle* that, then you shouldn't even be here."

"Here it is," Caleb announced as he marched into the kitchen. He stopped suddenly. "Are you fighting again?"

Gretchen's throat tightened. "No, Cricket, we're not. Now, tell me about that octopus."

"Bug said you don't remember."

Gretchen shook her head, unsure of how to explain such a crazy thing to a four-year-old. "I hurt my head really bad, and now I don't remember some things."

Caleb traced the lines that connected the arms of the octopus to its body. He didn't look away from the picture. "Do you remember me?"

Gretchen heard Jax sniffle, and she fought to maintain her own composure. "I don't remember the things we've done together or the places we've gone, but I remember you. Of course I remember you."

"You said I wasn't your baby." His frown was so deep, so intense, that he looked years older.

Gretchen hated herself. "I wasn't feeling very good that night, but you know what's cool?" She forced a cheery smile when Caleb raised his big brown eyes. "I'm going to be home every day for a while, so you can tell me about everything."

"Everything?"

"*Everything.* Tell me about school, your friends, your teachers, and what we did over the summer."

"Mrs. Henderson is my teacher. She's nice. My friends at school are Tommy, Lila, Danny—"

Gretchen laughed. "Okay, Cricket. Why don't you go get comfortable on the couch? I'll be in in a minute to lie with you and listen to all your stories."

"I need my blanket!" Caleb jetted off to his room.

Jax leaned back against the counter. Her expression was more relaxed, easier than it had been minutes before. "You might regret that."

Gretchen knew Jax was speaking specifically about Caleb's motormouth, but all she thought of were hours of Caleb in her arms telling her about his life and giving her a new memory to cherish. "Never. I'll never regret it."

CHAPTER FIFTEEN

24 days, 9 hours, 47 minutes

Gretchen was cranky the next morning. Her bed felt right, but the space was all wrong. Jax was upstairs, completely detached from her, and Caleb no longer needed to sleep with his mother. The quiet led her to so many of the thoughts she tried to avoid.

Who was Jax's girlfriend? How long had they been together? Did Jax miss her the way she missed Jax? Did Jax have a hard time sleeping without her, too?

She tried to count the questions like counting sheep, but they were better than caffeine at keeping her awake. She opened the wrong cabinet in the kitchen yet again, grumbling to herself. All she wanted was to get a pot of coffee ready for when she got back from her run. A run she desperately needed. Why was everything in the wrong place? The coffeemaker should be on the corner of the countertop, the coffee mugs should be in the cabinet above it, and the coffee should be in the fridge. She really should've given Amanda a list.

"I thought I heard you down here. What are you doing?" Jax wiped sleep from her eyes as she shuffled slowly into the kitchen.

Gretchen hated Jax's bedhead, and the way her stiff nipples caught her attention. And she really hated the strip of bare skin that peeked out from under her T-shirt when she stretched. Gretchen hated every single inconvenience this morning.

"I just want coffee."

"You gave up coffee. You're all about teas now." Jax opened the slender cabinet beside the range hood, the only one she hadn't opened. So many boxes of tea were piled up.

"Why would I give up coffee? Was I insane?"

Jax chortled. "I wondered the same thing, but it was for your health."

"Real good that did me."

"A new place opened up right on Broad Street. I can run and get you a cup if you'd like."

"No, that's okay. I'm sure you have to get ready for work or stop home or something."

"It's really no trouble."

"I'll have Amanda bring me some. I wanted to have a pot ready for when I get back from my run." Gretchen thought about what she had just said. "If I cared enough about my health to give up coffee, why would I stop running?"

"For work. You gave up a lot for work. I'm going to shower really quick, and then I'll get breakfast started for the little one."

Gretchen waved her off. "I can do it. Breakfast is one of the few meals I can handle."

Jax's smile was odd but soft. "I remember." She walked away but turned back just before she was out of earshot. "I'll be out in ten minutes, just in case you do need help." Maybe it was the delicacy of an early morning or the sleep fogging her mind, but Jax was much more like the Jax from her memories.

She went back to the kitchen and started to pull pans and bowls from the cabinets but quickly realized her preparation was for naught. The refrigerator was bare. All she had was one stick of butter, a couple yogurts nearing expiration, and something that used to be leafy. She hoped her pantry was more plentiful.

Oatmeal would have to do, and thankfully she could boil water without incident. She checked the time and knew she'd have to wake up Caleb soon, but the silence in the house was peaceful.

"Playing it safe with oatmeal, are you?" Jax was towel-drying her hair as she peeked at the ingredients.

Gretchen set out three bowls. "That was faster than ten minutes."

"It was actually twelve. Do you have any nuts?"

"Um…" Gretchen opened her cabinets but again ran into dishes where food should be. "Why would we switch the cabinets around?" she said much more loudly than necessary. "I can't find anything."

"Spring-cleaning fever a year and a half ago. That's when we redid Caleb's room, too." Jax stepped around Gretchen and opened the last upper cabinet. She pulled out a container of raisins and a small bag of almonds along with brown sugar and cinnamon. "Caleb prefers syrup in his oatmeal, but you haven't allowed that for a while. I sneak him some brown sugar, though."

"That's fine," Gretchen said, stepping back and allowing Jax to take over. She observed and ached, wishing she could understand the hows and whys. Jax prepared the simple breakfast with a sexy flair Gretchen watched keenly. Jax counted each raisin and placed it carefully, and the sprinkle of melting brown sugar looked beautiful. "I could watch you all day." Her small confession felt silly leaving her lips. She stuttered to save herself from embarrassment. "N-not like *that*, I just mean you're so artistic in everything you do. It's soothing to watch."

Jax rubbed sugar off her palm, her eyes down, and she didn't speak.

"I love watching you work," Gretchen said. "Painting especially, but when you carve or sculpt I could get lost in it for hours. Have you been working on anything recently?"

"No," Jax said, her expression completely closed off. She turned her back to Gretchen.

Gretchen looked at Jax's broad shoulders and the way her sweater hugged her body. Jax was only eight feet away but it felt like miles. "How did we get here? How the hell—"

"I'm going to get Caleb." Jax left the room.

She was so damn frustrated that she wanted to scream. She reminded herself to keep calm and breathe. In and out. In and out. Her heart rate was under control by the time Caleb came bounding into the room.

"Oatmeal! Oatmeal! Oatmeal!" he chanted. The dance that accompanied his excitement for something so mundane made her smile.

She brought each bowl to the small kitchen table and sat next to Caleb. He ate with gusto, she ate slowly, and Jax's bowl went untouched. Caleb talked nonstop about school and what they were learning. He was talking about someone named Rachel when the doorbell rang.

"Come in," Gretchen hollered. "Guess who that is?"

"Good morning." Amanda's voice carried through the house. She walked into the kitchen with a large shopping bag in one hand and her ever-present gigantic purse in the other. "Ooh, oatmeal. Today's the perfect day for a hot breakfast."

"What's in the bag?"

"Necessities."

Caleb's eyes lit up, and he dropped his spoon. Breakfast was obviously old news. "Presents?"

Amanda scrunched up her face. "Sorry, Cricket, this bag is full of boring adult stuff that'll help Mama feel better."

He sat back with force, wearing a pout.

"Hey, Caleb," Gretchen said gently. He shot her wicked side-eye. "Why don't you go pick out some clothes for today, and maybe I'll talk to Bug about getting you a present."

The kitchen chair nearly tipped over from the velocity of his body leaving the room. Gretchen and Amanda laughed.

"The old Gretchen would've never bargained like that."

"Yeah, well, the new Gretchen wants any and all peace she can get."

"Will this help?" Amanda asked as she reached into the shopping bag. She pulled out a bag of freshly ground coffee from Gretchen's favorite coffeehouse.

Gretchen snatched the bag and held it to her chest. She inhaled the heavenly aroma deeply. Coffee was the only medicine she needed. Now and forever. "How did you know?"

"You drank hospital coffee once a day after you were cleared to have caffeine. You deserved something better, and I knew you wouldn't have any here."

"So you know I went insane and quit coffee?"

"It was by far the strangest thing you've ever done."

Gretchen watched Jax walk past them directly to Caleb's room. She overheard Jax tell Caleb he wasn't allowed to wear whatever he had picked out and continue to direct him through his tantrum. She walked out with an impeccably dressed Caleb five minutes later. She stepped around Amanda, only offering a nod of acknowledgment as she grabbed Caleb's lunch from the refrigerator.

Caleb rushed over to kiss Gretchen good-bye. He hugged her so tightly her ribs hurt, but she wouldn't let go until he did.

"I love you."

"Love you, too, Mama."

"I'll be back later." Jax spoke to them in passing and led Caleb to the door. "If you need anything, text me. If you can't pick Caleb up, I'll ask Wyatt or Meredith." Her last word was barely out before the front door closed.

After a beat of silence, Amanda tentatively asked, "How were your first night and morning?"

Gretchen thrust the coffee into Amanda's hands. "Make a pot of this, and I'll tell you all about it."

Gretchen recounted how foreign she felt in her own bed. She detailed her awkward morning with Jax and how everything was just so weird.

"I hate feeling like a stranger in my life, to my son, and especially to my wife. Last night Caleb was telling me about school, and then he asked me where I put the Christmas tree he made me. Amanda, I had no idea what he was talking about. He was in a panic, thinking it'd be lost forever."

"Poor thing."

She sipped her coffee, the flavor and warmth comforting her deeply. "He's being so good, though. He wants to understand, but he's only four and a half." She ran her thumb along the inside of the mug's handle, deep in thought and getting lost in its smoothness. "The worst part wasn't even his panic. It was Jax not knowing where to find it, either."

"She's been out of the house for a while."

Gretchen looked out the window and noticed how gray the day was. "I think I'll skip my run."

"I don't think you should be running at all." Amanda's concern was still sweet, but still annoying.

"Dr. Melendez said I could."

"You need to take it easy."

"What I *need* is to remember what the hell happened over the past four years."

"You'll get your memories back."

"Will I?" Her tone lacked the hopefulness she should've felt. "At least if I remembered something, I could figure out how to fix my life."

"You can still fix it."

She eyed Amanda. "Where did all this positivity come from?"

Amanda laughed and went back to drinking her coffee, much lighter and sweeter than Gretchen's.

"I'm serious, Amanda. You're so different now."

Amanda leaned back in her chair, took a deep breath, and smiled at Gretchen. She looked peaceful. "After Mom died, I felt lost, like I didn't know who I was. I had no one to talk to or turn to. And before you say it, no, I couldn't come to you."

Gretchen lowered her head in shame. "I'm sorry for that."

"Don't be. You were dealing with your own mixed feelings. I got help, though, and I think I figured out who I am. I'm in a good place."

She gripped Amanda's hand on the tabletop. "I'm so happy for you, and I hope I get to be a big part of your life from here on out."

"You already are. We've been doing really well. Please stop feeling guilty for something we're past."

The relief of knowing their relationship had improved was huge and lifted Gretchen's spirits. Now if she could just get to the same place with Jax. Her next question made her feel slightly ill. "Have we been figuring out the divorce? What we'll do with Caleb or anything like that?"

"Oh, Gretchen. You don't have to worry about any of that right now."

"Don't I? Jax will be out of here the first chance she gets."

"You need to focus on healing and keeping calm. I'll be here even if Jax flies the coop."

"That's not fair to you. What about your life and your job? Do you work?"

Amanda shook her head. "I was an assistant for a bit, but then Mom passed. I've been able to live off the income from my inheritance."

"I forgot about the family money. Did we split the house, or did she leave it to the church, like she always threatened?" Gretchen said with a snort. God, her mother was such a piece of work.

"I'm still living in the house, and this is yet another thing I wish you remembered. Mom didn't leave you anything. She said you got more than enough when she helped you buy your house."

Gretchen sat stunned. She didn't think the chasm ran that deep, but what did she really know anymore?

"But," Amanda continued, "I insisted I give you what you were rightfully entitled to. You refused, I pushed, and we agreed to put it in trust for Caleb."

The unpredictable control Gretchen had over her emotions started to slip. "This is all so weird. I can't even explain it. It's like I'm living in a dream."

"I can't even begin to imagine, and I can't promise everything will be okay, but I am so happy you got a second chance."

Gretchen went to Amanda and hugged her. The position was awkward as she stood and Amanda sat, but she needed the comfort. She needed reassurance and to feel safe. She thought of Jax. "Do you think *she* could ever give me a second chance?" she whispered to Amanda.

"Anything is possible." Amanda pulled back and picked up Gretchen's coffee. She handed her the lukewarm mug. "You're even drinking coffee again."

"Thank God!" Gretchen laughed and let the lightness of the moment carry her through the day.

CHAPTER SIXTEEN

24 days, 15 hours, 31 minutes

Gretchen finally convinced Amanda she'd be fine for twenty minutes by herself. Caleb needed to be picked up, and Gretchen wasn't in the mood to hop in a freezing car and go to his preschool. A building full of screaming kids? No, thank you. After several rounds of back-and-forth, Amanda surrendered, but not without insisting Gretchen carry her phone with her at all times, even if she was walking from one side of the room to the other. She was beginning to feel like the elderly woman in the Life Alert commercial.

She finally felt up to unpacking her bag from the hospital. Even with Amanda and Jax bringing home her extra clothes and flowers ahead of time, she still had a bunch of odds and ends to deal with. She dumped the bag on her bed and sat beside the small pile. She had to shift around to find a comfortable position, reminding herself she was healing and her body would ache less eventually. She tossed the nonslip socks and piled the many get-well cards off to the side. She'd have to go through them again later once she was more comfortable. Her phone buzzed. Gretchen sighed at the message from Amanda.

Checking in.

For a split second, she considered not answering. But that wouldn't be nice. Funny? Yes. She typed out a quick message, assuring Amanda she was fine, and she put the phone back on the bed. The corner of the letter from Jax she had found in the hospital caught her eye. She shouldn't read it again—she already knew every word. She didn't even know if Jax was aware the letter was lost. If she didn't know, then maybe Jax really had stopped caring.

Gretchen went to her closet in search of the tattered craft box she kept her own letters in. The top shelf was stuffed with pillows and extra comforters, and the bottom was lined with shoeboxes and boots. The box was gone, but where? She couldn't have thrown away over fifteen years of love notes from Jax. Or could she? She couldn't have four years ago, but with everything that had happened since, anything was possible.

The thought of discarding such beautiful words was overwhelming in the worst way. Jax had declared so much, shared many confessions, and written endless sweet nothings. Gretchen refused to accept such a possibility. She went to her other closet and searched high and low. She didn't care about the pain in her ribs or the way her neck ached when she held her head a certain way. Not even the throbbing in her skull mattered. She was on a mission that took precedence over the rest of her meaningless daily tasks.

She spent ten minutes feeling like an alien in her own wardrobe before thinking to check upstairs. She rushed up the steps and paused at the top, winded. She held her aching side and breathed carefully. Three doors were closed. She knew one was the guest bedroom Jax was staying in, and the other her studio. The first door on the right was the bedroom. Gretchen almost let herself in. The desire to snoop through Jax's stuff was powerful, but she wouldn't be that person. She closed that door quietly and moved on to the next across the hall.

The room was nearly empty save for a drafting table and a bunch of boxes piled in the corner. She noticed a few easels sticking out from one box. She always poked fun at how Jax had collected a family of easels. The memory made her sad, so she kept searching. She checked the small closet, which was completely empty. Relief washed over her once she stepped out of that room and shut the door. Seeing such a stark, physical representation of Jax leaving her life made Gretchen's chest tighten. She needed to remain calm and find the craft box. If she still had those letters, that meant she hadn't given up on Jax completely.

And that was really it about the letters. If she *had* gotten rid of them, she was just as willing to divorce as Jax was—an idea she couldn't believe without proof. She opened the last door at the end of the hallway, dismayed to find a bathroom.

Disbelief slowed her footsteps as she walked back downstairs. The front door flew open, and Amanda rushed in with Caleb in tow.

"What were you doing?" Amanda said in a panic.

She opened her mouth, ready to confess how she had given up

on her marriage, but stopped herself. "I just wanted to check out the addition."

Amanda encouraged Caleb to go put away his things and get ready for a snack. She watched him turn the corner before piercing Gretchen with a harsh stare. "Did you go through Jax's stuff?"

"No!"

"Tell me the truth."

"I didn't. I wouldn't do that." She was offended by the accusation and the disbelief on Amanda's face. "I thought about it for a split second but didn't."

"That's my sister." Amanda walked around her.

She noticed a bag in Amanda's hand. "What did you get now?"

"More necessities and a *G-I-F-T* for Caleb since Jax left without knowing you struck a deal with the devil."

"You really are the best sister ever."

The afternoon passed in a flurry of Caleb talking, Caleb demanding different snacks, and Caleb crying about one thing or another. Gretchen finally got him settled by agreeing to watch his favorite Disney movie. She was exhausted before six o'clock and decided she needed a nap.

"You don't care if I lie down for a bit, do you? I can barely keep my eyes open."

Amanda glanced at Caleb, who was completely enchanted by the movie. "I think we're good."

She dragged herself to her bedroom and practically collapsed on the bed. She didn't bother to cover herself even though she was chilly in her T-shirt and flannel pants. She dozed off the moment her head hit the pillow.

She heard Jax come home and walk into her bedroom. Her eyelids felt sluggish, but when she finally looked at Jax fully, she was floored by Jax's bright smile.

"Hey you," Jax said as she sat on the edge of the bed. She took Gretchen's hand. "How are you feeling?"

"Tired, but good. We were watching a movie, and I couldn't stay awake." Gretchen pulled herself into a seated position. Her ribs didn't hurt. "I feel like I'm healing faster now that I'm not in that hospital bed anymore."

"I would hope so. We paid almost two grand for this mattress."

"Did we?"

"You insisted."

"Worth every penny." Gretchen let out a comical yawn. "It's wonderful."

Jax traced Gretchen's palm delicately with her fingertip. "We christened it four times that night and again in the morning."

Gretchen shivered. "That's a memory I wish I still had."

Jax ran her fingers up the inside of Gretchen's wrist, up her forearm, and to her cheek. She then fingered the ends of Gretchen's curly hair. "I could tell you about it. Tell you how I made you feel, where I touched, and what I used to fill you up." Jax caressed the sliver of Gretchen's abdomen left bare when her T-shirt had ridden up. "You were insatiable." Jax started to lean in slowly, her eyes trained on Gretchen's lips.

Gretchen needed Jax's kiss. She needed to feel their physical connection to prove they still shared a spark after all these years. She needed Jax to remind her she was still alive. Jax's breath tickled her sensitive lips.

Gretchen awoke with a start, a prominent throbbing between her legs. Sweat beaded her brow and her heart was racing. She started to cry a moment later, burying her face in her pillow so her sobs didn't grow too loud. There was so much sadness coming at once, Gretchen couldn't handle it. Her body clearly needed release, and crying was its method of choice.

Sorrow quickly turned to anger, anger that drove Gretchen to her feet. She pulled all her clothes from her closets and threw them on the bed and the floor. Her dresser and wardrobe were next, followed by her shoes. She held her head in her hands while she looked around at the mess.

The door creaked open, and Jax poked her head into the room. "What the hell is going on in here?" Her eyes widened at the disarray. "I just walked through the door, and Amanda sent me to check on you."

"I was looking for your letters and…" Gretchen picked up a green sweater. "Who wears this?" She picked up a pair of pants and another blouse. "I don't recognize these clothes. I hate them."

Jax bobbed her head from side to side. "You became more conservative and professional over the past few years."

"Who is your girlfriend?" Gretchen said the moment Jax stepped into her bedroom. She was done dancing.

Jax's mouth flapped but no words came out.

"How easy was it for you to move on?"

"Gretchen…" Jax's tone was firm, a warning.

"All I want to know is how. How are we here? What happened and how are you already with someone?"

Jax shut the door. "You need to calm down."

"No. What I need is answers. When did we split up?"

Jax lowered her head and shoved her hands in her pockets. "The end of September."

"When did you start seeing your girlfriend?"

Jax ran her fingers through her hair. A few strands stayed standing. "October."

"October?" Gretchen said loudly. "Was it really so easy to replace me?"

"Meredith isn't—" Jax froze. She exhaled loudly through her nose.

"Meredith?" The name sounded familiar but was hidden deep beneath the blur of the last few weeks. And then it came to the surface, loud and clear with a million possibilities of how and when. "Caleb's nanny?"

Jax balled her fists. She just stared at Gretchen for at least a minute, but time seemed to stretch on forever in silence. "It's not like—"

"It's disgusting," Gretchen said, turning away from Jax. "You said you didn't cheat." She felt like she was being torn apart at the seams.

"I didn't cheat, and it's not disgusting. Meredith is twenty-five and brilliant. She was there every day. She talked to me when I got home from work, she helped me potty train Caleb, and she cares about me."

Gretchen spun around and jabbed her index finger into her chest over and over. "I care about you!"

Jax shook her head sadly. "You didn't, though. Not for a while."

Gretchen sat on the edge of the bed, barely holding steady on the uneven pile of garments. She clamped her eyes shut. "That's impossible."

"You worked every day, from morning until night. You practically stopped coming home for any other reason than to sleep. Caleb barely saw you, and whenever I did, we argued. I was tired of feeling like a single mother who slept next to a stranger."

Tears distorted Gretchen's vision, and she could no longer read Jax's face. "I couldn't…"

"You did."

Gretchen started crying again, and this time she welcomed the way her ribs felt like they were separating. She deserved this pain, all of it.

"Please calm down. It's okay," Jax said softly. "I should leave you alone. All I'm doing is upsetting you." Jax started to go, but she stopped just inside the doorway. "We can get to a better place now and be the best mothers we can be. I do believe that." Jax left the room and it took six consecutive, counted breaths for Gretchen to start to calm.

She swallowed back her last cry and whispered, "But I still love you."

CHAPTER SEVENTEEN

25 days, 14 hours, 7 minutes

"None of it makes sense. How was I living like this?" Gretchen took the mugs from the cabinet and placed them on the granite countertop. She turned one mug in a circle. "This is nice. Where are the rest of the mugs? Did Jax take them?"

Amanda paused her meal prep and wiped her hands on a towel. "What mugs are you talking about?"

Gretchen used a chair to look in the inconvenient cabinet above the stove. "We had all these colorful, fun mugs. I'd pick one up everywhere we went and sometimes Jax would need one from Target just because. All of these are plain and part of a set."

"I have no clue. I've only ever seen these."

Weird. If she had been spending more time with Amanda over the past two years since her mother's death, when did she change the mugs? "I shouldn't have the spices all the way in the pantry. They were perfect right here." She stacked the containers closer to the oven. "I have to go up in the attic later."

"I will go up for you. The last thing you need to be doing is going up and down scary steps."

"Fine. When you're done with that salad, you're going up."

"And what exactly will I be looking for?"

"Mugs and clothes. I can't imagine I actually got rid of all my old clothes." Gretchen tugged at the hem of the sweatshirt she had been wearing for days. None of her other clothes felt like her, like they belonged on her body or like they were ever worn.

"Did you get any sleep last night?"

Gretchen was caught off guard. "A little. Why?"

"You look tired."

Her sleepless nights weren't Amanda's problem. "It's been hard, but I'm sleeping."

"What happened with Jax last night?"

"You are just full of fun questions this morning."

"You were making a lot of noise. Jax checked on you, I heard some things, and then Jax avoided you and breakfast before she left." Amanda shrugged. "I'm curious."

She chuckled. "I'm honestly surprised it took you this long to ask." She ran through her conversation with Jax in her head and didn't really know what to tell Amanda. "I'm sure you already know most of it. I ruined our marriage and am a terrible mother, so on and so forth."

Amanda dropped the cucumber she was slicing. "You're supposed to remain as calm as possible, Gretchen. What makes you say that?"

"Coming home to a stranger's life," Gretchen said, finding it unbelievable Amanda didn't already understand. "Everything's different, and I don't like any of it."

Amanda placed the rest of the salad ingredients in the fridge and squared her shoulders. "Let's get in that attic."

Gretchen all but ran to the rope hanging from the ceiling. The attic was at the far end of the house and went untouched by the addition. She was grateful for at least that remaining the same. Reaching for the rope, Gretchen was surprised by Amanda's firm grip on her shoulders.

"You're on the sidelines completely. No straining, no lifting, no *climbing*. I'll tell you what I see, and you let me know if you want it." Amanda pulled down and unfolded the stairs.

Gretchen stepped out of the way. "Bring your phone so you can send me pictures."

"It's already in my pocket," Amanda said over her shoulder as she ascended the narrow wooden stairs.

Gretchen clasped her hands together and held them to her chest. She felt hopeful that scattered pieces of her former life, her *better* life, still existed. She couldn't wait for Amanda to uncover them. "What do you see? Take a picture."

"I'm barely standing. You didn't tell me it was so cramped."

"It's a tight fit."

"I see a container labeled *house stuff*, and there's a garment rack wrapped in plastic."

"Look on the garment rack."

"I don't know if I can. You took your mothproofing very seriously. I probably need scissors."

Gretchen started to grow antsy. "I can throw scissors up to you."

"That is a terrible idea," Amanda said. Her voice sounded farther away. "I'll figure something out. Oh, hey, you have a bowling ball."

"That was up there when we moved in." Gretchen mentally walked through her attic—a tubful of decorations, their artificial Christmas tree, unmarked boxes. "Check the corner toward the front of the house. There should be a stack of three boxes."

"Okay. I see them." A thud followed. "Dammit."

"What happened?" Gretchen strained to see up the stairs, even though she knew it was impossible.

Amanda cursed a few more times. "I'm fine. I just slammed my knee into the chest you have up here."

"A chest? What does it look like?" Gretchen searched her unreliable memory for a chest.

"Large. Wooden. Looks haunted."

"What's inside it?" Gretchen's mind reeled. She hoped the letters were in there, but she also hoped it was full of discarded clothing.

"Looks like baby blankets, lots of baby blankets. Some stuffed animals and photo albums, but the albums don't have any pictures in them."

"My marriage probably fell apart before we got around to it," Gretchen said with a clenched jaw.

"What?"

"Nothing. Do you see the boxes? One of them has old tools in it. I'm sure there'll be something sharp enough for you to break into that garment rack."

"Old tools? How are you not even forty with a box of old tools in your attic?"

Gretchen found humor in it, too. "We collected tools as we moved from one apartment to the next, back when we could only afford to buy one at a time. If we needed a screwdriver we'd buy one, only one, and make sure it was the cheapest they had."

"Thankfully you also needed preschool scissors."

She remembered the day Jax came home to their first apartment with everything needed to wrap Christmas presents. She was so proud of herself for only spending six dollars on everything, including scissors. "Best ones the dollar store had to offer," Gretchen said as the memory ended.

"Got 'em."

She listened to Amanda's hurried steps and followed her back to the other side of the attic. The sound of crinkling plastic came next, followed by more cursing. "Your language has certainly improved."

"I've learned to express myself more fully by saying *fuck* a lot. It's very therapeutic. There's a lot of clothes packed on this thing."

Gretchen's phone buzzed. She opened the photo and grinned. "Bring it all down."

"All of it?" Amanda sounded overwhelmed.

Thirty minutes later, Gretchen spun in the middle of her bedroom and smiled. She felt a shift within, like she was finally becoming herself again. "I loved this dress." She smoothed her hands over the golden material. The small navy-blue flowers sewn into the cotton cheered her up immensely. "It's a shame we're in the dead of winter. I want to wear this every day."

"I don't think I've ever seen you wear it."

"You will now, once the weather warms up. I can't believe I didn't have any warm clothes up there." She shook her head at the pile of skirts, dresses, and linen shirts covering her bed.

Amanda shrugged from her place in the doorway. "Maybe it didn't fit."

Gretchen frowned. "We have to go shopping. Wait. Do I have money? How have my bills been getting paid?"

"About that," Amanda said just before walking away. She came back into the room with a checkbook. "I should probably give this back to you. After your first few days in the hospital, I went searching for it. Thankfully you are very, very meticulous when it comes to your finances."

"I can't believe more people aren't." Gretchen flipped through the pages.

"You have everything on autopay. Your car, phone, and credit card payments are all taken care of. Stepping in for you was easy."

"Well, thank you for thinking of it. I'm sure Jax didn't since our finances seem to be separate now. I'm sure you're sick of this woe-is-me attitude—"

"No." Amanda stepped up to Gretchen and put her hands on her shoulders. "You have a lot to process, and I'm here to listen and help. If you need to talk about the same things over and over, go for it."

Gretchen stepped into Amanda, just needing the comfort of a hug. "It's so bizarre, and I don't understand any of it. But what I do know is I need to go shopping, and today is the perfect day for it." Gretchen stepped back and tapped the checkbook against her palm. "I deserve it."

"Then I say we pick up Caleb along the way and make an afternoon out of it."

"Let's do it."

After three hours of mall hopping and stopping for treats to keep Caleb happy, Gretchen returned home with bags of clothing and a bright smile. She felt really good for the first time in weeks. She declined Amanda's help getting everything into the house. What was the point to having a kid if you couldn't put him to work? Caleb carried her purse and the lightest of the five bags.

"Where the hell were you?" Jax said, jumping off the couch the moment they walked through the door. Caleb froze and looked panicked. "Give me those." Jax took everything from Caleb and ushered him to the kitchen.

Gretchen was only a few steps behind, already annoyed at the fight she was in no mood for. "We went to two malls. I needed clothes. We had a great afternoon together—didn't we, Caleb?"

Caleb reached into a bag and pulled out a pair of socks with Spider-Man on them. "I got this." He waved them back and forth to make sure Jax saw them.

"That's great, Cricket. Why don't you go put them with your other socks so they don't get lost." Jax's eyes never left Gretchen. Caleb scampered off. "What the hell were you thinking?"

Gretchen was clueless. "Excuse me?"

"I get home to an empty house—no Amanda, no Caleb, and no Gretchen. You have amnesia, you don't remember shit, and you're just gone. You should have told me where you went."

"I was with Amanda. You could have called or messaged either of us."

"I did message Amanda. That's the only reason I didn't call the cops."

"Oh." She had no idea. "Well, you knew where I was. And what does it matter? You're not my keeper."

"That is literally what I am while I'm living here."

"Then don't." The hair on the back of Gretchen's neck stood on end. The surge of adrenaline from anxiety and anger was sickening. "I meant it when I told you to go if you don't want any part of this. You don't owe me anything, and I'm sure Meredith misses you." Gretchen didn't have the energy for another case of emotional whiplash. Every time she was starting to feel good, another incident with Jax would pull her right back into the depths of being unwell. "Amanda won't mind staying until I get clearance from Dr. Melendez to be on my own. She'll bring me for my checkup, and you won't have to worry about anything else but Caleb. No other responsibilities, free and clear, which is exactly what you wanted."

"I don't—"

"Save it. You don't love me, and I don't think you care about me, either. That's a tough pill for me to swallow, but I will. So please go. Having you here like this won't help me get better."

"You don't love Mama?" Caleb's small voice came from the edge of the kitchen. His big brown eyes were full of tears.

Gretchen's anger turned to guilt and regret immediately. "Oh…"

"I guess you also forgot how kids hear *everything*," Jax said before rushing to Caleb. She knelt in front of him. "Of course I do, Cricket."

"Mama said you don't."

"That's not what Mama meant."

Gretchen watched the exchange in horror. She backed out of the room, unable to listen as Jax scrambled to clean up her mess. She walked to her bedroom, bags of new clothing forgotten. She pulled out her phone and opened her messages to Amanda.

I hope you're ready to be roommates again. I'll explain more tomorrow.

CHAPTER EIGHTEEN

31 days, 14 hours, 12 minutes

Nearly a week passed, and Jax didn't leave, but Gretchen had stopped expecting things from her. She relied heavily on Amanda for what she couldn't do herself. Every day she felt stronger physically. Her pain was nearly gone, and the lingering fuzz in her head was gone. She felt more like herself, whoever that was. She had been in touch with her boss and explained the details of her current situation to him. The better she felt, the more eager she was to get back to work. Gretchen craved normalcy. She was happy to know Omar would hold her position for as long as necessary, and all her clients were in good hands. She missed helping people and everything that went into occupational therapy, even the paperwork. The moment Dr. Melendez cleared her for work, she'd run back to the office. But for now, she was a prisoner.

She stared out her window and watched the naked trees sway in blustery wind. She was about to spend Valentine's Day with her doctor and sister. Oh, how life had changed. She watched a cyclone of dead leaves grow higher and higher as she thought back to the last Valentine's Day she could remember.

She and Jax managed a romantic dinner at a local Thai place. They had left Caleb with their new nanny, Meredith. They spent a lovely evening together, eating and laughing. Jax talked about how jealous she was that Caleb was a summer baby, unlike her, and how she planned to do *everything* with Caleb over the summer, including throwing pool parties in the pool they didn't have. Later that night, after staring at their slumbering infant for an embarrassingly long time, they climbed into bed together and fell asleep immediately. Jax woke her in the middle of the night with pleasurable touches and promises of love and forever.

"Are you ready to go?" Jax's sudden words caused Gretchen to jump, and she spilled coffee down her front. "Sorry."

Gretchen looked down at the stain in defeat. She had just bought the blue sweater. "Yeah. Amanda should be here soon."

"I told her not to worry about it. I'll take you."

"I'd rather you didn't." Gretchen placed her mug in the sink and walked to her bedroom. She grabbed another sweater from her dresser and started to change. She was standing in her bra when Jax walked in.

"Oh. Sorry," Jax said, turning.

Gretchen rolled her eyes. "You watched a human come out of my vagina. I hardly think my bra is scandalous at this point."

"I'm just trying to be respectful." Jax turned back slowly, her gaze lingering on Gretchen's bare skin.

Respectful, huh? Gretchen fought to hide her smirk and took her time putting on a new sweater. "You really don't have to take me."

"Take you?" Jax's eyes flew up to meet hers. Gretchen let herself smile then. Jax knew she was caught and smiled back. "I already requested the day when the appointment was booked. I figured it'd be nice to give Amanda the day off."

"You know, Jax, some people don't think of spending time with me as work." She pulled her bouncy hair out from the collar of her sweater so it fell on her shoulders. It was so unruly—she really needed to go for a keratin treatment.

"I don't think that," Jax started to say, but Gretchen shot her an incredulous look. "It's a responsibility, and if I can be honest, it's kinda scary sometimes."

"Sorry to be a scary burden."

"Gretchen, please, I'm just trying to explain what it's like on our end. I can't begin to understand what it's like for you, but I'd listen if you ever tried to explain it to me."

She saw the sincerity in Jax's eyes and softened. "I'm really okay. I feel fine, and I think my MRI will come back good."

"Let's go find out."

The drive to the medical imaging lab was spent in silence, save for the classic rock Jax had playing. Gretchen would've preferred pop, but she was aware of her place. She couldn't make requests in Jax's truck. Once they arrived and she signed in, she filled out the paperwork and was called back almost immediately. Jax stood with an unreadable look, but Gretchen swore she looked sad.

"Good luck," Jax said awkwardly.

Gretchen lay still as the loud MRI machine took scan after scan. She spent the first thirty minutes inhaling and exhaling rhythmically. She wasn't a fan of confined spaces, and MRI machines took confined to a whole new level. Once the tech removed Gretchen after her first round of scans, she gave Gretchen an injection of contrast dye and pushed the button to send her back in. The young girl looked sympathetic as she forced Gretchen back into stillness.

She knew from her training and from the speech the techs gave her as she removed all the metal and jewelry from her body that the second round of images would be quicker. About fifteen minutes stood between Gretchen and being able to move all her parts as furiously as she craved.

She tried to distract herself with thoughts of what she'd have for lunch or the laundry that had to be done once she got back home. A thought hit her then: she lived a boring life. Before the accident, all she did was work, and now the most distracting thought she could conjure up was laundry.

What had changed? What had happened to the Gretchen who'd spend weekends away with the love of her life at the drop of a dime? They were always on the go, always looking for an adventure of some sort. At their most stir-crazy they'd leave the house in search of the best slice of pizza in a twenty-mile radius. Anything to feel alive together.

The startling silence of the machine stopping scattered Gretchen's thoughts. She let out a long breath in relief. She could move, really move, finally. She watched as the ceiling became visible inch by inch.

"Okay, hon, let me take this off," the older tech said as she pulled the cage-like apparatus from around Gretchen's head. Gretchen's chest felt instantly lighter with less anxiety. "Do you need help sitting up?"

"No." Gretchen practically shot to a seated position. Her head spun slightly from the sudden move. "The results will be sent to Dr. Melendez, right?"

"Immediately. As per her request."

"Thank you." She left the small room. She changed back into her sweater and replaced all her jewelry. For a split second she worried she had lost her wedding ring, and then remembered she wasn't wearing it anymore. When she got back out to the waiting room, she couldn't help but smile at Jax, who was watching *The Price Is Right* intently. She didn't notice Gretchen approach. "Do you want to stay and see who wins the Showcase Showdown?"

"Hey!" Jax stood. "How did it go?"

"I was stuffed into a narrow tube and wore a cage around my head. I'm glad I was unconscious for everything else."

Jax shuddered. "At least it's over."

"Now we go to Dr. Melendez's office and find out my fate."

Jax twirled her keys around her middle finger and ushered Gretchen to her truck. Ocean County Neurological Center was only fifteen minutes from the imaging building, and Jax spent the time on a call with her office.

Gretchen barely listened to the conversation, even with both sides being too loud for her liking. Hands-free communication was great, but unfortunate for a passenger stuck in the car. She watched Jax's face instead, and the clear dislike written in her ever-changing expression.

"Fine. I'll make the changes first thing when I get to the office tomorrow. Bye." Jax disconnected the call and then gripped the steering wheel so tightly her knuckles were white.

"You hate your job."

Jax looked at her quizzically before turning back to the road. "Yeah. Very much so."

"Why don't you quit?" She couldn't understand why Jax would suffer like that, day in and day out, for a job. She was the most passionate person Gretchen knew, and none of that was reflected during her conversation.

Jax pulled into the parking lot and took the first available spot. She unfastened her seat belt and turned to Gretchen. "It's so crazy hearing questions like this coming from you."

"Why?" Gretchen asked, genuinely confused. She'd never want Jax to be anything less than happy.

"We've had more than a few fights about this. I wanted to quit, but you'd remind me that we have bills to pay and a kid to raise. Neither are cheap."

"So find another job before you quit."

"It's not that easy." Jax's impatience was in her tone. "Every job I come across is either too far away or sounds worse than the gig I have now."

"If there's anything I can do to help, let me know, but I do think you should quit. You hate it so much—I could see it in your eyes when you were talking on the phone, and I see it in your posture when you get home." She placed her hand on Jax's forearm. The polyester of her puffer jacket was cool to her touch. "You are too talented to not be doing something you love."

Jax's head was down, and she looked at Gretchen's hand. She pulled back and said, "Let's get inside. Your problems are bigger than mine." Jax got out of the truck without another word.

The awkward tension followed them into the waiting room and all the way to Dr. Melendez's impressive office on the top floor of the large building. Jax bounced her leg and Gretchen wanted her to stop. The movement wasn't helping her nerves.

"Sorry to keep you both waiting," Dr. Melendez said as she entered her office. She took a seat behind her desk and smiled at Gretchen and Jax. "It's nice to see you both again outside of the hospital. How are you?"

"Okay," Jax replied.

"Good," Gretchen said confidently.

"How's Amanda?"

Both Jax and Gretchen snickered at the question.

Gretchen decided to answer. "Amanda is doing very well. She's been a trouper with keeping an eye on me. So has this one," she said with a tilt of her head.

"Very good." Dr. Melendez typed for a moment on her desktop. Judging by the way she used her mouse, she was doing a lot of scrolling. "Your scans came back great. There are a few shadows where the original damage was, but nothing out of the ordinary. You're healing beautifully. How are you feeling physically?"

"Good. I'm not back to what I was, or what I remember I was. I'm still getting winded after a lot of activity, but my ribs don't hurt, and my face, as you can see, is back to normal. I run a little bit every morning—nothing crazy, but it's felt very good."

"Any headaches?"

"Mild ones, from time to time, but nothing really painful. Honestly," she said, leaning forward and lowering her voice, "I think they're just the usual headaches that come along with having a kid."

Dr. Melendez's smile was radiant as she laughed. "And people ask me why I don't plan on having children."

Gretchen felt compelled to clarify. "Caleb is wonderful, but he's always making noise."

"How has he adjusted to all this?"

"He's been great," Jax said. She twirled her keyring around her finger. "He's only had two meltdowns, which is a personal best for him. He understands just enough to not add stress to Gretchen's situation."

"That's very good to hear." Dr. Melendez typed for a minute

before regarding Gretchen again. "Have you been taking your seizure medication?"

She gave a thumbs-up. "Every morning with breakfast like clockwork."

"I hate to ask, but have you remembered anything new since the last time we spoke?"

Gretchen shook her head. She was afraid to speak, knowing how quickly she could get angry when talking about her lost memories.

"Do you think she will?" Jax said.

Dr. Melendez sat back in her chair. The leather made no noise. "There's no way of knowing. Ideally, she would've regained some by now since it's been a month and her brain is healing well, but sometimes you do, sometimes you don't."

Gretchen already knew the truth of her situation, and she had heard enough at this point. She was ready for a subject change. "When can I go back to work?"

"Of course," Jax said.

"What?" she said to Jax. "Those bills and that kid you mentioned earlier still aren't cheap. My medical leave will be up soon, and I looked into disability, but it's a joke." She looked back to Dr. Melendez. "I just need to know if I'll be back at work before any assistance will kick in."

Dr. Melendez steepled her fingers and looked between them. "Your progress is great, and I think you're ready for a few changes. First, you don't need around-the-clock care, but I don't want you alone overnight just yet. Not just because you're still adjusting, but because you're caring for a child."

Gretchen nodded eagerly, already feeling more positive. "Okay, that makes sense."

"No driving until your six-month mark, I'm firm on that. Give yourself one more week before you return to work. Amnesia is tough to deal with, and while you may be growing comfortable with your home life, work will be a new challenge for you. Take one more week, and then I'll clear you for part-time. Can you agree to that?"

Gretchen knew her eyes were wide with excitement. "I can."

"Great. If you have any questions or concerns, give me a call. Otherwise, Gretchen, you're doing great. You should be very happy with your progress."

"I am. Thank you for everything." She stood and shook Dr. Melendez's hand firmly.

"I want to see you back in four weeks. You can schedule that with the receptionist on the way out. Take care."

Gretchen had a new spring in her step as she left the office. Normalcy was one week away. When she got to the elevator, she noticed Jax had stopped about fifteen feet away and seemed annoyed.

"Shit," Jax said, searching the pockets of her jacket and jeans. "I left my keys in her office."

"I'll wait here." She stood in the hallway and swayed back and forth.

Jax was oddly quiet on the drive home. After they'd left the office, her whole demeanor had changed. Gretchen knew Jax wasn't excited about her returning to work, but she was going to. No matter what. Gretchen let the subject drop, not in the mood to kill her good news with another fight. Jax stopped the truck in front of the house.

"Are you hungry? I can make you lunch," Gretchen said.

"I should get going. You don't need around-the-clock supervision anymore, remember?"

She didn't expect to be so reluctant to give up Jax's presence. "It's just a boring turkey sandwich."

"I'm meeting Meredith for an early dinner."

Gretchen felt stupid. "Valentine's Day. Of course." She got out of the car. She heard Jax talking, but she didn't care enough to listen. "I'll have Amanda stay the night, so you don't have to end your night with me."

"I'll pick up Caleb and drop him off."

"Good-bye, Jax." Gretchen turned and walked up to her house. The cold wind made her eyes water. At least that was where she placed the blame, not on her broken heart.

CHAPTER NINETEEN

31 days, 22 hours, 19 minutes

Gretchen kept stirring and stirring, but something didn't look right.

"It smells wonderful in here," Amanda said as she entered the kitchen. She took off her jacket and bent to kiss Caleb on the head. "Hey, Cricket."

"Hi, Aunt Man."

"Aunt Man? Sounds an awful lot like you're implying I'm a man made out of ants." Amanda started tickling Caleb. His giggles echoed in the room. "Was that your idea?" Amanda stepped up to Gretchen and gave her shoulder a squeeze.

"Ant-Man is a very popular superhero, and I just figured if everyone else was part of an insect family…"

"What's your name, then?" Amanda asked.

"Mama!" Caleb declared.

"I see how it is," Amanda said with a chuckle. "What are you making?"

"It's supposed to be Mom's macaroni and cheese, but I'm a little unsure." Gretchen lifted the wooden spoon from the saucepan and frowned at the lumpy mess that dripped from it.

"Oh, honey, that's ruined. Step aside." Amanda bumped her hip into Gretchen's to get her to move. "The only thing I can use here is the pasta. Do you have more milk and cheese?"

She grabbed the ingredients from the refrigerator. "I really tried."

"You really did." Amanda did a double take when she finally looked at Gretchen. "Are you okay? You don't look like someone who had a great visit with the doctor today."

"Do I look like someone whose wife is spending Valentine's Day with their not-so-new girlfriend?"

"Ooh. Ouch. I'm sorry."

"It's okay." Gretchen leaned back against the counter and crossed her arms. "My scans came back fine, and there's no one I'd rather spend the day with than you two."

"You're lying and it's sweet."

"I'm not lying," Gretchen said. "She's moved on. It's that simple. So I'm trying to be happy with where my life is now. I love having a dinner date with my sister and my son."

Amanda started to shred the cheese but paused. "Can you drink?"

"Amanda, I swear, I'm really okay."

"I know, but I think we should feed the kid, put him to bed, and then open a bottle of wine."

"Who knew you were so romantic?"

"Shut up and help me shred this cheese and fix your disaster."

She worked very well under Amanda's direction, and in no time they had macaroni and cheese on three plates next to thickly sliced ham steak.

"What do you think, Cricket?"

Caleb pushed the ham off his plate but kept shoveling the macaroni and cheese into his mouth.

"Take it as a win," Amanda said with a laugh.

"Hey, Caleb, wanna tell me about Meredith?"

Amanda choked on her water. She wiped a drip from her chin and looked at Gretchen with comically large eyes. "What are you doing?"

"I'm curious, and Jax won't tell me much. Who better to spill the girlfriend beans than the chattiest boy on the planet?"

Caleb must've considered the title to be a compliment because he shot them a cheesy, orange grin.

"Do you like her?" Gretchen needed to know the answer but absolutely didn't *want* to know it. What if he liked Meredith more than her? She instantly regretted having hired the perky young woman so many years ago. As present as Meredith was in her memory, Gretchen couldn't conjure up a clear picture. "Is she pretty?"

"Oh my God," Amanda said around a mouthful of food.

Caleb looked thoughtful with one eye closed and his mouth turned up. "Yes," he said simply. That told Gretchen nothing.

"But what does she look like?"

Caleb laughed. "You know what she looks like."

She wished for just this one moment Caleb could fully comprehend what amnesia was. "I don't really remember, sweetie."

He stabbed at his macaroni a couple times before eating another mouthful. "She ash te—"

"Chew with your mouth closed and swallow before speaking." Gretchen cringed.

Caleb made a show of chewing and swallowing. He pulled himself up to kneel on the chair. "She's pretty."

Gretchen blinked a few times, her smile stiff. "Pretty like Mama?"

Caleb shook his head. "No, really pretty."

Gretchen's heart sank and she pouted. "Thanks for your honesty, kid."

Caleb laughed and Amanda joined in.

Amanda took over for Gretchen and asked, "Do you have fun when you're with Meredith?"

He nodded and started to squirm. "We play a lot and she buys ice cream."

"How can I compete with that?" Gretchen knew she was overreacting, but that didn't stop her from panicking slightly. "She's really pretty and fun. She's obviously more fun for Jax, too."

"Done!" Caleb announced loudly.

"Great job, Cricket. Now, go get cleaned up and put on your pajamas. I'm going to put on your favorite movie and build a fort for you in front of the television." Amanda held his arm as he slid off the kitchen chair. He sped off for his room. "Why are you torturing yourself?" Amanda leveled Gretchen with her hard stare.

She slouched. "I don't know. I guess I feel like I'll accept it if I understand it. Meredith is younger and prettier. There's nothing to not understand."

"Listen to me, age and looks have nothing to do with it."

"Amanda—"

"*But* she's not prettier than you. She's a very cute girl, but she's nothing compared to you."

Gretchen's chin started to quiver. "You have to say that because I'm your sister."

"I'm actually more likely to compliment other people because I'm your sister." Amanda smiled when she laughed. "I think whatever connection Jax has with Meredith is real, but not serious."

Gretchen swallowed thickly. "I want her to be happy but…I want to be happy, too, and I don't think I can have both."

"Hold that thought." Amanda rushed out of the room and came back with a sheet. "Gotta build a fort," she said to Gretchen as she walked past. In a few minutes, Amanda had constructed a sizable fort from couch cushions, sheets, and one kitchen chair. She had Caleb's movie ready to go the moment he came running back into the room. "Get comfortable, and I'll start the movie." Amanda got everything started and made a promise of popcorn if he was good. She sat back at the table with a sigh. "Go ahead."

"You're so good with him. Sometimes I still feel like he's a stranger. The other night he cuddled up to me while I was reading him a story, and it took me a minute to fully understand that this was my life. But that maternal connection people talk about? It's real." She glanced at the fort and heard him laugh. "I didn't recognize him, but my heart knew exactly who he was."

"What about Jax?"

Gretchen smiled in spite of her sadness. "My heart knows her, too. Without a doubt."

"Do you love her?"

"With everything I am."

"Do you think you ever stopped?"

Gretchen struggled to imagine a life where she'd stop loving Jax. She just couldn't. "No. As sure as I was that Caleb was my son, I am sure I never stopped loving her."

"Maybe this can be your second chance. She may not have forgotten the past four years, but maybe she has forgotten all the good that came before. You can remind her."

As wonderful and hopeful as that sounded, she couldn't believe in such a beautiful possibility. "Have you seen the way she acts when we're in the same room? She hates me. I left her to feel like she was raising our son alone. I was not a good person, and I can't really blame her for wanting a divorce."

Amanda hummed. "I think if you both had a conversation, maybe there would be a chance. Tell her how you feel and let her talk."

"We could, but I don't know if she'd be up for it."

"That last part is the most important. Did you hear it? You have to let Jax talk. Hear her out."

"Was I really the monster she said I was?"

Amanda was quiet for several minutes. The television sounded loud. "You worked a lot. I knew you two fought a lot, almost every time I came over, which honestly wasn't often. Jax didn't invite me, and you were—"

"Busy with work. I love my job, I do, but I just can't understand loving it more than my family. They're my whole world."

"You need to make sure Jax knows that."

"I don't think I'd be able to handle it if she said no to us trying again. You can't force yourself to fall back in love with someone."

"You can't," Amanda said, shocking Gretchen with the easy agreement. "But I don't think she ever stopped loving you."

"You don't see the way she looks at me."

"And *you* don't see the way she looks at you. I was there, Gretchen—I watched her sit at your bedside every day. I saw the haunted look in her eyes when we thought we were going to lose you. Splitting up hurt her, but this nearly destroyed her."

Gretchen was too afraid to believe it. "She was worried for Caleb."

Amanda shook her head firmly. "It wasn't just that, and you need to trust me. There's the fear of your child losing his other mother, and then there's the fear of losing the love of your life. My heart broke for her every single time I looked at her."

Gretchen needed to know one last thing before she'd let herself consider the possibility of a second chance. "Is it fair for me to want this?"

"If I didn't believe Jax wants the same thing, I wouldn't let you get hurt. But I think she's trying to put a Band-Aid on a bullet wound. You are the only way she'll ever heal because you need each other."

"I wish I had your positivity."

"If I can get there, so can you." Amanda stood and popped some popcorn. "Tell me, what are you going to do?"

"I have to know if she wants the same thing, which means I'll talk to her and listen. Like you said."

"I'm so smart."

"Don't break your arm patting yourself on the back."

"Har-har." Amanda poured the popcorn into a bowl and delivered it to Caleb, who squealed in delight. When she came back into the kitchen, she slid Gretchen's phone closer. "Tell Jax you want to talk. Tomorrow night. Order a nice dinner, something you both love, and open some wine. Make sure she's relaxed. Don't just bombard her like you tend to do."

Gretchen opened her messages and felt her palms start to sweat. She shouldn't be this nervous about asking the woman she had been with for over fifteen years to talk. They'd eaten a million meals together and talked about everything under the sun, but Gretchen was more nervous for this than anything else she could remember. She took a deep breath and started typing.

I know you're out, and I'm sorry to interrupt you, but I think we should talk. Please have dinner with me at the house tomorrow night. I'll have everything ready for when you get out of work.

The send button was the most daunting thing on earth. Gretchen held her thumb over it, hovering and trembling, and hesitated to touch it. She stared, unblinking, then finally hit *Send*. Her stomach flipped.

"Oh God, I feel sick."

Amanda rubbed her back. "It'll be okay. Even if it doesn't go your way, at least you'll have closure."

Gretchen read and reread her message. She placed her hand over her face and groaned. "I apologized for interrupting. They're probably having *S-E-X* right now."

"Caleb can't hear you, and you don't know that."

Gretchen raised her eyebrows as high as they could go. "It's Valentine's Day. If I were with Jax, I'd be having sex with her."

"Nope," Amanda said, pinching her face in disgust. "Do not need to know that."

"I miss the sex." Gretchen folded her arms on the table and laid her head down. "It was *so* good."

"You almost died a month ago, and you're going on about how you miss sex right now?"

Gretchen peeked at Amanda with one eye. "What better time to think about what makes you feel alive?"

CHAPTER TWENTY

32 days, 21 hours, 30 minutes

Gretchen barely slept after Jax replied to her invitation. Sure, the reply was a simple *okay*, but that didn't stop her nerves from nearly fizzling out. She thought of the perfect meal, the perfect words, and the perfect way to present the crazy idea of trying to mend their broken marriage. Gretchen's head injury must've made her a little insane, because she actually believed this could work. She had years of history with Jax—they were family. Nothing was stronger than that.

Amanda excitedly agreed to take Caleb for the night. Gretchen wasn't sure if her excitement came from having a sleepover with her nephew or from knowing she was taking Amanda's advice. For once.

She set the table. The delivery guy had brought their dinner five minutes earlier, and Gretchen scrambled to put the Thai food into more presentable serving dishes. Everything had to be perfect. She couldn't risk a distraction. She checked the time and knew Jax would be home any minute. She smoothed her palms down her fitted T-shirt and knew the pale pink color made her dark complexion pop. She applied light makeup and felt mildly silly when she struggled. It had been about four weeks since she'd worn makeup, since she'd looked like her everyday self. She even paid extra attention to her hair, using a small amount of product to gather her puffy mess into defined curls. She felt attractive, and if she still knew Jax as well as she used to, Jax would most definitely agree.

Gretchen sat at the kitchen table and waited. And waited. And continued to wait. Five thirty turned to six and before she knew it, she had been waiting for an hour. She checked her phone constantly, hoping to hear from Jax. She should've messaged her, but she felt like she was on thin ice. She wanted to do anything in her power to repair their marriage, not drive Jax farther away. But was expecting respect really that wrong?

She picked up her phone and typed out an innocent message, keeping the words light and telling Jax her food was getting cold. No answer came. She sent another message twenty minutes later, just asking Jax if she planned on coming home. Gretchen was happy to see Jax was typing a response.

Not until late. Sorry.

Gretchen's heart broke a little more. Why she felt like this was her final chance, the only night she could approach Jax, was beyond her, but she felt like her final hopes for happily ever after were just extinguished. She looked at the spread of food before her sadly. Tears ran down her cheeks as she felt the side of a dish for warmth, and she continued to cry while eating her pad thai. She should've never been dumb enough to fall for Amanda's hope. But Jax was her entire world, and she refused to believe a love like that could just disappear in four years. She let out a pitiful laugh. She had fallen in love with Jax in a matter of minutes. Jax must have fallen out of love just as quickly.

She left the dirty dishes on the table and went to the couch. She wanted to lie back and let the pain and tears overwhelm her, but her body kept moving. Something drove her up the stairs. She barely knew what she was doing by the time she stood outside Jax's bedroom door. She placed her palm against the door, feeling the cold wood and its grain. Ignoring the small voice in her head, Gretchen opened the door and stepped into Jax's room. Immediately she smelled the Dior scent Jax had been wearing for years. The room was tidy except the corner with her hamper, which overflowed. She picked up a discarded shirt and held it up to her nose. Just like the first moment she'd held Caleb in the hospital, her heart was triggered by Jax's scent. Gretchen knew that would never, ever go away.

She sat on the edge of the bed and stared at the far wall. Even though Jax spent most of her time in the room, it still lacked her presence. Gretchen felt that way about the whole house at this point. Her thoughts turned to Jax's art studio, which was just as sterile as this bedroom. Jax used to live in her studio, spending any free moment working on something new, something exciting she'd tell Gretchen about for hours. When had all that stopped? When had all the passion died?

Gretchen shot a hesitant glance over her shoulder to the closet. She wondered if Jax was living out of a bag or if she had bothered to move at least a few of her belongings into the room. She opened the closet, mildly disappointed to only see a few articles of clothing hanging. Gretchen touched each piece, smiling at the soft textures and patterns that fit Jax so well—button-ups that would hug her body perfectly and sweaters that would show off her defined muscles. Gretchen closed her eyes and thought back to the many times they'd gone to the gym together, to the workouts she barely participated in because she was too in awe of Jax's body. She'd felt shallow every time, but she was so proud of having the sexiest wife in the world. Most times she wouldn't even let Jax shower when they got home because of all the pent-up desire and need to touch her.

Jax's shoes caught her attention next, all colorful and clean. Gretchen looked up to the top shelf and noticed the craft box. She stood on tiptoe and reached, hurting her injured shoulder, but she didn't care about the pain. She held the box in triumph and poured its contents on the bed, covering most of the mattress. Gretchen smiled in relief and joy. She hadn't thrown them away; she hadn't thrown away the love she knew she had for Jax. The first letter she unfolded weakened her knees.

Gretchen,

I'm sorry. I really don't know what else I can say. I'm an idiot and a fool and I don't deserve you. I thought making you choose between us and your family was the only way I could make you see how much they hurt you. Please forgive me.

Gretchen held the letter to her chest and sobbed. She remembered that day so clearly and the icky pain that had filled her chest when she thought she had lost Jax forever. That was ten years ago and here they were again. She picked up another letter, hoping for one that could remind her of all the happiness they had at one time.

Mama Bear,

I know you hate the nickname, but I also notice the way you smile every time I say it. Our cubs are so lucky to have you.

Gretchen scanned the paper and flipped it over, hoping to find a date. She examined Jax's handwriting, and there was no way she had made a mistake.

> *Caleb is going to be an unbelievable big brother, and you, my beautiful, amazing wife, are everything I need to believe I can do this. Two kids seems like a crazy idea, but when I look at you, I want sixteen more because they are all a part of you. I'm watching you sleep, and I can't stop thinking how incredible my life is all because one day I was avoiding my public speaking class and hiding in the library. I want to remember this moment forever, and since you're asleep and I want to share it with you, I'm writing it all down. Thank you for being you, the mother you are, and the woman who loves me. But most of all, thank you for being a book nerd.*
> *Love you till the very end,*
> *Jax*

Gretchen dropped the letter like its edges had sliced her. She backed away from the bed and took calming breaths. How did she not remember? Her stomach turned and she fought against rising bile. What had happened with the baby, and why hadn't Jax told her? She remembered the blankets and empty photo albums Amanda found in the attic. Her head felt like it was spinning.

"Calm down," she said aloud, hoping to engage all her senses in trying to remain calm. Her nose started to run from the tears prickling her eyes. "You need to calm down right now." She flexed her toes into the carpet and took another deep breath. "You're okay. This is something that happened to you, and you survived. It is sad and it is devastating." The rational facts ended there. She turned and looked at herself in the mirror. "No wonder Jax stopped loving you."

Feeling herself start to spiral, she started to open the rest of the letters frantically, praying one would tell her more. Praying one would tell her Jax hadn't left her because of that.

An hour later, she sat at the center of the bed, surrounded by folded and crinkled papers. What little makeup she had applied was now dried-up salty black trails that ran down her cheeks. She held one letter in her hand and lay back. She found no answers, no help, and not one word that made her feel better. She felt alone, abandoned, like she had let Jax down.

Gretchen was emotionally and physically drained, but her mind wouldn't rest. She picked up her phone and dialed the only other person who had the answers she needed. She just prayed he'd be willing to talk to her about it.

"Hello?" Wyatt answered after one ring.

"You still sound scared when you answer the phone. I'm glad that hasn't changed."

His laugh sounded deeper over the phone. "How are you, Gretchen?"

Gretchen blew out a long breath, unsure of how to answer such a deceivingly complex question. "I'm not doing so great."

"What's wrong?" he said, worry coming through clear.

Gretchen didn't have it in her to beat around the bush. "Tell me about the baby, our second baby." Wyatt didn't answer. Gretchen checked her phone to make sure the call was still connected. "Wyatt?"

"Yeah, I'm here. I just don't think I should be the one you talk to about this."

"Please. Jax won't tell me. I'm pretty sure she'd keep it from me forever."

"I don't think so. It was a hard time for both of you, and Jax probably wants to keep you both from reliving it again."

Anger flared within Gretchen. "That's not fair and you know it." Wyatt went quiet again. "Is that when everything started to go wrong?"

"Honestly, Gretchen, I don't know. I had no idea things had gotten so bad between you two. I was floored when I found out you had split. One minute you were dancing at my wedding, and the next Jax was telling me she moved out."

Gretchen balled up the letter in her hand and threw it. "This is so hard to explain, but I have no recollection of losing the baby, absolutely none, but knowing I did…I feel hollow now. Like my body remembers the loss even when my brain doesn't."

"I'm so, so sorry Gretchen. And I'm sorry you didn't hear it from Jax. I don't know what's up with her lately, but she's barely speaking to me, too."

She hated the way her mind and heart betrayed her by instantly worrying about Jax. She had no one else to turn to. Wyatt was her family, but she supposed Jax had Meredith now. "My injury hasn't been easy for anyone."

"Aside from all this horrible shit, how are you feeling?"

She wanted to laugh and scream and cry. "Physically, I feel great.

My body has bounced back, and the doctor said I could go back to work next week."

"That's great. I'm sure you'll feel even better once you're back into the normal swing of things."

"I hope," she said sullenly, knowing the normal swing would never feel normal without Jax. "What about you? How's Carly feeling?"

"She's gonna go into labor any day now, and I don't know how I feel about that." Wyatt and Gretchen laughed together. "We're both tired of waiting. We're just ready to have this kid already."

"Are you having a boy or girl?"

"We don't know, actually. We still want to be surprised."

"That's wonderful. Either way, Caleb will be lucky to have them as his best friend."

"I couldn't agree more."

Silence stretched on, and Gretchen decided to end the call before it grew awkward. For as much as she loved Wyatt and considered him family, she understood he was Jax's friend. "Thank you for talking to me tonight. I was in a bad place, and you helped me a lot."

"Anytime, Gretchen. I love you both very much and nothing will change that."

She was overwhelmed with gratitude for all the small things in that moment. "Thank you. Give Carly my best and have a good night." She hung up and looked at the ceiling.

Gretchen was hit with exhaustion instantly and closed her eyes. She thought of what to do next and what to say to Jax. She knew it was time to let go and surrender to all the damage that had already been done. She fell asleep with the lingering scent of Jax in her nose.

CHAPTER TWENTY-ONE

33 days, 4 hours, 15 minutes

A loud slam startled Gretchen awake. She struggled to focus when the overhead light came on. Jax was standing next to the bed, and she looked angry.

"What are you doing in here?" Jax's nostrils flared.

Gretchen only had one eye open when she fully realized where she had fallen asleep. "I'm sorry. You didn't show up and—"

"And that gave you the right to go through my stuff?"

She was fully awake now. "You moved out, which makes this my house."

"Hasn't it always been?"

She sat up and started picking up the discarded letters. "Glad to see that insecurity is still alive and well." She shoved the letters back into the box.

"You didn't answer me. Why are you in here?"

Gretchen had no fight left in her. "Because we're done, and I have finally accepted that. I wanted to feel close to you one more time, so I came in here. I didn't go through your things. All I did was sit here and open the closet." She sat on the bed and held up the box, its weight nearly too much for her tired body. "I found these. I thought I had thrown them away."

Jax stared at the box, her throat flexing with a hard swallow. "I told you I couldn't make it tonight."

"It wasn't just about dinner. I had planned on talking, really talking to you. Not fighting." She decided to lay it all on the line. "I wanted to ask you for another chance."

Jax's eyes flashed with surprise.

"I really thought we could make it work, even with whatever we had been through, because I love you so much."

"Gretchen..."

"I know. I was horrible, and you don't love me anymore. I heard you loud and clear, and I'm moving on from the fairy tale." Even as Gretchen spoke calmly, Jax seemed to hold on to her anger.

"It's not that simple. You've forgotten four of the worst years we've ever lived." Jax paused, and her eyes started to well up.

"It doesn't feel good, you know? You think it's a gift when it's actually torture—to be surrounded by complete destruction and not have any memory of causing the explosion." Gretchen pressed her fingers to her lips to try to keep from crying. "So yeah, this is a real fucking gift." Gretchen wiped her tears away with the back of her hand. She threw the box of letters in a small wastebasket and stepped around Jax to leave.

Jax grabbed Gretchen's wrist and pulled her into a bruising kiss. Jax kissed her with such force that she was sure she'd be imprinted for the rest of her life. Jax backed her into the nearest wall and forced her legs apart with her knee. She breathed heavily against Gretchen's parted lips and ran her hands down Gretchen's body, cupping her full breasts along the way.

Gretchen whimpered, all of her sorrow replaced by desire, and she felt dizzy. She opened her mouth wider and licked Jax's lips, tasting them. Her hips canted forward when Jax tugged at the button of her jeans. She kissed Jax slowly, relishing how well they fit together. Gretchen started moving her hips, grinding her center against Jax's thigh. She wrapped her arms around Jax's neck and held her body close. Nothing compared to the feeling of safety she felt when she was surrounded by Jax. Every piece of wreckage that lay at her feet was finally starting to fall back into place.

She lifted her arms and let Jax remove her T-shirt. The air was cold against her bare skin. Gretchen shivered.

"Are you okay?" Jax said, pulling back just enough to look Gretchen in the eyes.

She held Jax's face in her hands and smiled. "I'm okay."

Jax lifted Gretchen and carried her to the bed, putting her down carefully. Gretchen was greedy with her hands, pulling at Jax's sweater and tugging it frantically to get it off her body. She needed skin and warmth and the softness she had been missing.

Jax sat back to take off her pants. She kneeled between Gretchen's legs in nothing but her sports bra and boxer briefs and smiled down at her. Jax pulled Gretchen's jeans down her curvy legs. Once the pants were discarded, Jax leaned forward and kissed her panty line. She trailed her mouth up Gretchen's soft stomach and stopped at her sternum. "I don't want to hurt you," she said in a whisper against Gretchen's skin.

"You won't." She ran her fingers through Jax's lilac hair. "You feel so good." She sucked in a breath when Jax traced her folds over her panties. Her body was so sensitive. She felt like a million flames were lapping at her skin. "When was the last time you touched me?"

"It's been a long time." Jax bit at the swell of her breast. She pulled down the cup of her bra with one hand and slid her panties to the side with the other. Jax scraped her dark nipple between her teeth as she entered her with two fingers.

She burrowed her head back into the pillow and keened. She had never felt like this before, like it was her first time and the hundredth all wrapped into one. Her body was starving for every little thing Jax was doing to her. Gretchen nearly came the moment Jax rubbed her clit with her slick fingers.

"So wet…" Jax teased the shell of Gretchen's ear with her tongue.

She opened her eyes and reached down to grab Jax's firm ass. Gretchen couldn't just lie there and let Jax touch her—she needed to touch Jax just as badly. She pulled Jax's hips into her, moaning at the added pressure against Jax's working fingers. She ran her hand up Jax's lower back, around her sides, and up to scratch her hard nipple through the tight material of her bra. Jax's breasts weren't large, but Gretchen salivated at the sight of them every time. She knew Jax's nipples were dusky against her pale skin, and they'd beg for her tongue and touch. She tugged roughly at Jax's sports bra, hating how tight and restrictive it was.

Jax chuckled. "Patience."

"I want you naked. Now." Gretchen let all of her desperation bleed into her tone. "I need you."

Jax got up on her knees and peeled off her sports bra. Her body was as glorious as Gretchen remembered and expected, but something new caught her eye. She found a small tattoo just below her right breast. Four little birds flew along her ribs—three black and one red.

She reached out to touch it. "This is beautiful," she said, but Jax pinned her hand to the mattress before she could touch the inked skin.

Jax pulled her panties down to her knees and licked along her slit. Jax's movements felt more hurried and desperate now. She let go of Gretchen's hand only when she needed to take her panties off the rest of the way. She moved her tongue in practiced patterns, humming as Gretchen's wetness increased.

Gretchen didn't want to rush the moment, but her climax was fast approaching and Jax's expert tongue was unrelenting. She opened her mouth and screamed the moment her inner muscles spasmed. Her orgasm was so powerful, nearly painful. She felt the years of pent-up tension break apart in her chest. She cried as she came down, breathing heavily and caressing every inch of Jax's skin she could touch.

Jax wore a predatory smile as she crawled back up Gretchen's body. She kissed her hard, driving her coated tongue into Gretchen's mouth.

She savored the familiarity of her taste on Jax's tongue. She touched Jax's hair, face, and strong shoulders. Reaching down between her legs under the waistband of Jax's boxers, she pinched Jax's clit. She swallowed Jax's surprised whimper and moan. She rubbed tight, firm circles against Jax's flesh, wanting to give greater pleasure than she ever had. Jax rivaled everything else. She continued rubbing Jax's clit while focusing on Jax's addictive lips. Even while being pleasured, Jax was able to focus on driving Gretchen crazy.

Jax would kiss her slowly, pulling back every time Gretchen tried to gain the upper hand. The pressure went from featherlight to firm instantly and back again in the blink of an eye. Gretchen grew wetter every single time.

"I love you," Gretchen whispered. "I love you, I love you, I love you." She was able to say it now and not feel like she was begging. She looked into Jax's eyes and circled her entrance with the pads of her index and middle fingers. She knew Jax didn't like penetration, but she loved every inch of her pussy to be touched and the copious arousal coating Gretchen's fingers told her that hadn't changed. Gretchen spread her fingers and rubbed the length of Jax, back up her clit.

Jax's arms went weak, and she fell atop Gretchen, her weight stifling Gretchen's movements slightly. She got back up on her elbow and looked down at Gretchen in concern. "Did I hurt you?"

Gretchen shook her head and grinned. She increased the pace, knowing by the way Jax was breathing against her she was going to come soon. She pinched Jax's nipple and pressed harder against her clit. Jax started to shake, and she choked out a strangled moan. She said Gretchen's name and rode out her pleasure against her hand. She wrapped her arms around Jax's limp, sweaty body and held her tight. Their breathing evened out and synched up.

Gretchen closed her eyes and pressed her lips to the side of Jax's neck. She finally felt like she was home.

Chapter Twenty-two

33 days, 11 hours, 51 minutes

Gretchen watched as Jax got ready for work, unabashedly and silently. They hadn't spoken a word since waking up, and she was happy in the peace. It allowed her to think and fully feel the moment. She still couldn't understand how her physical self and her brain were so at odds. Her body buzzed after their night of lovemaking. But her mind? Her mind was filled with images of happiness. Gretchen propped her head in her hand and started to laugh.

Jax looked over her shoulder as she fastened her belt. "What's so funny?"

"Nothing. I really can't explain it."

"Try." Jax sat and pulled on her oxblood Dr. Martens, distracting Gretchen with the flex of her back muscles beneath her thin tan sweater.

"I get these sensations," Gretchen said. She saw Jax smirk. "Not like that. Not one memory has come back, not even the ghost of one, but I swear my muscle memory is perfect."

"What do you mean?" Jax twisted on the bed to face Gretchen fully.

"Last night, when I touched you, I knew exactly what I was doing, but I also knew it had been a long time since I had done it."

Jax didn't say a word. She just turned her attention to Gretchen's foot, poking out from beneath the white bedding. She touched each toe and then traced a delicate tendon. Her touch tickled, and Gretchen couldn't fight back a giggle.

As much as this moment felt like old times, she knew it wasn't. They still had so much between them. Spending the night together could've helped, but it also could've harmed.

"Are you okay?" she dared to ask. She was absolutely terrified of any answer Jax could give her.

Jax glanced at the bedside clock and stood. "I'm going to be late."

A new unease washed over Gretchen. "Will I see you later?"

"It may be late, but yeah."

Spiraling thoughts of Meredith and regret strangled Gretchen, but she refused to stop believing in the undeniable connection she still had with Jax. "Maybe we can spend the weekend with Caleb and possibly talk about us? There's obviously a lot to talk about." She tried to ease the tension with a laugh, but it sounded painfully fake.

Jax grabbed her jacket and messenger bag on her way. She paused with her hand on the doorknob. She looked back at Gretchen and winked. She left a second later.

Gretchen lay back on the mattress and blew out a long breath. She started to analyze and overanalyze Jax's behavior. Last night wasn't supposed to happen, and as hopeful as Gretchen felt, she knew Jax would need more time. A weekend with their family would be good for both of them.

Gretchen spent the day taking phone calls and responding to emails from her boss. She sorted through most of her inbox, feeling confident she'd be returning to work soon. She needed to refresh her memory. Emails dated nearly twelve months earlier caught her eye. A conversation thread between herself and the head of the practice, Omar Runge, detailed her eagerness to pick up as many clients as she could and how she was more than happy to work overtime. Going back farther, she noticed a promotion two years ago, and an early retirement option with her 401(k).

Gretchen squinted at her computer screen. She sat back and finished the last bite of her breakfast. The phone rang as she picked up her plate. The chorus of Montell Jordan's "This Is How We Do It" seemed like an odd choice for a ringtone, but when she saw Amanda's name on her screen, everything made sense.

"Did you set this ringtone or did I?" Gretchen said.

"It was a joint effort."

"Mm-hmm." Gretchen went to refill her coffee. "What's up?"

"Nothing really. I'm just doing laundry and wondering why my sister hasn't called to see how Caleb did overnight or tell me what happened with her almost ex-wife. I'm separating my darks from my lights and trying not to be offended or mad."

She shook her head at Amanda's dramatics. "How was Caleb?"

She knew dodging the Jax topic would irritate Amanda, and that was fun.

"Fine. He loves his Aunt Man."

"There's not much to say about Jax." She was so happy Amanda couldn't see her grin.

"Did you talk?"

Definitely no talking. "She actually stood me up."

"I'm going to kill her."

"It's okay," she said quickly even though she was getting used to Amanda's protective side. "I think we're going to try to spend the weekend together with Caleb and really talk."

"That's great! I know Caleb would really love that."

Gretchen thought of how Caleb had been affected by everything going on. "This has all been so hard and bizarre. Have I been unfair to him or neglectful?"

"Gretchen, considering your situation, I think you're handling everything very well, including Caleb. He's happy, and he talked nonstop last night about how helpful he's been." Amanda laughed. "You really have nothing to worry about."

"What about before? Jax said—"

"Jax has said a lot of shitty things."

"But that doesn't mean she's wrong." She scratched at her forehead. The emails and work hours only supported everything Jax had said. "I feel like I've let them both down so much already."

"Hey. You have so many years ahead of you, Lord willing, and Caleb will barely remember any of this. Before you know it, he'll be sixteen and hating you."

"But he won't hate Jax because she's the cool mom," Gretchen said.

"What prompted these weekend plans? You said she stood you up last night."

Gretchen listened to Amanda sip on something. "She got home late and...we talked a little this morning before she left for work. She didn't exactly agree to the weekend, but I'm feeling good." Gretchen thought back on the night spent with Jax. "Yeah, I'm feeling good." She walked to her bedroom and grabbed the pill vial from her nightstand. "I really want to spend the weekend away, but she'll probably say it's too soon for me. If I can go back to work, I can go away for a weekend."

"Just book something. Surprise her. Why wait for a long conversation to start trying?"

She knew Amanda was right. "Thanks for the advice, sis."

"Any time. Are we having dinner later when I drop Caleb off?"

"No. I have a trip to surprise my family with."

"Good luck. Tell me how it goes."

"Will do." They said their good-byes and Gretchen ended the call. She tossed her medicine up in the air and caught it. She wore a grin as she walked back to her computer. She put the pills down next to a glass of water and started typing. She searched different resorts and inn options within driving distance. Thankfully, it was off-season for all of New Jersey, and rates were low. She searched for a place that would entertain Caleb but would lend a small air of romance for Jax. If she was planning on wooing and convincing Jax that they were worth fighting for, she was going to have to pull out all the stops. She had to win Jax back from Meredith and keep her this time. Gretchen filtered her search to view only five-star establishments.

The front door opened and slammed shut, pulling Gretchen's attention from the search. Heavy footsteps could be heard. Jax stepped into the kitchen a moment later.

"Why did you call Wyatt?"

Gretchen closed her computer and stood. "You're home early."

"I took the afternoon off because I couldn't concentrate. Why did you call Wyatt?" Jax said from just inside the kitchen, like she was afraid to be near Gretchen.

"You blew off dinner and I had so many questions—"

"Questions you should ask me."

"But you're never here! Not with me, anyway. I'm tired of being in the dark and learning about my life one bit at a time. I'm tired of you and Amanda deciding what parts I get to know about." She felt a familiar queasiness flash in her gut, and she took a deep breath. "I should've known about the baby."

Jax's nostrils flared. "Dr. Melendez said we shouldn't upset you."

"That means taking care when you tell me things, not hiding them from me. Were you planning on ever telling me?"

Jax looked away and said, "Yes."

Gretchen let out a sad, airy laugh. "When did we start lying to each other?"

Jax closed her eyes and shook her head. "Everything changed so much."

"And I want a chance to change it again." She walked over to Jax and took her hand. Jax pulled away. "I'm looking for a place we can go this weekend, just the three of us. Leave all of this behind and be a family so we can see if we can make this work. One last try." Gretchen grew annoyed at Jax's uncharacteristic silence, but she tamped it down to let her desperation show through. "We owe it to ourselves and to Caleb to try, and if last night was any indication, I think I'm right."

"Gretchen…"

"I know you felt it, too. Our connection, the love between us. Last night felt like a new beginning to me."

"It always does, and that's the problem." Jax stepped back and away from Gretchen. "This won't be the first or tenth time we try to make it work. That's what I've been trying to tell you. All these forgotten memories have you living in a fantasyland."

Gretchen refused to believe it. She shook her head forcefully. "No," she said with a raised hand, "I know you felt what I felt last night."

"It's not about that, goddamn it." Jax's voice started to rise, and she pointed between them. "It's about this, the fighting every day. We were at each other's throats constantly, and nothing helped. We tried counseling and trips and retreats, and nothing ever worked. We'd have sex and feel so in love and then hate each other in the morning. It was vicious and ugly, and I can't do it anymore."

"Things are different now," Gretchen said, begging. "I'm different. What will it take? Less work? I'll cut back my hours for good." Gretchen turned back to her computer and opened it. Panic caused her fingers to shake as she typed. "I'll email Omar right now and tell him I'll be part-time."

"It's too late."

Gretchen looked over her shoulder at Jax, and her heart shattered all over again. Jax's expression screamed resignation and sadness. The tears running down to Jax's square jaw punctuated the finality of her statement. "One more try, please," Gretchen said, her voice crackling.

"We've had all the tries I can handle. You don't remember them, but I do. I remember every painful word, the tear-filled nights, and the way you watched me leave. You don't have any of that haunting you, and I fucking hate you for it." Jax reached into her back pocket and pulled out folded papers. She dropped them beside Gretchen's computer. "I signed them."

Gretchen's vision blurred from tears. "Please…"

"See if Amanda can start spending the night. I can't do this anymore." Jax turned and left.

Gretchen wanted to chase after her, but she felt paralyzed. She sat heavily on a kitchen chair and started crying. The force of her sobs hurt her throat. She felt nauseous and tired. A headache came on and she didn't care. She welcomed the pain, until the edges of her vision started to go dark. Something didn't feel right. She took rapid breaths, trying to calm herself, but her heart continued to pound. The lingering smell of lunch made her stomach lurch, the room started spinning, and Gretchen reached out to steady herself with a hand on the kitchen table. She gripped the divorce papers as she fell forward. They bumped into the vial of antiseizure medication. She fell to the kitchen floor, and the last thing she saw was the orange bottle spinning beside her.

CHAPTER TWENTY-THREE

14 days, 23 hours, 14 minutes

Jax pressed her fingertips into her temples. Her mind was reeling, and not one bit of the information Dr. Melendez threw at her helped. "What does this mean?"

"Like I said, sustaining an injury to the occipital lobe—"

"English," Jax said firmly. "Just tell me if this set everything back or if…" Every ounce of hopefulness drained from Jax's heart. "Did we ruin our chances of Gretchen recovering?"

"Having a seizure at this point isn't detrimental, and it's better it happened now rather than later, when we were less prepared for it. It's impossible to say how it'll impact her, but we need to stay positive." Dr. Melendez grabbed a pen from the pocket of her lab coat and jotted something in her notepad.

"That's it?"

"Until she wakes up again, yeah."

Jax felt like she was living in an infinite, frustrating loop. She ran her fingers through her hair. "Okay." A hollow knock caught Jax's attention. She spun on her heels and smiled when she saw Gretchen was awake. She was grateful this wait was considerably shorter than the first. "Hey," she said, walking to Gretchen's bedside. She touched Gretchen's forehead gently. "You're awake. You gave us quite a scare." She looked into Gretchen's drowsy eyes.

"Gretchen? Can you hear me?" Dr. Melendez took her spot across from Jax. "It's me, Dr. Melendez." She encouraged Gretchen to open her eyes and shined her penlight into them.

She hated watching the way Gretchen winced and tried to pull away from the bright light.

"Do you remember me, Gretchen?" Dr. Melendez asked as she slid the light back into her pocket. She and Jax waited patiently for Gretchen to answer.

Jax studied Gretchen's face. Apparent on the surface were frustration and fear. She felt relieved at Gretchen's small nod.

Dr. Melendez smiled softly, showing her relief, too. "Do you know where you are?"

Jax laughed at Gretchen's incredulous look. Her face was so expressive, it said more than words ever could. She imagined Gretchen wondering where her doctor received her degree from and if it was real. The humor of the moment fell away when Dr. Melendez's expression turned to concern.

"Can you talk?" the doctor asked.

Jax's heart dropped when Gretchen looked at her with desperate eyes instead of answering. "Can you answer Dr. Melendez? One word, that's all we need." She took Gretchen's hand. She hated how awkward it felt to do something that was once second nature.

Gretchen's eyes started to tear, and her chin quivered. Her brow was pinched together, and she looked like she wanted to scream. Gretchen held her hand so tightly it hurt.

Dr. Melendez stepped back from Gretchen's bedside. Jax started to speak, wanting to demand answers and for them to do something, anything, to help fix her, but Dr. Melendez stopped her with a tilt of her head. She stood and followed her to the doorway of Gretchen's room.

"What the hell is going on?" She crossed her arms over her chest.

"Gretchen's main injury is to her occipital lobe, but in her scans we did notice faint bruising to the cerebrum. That's the part of her brain that controls speech."

"So she can't speak?"

"I think that's what we're dealing with right now."

"Why didn't you tell us about this?"

"Brain injuries are unpredictable. Her seizure must've triggered something."

She tugged at the neckline of her fuchsia sweatshirt, suddenly feeling hot and panicked, and above all else angry. She heard Gretchen knock again, but she couldn't even look at her. "Do you think it's permanent?"

"It's hard to tell right now." Dr. Melendez took out her notebook and wrote a few new notes. "I'll know more tomorrow."

"Hey!" The one word was loud.

Jax turned back to Gretchen immediately, grinning broadly at the sound of her voice.

Dr. Melendez chuckled and kept writing. "It's not much, but I'll take it as a word."

Jax knew she was being beckoned, even without Gretchen saying another word. She walked back to Gretchen, each step feeling slower than the next. Gretchen flipped her hand on the mattress and opened her palm to her. When Jax took her hand, she felt awash with happiness and confusion. Gretchen's eyes were clear and soft and looked the way they used to, when she still loved her.

Dr. Melendez started to leave. "I encourage you to rest some more. Sleep is the best medicine for a healing brain. I'll be back in the morning to check on you and ask some questions to figure out your progress." She smiled at Jax. "But for now, I'll let you relax and enjoy the rest of visiting hours." Jax felt overwhelmed in the odd silence that followed Dr. Melendez's exit.

Gretchen ran her fingertip back and forth over Jax's knuckles. The motion was soothing, and then it stopped. She worried at Gretchen's wide-eyed stare.

"Caleb?" Gretchen whispered, her voice crackling with dryness and instability. The name was said so quietly, it could barely be heard over outside noise.

Jax saw the panic and worry plainly written on Gretchen's face. The same look she'd had before the seizure. "You don't remember, do you?" A chill crept into her chest. She felt silly for hoping Gretchen's brain would cooperate just this once. She rubbed her face and walked to the window. The darkness outside matched her life. "Caleb is four and a half." Jax knew she shouldn't be mad at Gretchen for what was happening, but she couldn't keep the anger out of her tone. She looked at Gretchen's reflection in the window but couldn't bear to turn around yet. "He wants to have a bowling party for his birthday, and just last week you and I were fighting about him going to kindergarten." Jax turned to lean her back against the windowsill. She crossed her arms and stared at the doorway. "His preschool teacher recommended keeping him back because he has a hard time concentrating. I was willing to hear her out, but you cried. You insisted he was just energetic, and that there's nothing wrong with that. He needs to adapt, and we shouldn't cater to the whims of the school."

Gretchen shook her head. She touched her face and winced.

Jax rushed over and pulled Gretchen's hand away. "I wouldn't do that if I were you. The stitches are out, but your scabs are pretty fresh." Jax dropped Gretchen's hand and stepped back. She really needed to stop protecting and touching Gretchen so easily. She backed away awkwardly and found safety against the far wall. She felt helpless as she watched Gretchen look around in confusion, completely out of sorts.

Gretchen raised her hand weakly and motioned for Jax to come closer. She wanted to stay where she was—she wanted to keep her distance and not make anything more difficult than it already was. But Gretchen looked so fragile and damaged. Jax stepped forward helplessly and sat on the side of the mattress Gretchen patted so invitingly. She couldn't look in Gretchen's eyes without wanting to cry, so she chose to look at a small piece of Gretchen's curly hair that clung to her white pillowcase.

"Did you know Caleb's four?" Jax said, terrified. She blew out a breath when Gretchen nodded. Maybe not everything was lost. Maybe their lives hadn't been flushed away in one split second.

Gretchen clamped her eyes closed and moved her lips, struggling to speak. "In kit-kitchen?"

Jax frowned. "What about a kitchen?"

"Fell…kitchen," Gretchen said more firmly.

She might be speaking clearly, but now Jax worried Gretchen's brain injury affected more of her memory. Jax slumped forward in disappointment. "I have to get Dr. Melendez."

Gretchen gripped her hand tightly and gave it three little squeezes, something she hadn't done in years. Her watery eyes were filled with fear. "Don't," Gretchen said, intertwining their fingers. "Please."

Jax didn't dare move, but she also said not another word. She watched Gretchen's eyelids grow heavier and heavier by the minute. Visiting hours ticked away, and Gretchen eventually fell asleep. Jax pulled away from Gretchen's surprisingly tight hold and grabbed her jacket. She slid on her heavy coat and looked at Gretchen. She looked so peaceful, the complete opposite of how Jax felt.

"It's not fair, you know?" Jax spoke into the silent room. She studied Gretchen's eyelids carefully to see if she could hear her. Gretchen's chest rose and fell rhythmically. Jax sighed, a sound that came out louder than her next words. "I don't want to be the only one who remembers the past three years. So you better remember." She hated herself for being so resentful, but she felt strangled by her anger. She needed fresh air to help clear her head.

Jax left the hospital and sat in her truck for nearly ten minutes before driving away. She felt completely drained, but she knew she wouldn't be able to sleep. She stopped by Wyatt's to pick up Caleb, who was sound asleep in Wyatt's arms. She couldn't thank him enough for taking care of Caleb. She waited until she was home and had Caleb settled in his own bed before typing out an email to her boss explaining the situation and how she'd be out of the office again. She struggled to not end the email with her resignation. Her nightly routine felt robotic, and Jax walked into her bedroom just after nine o'clock, hours earlier than her normal bedtime.

She lay in bed that night and stared at the ceiling. She considered calling Meredith for a distraction, but the last thing she needed was the added guilt of using the one good thing in her life. No, she would force herself to sleep. But when she tried, she started to think about how she was going to explain Gretchen's memory loss to Caleb. How would their four-year-old, no matter how brilliant, understand his own mother didn't remember most of his life? He was already traumatized by Gretchen's outburst. Gretchen might be lying in a hospital bed, but Caleb was the real victim.

She shifted on her side and sighed. Her eyes did not want to close. She picked up her phone from the nightstand and was not at all shocked to see an email response from her boss already. He insisted she show up for their morning meeting. She would've broken her phone in half if she could afford a replacement. Instead, she opened a message to Amanda and updated her.

She woke up again and you didn't tell me?

Jax felt a different kind of guilt then. She grimaced at the bright screen. *I'm sorry.* She sent the message but knew it was inadequate. *Visiting hours were almost done and we sat together for a bit. Her speech isn't good, but the doc didn't seem overly concerned. Her memories are still gone.* Jax reread her message and knew it was a small lie. She'd never forget the look on Dr. Melendez's face when she asked Gretchen if she could talk.

I'll get there first thing in the morning and bring her some food.
I don't really know what she's allowed to eat.

She has to eat. Jax could hear Amanda's stern tone in her head clearly. *And when she does, it should be something good that she loves.*

Jax couldn't argue with that reasoning. The rest of Gretchen's life was shit—her food options shouldn't be. *Can I convince you to make a little extra for me?*

That'll depend on whether or not I'm still mad at you when I wake up.

She chuckled. *That's fair.* She told Amanda good night and tucked her phone away. She was still wide awake but exhausted. The thought of tomorrow being another day of this nightmare was daunting and something that'd undoubtedly keep her up all night. She pulled her phone out again and started typing. Jax lay back with a smile and ignored the small voice telling her she was wrong for hitting *Send.*

Chapter Twenty-four

15 days, 10 hours, 19 minutes

Jax stared at the ceiling. Her alarm had gone off fifteen minutes prior, but she couldn't bring herself to move. She ached with fatigue. Weeks spent going back and forth from the hospital, caring for Caleb, and trying to keep her head above water at the office were finally starting to take their toll. Instead of rising to the early morning light, she decided to watch Meredith sleep soundly instead. She reached out to touch the ends of Meredith's hair, the silky feel soothing her. Meredith had been so kind and patient, never expecting more from her than she was able to give. She touched Meredith's shoulder next, feeling the familiar soft cotton of an old shirt. Jax loved when Meredith chose to sleep in one of her T-shirts. Something about it struck her as more intimate than nudity.

"I saw the letters." Meredith hadn't opened her eyes, but she'd obviously been awake for a while.

"I'm sorry," Jax said dumbly, not entirely sure what she was apologizing for.

Meredith smiled slowly, her lips spreading into a sweet grin. She opened her blue eyes. "You don't owe me an apology, silly." She touched Jax's cheek.

"The doctor recommended talking to Gretchen while she was in her coma. I thought it was stupid and couldn't think of a damn thing to say. There was no way I was going to talk about the ham and cheese sandwich I had for lunch." She gripped Meredith's hip and ran her fingertips along the strip of bare skin between her shirt and shorts. The softness eased her racing mind. "I came across the letters and figured reading to her would be just as effective," she said, feeling embarrassed.

"I didn't read them…well, not all of them. I saw them and took a peek out of curiosity. Gretchen loved you very much."

She felt the sting of Meredith's choice of past tense, but she didn't let it show. Jax nodded and leaned harder into Meredith's warm palm. "She did."

"I remember when you two interviewed me to be Caleb's nanny. I was so jealous of what you had."

Jax could barely remember that day. "We were different people then." She kept her responses short, never feeling completely comfortable with sharing details of her marriage with Meredith. She was too involved already.

"I wish I could see the letters you wrote to her." Meredith shifted closer, pressing her breasts into Jax's front. "You're a wonderful artist. I'm sure you're just as talented with words as you are with pen and pencil."

Art. Drawing, painting, and sculpting were all the things Jax loved before her life started to fall apart.

"She probably threw those letters away," she said, leaning her head back as Meredith started kissing her neck.

"She's crazy if she did. If you wrote me a love letter, I'd keep it forever."

Jax looked away from Meredith, careful to keep her expression neutral. She'd never write Meredith a letter, not after pouring her heart into so many for Gretchen. She flipped Meredith on her back and lay atop her. Jax kissed Meredith hard, hoping to end the conversation.

"Caleb gets up soon," Meredith said evenly, but her wandering hands told Jax she wasn't too concerned.

Jax could feel Meredith's hard nipples against her chest. She slid her hand into Meredith's panties and touched her growing wetness. "You're right," she said, pulling back. "We should probably stop."

"Don't you dare."

She grinned. This lightness was what she found so addicting about Meredith. They had fun and simply enjoyed one another. She kept one hand between Meredith's legs while she held herself up with the other. She focused on the way Meredith's body moved and felt, and the scent of arousal growing between them. Her mouth watered. "I want to taste you."

Meredith ran her fingers into Jax's short hair. "Then get to it," she said deeply, pushing Jax down her body and moaning when Jax pulled her shorts off.

Jax wasted no time diving into Meredith's pussy. She wanted and *needed* the feeling of power and control. She brought Meredith to her first orgasm slowly but refused to stop there. She worked Meredith's body until she fell limp against the mattress. Jax left her to sleep while she got ready for the day.

Jax got herself together for work and Caleb ready for school in record time, sharing a sweet good-bye with Meredith before rushing to her truck. She blasted the heat and started toward Caleb's school. After drop-off, she was heading to the office with two hours to spare before the meeting—enough time to get some work done. But something made her turn right instead of left. Something told her to stop by the hospital first, even though she'd promised to visit later. Morning traffic kept her from making it to the hospital as quickly as she expected to, and by the time she parked, she was already aggravated and regretting her decision.

She walked into Gretchen's room and widened her eyes at the display in front of her. Both Amanda and Gretchen were crying while hugging each other. "Oh, shit," she said, turning away and moving to leave.

"Come in," Amanda said, waving to Jax. "Gretchen has been looking for you all morning."

She narrowed her eyes at Amanda, truly not believing her. "I didn't mean to interrupt. I'm on my way to the office and wanted to see if anyone needed anything." Jax quickly noticed a troubled look in Amanda's eyes. "Has Dr. Melendez been in yet?"

Amanda looked lost in thought before shaking it off and nodding. "Yeah, she stopped in earlier and gave Gretchen the lowdown on her injuries."

Jax knew there was more going on than Amanda was letting on. "Is she okay?"

"She's fine. Her vitals are where they need to be, and Dr. Melendez feels confident with how quickly she's healing."

"But…"

Amanda gave her a look she didn't recognize. "I'm afraid of her symptoms."

Her heart started to hammer. Before she could ask Amanda to explain, waving caught her eye. She saw Gretchen holding up a notepad, words written all across it. "You can write!" She rushed over to read what Gretchen had written.

We were just talking about you.

Jax turned to Amanda. "You were talking about me?"

Gretchen tapped at her notepad, regaining Jax's attention. She wrote quickly and showed Jax the paper.

When did you have time to change your hair?

Jax ran her fingers through her short hair. "I've been blond for a while now." Gretchen stared at her like she was a walking mathematical equation.

Gretchen opened and closed her mouth, her face twisting up in frustration.

"I'm going to get coffee," Amanda said, standing and leaving without another word.

She sat on the edge of the bed after Gretchen motioned for her to come closer. Gretchen grabbed her left hand and held it tightly. Jax felt uncomfortable in the moment. She pulled her hand back. "What else did Dr. Melendez have to say?"

Gretchen let out a long sigh and wrote aggressively.

You know. You already know all of this. Why are you asking me?

Jax read the note and felt thoroughly confused. "What do you mean I already know? Oh, right, she went over your injuries. I know, I was pretty freaked out when I found out they drilled a hole in your skull." Jax shuddered. "But your vitals improved immediately after, so as scary as it was…" Her curiosity was piqued when she saw a few words on Gretchen's paper. She took the notebook and started flipping through the pages. Gretchen talked about last week and Jax leaving. "Are you starting to remember?"

Gretchen snatched the pad back. Tears were in her eyes as she scribbled words.

I remember all of this. I remember you sitting here, and I remember talking about the doctor. I remember this conversation.

Jax looked between the written words and Gretchen. She stood and backed away from the bed. "You remember this? Like today?" She wasn't even sure what that meant. "That's good. That means your short-term memory is okay."

Gretchen shook her head. "Pens…and more pads." She kept writing.

"You want another pad? I can stop at the store and get you one. I'll get you gel pens, too. I know how you prefer those."

Gretchen held up her paper, tears streaming down her face.

I'm scared, Jax. I don't know what's happening to me. Please don't leave.

Jax's heart sank. "I'm sorry, but I really can't stay. They need me in the office today. I'll be back with Caleb later, if you're feeling up to it."

Gretchen was writing again already. She handed Jax the pad.

I'm living this day all over again, and I want it to stop.

She read the words slowly and twice. How was that possible? "Dr. Melendez said the side effects of the coma and your injuries could make you feel disoriented. I'm sure that's it. You're getting better and stronger by the minute. I'm sure it'll wear off soon. I'll get the pad and some pens, and I'll even stop and get some more flowers." Jax looked around the room at the many bouquets already lining the walls. "Maybe something different."

"Cactus."

Jax turned back to Gretchen's voice and started laughing, but that laughter died when she noticed how hard Gretchen was now crying. She panicked. "I'll get you a cactus. I promise."

Gretchen pressed her hand to her mouth and shook her head. She pointed to the door and said, "Doctor."

Jax peered at the empty doorway over her shoulder. "You want me to get the doctor?"

"I'm happy I heard some laughter coming from here," Dr. Melendez said as she entered the room. "And some tears. Is everything okay?"

Gretchen wiped her face and nodded.

Dr. Melendez looked between them. "Good morning, Jax."

"Good morning, Doc."

"Today will be a busy, tiring, and eventful day for Gretchen." Jax perked up. Dr. Melendez directed her next words to Gretchen. "I'm pleased with your progress in the last thirty-six hours. You're out of the ICU, following conversations, and your personality appears to be consistent with how everyone knows you."

Jax wanted to mention Gretchen's odd notes but decided to address the bigger concerns at the moment. "But she doesn't remember a thing."

Amanda rushed into the room with a coffee and a foil-wrapped sandwich in hand. "Did I miss anything?"

"No, I was just about to list today's itinerary. First, I'd like to get Gretchen up and moving," Dr. Melendez said, turning back to Gretchen. "Any little bit. I'd like to see if there's been any more physical damage, and I'd also like to avoid any muscle atrophy."

"I'm fine," Gretchen said in a harsh whisper. She pulled back the covers and started to slide out of the bed. Her grip on the bed's railing slipped and Dr. Melendez rushed to her rescue.

"Whoa, now." Dr. Melendez lifted Gretchen's leg back up onto the bed. "Let's wait for a nurse and the physical therapist. They'll get here in about an hour."

Jax evaluated the way Gretchen fell back and continued to cry. "Do you think the damage to her brain could've affected her body, too?" Jax crossed her arms over her chest and tried to look much calmer than she felt. Too many things weren't adding up. Dr. Melendez said she was doing great, but everything about Gretchen set warning bells off in Jax's mind.

"I'm not overly concerned, but she needs to be evaluated, regardless."

"She's writing," Amanda said excitedly. "Every word is clear, and her handwriting is exactly how it always was."

Jax thought immediately of the letters. "Exactly the same." Her thoughts wandered to her early morning with Meredith and whether she was right in assuming Gretchen had gotten rid of the many letters Jax had written her.

"That's very good." Dr. Melendez made a note. "I'm a bit envious of your handwriting and pad. I have to write so small to fit everything on this." She put the memo pad back in the pocket of her white coat. "Later this afternoon I'd like to do a thorough evaluation to determine what we're dealing with in terms of her amnesia."

"So you think she really has amnesia?" Everyone turned to Jax.

Dr. Melendez furrowed her brow. "That much is obvious."

"What does the evaluation entail? Will it harm her?" Amanda said.

Gretchen held up her paper. Jax read it over Dr. Melendez's shoulder.

Questions to determine memories and things like that.

"It will be tiring, but all I will do is ask a series of questions to determine her memories, mental state, and things like that."

Jax frowned at the similarity between Gretchen's words and Dr. Melendez's description.

Dr. Melendez continued, "I'll need you both to be present."

"Why?" Jax said loudly.

"How else will I know if her answers are correct? Can you both be back here around four?"

Jax looked at Amanda and wondered if she saw Gretchen's note, too. She shrugged when Amanda did.

"Great. I'll see you both then." Dr. Melendez left the room.

Jax had a million questions and needed to understand more of what was going on, but she had to get to work. She checked the time and realized she'd have to speed to make it to her meeting on time.

"I have to get going," Jax said, turning her back to Gretchen and leaning into Amanda. "Keep me updated, will you?"

Amanda's solemn nod told Jax she wasn't the only one who noticed Gretchen's odd behavior.

Chapter Twenty-five

15 days, 19 hours, 2 minutes

Jax packed up her work for the day. She was leaving the office with more than enough time to stop at the store and make it to Gretchen's evaluation on time. She couldn't stop thinking about Gretchen and the note she wrote. If the evaluation didn't go smoothly, she'd bring it to Dr. Melendez's attention, but until then she would allow Dr. Melendez to be the one to decide what was and was not normal at this stage of healing. Jax pulled her phone from her pocket and decided to finally respond to the messages from Meredith and Wyatt. Wyatt asked for updates on Gretchen, and Meredith asked if she would see Jax later. She had no clue how to answer either.

She gave Wyatt a brief rundown of Gretchen's vitals. She opted to share only facts. Gretchen's memory wasn't good, but she was healing and appeared to be out of the woods. They'd know more after the evaluation, and she promised to call him later. Easy. Meredith's message, however, proved to be much more difficult even though it only required a yes or no answer.

Jax loved spending time with Meredith, but the day so far had shaken something within her. Maybe it was the way Gretchen lay broken and desperate in her hospital bed. Maybe it was the reality of almost losing Gretchen finally hitting her. Or maybe it was as simple as her broken heart never getting the chance to mend at all before being shattered again. Whatever it was, Jax had a hard time picturing herself sleeping beside Meredith for another night right now.

She typed, erased, and typed again, multiple responses, but in the end, she sent the one that was closest to the truth. *Not tonight. I have to be at the hospital for a while, and I'm beat. Maybe tomorrow?* Jax hit *Send* and took a breath. She couldn't juggle worrying about her hospitalized wife, obsessing about her annoying boss, and hurting her girlfriend's feelings. Unfortunately, Meredith fell at the bottom of her priority list.

I understand. I'll be up late if you change your mind. Do you need me to pick up Caleb?

Yes, please.

Anything for you.

Guilt hit Jax like a punch to the gut. Meredith was too kind to be pushed to the side. She decided then and there that she'd make it up to Meredith in a big way once Gretchen was cleared and released from the hospital. Jax was imagining a weekend away where she and Meredith could just bask in each other's company and have a chance to really explore where their connection could take them.

"Leaving already?" Jax's boss said from behind her.

Jax started and faced him. "Yeah. I have to get back to the hospital. I emailed you the details."

He sipped from his protein drink. "You're missing a lot of work lately. Even though you're caught up on your accounts, I can't just let you make your own schedule. I'll need documentation to support your absences."

"Are you serious? Gretchen is getting evaluated to see how much of her memory is lost, and you think I'm making that up?"

"Nothing personal, Levine. I have to be a smart boss." He took another drink and started to back away. "Have it on my desk in the morning. Or the hospital can fax it over tonight." He turned his back and walked away without giving Jax another second to speak.

She clenched her jaw. Five years with the company, and she had earned nothing real. No trust, understanding, or even an ounce of compassion from the bastard. She couldn't wait to get a new job.

Instead of driving to the convenience store down the street, Jax decided to walk and let the frigid air calm her. The biting wind distracted her from her anger, and the crispness filled her lungs. She grabbed legal pads and two packs of pens, so Gretchen could choose between blue and black ink. She hopped in her truck once she was done and started for the hospital. She made one stop at a home and garden store for the most elaborate cactus they had, and before she knew it, she was parking in the same exact spot she had occupied only hours earlier. She stepped into Gretchen's room with five minutes to spare. Amanda and Gretchen looked at Jax in surprise.

"I know, I'm actually early." She handed Gretchen the cactus and felt proud of the smile she received in return. "These are for you, too." She placed the plastic bag of stationery on the bed and took off her jacket. "How did your walking go?"

Gretchen reached into the bag and pulled out the notepads. She turned them over before holding them to her chest. She looked up at Jax with tired eyes.

"She's exhausted," Amanda said. "And I think she's nervous for her evaluation."

"No." Gretchen's whisper was almost as quiet as the scratching of her pen against paper.

Going to ace it.

She thought about Gretchen's earlier prediction and felt uneasy. "I bet you will," she said.

"Hello again." Dr. Melendez walked into the room and pulled one of the chairs up to the bedside. She motioned for Jax and Amanda to take seats as well. She sat back and pulled out her own memo pad. She also had a folder with her this time. "Are you ready, Gretchen?" She waited for Gretchen to confirm. "Try to answer verbally as much as you can. I know you're having difficulty, but the more you try, the better."

Gretchen nodded and then forced out a weak, "Okay."

"Let's get started. What is your full name?"

"Gretchen Rebecca Mills," she said slowly but clearly. Jax felt hopeful.

"Date of birth?"

"November twenty-third. Eighty-three."

Jax was surprised Gretchen offered the year up so freely.

"Do you know where you are?"

Gretchen moved around a bit, her body language screaming of someone whose patience was waning. "Jersey Shore Med Center." She took a deep breath and cleared her throat. "I know this…all already."

"Do you know how you got here?"

"Stairs."

Jax perked up. She hadn't told Gretchen the details of her fall, and if no one else had, then she was remembering something. "What else do you remember?"

Dr. Melendez held up her hand but said nothing to Jax. "What's the last thing you remember before being in the hospital?"

Gretchen covered her face with her hands and growled in frustration.

She stood and started to pace. Gretchen's agitation was triggering Jax's own anxiety. "You already asked her this."

"Gretchen," Dr. Melendez said evenly. "Do you remember me asking you this?"

Gretchen's gaze was locked on hers, her eyes desperate and sad. "Yes. Every question."

"What's the last thing you remember before being in the hospital?"

Jax snapped. "Ask her something different, for Christ's sake."

"Jax, spending the night. Morning after, fight."

Jax looked at Amanda who stared at her, clearly surprised. "That didn't happen."

"Her answer is incorrect?"

"Correct," Jax said, embarrassment warming her cheeks as she imagined, for a split second, what Gretchen could be remembering.

"When was this?"

Gretchen looked panicked as she pressed her fingertips into her temples. "Not sure."

"What do you remember before your injury?"

"Caleb's first Fourth of July."

"How is that possible?" Jax said. "Dr. Melendez, how is that possible?"

"It's like her amnesia is spotty, like most of her memories are missing, but some still remain. And others aren't real. It's an unusual case. One I've never seen."

"They are real," Gretchen said.

Amanda sat down beside Gretchen and held her hand. "Can we keep going with your questions and worry about the rest later? She's tired and doesn't need this stress."

"Of course." Dr. Melendez finished writing a note and cleared her throat. "Tell me about your son."

"Caleb," Gretchen said with a huff, "Michael Levine. Named after Jax's foster father."

Jax looked at the linoleum. What she wouldn't give to have Michael in her life today to help her through this. He would know what to do—he always did.

"How old is Caleb?"

"Four." Gretchen picked up her pen again and started writing.

"I need you to speak as much as you can, Gretchen."

She held up the paper and looked at Jax. "Read it. Out loud."

"A jumping bean wouldn't help the evaluation. Caleb is with Meredith." Jax almost stuttered on the last sentence. "How did you know that?"

"How did you know about Meredith, Gretchen?" Amanda said.

Dr. Melendez raised her hand. "Who is Meredith?"

"She's my—"

"Caleb's nanny," Amanda said.

"Girlfriend," Gretchen said over Amanda. Unease settled over the room.

Jax was breathing rapidly, and she really wanted to flee the situation. "Do you have your memories back or not?"

"I remember what you all told me." Gretchen's impending tears could be heard in her wavering voice. Gretchen wrote out a list and showed it to Jax and Dr. Melendez. A series of follow-up questions and answers were listed.

Jax couldn't believe Gretchen knew any of this. The only real explanation was Gretchen was playing her. Was this all an elaborate plan to manipulate their relationship? Jax took over the questioning. "What did we do for Caleb's first birthday?"

Gretchen lowered her head and clamped her eyes shut. "I don't know."

"What about his second birthday?"

"I don't know."

"What did you tell him when I moved out?"

"I don't know!" Gretchen's volume startled everyone in the room.

Jax stepped back toward the door. "You told him it's better this way. I have to go."

"Hang on," Dr. Melendez said, standing. "I understand that emotions are running high, but we need to stay focused. Gretchen's memories are jumbled right now, and that's not unusual. Yes, this is a rare case."

"Or she's faking it," Jax said bluntly, feeling completely numb and detached.

Amanda stepped forward. "Are you fucking kidding me?"

"I don't think that's the case," Dr. Melendez spoke over them. "Symptoms like these are very hard to fake."

"She's an occupational therapist. She has knowledge of how the brain works after an injury."

"And I'm a neurologist whose specialty is brain injuries." Dr.

Melendez's firm tone made Jax close her mouth. "Believe me when I say we're dealing with amnesia. I'm just unsure of the kind right now."

"So, what do we do?" she said, barely reining in her annoyance.

"You can leave," Gretchen said. "All of you."

"The plan is to have Gretchen home next week."

"That soon? Really?" Amanda's skepticism was written plainly on her face.

"Yes. We'll need to discuss it further, and you two will have to make some plans. I'll want someone with her around the clock at first. She won't be able to drive for six months at the very least, and the most important things will be comfort and familiarity. Going home will be a shock to Gretchen. Although we've discussed what her life is like now, her memories are still unclear. She'll need help remembering what her everyday life is like."

Jax's head was already spinning with the thought of being forced to take part in Gretchen's every day. She had gotten over that loss once, but she wouldn't be able to do it again. "I don't think I should be that involved."

"Leave," Gretchen said loudly.

Amanda touched Gretchen's shoulder, but Gretchen never looked away from the ceiling. "Are you sure? I can come back later."

"No. I want to be alone. I don't want dinner, just something to take for sleep."

Jax felt a war waging in her chest. She was still so full of doubt, but her heart continued to break for Gretchen. She couldn't imagine feeling so helpless. Instead of saying another word and potentially making a bad situation worse, Jax started to leave.

Amanda and Dr. Melendez were right behind her when she walked out into the hallway. "I need documentation for my employer," she said, feeling small to make such a request at a time like this. "You can fax it over."

"Of course." Dr. Melendez wrote the fax number as Jax relayed it.

"How can you care about that right now?"

Jax looked at Amanda like she was nuts. "My job? How can I care about my job? I care because I need it."

"Gretchen needs you."

"And I've been here."

"I'll fax over the information tonight." Dr. Melendez left awkwardly.

"You're about to split. You know it, I know, and you basically just told Gretchen."

Jax pulled on her jacket and took a deep breath. "Look, I just don't think it's a smart idea for me to be with her every day."

"Why? Because you might realize you still love her?"

"What if that's exactly it? I'm not wrong for wanting to protect myself. You have no idea how hard it was the first time, and I know I won't be able to handle a second."

"I get it, but it still makes you selfish."

"Then I'm selfish." Jax turned on her heel and walked away, not wanting to explain herself any further. She left the hospital with her head held high even though all she wanted was to curl up in a ball and cry.

CHAPTER TWENTY-SIX

21 days, 12 hours, 11 minutes

"No!" Caleb screamed as he threw the third piece of waffle to the floor.

Jax took a deep, calming breath. "Come on, Cricket. They're your favorite, cinnamon sugar." Each day had gotten harder with Caleb, who only wanted his life to go back to normal. A sentiment Jax fully understood. "Just a few more bites, and then we gotta go."

"I wanna go with Mama."

She wanted to make it through one morning without Caleb demanding to see Gretchen. She had already made up every excuse for not bringing him to the hospital, and now she just felt like a villain. "You'll see her soon. I promise."

"You always say that."

Six days passed, and Jax had yet to feel like Gretchen was ready to see Caleb. Or maybe Jax just wasn't ready. Gretchen's behavior was consistent, but unpredictable, too. Her odd memories and lack of knowledge scared Jax, and she wasn't sure she wanted him to be around her. What if he got hurt? But she supposed keeping him from his mother wasn't exactly harmless.

"How about this," Jax said, kneeling beside his chair. "You finish that waffle without throwing any more on the floor, and I'll take you to see Mama later today."

His amber eyes lit up. "Really?"

"Yes." She had to slow Caleb down when he started shoveling the waffle into his mouth. "Chew. You're going to make yourself sick."

Caleb dressed himself quickly and practically bounced out of Jax's apartment into her truck. She worried Gretchen wouldn't want to see him, and she would, again, be the bad guy in Caleb's eyes.

She picked up her phone the moment she settled into her desk at the office. She dialed one of the few numbers she knew by heart and was relieved when Wyatt answered right away.

"Is everything okay?"

Jax laughed. "That's a tough question to answer, but yeah, everything's fine. I just needed to talk to someone who wasn't Amanda or four years old."

"What about Meredith?"

Jax knew Wyatt was teasing her, but she still felt it necessary to defend her relationship. "I can talk to Meredith about anything, but this is more best friend territory."

"What's up?"

She bought herself some time by opening her design programs and pulling up her latest project. "I know you've stopped by the hospital once—"

"I'm sorry I haven't been around more."

"Dude, you don't have to apologize for anything. I appreciate everything you've done, especially the supportive texts. I get it. Your wife is about to have a baby. That's sort of big."

"So is she. Don't tell her I said that!"

Jax laughed loudly. "Listen, I was wondering if you could possibly stop by the hospital today. Even if it's just for a few minutes."

"I'll talk to Carly and see what I can do. Other than Gretchen missing me, why the request?"

Jax shouldn't have been ashamed of her motives, but she couldn't help the icky feeling in her gut. "Gretchen's memories don't really add up, and I figured if you stopped by, you'd be able to get a feel of the situation."

Wyatt was silent for a minute. "Are you asking me to see if she's lying to you?"

"No," she said quickly, but the word felt bitter on her tongue. "Not exactly."

"Sure sounds like you are." She could hear Wyatt's displeasure.

"I'm bringing Caleb by soon, and I just need to feel more comfortable, with everything that's going on. She's been constantly evaluated and she's going through therapy. But there's still something that isn't right."

"What's her doctor saying?"

"That she has some kind of complex amnesia, and we have to take it one day at a time." Jax picked up a paper clip and started to bend it.

"But you don't believe her?"

"I want to." Jax twisted the thin metal until it broke. "But there's this nagging voice in my head telling me there's more going on here. What if she's lying to control me?"

"What's to control? You separated and she's the one who filed for divorce."

"Maybe she doesn't want me with Meredith." Jax filed through the many other reasons. "She could be doing this to make sure I don't go anywhere with Caleb."

"You wouldn't do that anyway." She didn't say anything, just stared at the metal in her hands. "Jax?"

She dropped the clip on her desk and sat back. "Once, when we were fighting, I told her that I would leave and take Caleb with me. That she was constantly working and made so little time for him that she'd never get custody."

"Oh my God."

"I know. It was disgusting, and I regretted it immediately, but I never told her. I let her believe I would do it, so now I'm wondering if she's doing this to keep me around."

Wyatt blew out a long breath. "I've known you and Gretchen for a long time, and even though you've been like a stranger lately, I think I still know you pretty well."

Jax fought back an apology. Wyatt made his point and she knew it was time to shut up and listen.

"You wouldn't take Caleb from Gretchen. I know that, and deep down Gretchen knows that, too," Wyatt said with more confidence than Jax had felt in a while. "Just like how deep down you know Gretchen isn't faking any of this, but I'll still stop by anyway."

Jax closed her eyes. "Thank you."

"Now I have to go because Carly is hungry, and I promised her hot and sour soup from the one Chinese food place in the area that doesn't deliver."

"You're a gem." Jax smiled and said a quick good-bye. She focused on her work for only so long before picking up her cell phone. The least she could do was give Gretchen a heads-up that she was planning on bringing Caleb by, but she thought for a minute before typing out the message to Amanda. It would be much harder for Gretchen to say no to her face. Jax decided a lunchtime rendezvous at the hospital was in order.

❖

Jax marched up to Gretchen's room. She was on a mission, but her bravado deflated when she saw nothing but an empty bed. She stepped back into the hallway and spotted Amanda walking toward her. "Where is she?" she said with a thumb pointing into the room.

"Therapy, like she is every day at this time. You would know that if you hadn't suddenly stopped visiting." Amanda blew into her tea to cool it off. The steam billowed around her mouth.

"I have to be careful about missing work. When will she be back? It's my lunch hour."

"Soon. I'm glad you're here, though. We have to figure out what we're doing once she gets out of here."

Jax had been trying her best to avoid this very conversation. "Did Dr. Melendez say when that was going to be yet?"

"Not yet, but it could be any day. She's walking and moving with only a little pain, and her speech is improving. What are we going to do?"

"I'm here because I need to tell Gretchen I'm bringing Caleb by later. I don't have time to plan our lives."

"You need to make time," Amanda said, her eyes going back to her tea.

Jax was so distracted by her growing anger that she didn't notice Gretchen until she was walking into her room. Amanda practically pushed Jax out of the way to get in the room before her.

"How was therapy?" Amanda said.

Jax barely heard Gretchen's response before she started talking. "I have to bring Caleb by. You can't keep avoiding him."

"Bring him. I never told you not to."

Jax stepped back in surprise. "But after the first time, I didn't think you were ready."

"*You* didn't think I was ready. You never asked. You just assumed. Bring him by after dinner. I miss my son."

"Why didn't you say something?"

"When? When you were rushing into the room or rushing out? Or should I have said something when you never came back?"

Jax felt properly chastised. "I handled this wrong, and I'm sorry. Will you be too tired after dinner? You get cranky when you're tired."

Amanda snorted.

"I'm cranky now."

Jax feared for her well-being if she didn't leave soon, which meant her job would have to be pushed aside again. "How about I go get Caleb now and stop for some ice cream on the way. Rocky road from the place across town, not the one right around the corner whose chocolate ice cream tastes like white."

"Great," Gretchen said. "You know my order and make sure you get strawberry for Amanda."

Jax did not want to get Amanda anything, but in the name of peace, she would get a cup of strawberry ice cream. "Okay." Jax left without a second glance at Amanda. She was excited to bring Caleb to see his mother, and that was going to be her sole focus for the day.

Caleb bounced around in his car seat, his excitement adding to his usual hyper state. "Mama," he screamed for the tenth time in less than fifteen minutes.

"That's right, Cricket. We're going to see Mama." Jax took the exit for the hospital too quickly, and the full-to-bursting bag of ice cream toppled over on the passenger seat. Spoons spilled out on the seat, and a container rolled out, headed for the space between the seat and the door. In a panic, she reached over to save it. She had to slam on her brakes to avoid a collision.

Caleb started to cry instantly, and Jax breathed rapidly to calm her racing heart. She felt the beating in her throat. She returned both hands to the steering wheel and gripped it until her knuckles turned white.

"You okay, Caleb?" Jax looked in the rearview mirror at Caleb, too afraid to turn around and take her eyes off the road again. Spit ran down his chin as he cried. Traffic started moving, and Jax decided to pull over. She parked and put on her four-ways. She hopped from her truck, but by the time she opened the back door, Caleb's tears had stopped. "You're okay."

Caleb nodded and continued to tug at the short arms of his stuffed dinosaur. "Ice cream gonna melt."

She took a deep, calming breath and let it out slowly through her nostrils. She got back in the driver's seat after a quick kiss to Caleb's forehead. She needed the reassurance.

By the time Jax made it to the hospital and found parking, she was frazzled and tired and was going to need more than a cup of ice cream to relax. "Should've gotten rum raisin," she muttered to herself as she walked Caleb to the elevators. The doors opened when they arrived on the third floor, and Jax almost walked right into Wyatt.

"Watch where you're going, crazy lady." Wyatt laughed and reached out for a high five from Caleb.

"You stopped by." Jax was genuinely surprised.

"Yeah, I told you I would. What's up, bud?" Wyatt flicked Caleb's earlobe, and he giggled. "What kind of ice cream did you get?"

"Bubble gum."

"Gross." Wyatt's smile faded when he looked back to Jax.

"How's Gretchen?" Jax said, holding Caleb's shoulder to keep him from running off.

"Quiet. She didn't say much other than asking about Carly. A lot of questions, actually." He chuckled. "She's probably desperate to hear about anything other than her own problems."

"What about her memories?"

Wyatt shrugged and turned up the corner of his mouth. "I don't know."

Jax's shoulders slumped in defeat. "Thanks for stopping by." She went to pat his shoulder, but Wyatt grabbed her hand and held it.

"Be patient with her, Jax. She's going through something that we can't understand. I see it in her eyes—it's hard and it's dark."

Jax had never heard him speak so seriously. "Okay. I will." They said their good-byes, Caleb hugging Wyatt tight around the neck.

They walked to Gretchen's room, and Amanda's voice could be heard just outside the open door.

"Are you sure you're okay? You've barely said a word since this morning."

Jax couldn't hear Gretchen's answer, and she started to have second thoughts about bringing Caleb by. What if he upset Gretchen and she had another seizure? Jax watched Caleb's curious eyes as he followed doctors, nurses, and patients. He was practically entranced by everything going on around him. This child was their whole world. He couldn't ever bring Gretchen harm.

"Remember, Mama is a little hurt, and she's having a hard time remembering things, but she's very excited to see you."

"She won't cry again?"

Jax wished more than anything she could erase that memory from Caleb's mind. "If she does, it's because she's so happy to see you, Cricket."

Caleb stood on tiptoe in an effort to see into Gretchen's room through the small window. "I see her!"

"Come on," she said, grabbing his hand and leading him into the room. "Go say hi to Mama."

She watched him run to Gretchen and climb up on her bed. Without hesitating, Gretchen wrapped her arms around Caleb and held him.

"Not too tight, Cricket, Mama's still healing," Jax said, hoping she didn't sound too concerned. She hadn't realized how deeply she feared the possibility of a disconnect between Gretchen and Caleb until now.

"She's the one crushing me." Caleb's voice was muffled against Gretchen's shoulder.

Gretchen released Caleb and wiped away her tears. "I'm sorry. I'm just really happy to see you."

Jax needed to lighten the mood before she lost her composure altogether. She raised the white paper bag in the air with a proud smile. "I can't imagine a better way to celebrate than with ice cream," Jax said, handing out everyone's treats. After everyone was armed with their dessert, a spoon, and napkins, she took a seat and opened her own mint chocolate chip. It was half melted, but Jax shrugged and dived in anyway.

"You just missed Wyatt," Amanda said between bites.

Jax pointed with her spoon and swallowed. "I saw him by the elevators." She was about to mention his concern over Gretchen's uncharacteristic silence, but she noticed Gretchen had yet to touch her ice cream. "Did they not give you enough sprinkles? I asked for double extra, the way you like it."

"It's fine." Gretchen rested her cheek against the side of Caleb's head as he ate his ice cream.

Jax felt what Wyatt had mentioned early. Something was up with Gretchen. "Wyatt said you didn't talk much when he was here. Are you okay? Is it your speech?"

"My speech is fine."

Amanda said, "Great, actually. Dr. Melendez feels confident she'll be back to one hundred percent in no time."

"I bet that makes you feel pretty good." She wanted more of a reaction out of Gretchen than a nod. "What's going on? Why are you so quiet?"

Gretchen looked directly at her with empty eyes. "I have nothing to say."

Jax fought to swallow her ice cream. She wished she had never asked the question.

CHAPTER TWENTY-SEVEN

22 days, 13 hours, 17 minutes

Jax ignored the fifth message from Gretchen and the third from Amanda. She was ready to turn off her phone completely. She didn't know how to talk to Gretchen, and she didn't want to worry Amanda or piss her off again. She figured keeping to herself until the meeting with Dr. Melendez was the best thing for all parties involved.

"I appreciate you inviting me to breakfast, I really do, but I'd enjoy it more if I felt like you were here with me." Meredith put her hand over Jax's. The diner was busy, but the bustling patrons did very little to kill the awkward silence between them.

She pushed scrambled eggs around her plate and flipped her hand over to play with Meredith's fingers. "I'm sorry. My mind is all over the place."

"You can talk to me. I know you try to keep me separate from things with Gretchen, but I can tell it's eating you up inside. You're not drawing or painting, and when you're not at work, you're at the hospital. I'm worried about you."

Jax felt the softness and sincerity of Meredith's words in her heart. "Something's wrong, and I don't know what." She pushed her plate aside and held Meredith's hand in both of hers. "Her doctor says everything's fine, and her vitals are good. It's just…"

"What?"

Jax stared into her coffee and wondered how to explain what her gut was telling her. "Gretchen's not Gretchen." She frowned at Meredith's laughter.

"Of course she's not. Think about everything she's been through. On top of that, she's been in the hospital for weeks. I wouldn't be myself, either."

"It's more than that. There's this blankness that was never there before. She was so scared the first few days, and now it's like she's just given up."

"I don't know Gretchen as well as I know you." Meredith rolled her eyes at Jax's amused look. "Not like that. I mean you always talked to me and got to know me, but Gretchen never did. She cared about my credentials and background check, and knowing she had hired the best. But one impression I always had of her was she's fierce, no nonsense, and that means she won't give up easily."

"I hope you're right."

"Are you still working on that?" the waitress said, interrupting the one hopeful moment Jax needed.

She handed over her plate and sat back. She took the check the moment it was placed on the table.

"You always pay for me," Meredith said coyly.

Jax smiled. "And you always make sure I'm okay. It's the least I can do." She paid and escorted Meredith from the diner with a hand on her back. They walked together to their cars and paused next to Jax's truck. She braced herself against the cold breeze. The sun was shining just enough to cut through the bitter cold. The air felt fresh instead of painful. "Thank you for meeting me."

"Thank you for the invite." Meredith leaned up and kissed Jax once, a sweet, short kiss. Her eyes were twinkling when she stepped back.

Jax got into her truck and started the engine. She looked at Meredith curiously when she climbed into the passenger seat. "What are you doing?"

"I hate seeing you like this." Meredith leaned across the center console and kissed Jax deeply. She ran her fingers through Jax's hair and scratched at her scalp.

Jax sank deeper into her seat at first, but then she pulled back and whispered, "I have to get to the hospital."

"Forget about the hospital." Meredith ran the tip of her tongue along the bow of Jax's upper lip. "For just a few minutes, think only about this." Meredith unzipped her jacket and brought Jax's hand to her breast.

Jax looked out the window to see if anyone was around, but not a soul could be seen. She kissed Meredith hard. Forgetting about her injured wife, her angry sister-in-law, and the meeting she had at work in less than thirty minutes seemed like the best bad idea she had heard in a while.

❖

Jax weaved through traffic and made it to the hospital ten minutes later than she was supposed to, but not nearly as late as she expected. She saw Dr. Melendez through the window of Gretchen's room and wasted no time letting herself in.

"What did I miss?" she said loudly. She couldn't look at Gretchen, fearing she'd know why she was late.

"Gretchen is being discharged tomorrow," Amanda said. "No prescription for her pain."

She expected more details to come, but apparently that was it.

Dr. Melendez wrote on a prescription pad instead of her usual memo pad. "I'll be sending you home with some antiseizure medication. I'm also writing a prescription for you to put on file with your pharmacy as soon as possible. It's very important you follow the instructions and take those on schedule," she said, handing Gretchen the prescription. "Avoid physical exertion and high stress situations. Just take it easy. Once I see you for your follow-up, we'll know what the next step is."

"No driving?" Jax said.

"Absolutely no driving."

"Can I run or not?" Gretchen said flatly. Her demeanor screamed disinterest.

"You haven't been running in a long time," Jax said.

Gretchen waved her off. "I want to go for a jog every morning."

"You *used to* jog every morning, but you can't just get back into it now. Not after your injury." Jax looked at Dr. Melendez for backup. Gretchen was crazy, and she needed to know it.

Dr. Melendez pursed her lips. "If you'd like to exercise, I encourage it. Just be careful not to overdo it with any physical activity—that includes running and even sex."

Gretchen snorted.

Jax shook her head and walked to the other side of the room. She was ready to scream. Was no one else worried about Gretchen's well-being?

Dr. Melendez continued, "Someone needs to be with you around the clock until we know you're less of a seizure risk."

"When will we know that?" Amanda asked.

Dr. Melendez sucked in a breath between her teeth. "Usually in anywhere from one to three months, but given some of Gretchen's symptoms, I won't really know until I know."

Jax's mind reeled. "Three months is a long time."

"And during the first two to three weeks, she needs as much familiarity as possible." Dr. Melendez turned her back to Jax. "Daily routines that feel good, not foreign. What's a typical day for you?"

Gretchen shook her head. Her features were drawn, and she paid more attention to her hands than Dr. Melendez. "Run, breakfast, work." Gretchen finally looked up and frowned at Jax. "I don't know what I've been doing for dinner lately. Jax used to cook every night."

Dr. Melendez was waiting for more, but Gretchen didn't say another word. "Okay. Stick to that for now and make strides each day."

Amanda raised her hand. "I can stay with you. I know I'm not a fancy cook like Jax, but I know a thing or two."

Dr. Melendez put the prescription pad in her pocket. "Whatever can be done to make you comfortable. It's important to avoid anything that'll trigger a seizure, so if a jog will help you feel better and keep you calm, then go for it. You'll have to accommodate for Caleb, but I think having your son around will only help you."

"Do you think I'll regain my memories this time?"

"This time?" Amanda said, her words heavy with concern and confusion.

"I like neurology because the brain is incredible," Dr. Melendez said, undeterred by Gretchen's phrasing. "It's the most powerful organ, but the one we understand the least about."

"Yeah, I know." Gretchen sighed. "But venture a guess."

"You're being rude," Amanda said in a firm whisper.

"It's okay," Dr. Melendez said. "I don't know. Even the simplest case is unpredictable, and your amnesia is more complex than most. What I do know is that your recovery is miraculous. Your life now should be cherished and lived, regardless of what you're missing from the past."

Jax took the sentiment to heart, even if Gretchen appeared to not care at all. "Thank you, Doc." She reached out to shake Dr. Melendez's hand before she left.

Dr. Melendez stopped to touch Amanda's forearm on her way out.

"Between that moment and this getup, I'll be disappointed if you two don't date after this," Jax said, trying to lighten the ominous mood choking her.

Amanda shook her head. "Get over it."

"Before you two start fighting, let's talk about tomorrow." Gretchen's voice grew in volume. "Amanda, you're staying with me. I don't care what plan the two of you came up with behind my back."

"We haven't been talking about it," Jax said defensively. She did not appreciate being accused of something so stupid in the grand scheme of things.

"You don't want to do it, and nothing good will come of it if you do. Amanda is more than happy to help, and soon enough I won't even need a babysitter." Gretchen pulled her cardigan around her and sat back in the bed.

She scrambled for something to say. "That's not—"

"Just stop. This is for the best. Forget about the familiarity bullshit Dr. Melendez just spewed. I know what's best for me, and having you there every day isn't it."

Jax stepped back, feeling every one of Gretchen's hurtful words chip away at her heart. Right there, in that moment, she had the clarity she'd lacked months ago to sign the divorce papers. She left the room.

Jax didn't get far before Amanda called her name. She turned around and said, "Do not ask me to go back in there."

"I'm sorry, Jax—she didn't mean it."

"I'm pretty sure she did, and I think we both know she's been feeling that way for a while now."

"She's not herself. I know you see it, too."

"That sounded a lot like her," Jax said angrily. She flexed her jaw over and over while looking into Amanda's helpless dark eyes. They were in the same boat, and they only had each other to keep it from sinking.

"I'm worried about her. She knew Mom died."

Jax was legitimately shocked. "What?"

"But she thought it was a heart attack. I had to retell how she only lived a month after her cancer diagnosis. Gretchen didn't even flinch, and that scared me. I'm hoping going home will help her get through whatever this is, and I think you need to be the one who's there."

Amanda must've lost her mind. "You heard her. Hell, everyone on this floor heard her. She doesn't want me there. She doesn't want me anywhere."

"But Dr. Melendez—"

"I don't care what the doctor said—I care what my wife said." Jax shook her head, hating the reality of her situation. "My ex-wife. You saw how upset she is. That's exactly what we need to avoid."

"She needs you and Caleb now more than ever."

"Caleb? Yes. Me? No."

"She loves you."

Jax laughed outright. Several people turned and looked at her in concern. "She stopped loving me a long time ago."

"You can't believe that."

"You have no idea."

"I don't, you're right, but I think the three of you being back under the same roof caring about one another will be good for everyone, especially Gretchen. She woke up remembering that life, and maybe being surrounded by it will help her remember other things, too. I'll come by when you leave for work or if you need a break. I'll be there, but I can't be there all day, every day. That's your place. It always has been."

Jax had to think fast. She had a child who'd be impacted by her decision. But she would hurt Meredith by moving back in with Gretchen for an undetermined amount of time. She wiped at her face roughly. Meredith didn't deserve an ounce of pain, but Jax's family had to come first.

"Fine, but you're stepping in if it's not working. No questions asked and no pressure for me to stay longer."

Amanda held up her right hand. "I promise I won't pressure you to stay longer than you feel comfortable, but I can't promise to not ask questions."

Jax chuckled in spite of her despair. "Fine." She turned and stepped back into Gretchen's room. Weariness caused her to approach slowly. "Gretchen, listen—"

"Don't," Gretchen said to the window. "Don't let Amanda guilt you into this. I made my decision."

She decided to just pull off the Band-Aid. "I'm moving back in until you get the all clear."

"I don't want you to," Gretchen whined. Her eyes were wide like she was only a second from a full-blown panic attack. "If you move in and stay, I'm just going to get hurt."

Jax wanted to scream about the ways they had already hurt each other, but she needed to avoid an argument. She shook off her aggravation. "It's for Caleb, not you. You need to be the best version of yourself for him, and the only way that can happen is if our family is together."

"Please, Jax." Gretchen's eyes filled with tears. "Please don't do this to me," she pleaded, so loudly her voice broke.

Jax needed to stay rational through the pain. Whatever Gretchen was so afraid of, it was her duty to make it go away. "Amanda will stay with you while I'm at work or if I need a break."

"Or if you need a break from Jax." Amanda stepped up to Gretchen and started rubbing her back. Gretchen started to sob.

"It'll be for the best. I promise." Jax stood back as Gretchen cried harder. Why was she doubting her promise, and why did it feel like she'd just sentenced Gretchen to a punishment worse than life in the hospital?

CHAPTER TWENTY-EIGHT

23 days, 14 hours, 58 minutes

Jax unpacked her duffel bag and started filling the dresser drawers with her clothes. She felt like she was in a foreign land even though she had picked out the furniture for the guest bedroom. She had never expected to use it, and now she hated herself for making decisions based on design and not practicality. She'd have to use the dresser and closet just for the few things she thought to bring along. Everything else could stay at her apartment for the time being.

She stopped moving and listened for Caleb, making sure he wasn't getting into too much trouble while she tried to settle in. She heard the TV and his giggles. She opened the closet and pulled the chain for the dim light to start hanging her work shirts and sweaters. She was shocked to see Gretchen hadn't taken over the spare closet, but then she remembered Gretchen now had the whole master walk-in closet to herself.

Jax lined her shoes up along the floor, and as she reached up to turn off the light, a box on the top shelf caught her attention. Deciding to mind her business, she closed the closet door and collected her toiletries for the guest bathroom. She lined up her shampoo, conditioner, and face cleanser. Her moisturizer and hair products went in the empty medicine cabinet, and she placed her toothbrush and toothpaste on the vanity. Making sure every little tube and bottle was in place only served as a distraction for so long, and in no time, she had convinced herself to march back to the closet and grab the box. She put it on the bed and flipped off the top. The contents were unmistakable.

She ran her fingertips along the many letters she'd believed were gone. Why would Gretchen ever keep them if she didn't still love her? She laughed at herself. You didn't have to love someone to keep mementos, especially when you'd been with her for over fifteen years.

Jax poked her head out of the bedroom. "You okay down there, Cricket?"

"Goofy's funny."

She would've preferred a yes or no, but she'd take what she got. She reached into the box and pulled out a random letter, unfolding it and placing it on the bed. She paced at the foot of the bed four times before she even looked at the date. The significance of the year made Jax's stomach drop. The same wave of nausea hit her just like it always did. She started to read.

> *My Love,*
>
> *We're both hurting so much right now, I know it's hard to talk about it. But I never want you to forget I'm here and I love you. We're in this together, forever, and that means dragging each other through the hardest days. I'll drag you and you drag me, and one day we'll smile again. And I cannot wait to see that beautiful smile of yours.*
>
> *Unconditionally forever,*
>
> *Jax*

Jax's hands shook as she folded the letter back up. She replaced the lid on the box and put it back in the closet. She wanted to weld the door shut to ensure that monster stayed inside. She already remembered so much of that day when she closed her eyes: the way Gretchen cried in her arms, the way not one doctor or nurse would look them in the eyes, the way they held their stillborn. For the first time since the accident, Jax was genuinely jealous of Gretchen for losing her memories.

"Maybe I should fall down some stairs."

"Mama's home!" Caleb's voice carried up the stairs and scared her.

She ran down the stairs, wanting to get the door for Gretchen and shield her from Caleb if he was going to be rough. She peeked through the small window in the front door and saw Amanda walking up the path with a bunch of shopping bags. She threw the door open and rushed to help her.

"Did you buy the whole supermarket?" Jax grunted when she took a particularly heavy bag.

"She needed coffee and a few other things." Amanda shrugged the best she could while her arms were weighted down.

"A few other things?"

"I thought I had a BMW," Gretchen said, stepping around Jax and Amanda.

Jax noticed how much healthier she looked in the daylight rather than the buzz of fluorescents. Even after weeks in the hospital, Gretchen still managed to glow. "You couldn't choose between the BMW and the Audi, but the Audi won because you liked the color better." Jax peeked in the bag she held. "Sprite *and* coffee? You haven't had either of those in years."

"I want them again." Gretchen walked into the house, and Jax couldn't get around her fast enough to block a charging Caleb.

She watched with a grimace as he squeezed Gretchen. "Careful, Cricket, remember what I told you."

"Me and Bug will make you better."

"I'm Bug," Jax said for clarification. "You didn't like me calling him Cricket, so you started calling me Bug."

Gretchen looked disinterested as she nodded. This reunion was not off to a promising start.

"I think this is everything," Amanda said, placing Gretchen's large hospital bag on the couch just inside the front door. "Do you want me to stay? Do you need anything else?"

Jax was already nodding. "You should stay."

"You can go," Gretchen said at the same time. "We're fine. I'll talk to you later."

Amanda was hesitant to leave, but she eventually did, and all that could be heard in the house was Goofy.

Jax followed Gretchen into the kitchen. "We opened up the wall after Caleb was born. So we could watch him and eat in the kitchen still." Gretchen said nothing. "You were really happy with the result." She watched Gretchen until she turned the corner toward the bedroom. She dashed back to the living room for Gretchen's bag and walked into the bedroom just as Gretchen took a seat on her bed.

Her last memory in the space was far from pleasant. Jax hadn't been back in this bedroom since the night she left. She needed to keep talking to stop herself from reliving it all in her head. "We moved my office upstairs to the addition, so the nursery could be down here. The guest room is where I'll be." When Gretchen remained silent still, Jax knew it was time for her to go. "If you need anything, just holler. I'll be in the kitchen cooking."

She stepped out of the room and tried to shake off her unease. She had no idea how to be around Gretchen, especially this version of Gretchen. Caleb went zooming past Jax right into Gretchen's bedroom. She wasn't fast enough to stop him, and quite frankly she was too tired to care. She had to focus on cooking and making it through the night without losing her patience, which led her to wonder if Amanda had picked up any wine or beer at the store. The next sound she heard was the door slamming, and then Caleb was next to her.

"Mama told me to help you."

"Okay," she said, peering over her shoulder and down the hall. Gretchen probably just needed some peace. "I don't have much for you to do, but do you think you can put the cereal away for me?"

Caleb nodded so seriously that his whole body bobbed.

She unpacked the groceries and checked the cabinets for possible lunch options. She said she would cook, but she probably should've known what ingredients she had on hand. Simple comfort food was the answer.

She started a pot of water on the stovetop and walked down the hallway. She knocked on Gretchen's closed bedroom door. No answer. In a panic, she swung the door open to find the bedroom empty but the bathroom door shut. She knocked again.

"Are you okay?" Jax pressed her ear to the door.

"Fine. I'm going to shower. I'll be out in fifteen."

"I'll have lunch ready when you get out."

"What are you making?"

"Lipton noodle soup. I know it sounds boring—"

"I can't imagine eating anything else after being in the hospital."

She smiled. "That's what I was going to say. I'll have it ready." Jax rushed back to the kitchen, only to find Caleb in front of the television and the cereal boxes still on the floor. "I thought I told you to put those away."

"I forgot," Caleb said, never looking away from the screen.

"Sure you did." Jax did it herself and went back to the task at hand. She lost herself to the hypnotic rise and burst of bubbles in the boiling water for a little too long before emptying a packet into the pot. The soup was done, and Gretchen was still not out of the bathroom. Jax knew she should wait a little longer, but images of Gretchen slipping and falling or having a seizure in the shower poked at her conscience until she went to check on her again.

Her hand was poised to knock on the bathroom door when the door opened.

"I'm sorry," Jax said immediately, but Gretchen didn't look at all surprised. She must've heard her coming. "I was about to check on you."

"You don't have to check on me constantly."

"It's going to take me a while to believe that." She laughed nervously. The dim lighting of the bedroom caught just so in the droplets of water on Gretchen's skin. Jax glanced quickly at her bare chest and the way the towel pushed her breasts together. She turned abruptly and went back to the kitchen.

She filled three bowls with soup and buttered a few slices of the bread Amanda had gotten from the store. By the time the table was set, Gretchen joined them in the kitchen.

Jax was instantly transported back to lazy days at home with her family. Nights off and simple dinners that made them all feel good. She wanted nothing more than to break down into tears of remorse, but she forced a happy face. She sat at the table and Gretchen took her usual spot across from her. Caleb's nose was buried in a picture he was coloring. He'd only paused to slurp his soup or take a bite of his bread from time to time.

"We're lucky he loves coloring so much," Jax said offhandedly. "It keeps him in one place and…" She mouthed the word *quiet*. Jax expected Gretchen to say something, but she just stared at her soup and held her bread in one hand. "I hope you're not worrying about the carbs. You need to worry about getting better, not what you eat."

Gretchen's eyes were brighter and more alert than they had been all day. She stared at Jax and examined her for a moment. "It's like you remember, too."

"Remember what?"

"But you don't," Gretchen said sadly. She dipped her bread into the broth and ate slowly, seemingly shutting down again.

Jax wanted to ask a million questions, but Caleb launched into a story from his day at school, and Gretchen looked happy to listen. She couldn't interrupt that. Gretchen was getting a good dose of her normal, daily routine, even if it was one of the louder parts. Caleb showed off the frog drawing he made in preparation for Gretchen's return home, and she fawned over it just as she did every picture he colored or drew. Jax settled back in contentment. If things between her and Gretchen were rough from here on out, it'd be okay, because Gretchen was still the loving mother she always was.

"Hey, Cricket, why don't you get the picture of the sea turtle you drew with Mama."

"Octopus," Gretchen blurted out.

"What?"

"We drew an octopus."

"You remember drawing an octopus with him?" Jax felt hopeful as she saw Gretchen's mind work to figure out what she remembered. Maybe this was the start of her memories coming back.

"No. No, I don't."

Jax tried to hide her disappointment, smiling when Caleb came hopping back into the room. "See that."

"A sea turtle." Gretchen sounded confused and astonished. She took the picture from Caleb and examined it. She ran her fingertip along the lines of the fins like she was redrawing it all over again.

"It was one of the first drawings you did with him after he was diagnosed. We were trying out art as a therapy for him, not just as something fun and messy for him to do." She found Gretchen's silence rude and uncharacteristic. She decided to answer the question Gretchen *should* be asking about their son. "ADHD."

Gretchen hummed instead of speaking. She kept tracing the same lines over and over.

Jax felt her anger start to build. "Go get your sketchbook to show Mama." She waited for Caleb to be out of the room before taking the picture from Gretchen's hands. "What's wrong with you?"

"What do you mean?"

"I'm telling you something really important about our son, and it's like you don't even care."

"Because it's not news to me."

Those words detonated Jax's ire. "Because you know it all, just like you did the day you told me he should be tested. I shouldn't be surprised that a year later you're still saying I told you so."

"I'm not—"

"If I'm going to have to relive all of these arguments again…"

"You won't. Don't worry."

"Are you fighting?" Caleb's voice sounded so small from the edge of the kitchen. His sketchbook was too large for his small body.

"No, we're not." Gretchen crooked her finger to call Caleb over and lifted him on her lap. "Show me what you've been drawing."

"Bug says you don't remember."

"I hurt my head pretty badly, and now I have a hard time remembering things."

Caleb pulled back the cover of his sketchbook. "Do you remember me?"

Jax couldn't watch anymore, so she collected the bowls from the table and ran the water with as much force as the faucet would allow. She needed to drown out Caleb's voice as he recounted the way Gretchen told him he wasn't her baby. By the time the dishes were done, Caleb had moved on to much lighter topics.

"Why don't you go get your blanket and get comfortable on the couch," Gretchen said, kissing the side of Caleb's head. "Then you can tell me all your stories from school." Caleb bounced off her lap and ran for his room.

Jax dried off her hands and leaned back against the counter. "You might regret that." Her mood already felt significantly better.

"Never," Gretchen said with more confidence than Jax had heard from her in weeks.

CHAPTER TWENTY-NINE

24 days, 9 hours, 47 minutes

Jax stayed in bed well after her alarm went off. The first night back in her old home could only be described as odd. She was up late listening to familiar sounds and the echoes of her family stirring. So much noise carried up the stairs into the guest bedroom. She should've closed the bedroom door, but the small sounds actually brought more comfort than annoyance. She could never have this in her apartment.

She didn't spend much of the previous night with Caleb and Gretchen. The scene was too warm and inviting. They didn't sit in a blanket fort to talk about their days anymore. All of that was gone. They were no longer this close family unit, and believing they could be would be dangerous. Jax was torn between diving in and spending every moment with Gretchen and Caleb or fleeing for good.

She felt hopeful and at peace when she opened her eyes, the complete opposite of the night before. She had no idea where the feeling came from, but she wasn't about to question it. Jax knew whatever was going on could be fleeting, so she had to embrace it. She listened carefully to the sounds from the kitchen. She checked the time and knew she needed to get moving. She also knew if Gretchen was already in the kitchen, she'd be walking into a disaster if she waited too long. She got out of bed and pulled on a pair of worn sweats over her boxers.

She took the steps slowly and quietly and turned the corner to find Gretchen filling the kettle with water. Jax observed her back and long legs. Yoga pants always looked good on Gretchen. "I thought I heard you in here," Jax said, stepping into the kitchen and stretching. She wiped at her face and pushed her unruly hair from her forehead. Gretchen didn't look at her. "Are you making tea?"

Gretchen placed the kettle on the stove and turned the flame to high. "Oatmeal. The coffee's set to brew at eight."

"You don't have to make coffee just for me."

"It's for me."

"I guess I didn't believe you. You gave up coffee a while ago and became all about teas." Jax opened the cabinet and pointed to the many boxes of tea to make her point.

"Clearly I went crazy. But I was sane enough yesterday to get Amanda to stop on the way home to get some. I won't be without coffee again." Gretchen still wouldn't look at Jax. "I'll go for my run, and then I'll have my coffee. Those two things make me happy."

"They really did," she said with a smile, wanting to share her lightness with Gretchen. "I hope I'm here when you take your first sip. I know you had coffee in the hospital, but this will be different."

Gretchen's eyes sparkled. "This will be heaven."

Jax lost herself to the delicacy of the early morning, the pure joy on Gretchen's face, and the intimacy of the quiet kitchen. She could've sworn Gretchen was back to her old self, like she was the woman who eagerly married her in Las Vegas.

She cleared her throat. "Do you need help?"

"With oatmeal? No. Breakfast is one of the few meals I can handle," Gretchen said with a small laugh.

"I'm going to shower really quick. I'll be out in ten minutes in case you change your mind." She didn't give Gretchen time to say anything more before she dashed back up the stairs. She wanted to be back as quickly as possible to ask her a few questions, like how she was feeling or what she had planned for her day—all the things Jax had been wondering but couldn't pull out of Gretchen. She'd been so eerily quiet, but maybe now that she was back in her own house with her family, she'd open up and start talking.

Jax showered quickly and threw her sweats back on. She'd get dressed for work later. She was still towel-drying her hair when she returned to the kitchen.

"That was more like twelve minutes."

Jax chuckled and tossed her towel on the back of the kitchen chair. She leaned against the counter next to Gretchen and surveyed the ingredients. "You got everything for a good bowl of oats. The only thing missing is—"

"Nuts," Gretchen said, raising her finger. She rushed to the cabinet and stepped back in shock when she opened it and stared at dishes.

Jax laughed outright. "Spring-cleaning fever a couple years ago. That's when we redid Caleb's room, too." Jax stepped around Gretchen to get to the correct cabinet. She leaned into her space, indulging in their closeness but still being appropriate. She was happy to see Gretchen still had a plethora of nuts to choose from. She grabbed the almonds. "Caleb prefers syrup in his oatmeal, but you won't allow it."

"I got some brown sugar for him."

Jax dropped the almonds on the counter. Caleb hadn't started to really enjoy oatmeal until recently. She studied Gretchen's face, looking for any sign of her mental state. Gretchen looked frustrated and confused.

Gretchen shook her head. "This isn't how the cabinets were."

"You don't remember the cabinets, but you remember the brown sugar?"

Gretchen stared, wide-eyed and speechless. Instead of talking, she turned her attention back to the food. Her hand was shaking when she lifted the steaming kettle.

"Let me." She placed her hand on Gretchen's and encouraged her to set the hot water down. They switched spots, and Jax went about prepping breakfast. She preferred more nuts than raisins, and Caleb only liked the sweet stuff in his. Jax was unsure how to make Gretchen's and when she looked up to ask, Gretchen's eyes were on her. Jax could feel her stare like a hot touch. "What?"

"Nothing," Gretchen said, licking her lips. "It's just, everything you do is so artistic. I could watch you work on even the silliest thing all day."

Jax wiped the brown sugar from her palm into the sink. She felt a blush creep up her cheeks. She hadn't received attention like this from Gretchen in a long time. "I'm just making oatmeal."

"I always loved watching you. Whether you were painting or drawing. What have you worked on recently?"

Jax froze with a hot bowl in her hand. She put it down when it started to burn. "Nothing."

"What do you mean? You were always in the studio."

She didn't want to talk about the packed-up studio or the boxes of art supplies gathering dust in her apartment. She didn't want to explain how she saw Gretchen's face every time she held a pencil, and how the one thing that had always given her inspiration now hurt her the most. Jax composed herself enough to take two of the three bowls to the table. Gretchen wasn't far behind with the third.

"I'll get Caleb."

Gretchen held up her hand. "No, you get ready for work. I'll get him. Just, please take this and eat a little something." Gretchen grabbed the bowl with a spoon and napkin, and she handed it to Jax with an expression of surrender.

Jax was startled by her own desire to kiss away that forlorn look. She took the bowl and fled to the safety of the guest bedroom. She was no longer angry, and she didn't need breakfast. What she needed was to get her head on straight. Jax couldn't allow herself to fall for this all over again, especially this quickly. She knew the way she and Gretchen so easily fell together. But she had barely healed from the first time Gretchen let her go. How would she ever survive a second time?

Already knowing the answer, Jax set about getting ready for her workday. Eight hours in a miserable office surrounded by miserable people would undoubtedly distract her from the tiny blip her heart and body had just made. She walked to the guest bathroom and stopped in front of the door to her former studio. The door was shut. She couldn't see a thing inside, but it still called to her. She had given up on ever feeling creative again, so she couldn't understand why the room scared her so much.

Jax laughed at herself. A room couldn't be scary. She turned the knob and swung the door open. The early sun barely lit the room enough to see the inside. With tentative steps, she went deeper and flipped the light switch. Not one thing was in a different place—every box she'd packed remained where she had left it. Several portfolios were stacked against the far wall. She'd planned on taking it all to the apartment, but she didn't have the room. Or maybe she never really wanted to anyway. Jax was still so unsure of her every motivation over the past year.

Against her own good judgment, Jax opened one of the portfolios. She recognized the work inside as a watercolor series she did. Simplistic, minimal strokes forming a beautiful nude silhouette. Gretchen's silhouette. She ran the tip of her index finger along the textured paper, following the curve of Gretchen's enticing hip. No other woman would be this captivating to Jax, either as an artist or as a lover.

Jax zipped up the portfolio and jumped away from it when the doorbell rang. She left the spare room and hurried back to her own. She didn't know why the idea of being caught in the old studio shook her so, but she wanted to keep that short foray to herself.

"Guess who's here?" Gretchen's voice boomed through the home. "Come in."

Jax heard Amanda entering the house and greeting Caleb. She knew this was her chance to leave the house quickly and with very little interaction. She didn't trust herself around Gretchen that morning. Something had slipped that should've stayed in place, and they had only been under the same roof for one night.

Jax threw on the first work outfit she could find that looked halfway presentable and grabbed her bag. She threw her jacket on and left her bedroom. As soon as she got to the top of the stairs, she stopped walking. She didn't want to eavesdrop, but Gretchen's tone caught her ear.

Gretchen was talking to Amanda. "Yeah, well, maybe this really is the old Gretchen."

"What do you mean?" Amanda's volume and inflection told Jax exactly what face she was making, and Jax almost laughed.

"I can't explain it without sounding crazy, but I swear I saw things when I was in that coma, or after, or maybe I was really awake."

Jax stepped down to get closer, not wanting to miss a word. She waited, barely breathing.

Gretchen finally continued, "It's like, I saw what I had become, what my life had become, and it was miserable. I don't want to be that person. Not for myself or for my kid."

Jax wanted to be surprised that she wasn't included on that list, but she had no reason to be. Gretchen wanted to be a better person for the right reasons, and she should be happy about that. She continued down the stairs and started straight for Caleb's room, knowing he wouldn't be ready for school yet. She bumped into Caleb along the way. He was perfectly dressed and smiling at her.

"You're ready," she said in shock.

Caleb nodded.

"Here's his lunch and a little something for you, too. I'm not sure what you eat lately while you're working, but I figured a snack couldn't hurt." Gretchen handed Jax a bulky Spider-Man lunchbox and a brown paper bag.

Jax didn't know what to say. "I'll be home later. Text me if you need anything."

"I'll be fine."

"Thanks." Jax held up the bag and walked to the door. She was so blindsided by Gretchen's behavior that she almost forgot Caleb.

Chapter Thirty

24 days, 16 hours, 33 minutes

Jax sat back at her desk and felt good about the progress she had made for the day. No longer having the stress of Gretchen being in the hospital made a huge difference. She could focus completely on the task at hand and give work her full attention. She even opted to order pizza delivery to the office to ensure she stayed on task, and her coworkers were grateful she ordered plenty to share. Jax didn't take a real break until a little after two in the afternoon when she sat back and pulled her phone from her pocket. She had ignored several messages throughout the day, only making sure there weren't any from Amanda or Gretchen.

Wyatt invited her over for dinner, and the idea made Jax smile. Wyatt was a phenomenal cook, and she hadn't spent much time with Carly recently. She knew accepting the invitation was a good idea, without a doubt. Especially if the weirdness with Gretchen just that morning was any indication. Jax needed a little extra time to clear her head.

Meredith sent a selfie, puckering her full, moist lips. She was tantalizing, but Jax wasn't in the mood to talk about the first night back in her old house, and she definitely didn't feel like dancing around the awkwardness that'd surely follow. Meredith had to remain as separate from Gretchen as possible, or Jax's life would become a huge mess. Well, messier than it already was.

Seth propped himself against Jax's desk. "Did you order these from Rosie's?"

Jax didn't mind Seth. He was one of the few guys in the office who didn't treat the job like a competition. She watched him shove half a slice into his mouth before she answered him. "I did."

He chewed remarkably fast and swallowed. "I always forget they're there. Which means I always forget how great their pizza is." Seth was a tall string bean of a man who always seemed to be eating.

"You think all pizza is great." She felt her point was somehow proven by the crumbs in his copper mustache.

He bobbed his head from side to side as he chewed another large bite. "Oh, cool," he said, pointing his greasy crust at Jax's monitor, "are you working on the summer fest flyers?"

Jax turned back to her screen. "Yeah. I've been working on it for a few hours now. I'll probably have the first set of proofs ready to go within a day or two." She looked over the fonts and graphics. Summertime was months away, but plans were already in full swing.

"It's looking good already." He tore the crust in half, small crumbs raining down on the floor.

Jax followed the trail and tried her best not to let the mess annoy her. "Thanks. What are you working on?"

"The new golf place in Oakhurst."

"I'm doing the new golf place in Oakhurst."

Seth paused with the last bit of crust between his lips. "Did Randy not cc you on the email?" He widened his eyes when Jax shook her head. "He's such a dick sometimes."

"Sometimes?" She stood and started for Randy's office.

"Wait." Seth reached out and grabbed her arm. Jax looked at his hand on her. They were friendly, but not that friendly. He let go immediately and put his hands up. "I'm sorry."

"It's okay."

"You're very muscular."

"Why did you stop me, Seth?"

He pursed his lips, fanning his mustache out slightly. "It's not worth it. And I'm not saying that as the coworker that got your account. I'm saying it as the coworker that has heard quite a bit about what you've been going through."

She racked her brain for a time when she'd confided in anyone at work.

"Word travels," Seth said before she could even question him. "Randy has been fair to you, but in the most unfair way, if that makes any sense. He's giving you the time you need, but also punishing you."

She never suspected that anyone in the office ever noticed the way she was treated. "He's always been this way with me."

"He has, and I have no idea why. Maybe it's because you look the way you do or maybe it's because you don't kiss his ass."

"I hate that guy."

"We all do." Seth laughed. "But if you want my theory, I think it's because you're very good at your job, and Randy hates that."

One thing that killed Jax's artistic spirit was office politics. "That makes zero sense."

"You shouldn't be making flyers or menus. We all know it. We knew after your first week here. I think Randy treats you the way he does to keep you in check."

"Do I look like someone who needs to be kept in check?"

"To Randy, yeah. He obviously knows your dick is bigger." Seth started shaking his head immediately. "I should not have said that. I'm sorry again."

"It's okay. Again. Why don't you go have some more pizza?"

"I think I will."

"I think you should."

"Thanks again. For the pizza."

She hummed and watched Seth slink awkwardly away. She replayed the short conversation over and over again in her head as she got back to work. Knowing other people saw the way she was treated somehow made her feel better, like she wasn't overly sensitive or imagining things.

She finished up her workday with no more interruptions. Randy only walked around and made his presence known once, and he chose someone else to hover over that time. Jax packed up her stuff, ran out the door at five, and headed straight to the liquor store. She grabbed a six-pack of dark lager for herself and Wyatt, and a bottle of sweet wine for Carly to enjoy when she was no longer pregnant. Jax knew not every pregnant woman was the same, but Gretchen couldn't wait to have a glass of chardonnay after Caleb was born. Jax was in front of Wyatt's simple bungalow before six o'clock.

"Hey, bud," Jax said the moment Wyatt swung the door open.

He threw his arms around her and pulled her into a tight bear hug. "I'm so glad you could make it. She's driving me crazy."

"She's your pregnant wife," Jax said firmly. "Imagine how she feels."

"Get your ass in here." Wyatt held the door open for Jax.

Jax made a beeline for Carly, who was propped up on the sofa and bigger than Jax could've ever thought possible. Her eyes were on Carly's belly as she approached. "You look—"

"Don't even say it, and you're gonna have to come down to me."

Jax couldn't contain her smile as she bent to kiss Carly's rosy cheek. "You look wonderful," Jax said quietly and cautiously. "I bet you're ready for this to be over, though." Jax took a seat next to Carly and lifted Carly's bare feet onto her lap. Without a second thought, she started to give Carly a foot massage.

"Holy shit." Carly threw her head back and moaned. "Your hands are better than Wyatt's."

Jax shot Wyatt a wink. "They're not better—I've just had more practice with pregnant women's feet."

"And you couldn't bestow me with this special technique a few months ago?" Wyatt threw his hands up and walked to the kitchen.

"How's Gretchen?"

"She's okay."

"You knew I was going to ask about her. Get the arches, please."

Jax dug the pads of her thumbs into Carly's feet. She watched in amusement as the very pregnant woman squirmed. "She's getting better, stronger each day. I think."

"You think?"

"She's been mostly quiet."

"Why haven't you been asking?"

She didn't have an answer. "I don't really know. I guess I got so used to everyone checking on her in the hospital and just trying to stay out of the way. And when I would ask, she didn't always answer."

"Make sure you keep asking—check in with her constantly. Just in case she's trying to hide anything. You know how Gretchen can be sometimes." Carly switched feet. "How was being back in the house?"

"Wyatt really caught you up, didn't he?"

"My husband loves to talk."

"And cook," Wyatt said from the kitchen.

She inhaled deeply. "Are you making fajitas?"

"With homemade guacamole."

"Are you looking for a third party in your marriage?" She kept her face serious as she propositioned Carly. "I cook, too, and I fold laundry like I came from the military."

"With hands like these? You can have the bed, too. Wyatt can sleep on the couch."

Jax could hear Wyatt laughing. Carly nudged her to answer. "Oh, um, it was fine. Weird, definitely, but fine."

"Where did you sleep?"

"The guest bedroom."

"All night?"

Jax didn't hide her surprise. "Yes. All night."

"Really? You didn't try to sneak between her sheets?"

"What?"

"Carly," Wyatt called out. "Go easy on her."

"Yeah. Go easy on me or I stop." Jax paused the massage to prove her point.

"Fine. Just wishful thinking on my part. I love you guys together, and I guess I was hoping you'd give it another shot."

"I know, but it's not going to happen. I've made my peace with it, and I think Gretchen has, too."

Carly's eyes were closed as she soaked up Jax's touch. She looked so peaceful, like she had fallen asleep, but then she opened her mouth unexpectedly. "Gretchen will always be in love with you."

Wyatt poked his upper body out of the kitchen, proud smile on his face and apron hugging his slight belly tightly. "Dinner's ready."

Jax arrived home nearly two hours later with a full stomach and rattled mind. She'd never asked Carly what she meant, and quite frankly she was too scared to want to know. She knew Gretchen would always love her, just as she would always love Gretchen, but Jax had long since resigned herself to believing Gretchen had fallen out of love with her. What exactly did Carly know that she didn't? This was not a seed Jax needed planted. She stood at the front door and shook away any and all thoughts of Gretchen's possible but completely impossible feelings for her.

She smiled the moment she opened the door. She could see Amanda curled up with Caleb, watching *Finding Dory*. Again. She scanned the rest of the great room.

"She's been in her room for a while," Amanda said in a hushed tone. "You should probably check on her."

She wanted to tell Amanda to check on Gretchen herself, but she noticed how peaceful Caleb was. Nothing was worth more than that.

The closer she got to Gretchen's room, the more commotion she started to hear. When Jax poked her head into the bedroom, she immediately wanted to retreat.

"I'm fine," Gretchen said without ever turning to Jax. "I just still can't believe this is what I've been choosing to wear."

She had to laugh at that. She could still remember the start of Gretchen's evolution from carefree boho stunner to professional woman who wore her maturity on her very monochromatic and buttoned-up sleeve. "You did turn to a more office chic look over the years."

"I'm sorry."

Jax shook her head, dumbfounded, and stepped into the room. She shut the door behind her. "For what?"

"For changing so much. For becoming this." Gretchen held up the sleeve of a tan blazer.

"You didn't—" Jax couldn't bring herself to lie. "You're not the only one who changed." Jax could only see Gretchen's back, but she could feel her sadness. You didn't love someone for over fifteen years and not learn every nuance of their behavior, or how their heart reacted to shock and pain.

Gretchen tossed the blazer aside. "Except you didn't drive *me* to fall for someone else." Jax wanted to explain that everything was so much more complicated than that, but Gretchen kept talking. "What was it about Meredith? I know you well enough to know it wasn't about age or looks."

Jax got angry in an instant, but she wasn't entirely sure anger was really what she felt anymore. She was sad and broken, and even a little embarrassed. "Age and looks had nothing to do with anything, ever," Jax admitted quietly.

"Yeah. You're not like me with left-handed women."

Jax laughed, surprising herself. Gretchen hadn't joked about her odd fetish in years. "They'll turn your head every time, even though you're married to one." Jax nearly choked on the words, wanting to correct herself for speaking so presently of their marriage.

"So what was it?" Gretchen said, turning to Jax. Her eyes were full of tears and her tone held no malice.

"We talked a lot when you weren't around. She asked about my day and really cared and listened. She's very kind and…" Jax looked at the hardwood floor. The distance between her and Gretchen felt like a mile. Shame kept her from continuing to talk.

"Everything I wasn't."

Her eyes met Gretchen's, and for the first time in over a year, Jax didn't see the woman she blamed for every bad day. She saw the woman she married, and the woman she knew she'd love until her dying day.

"We're okay, Gretchen, you and me. We'll be okay."

"But not together."

She saw every ounce of pain shimmering in Gretchen's amber eyes, and she saw what Carly claimed existed. This moment of vulnerability and sadness was what Jax needed to save her marriage, but she needed it a long time ago. Jax conjured up the strength to say the one thing her brain forced her to believe. "It's too late. I'm sorry."

Gretchen forced a watery smile. "You should probably go because I need to clean this up, and I'm going to cry a lot while I do it."

She stepped forward, fully intent on wrapping her arms around Gretchen and holding her until she felt strong enough to stop crying. But Jax stopped and thought, and she knew her touch was likely unwelcome. She left the room without another word but paused just after she closed the door behind her. Did her heart believe it really was too late?

CHAPTER THIRTY-ONE

25 days, 18 hours, 9 minutes

Jax knew with complete certainty her day couldn't possibly get worse. She was running late because Caleb threw a temper tantrum, she spilled her coffee during her dash to her truck, traffic was backed up due to heavy rain, and she had forgotten her umbrella. Jax spent her morning in cold, wet clothes, and the conference room she needed for her eleven o'clock meeting was double-booked. Jax wanted to scream at everyone around her. So when Randy called her into his office just after she had finished her lunch, Jax knew there was no way for this to go well.

"Jax, thanks for stopping in. Have a seat."

She bit her tongue to keep from expressing to Randy how little she wanted to be there. She breathed in deeply as she sat, stealing one of Gretchen's calming techniques to aid in her own survival. "What's up?"

"I like what you did with the festival flyers. Good job."

"Thank you."

"But I need you to redo them."

"Redo them?"

Randy scratched at his chin where no more than fifteen hairs sprouted, but he still called it a beard. "It's a family festival, and this just isn't giving me a family vibe." He turned his computer screen around to point at her proof image.

"The first three attractions I listed are bounce houses, face painting, and the petting zoo." Her phone buzzed in her pocket.

"The font you chose is very mature."

"Helvetica bold is one of the easiest fonts to read and the one we use for all of our flyers."

"It could look younger."

Jax's phone buzzed again, and she itched to check it. "Okay…"

"You have a kid, don't you? How old is she now?"

She gritted her teeth. "My son, Caleb, is almost four and a half."

"Right," Randy said, snapping his fingers. "Caleb. Would he be interested in this?"

"Since he cannot read, I can assure you he'd be very excited as soon as I mentioned animals."

He closed out of the proof and turned his computer back. "Kids need to be drawn to it. Change it and please have it to me by the end of today."

She took another calming breath as she walked to the door, but this time she decided Gretchen's techniques were bullshit. She turned back to Randy and said, "Do you have a problem with me?"

Randy didn't bother looking away from his computer when he answered her. "Excuse me?"

"This flyer and the Oakhurst golf club." Her frustrations peaked when Randy looked at her with complete disinterest. "Are you trying to make me quit?"

He arched his eyebrow. "Do you want to quit?"

The urge to say yes was strong, but she thought of Caleb and Gretchen, her family, and how that wasn't quite true anymore. But her apartment did have a rent bill to be paid. "No."

"Okay then." End of conversation.

Jax resisted slamming Randy's office door behind her. Several coworkers turned their heads as she walked by, but no one said a word. She pulled out her phone as she got back to her desk and sat. Gretchen had messaged her twice, and Jax only felt mildly worried.

Caleb and I are with Amanda, shopping. Don't get mad about it.

Her defenses went up immediately. Who the fuck was Gretchen to tell her not to get mad? Jax threw her phone on her desk without answering the text.

She started working on the flyer right away. She broke it down piece by piece, deleting the aspects she felt most proud of first and inserting complete nonsense that would only appeal to Caleb's preschool class.

She inserted balloons and clowns—she didn't even know if there would be clowns at the festival. Jax worked and worked past the time other people had started to pack up for the end of the day. She finished off the flyer with a knockoff version of Thomas the Tank Engine and sent the proof off to Randy. He wanted childish and she'd delivered.

She loaded her messenger bag and pulled on her jacket. She hated how early the sun set during the winter. It seemed like she spent every minute of daylight at work. Once upon a time she would spend her lunch hour with Gretchen, taking strolls and getting fresh air no matter the time of year. Sometimes they'd play hooky and try a new restaurant in the city. Now, she woke up at the last minute, went to work, and went straight home. Day in and day out.

Jax started a message to Amanda on her way to the door. She and Gretchen had been very quiet all day, and although that seemed like a blessing, she kinda missed getting the usual updates and being part of their day.

"Levine, before you go."

She stopped at the door and considered acting like she didn't hear Randy at all, but professionalism, the thorn in her side, forced her to remain in the building. She turned to him slowly. "Yeah?"

His face turned into a goofy grin. "The flyer is great," he said, giving her a thumbs-up.

Jax really needed to find a new company to work for.

She nodded and left. She dodged freezing puddles as she walked to her truck. Each patch of fresh ice made her think of Gretchen. Jax held the door handle and swallowed back a swell of nausea. She'd never forget being told how Gretchen had been bleeding on the frozen ground for an undetermined amount of time.

What if they had still been together? What if Jax had been home and noticed Gretchen's absence? What if she had been enough for Gretchen to fight for? Jax pulled open the door and sat in her truck. She shivered and thought about her foster father. Michael always taught her that thinking about what-ifs never led to anything good. She needed to focus on what was. Gretchen was hurt badly but survived. Caleb still had his mother, and Jax's relationship with Gretchen seemed like it was on its way to improving. The facts of her situation weren't all bad—she just had to figure out the most tactful way to navigate the choppy waters.

The drive home was slow thanks to black ice and pedestrians who seemed to enjoy the deep freeze. She stopped along the way to pick up pizza, not having the energy or desire to talk about what to eat. When she was three blocks from home, she could feel the tension start to release from her shoulders. She stopped at a red light and took the opportunity to roll her neck. The popping sounded loud in the quiet cabin.

She took her foot off the brake as the light turned green. The truck crawled forward, and just as she started to give it gas, a minivan went through the red light. Jax slammed on the brake, and the pizza slid off the seat. She picked the pizza box up and looked again before going through the intersection. She needed to get home.

She drove carefully the rest of the way, more shaken than she should've been for such a small incident. But her nerves were frayed, and the horrible day had completely worn her down. When Jax pulled into her driveway, she breathed a sigh of relief. She threw the truck door open and jumped down on the beaten rocks of the driveway with a heavy thud. Jax slammed the door as hard as she could, releasing just a hint of the pressure building within. She grabbed the pizza and her bag from the passenger seat and headed inside.

Jax tried her best to be calmer when she entered the house, not wanting to startle anyone who might be home, but the house was silent. One lamp illuminated the space.

"Gretchen?" she said, her deep voice echoing faintly. She went to the kitchen and flipped on the lights with her elbow. She placed the food and her bag on the table so she could get her phone out. No messages. Zero consideration. Gretchen should have told her what time she planned on being home. Jax had flashbacks to many dinners gone cold, unexplained absences, and the sinking feeling that Gretchen would rather be anywhere but with her.

She paced until the balls of her feet started to ache. She sat on the couch and placed her head in her hands. She still wore her jacket and work clothes, not caring at all about her comfort.

The front door creaked open forty-five minutes later, and Caleb came charging into the house. Jax was on her feet the moment she heard Gretchen's voice.

"Where the hell were you?"

Gretchen froze just inside the doorway, her hand still on the doorknob. Her hair was half pulled back, a style she hadn't worn in a long time. "We went shopping with Amanda."

"All day?"

"Yeah." Gretchen held up the shopping bags in her hands. Caleb was already digging through one of the two bags he was carrying. "I told you this."

"It would've been nice if you had told me how long you'd be out for. Now your dinner is cold."

"We already ate."

"We had Burger King," Caleb said with his face in the bag.

Jax flared her nostrils and clenched her fists at her sides. "Wish you had told me that, too."

"Why do you still have your jacket on?"

Caleb held up a pair of Iron Man socks and waved them about. "I got this."

"That's great, Cricket." Jax forced a smile and put her hands on Caleb's shoulders. "Why don't you go and put those with the rest of your socks?" She waited for him to leave the room before looking at Gretchen again. "You need to be more considerate. You can't just go out all day and not tell me your plans."

Gretchen closed her eyes and tilted her head back. When she faced Jax again, she looked tired. "I told you where we were."

"In the vaguest way possible."

"I would've told you anything you wanted if you had answered me."

"I was at work."

"This is unbelievable," Gretchen said with a huff. "I can't believe we're having this fight again."

Jax flinched with confusion. She kept hearing Gretchen speak like that, but it still didn't make sense. "What do you mean *again*?"

Gretchen stared and pursed her lips. "Nothing. It just feels like we're destined to fight, no matter what."

"Then stop doing things that'll make me mad."

"It wouldn't matter, so you should just go. And I really mean it this time."

Jax racked her brain for a moment that would clue her in to this past Gretchen kept hinting at. But she had nothing. "What?"

"You won't believe me, but I know how this plays out. We fight, I tell you to go, you stay, we fight some more and then—" Gretchen pressed her lips together abruptly.

"Then what?"

"Something *really* bad happens."

She saw something deep in Gretchen's dark eyes, and her stomach twisted with dread. It felt like déjà vu, but also bigger and scarier. "To you?"

Gretchen smiled sadly. "I think I get it now. We were never supposed to have a second chance, and trying to make it work last time caused all this." Gretchen was visibly shaking now.

Jax started to panic. "What are you talking about?"

"Move out. Amanda will stay with me, and then maybe everything will be okay. I mean it. Go be happy with Meredith. Remember all the reasons why you hate me."

"You hate Mama?"

Both Jax and Gretchen turned to Caleb, who stood at the edge of the room. Jax rushed to him. "Of course not, Cricket. I could never hate her." Out of the corner of her eye, she noticed Gretchen sneaking out of the room. "I love your mother very much," Jax said, feeling betrayed by the honesty of her words.

Caleb pouted. "Why'd she say you hate her?"

Jax smoothed her palm over his bouncy tight curls and held his small face in her hands. "Her head isn't quite right, so it's our job to keep reminding her how loved she is. Think we can do that?" Caleb's nod lacked confidence, but she pulled him into her arms. "Good."

She stared at the wall while holding Caleb. She had no idea whether Gretchen's condition was getting better or worse, but something was very, very wrong.

CHAPTER THIRTY-TWO

31 days, 16 hours, 24 minutes

Almost a week had passed since Gretchen told her to go, and they had been nothing more than cold, cordial, and parents when together. But even at Gretchen's urging, Jax wouldn't leave. She stayed with Gretchen but kept her distance. As awkward as it had been, she knew it was the right thing to do.

She waited for Gretchen to get herself together for her checkup, and her every pleasantry was met with silence. Jax sat in the waiting room of the imaging center and zoned out to immortal game shows on the television. When Gretchen stepped out of the restricted area, she barely cast Jax a glance. They even remained quiet as they drove to the doctor's office together on Valentine's Day.

"How did it go?" she said. She was ready to crawl out of her skin from discomfort.

Gretchen continued to look out the window. "You should quit your job."

She did a double take. "What?"

Gretchen turned to Jax with an odd look in her eyes.

Jax's phone started to ring through the speakers. She answered and immediately regretted it when Randy's voice filled the cabin. "Hey, Randy. What's up?"

"The brochures you made for the youth center need to be revamped."

"Why?"

"Because it's not exactly what they were looking for."

She watched Gretchen out of the corner of her eye. "I carefully followed the very extensive list of specs they sent."

"I guess it wasn't good enough. I sent the revisions to your email, and I hope you can have it done by the end of the workday tomorrow."

She gripped the steering wheel so tightly she felt the skin of her palms burn. "Fine."

"Great. I'll see you tomorrow."

Jax disconnected the call and shut off the radio, plunging them into complete silence. She drove a few blocks before speaking. "I can't just quit."

"I know, but I hope you're looking. You're miserable."

Jax was struck by Gretchen's sincerity. "I'm working on it," Jax said, keeping her reply simple. The last thing she wanted to admit was how losing Gretchen was the greatest source of her misery, because a rough day at the office wasn't so bad when she came home to the woman she loved. "We're here." Jax pulled into the parking lot.

They rode the elevator up to Dr. Melendez's office in silence. Jax watched Gretchen out of the corner of her eye, worry overwhelming her. She knew their relationship had hit another setback, but in the past week it was like Gretchen had completely shut down again. She only opened up when Caleb or Amanda was around.

Gretchen stepped off the elevator and looked around, clearly lost in the expanse of the building. After glancing at the directory in front of her, Gretchen turned to the left and walked away, leaving Jax behind.

"Wait up." She jogged to make it to the door before Gretchen. Regardless of circumstance, she still wanted to be polite. Or maybe it was more automatic than wanting. Jax waited for Gretchen to sign in and take a seat before sitting beside her. "Are you nervous?" she asked in a whisper.

Gretchen looked at her like she was nuts. "No. I feel good and I know everything *is* good. I have nothing to worry about."

Jax envied that confidence. "Good. That's good." She spun her keys and grimaced at how loudly the metal clanked together in the quiet waiting room. She opened a *Reader's Digest* with zero intention of actually reading it. She scanned an ad for an erectile dysfunction drug, and her thoughts went to the only dick in her life. "What if I did quit my job?" She tried to read Gretchen's soft smile for a possible meaning.

"You would be happier." Gretchen took the magazine from Jax's hands and started flipping through the pages. "If we were still together, I'd tell you to do it today and get a simple job just to bring a little money in, anything that would leave you time to work on your art again."

She shook her head and opened her mouth to speak, but Gretchen wasn't done.

"I know," Gretchen said, her smile faltering. "I wasn't like this before."

"You weren't."

"I reminded you of how expensive a child and a home can be. I forced you to stay in a job that made you unhappy."

She lost her breath. "You remember?"

Gretchen closed the magazine and dropped it on the table beside her. "No. But like I've said, you told me."

"I never…"

"Gretchen Mills?"

Jax and Gretchen both looked at the open door. A young woman stood with a folder in her hands and a smile on her face. They followed her to the very back corner of the office, into what was obviously Dr. Melendez's space. Jax took a seat immediately while Gretchen browsed the many certificates and pictures on the walls. Jax couldn't imagine the manpower it must have taken to get the large wooden desk into the office.

"She really likes New York," Gretchen said casually.

Dr. Melendez walked in and went straight for her big leather chair. She extended her hand to Jax first. "Good afternoon, Jax." She shook her hand and then motioned for Gretchen to take a seat. "It's nice to see you two again, outside of the hospital for once. How are you feeling?"

"It's been exhausting," Jax said, running her hand over her face. "But we've gotten into a routine." She felt Gretchen's eyes on her and noticed Dr. Melendez's odd stare. Her stomach clenched. "You weren't asking me."

Dr. Melendez's smile was tight. "No, I wasn't, but I am happy to hear you've worked out a routine."

Gretchen laughed outright, removing some of the tension from Jax's shoulders. "I feel fine. My ribs don't ache, my shoulder only hurts when I either move it too much or too little, and my face is all healed." Gretchen pulled her hair from her face and Jax was struck by her stunning silhouette.

"That's very good." Dr. Melendez made a few notes in Gretchen's file. "Exercise?"

"Running every day, but only a little. I still get winded pretty quickly."

"Don't push yourself."

"I'm not." Gretchen fiddled with her hands. "No headaches other than the usual mom headaches. I'm taking my medication as directed."

"Uh, okay. Good." Dr. Melendez jotted something down. "Your scans came back, and while there are some shadows where your injury was, I don't see any reason for concern. You're healing well and your speech has fully returned."

Unexpectedly, Jax had the desire to hold Gretchen's hand.

"What do you think, Dr. Melendez? One more week before I can get back to work?"

She wished she hadn't heard Gretchen correctly. "Of course you care about work," she said.

"I do. I have bills to pay, and disability is a joke." Gretchen pinched the bridge of her nose, as if she was annoyed with Jax before the conversation even started.

"One more week, and then I'll clear you for part-time. I'm not changing my mind about the six months for driving, though."

"That's fine."

"How's Caleb with all of this?"

Gretchen chuckled. "Loud, but wonderful."

"I knew he was smart," Jax said, pride filling her chest and voice, "but the way he's been and how much he understands has really floored me."

"Sometimes kids are better than the adults." Dr. Melendez's eyes sparkled knowingly. "I want to see you back in four weeks. You can schedule that appointment on your way out. Other than that, you're healing very well, and I hope you are looking at this as a second chance."

Gretchen tilted her head but didn't say anything.

"We'll see you soon, Doc." Jax stood.

"Tell Amanda I said hi." Dr. Melendez closed the folder and opened the door for Gretchen and Jax.

She waited while Gretchen made her appointment, and they walked back to the elevator side by side. An odd tension surrounded them, one Jax had never felt. "We should just give her Amanda's number and get it over with." Jax waited for a response, but none came. Gretchen's sporadic memories and mood swings were starting to terrify Jax. She needed a minute alone with Dr. Melendez, and now was her chance.

Gretchen stopped in her tracks, almost causing Jax to collide with her. "You forgot your keys," she said with her back to Jax.

Jax's mouth fell open, and the hairs on the back of her neck stood on end. "Yeah, I'll be right back." She started back toward the office, hand pressing into the lump of keys in her pocket. She gave the receptionist her excuse and was ushered back to Dr. Melendez's office.

Dr. Melendez showed surprise at seeing Jax again. "Did you forget something?"

"No, actually." She scrambled for a way to explain what was going on. "I'm worried about Gretchen."

Dr. Melendez seemed to understand immediately. "I won't approve her for work if I don't think she's ready."

"It's not that. It's her memories."

"Is she regaining any?"

"It's more like she's telling me what's going to happen. Remember how she was acting in the hospital? When she wrote down exactly what we said? That hasn't stopped." Jax knew she sounded crazy. "She told me to move out because bad things were going to happen if I didn't. She knew her scans would be fine, and just last week we got into a fight, and she kept saying how fighting was inevitable. No matter what she did to avoid it, it was going to happen."

"Please don't take offense to this, but you two do argue a lot."

Jax scrubbed her face roughly with her hands. "This isn't just a blip, doc. You have to believe me. Something's up."

Dr. Melendez's face fell into a serious scowl. "Since discharging Gretchen, I've been doing some research, looking into similar cases and reading studies done on amnesia victims. There have been a few where the vivid dreams or nightmares a patient experiences during an induced coma can mimic reality by merging with faint, forgotten memories." She leaned back against a bookcase and ran her fingers through her long dark hair. "It's not at all common, but I've read a few reports."

Jax knew her face reflected her feeling of disbelief. "That sounds more like an episode of *The Twilight Zone*. Do these reports seem legit to you?"

Dr. Melendez bobbed her head from side to side. "I can't confirm that, but it is possible that Gretchen had something like that happen to her."

Jax raised her eyebrows as far as they could go. "She predicted the future in her coma?"

"Not exactly. I think of it more as the brain dreaming and filling in the blanks. She knew she was in the hospital and injured, she knew who was with her at the time, and small details like that. While healing, her brain worked overtime and told her a story."

Jax stared at Dr. Melendez, agape. "You don't think this sounds completely bonkers?"

"I wouldn't say bonkers." Dr. Melendez pinched her features together and then smiled. "The brain is a wild card. Think of the tricks it can play on you when you're completely healthy. If there's one thing I've learned during my twenty years practicing it's that I will continue to be surprised until I retire. Maybe I'll even write my own paper."

Jax couldn't understand how she felt more confused and yet very relieved. "So what do I do?"

"Keep being there and keep helping her."

She could hear Gretchen's pleading voice in her head. "She's afraid of what will happen if I stick around."

"Gretchen's going to believe those memories until they're proven wrong, and you can help her with that." Dr. Melendez sat back and opened a chart. "Good luck, Jax."

"Thanks, I think." Jax left the office again, just as unsure as when she entered, but with a bit more understanding. She looked up to see Gretchen leaning against the wall beside the elevator. Jax wanted nothing more than to fix everything wrong, starting with six months ago when she'd walked out.

"Took you long enough. Did you find them?"

She nodded. "Let's go."

Jax didn't say another word until she pulled up in front of the house. "I'll pick Caleb up and drop him off here after school." Gretchen started to climb out of the truck, but something forced Jax to speak again. "Gretchen."

"Yeah?" Gretchen said, turning quickly enough to cause her hair to bounce. The darkness and sparkle in Gretchen's eyes wrapped around Jax's heart and clenched it so tightly her chest ached.

"Happy Valentine's Day."

Gretchen didn't respond. She simply leaned across the front seat and kissed her cheek. The tip of her nose was cold. "Have a good night." Gretchen got out of the truck and never looked back.

Jax watched her go.

CHAPTER THIRTY-THREE

31 days, 22 hours, 19 minutes

Candlelight. Rose petals. Lingerie. Jax couldn't think of anything else to make the perfect Valentine's Day. Meredith stood before her in a lace bodysuit. Her pale nipples were barely visible beneath the violet material, but Jax's hungry blue eyes still saw them. She sat back at the kitchen table, eager to ask about dinner but much more interested in having dessert first. Meredith walked around her chair and started massaging Jax's shoulders.

"Happy Valentine's Day," she said in a near purr.

The tone settled between her legs. She reached behind her and grabbed Meredith's thighs, tilting her head back to look up at Meredith. "Happy, indeed."

"I hope you don't mind. I know we were supposed to go out."

"We were?"

Meredith caressed the sides of her neck and cradled her jaw. She bent just enough to place an upside down kiss on her parted lips. "You've been so busy and distracted, I figured this would be more your speed."

She wove her fingers into Meredith's hair, tangling the thick strands tightly around her fingers before going in for another kiss. She deepened it, even at the awkward angle. Jax was hungry for the connection, the warmth, the arousal. Jax was starved for normalcy. She inhaled deeply and basked in the scent of Meredith. She smelled of wildflowers and saltwater.

"Do you want to eat?" Meredith spoke against her wet lips.

Jax smirked. She grabbed Meredith's hand and led her around to stand between her parted legs. She took her time scanning Meredith's body. She sat forward and kissed just above Meredith's navel, and then between her breasts. She felt Meredith's toned calves up to the backs of her thighs, and palmed her ass roughly.

Meredith was watching her intently when their eyes finally met. "I'll take that as a yes."

"I think we should eat." She toyed with the rough edges of Meredith's enticing clothes. "I wouldn't mind looking at you in this for a little longer."

"I'm happy to hear that," Meredith said, running her fingertip along Jax's jawline, then dipping her index finger between Jax's lips.

She ran her tongue along Meredith's finger, then sucked eagerly the moment Meredith responded. She released the finger with a pop and enjoyed Meredith's dazed expression. "You look like you need to sit down."

"Not yet." She gripped Jax's shoulders firmly before pushing back. "I have something for you." Meredith walked across the room.

She gawked at Meredith's body and her perfectly formed ass. "You're gorgeous."

Meredith turned, flipping her long hair over her shoulder. "Try saying that to my face next time."

"You know I will."

Jax watched, enamored, as Meredith turned on a small speaker and looked through her phone. Her heart was beating hard with anticipation for what was to come. The opening bass line of the song caused her throat to tighten and stomach to drop. Toni Braxton's "You're Makin' Me High" brought back a hundred memories, all good and all involving Gretchen.

"This song…"

Meredith smirked. "I snooped through your music. This is one of your most played."

She kept her eyes on Meredith's hips as they swayed in time. Her mind, however, went places they shouldn't have. Like Gretchen driving her beat-up Chevy, windows down in the heart of summer with the same song blasting on the radio. She could still recall watching the mirrors shake with the vibrations.

Meredith pressed her ass into Jax's lap and moved in tight circles. Jax closed her eyes.

Gretchen was walking toward her in the living room of their first apartment. The carpet was tattered, and they had no food in their refrigerator, but the place was theirs, and Gretchen wanted to celebrate.

Meredith took her hands and placed them on her breasts. Arousal lit Jax's body on fire, but her heart and mind were betraying her. She stood and grabbed Meredith by the waist. She spun them and pushed Meredith up against the edge of the small dining table. Jax needed to concentrate and be in the present with Meredith. Not in her past. She kissed Meredith roughly, pouring every ounce of desperation and need she felt into it. She flinched as Meredith ran her icy fingertips along the heated skin beneath the hem of her T-shirt. Her belly quivered. She pulled Meredith's legs around her waist and smiled at how tightly they held her. Meredith wove her fingers through Jax's hair, but all Jax could think of was needing a haircut. Gretchen always made sure she never missed an appointment.

Jax pulled back from the embrace and looked into Meredith's concerned eyes. "I…" She licked her lips. Why her mind couldn't cooperate was beyond her. She had this gorgeous, caring, interesting woman in front of her, and she couldn't focus. Or maybe she was focusing on what her heart cared about most.

"Fine," Meredith said, amusement shining through her small smile. "You can have your gift first."

"Gift?" She watched Meredith walk to the other room and felt more panic than anything. "I didn't get you anything."

Meredith returned wearing a silk robe. "You don't have to get me anything, silly." She handed Jax a small, rectangular box.

The plain white packaging was wrapped simply with a red ribbon. "You really shouldn't have."

"It's nothing much. I just noticed how you've been struggling lately and wanted to help." Meredith had wrapped her arms around herself.

She pulled the ribbon loose, nerves causing her to go slow. She opened the box and a flash of confusion came and went. Inside were three pencils and two pens.

"I asked the guy at the art supply store which were the best, and he pointed these out. I hope he wasn't lying." Meredith laughed nervously.

Jax turned over the pencils, feeling the quality of the wood.

"He wasn't," she said quietly.

"You used to spend so much time in your studio, and now all of your supplies are still packed up. I figured maybe you needed a little bit of a fresh start." Meredith's sentiment chipped away at her heart.

Realization hit her like a ton of bricks. She closed her eyes when they started to burn with tears. "That's really sweet. Thank you."

"Hey." Meredith wrapped her arms around Jax's neck and drew

her into a sweet kiss. She felt it in her gut when Meredith pulled back and looked into her eyes. She knew what was coming and was too slow to stop it.

"I love you, Jax."

Jax opened her mouth, wanting nothing more than to speak the words but knowing deep in her heart they weren't true. They would never be true. "I'm sorry."

Meredith cradled Jax's cheek. "Please stop apologizing. You don't have to say it back. I just needed you to know how I feel. When you're ready to say it, I'll be here."

She shook her head and wished she could lie, but Meredith deserved so much more than a lie and a brush-off. Meredith deserved so much more than Jax could ever be for her. "I can't—I won't." She cleared her throat and grabbed both of Meredith's hands. She held them to her chest. "I'm sorry because I've been very selfish and unfair to you."

"You've been dealing with something unimaginable. But soon enough we'll be back to normal, and we can focus on us."

She took a deep breath through her nose and looked away from Meredith's innocent, hopeful face. Why did Meredith have to say the exact words she wanted to hear from Gretchen? Words she still wanted to hear in spite of everything.

"I wish I could go back," Jax said. "I'd fight more, and maybe I could avoid hurting you." Jax didn't fight when Meredith pulled away. She looked Meredith in the eye, knowing she owed her at least that respect. "I'm sorry because I think I've always known I'll never love someone the way I love my wife."

Meredith pulled the robe tightly around her, covering as much exposed skin as she could. "Your ex-wife."

"I really am so—"

"Save it. I don't need your apologies," Meredith said as she paced. "Just tell me how. Gretchen did nothing to save your marriage, and you hated her up until last week."

She had no way of explaining herself. "Gretchen's my family, her and Caleb are my world."

"I remember envying her so much. She had this sexy, gorgeous, sensitive artist following her around like a puppy dog, and the love and admiration you have for her made me weak. But she broke you down and stole your spark."

"We both made mistakes. I expected so much from her without

ever really telling her what I needed. I eventually shut down and shut her out. I was just as hurtful, but in a less obvious way."

"Do you really think this changed her?"

She shrugged. "I don't know about changing, but I do think it's given us a second chance."

Meredith smiled sadly as tears ran down her cheek. "I gotta admit, I did not see this coming."

"Neither did I," she said honestly.

"I'll stick around long enough for you to find a new nanny."

She hadn't considered Meredith's job yet. "You don't have to quit."

"We both know I do." Meredith tilted her head. "I want you to be happy, and it really fucking hurts to know I'm not the one who can do that. Even so, I'll cheer for a happy family every time."

Jax held her hand over her chest. "I do love you, Meredith, and I consider you part of our family."

"I get it, I do. You and Gretchen are meant to be."

Meant to be. The concept had become so foreign to Jax over the past two years. "Seventeen years of heartbreak and happiness," she said, shaking her head at the enormity of it all. "I think we are."

Several minutes of awkward silence passed. Jax had no idea what else she could say, and Meredith looked like she was on the brink of speaking, but she never let the words loose. "I'm going to get dressed and go," she finally said.

Their good-bye was sweet. Jax held on to Meredith and breathed her in, taking the last opportunity to soak up the peaceful presence Meredith had been for her during the rockiest months of her life. Meredith held her just as tightly.

"Good-bye, Meredith." She framed Meredith's face with her hands and kissed her. When she pulled back, she knew her eyes were as wet as Meredith's.

Meredith walked out of Jax's apartment without another word.

Jax went to her bedroom, leaving dinner on the counter. She got undressed slowly, feeling emotionally and physically drained, and she crawled under the covers with a sigh. The silence and darkness of the room felt haunted with a million unexamined thoughts. She grabbed her phone from the nightstand and felt disappointed when no one had messaged her. More specifically, Gretchen. But why would she? Jax opened her messages and started typing before she lost her nerve.

I think we should talk. Not now, I know it's late, but maybe we can have dinner tomorrow? I should be out of work on time and Caleb can spend the night with Amanda.

She sent the message and placed her phone down on her chest. She knew she was crazy for even thinking this chance would be any different than the many times before, but Jax couldn't remember one moment of their relationship where she felt completely sane. She had always been crazy for and about Gretchen, and she truly believed the part of Gretchen that had felt the same way was still alive. Her phone buzzed.

There's nothing to talk about.

Jax pushed aside the sting of rejection and typed quickly.

Have dinner with me. Please.

Jax barely breathed as she waited for Gretchen's response.

Okay.

She stared at the ceiling, fully accepting sleep would not come easily that night.

CHAPTER THIRTY-FOUR

32 days, 22 hours, 13 minutes

The bag of takeout was too full for just two people. Jax was startled by Gretchen's look of surprise when she walked through the door just before six o'clock. She held up the bag and smiled. "I brought dinner."

"You're here." Gretchen looked completely stunned but gorgeous in a multicolored skirt and marigold sweater. Her dark skin glowed.

"We're having dinner." Panic hit her. "Do you not remember?"

"I remember, I just didn't expect you to show up." Gretchen took the bag from Jax and walked to the kitchen.

Caleb came running out and launched himself into Jax's arms before she could even get her jacket off. "Bug!"

"Hey, Cricket." She ruffled his hair and kissed his temple. He pulled away and giggled. "I thought you'd be out with your aunt." She looked at Gretchen, curious for answers.

"Aunt Man," Caleb said seriously.

"Ant-Man?" Jax was now thoroughly confused.

"Amanda's new nickname, and like I said, I didn't expect you to show up." Gretchen opened the bag of food and jumped back like it had bitten her. Her eyes were wide when she looked back at her. She looked completely frightened.

"What is it?" she said, walking over to check the bag. "Do you hate Thai food now? I didn't know brain damage could do that." She knew it was a tasteless joke, but she felt desperate to shift the odd mood.

Gretchen left the room abruptly.

"Is Mama okay?" Caleb's concern was endearing.

"She's fine. How about you grab your Legos and bring them out to the living room? I'll check on Mama, and then we'll eat and play."

"We're going to eat in the living room?" Caleb was clearly excited by the idea of breaking a rule. He raced out of the kitchen.

She walked to Gretchen's bedroom slowly and pushed the door open. Gretchen was sitting on the foot of the bed, staring at her folded hands. She wanted to sit beside her but played it safe by standing closely. "Are you okay?" she said.

Gretchen nodded, but she broke down into unrelenting sobs a second later. Jax sat and pulled Gretchen into her arms. She let her cry and cry, trying her best to soothe Gretchen by rubbing her back and kissing the top of her head.

"I need you to calm down, please, Gretchen. Calm down."

Gretchen took a deep, shuddering breath and pulled away from Jax. She wiped at the tears on her face angrily. "I have no control. No matter what I do, it's going to happen."

"What's going to happen, baby?" Jax let the endearment slip out.

Gretchen distanced herself from Jax. "You won't believe me, and you'll probably call Dr. Melendez and tell her I'm crazy and broken."

She could hear the panic beneath Gretchen's harsh tone. Jax brushed away the accusation and focused on Gretchen. "I promise you I won't."

Gretchen stared at her for a silent, still moment. "I've been telling you, and you just won't believe me. I've lived this before."

Jax reminded herself of the studies Dr. Melendez found. "Your brain is wacky and probably came up with a believable story while you were in the coma. Yeah, there's been some coincidences, but that doesn't mean everything's going to play out the same."

"It will. I know it will. There's small differences, but almost everything is exactly the same."

She wanted to believe Gretchen and figure out a way to make her feel better, but how was she supposed to handle something like this? "Are you sure you don't want me to call the doctor?"

"I'm sure," Gretchen said, deflated.

She didn't want to let Gretchen down, so Jax played along in the hopes of helping her heal. "What happens next?"

Gretchen looked at her with fear-filled eyes. "Something bad."

"Tell me."

"You spent Valentine's Day with Meredith, and I asked you to have dinner with me the next night."

"But *I* asked *you* to have dinner." She got a stern look from Gretchen, telling her not to interrupt. She shut her mouth.

"I asked you to have dinner, and you said okay, but you never showed. Not until later…" Gretchen seemed hesitant but rebounded quickly. "Which is why I'm so surprised you showed up tonight. I found my letters from you and called Wyatt to talk. That's how I found out about losing the baby."

Jax exhaled sharply. "You know about the baby."

"I still don't know why you kept it from me."

Jax pressed her thumb into her palm as hard as she could. "Because you're not supposed to get upset and…" The tear running down her nose tickled. "If anything good could come of this, you'd at least be free from that pain for a little while. That's all I've ever wanted," she said, looking at Gretchen. "I wanted to take that burden from you. You blamed yourself for everything." She recalled the late nights spent crying on the floor. Maybe the accident was fate's way of giving back to Gretchen.

"Was it my fault?" Gretchen's tone was exactly the same as it was three years ago when the doctor's tried to explain how tragic things just happen.

"No. There wasn't enough blood flow to the placenta. We couldn't predict it, and none of the tests picked it up until it was too late."

"How far along was I?"

"Thirty weeks," she said, swallowing hard. She hadn't spoken about the loss in a long time. "They let us hold her."

"Her…?"

"Aurora."

"That's a beautiful name."

She smiled softly. "I wanted to name her Tracy, but your eyes would light up at the mention of Aurora every time we talked about names. I knew that was her name. I knew that was exactly how you'd look at our daughter every day."

"Did we try again?"

Jax shook her head. "I wanted to, but you weren't ready. And then you threw yourself into your work and I—"

"Hated me for it."

"I didn't hate you," she said quickly. "I wanted us both to heal, and I resented how you found that, anyplace but with me."

"I wish I had an explanation for you. I wish I could remember why or how I left you."

"I left you," she blurted out. She felt Gretchen staring at her, but she couldn't bring herself to look at her. "I thought I could get your attention, make you see just how much I was hurting, but it didn't exactly work out as planned. And then you filed for divorce." She finally looked at Gretchen. "I'm sorry."

"I don't understand any of this."

"I should've tried harder to make you understand back then, and I should've told you how badly I needed you."

"But why did I let you go? Even with everything that had happened, I'd loved you for so long. I wouldn't just throw it away."

She didn't want to hurt Gretchen with the truth, so she brought the topic back around. "You didn't tell me what happens next."

Gretchen stood and walked to the door. She placed her hand on the doorframe and looked back over her shoulder. "We argued, and then we had sex." Jax didn't hide her surprise, not at Gretchen's words or the shot of arousal she felt. "But then you found out I talked to Wyatt. You came home from work so angry. You ended things for good."

She narrowed her eyes, examining Gretchen's expression. "You're not telling me everything."

"I collapsed, everything went black, and then I was forced to relive it all."

Gretchen left the room.

Jax looked straight ahead and caught her reflection in the dresser mirror. She couldn't make sense of it. She'd give anything for an answer or a clear path. She refused to believe Gretchen's premonition—or whatever she wanted to call it—was set in stone. Jax was determined to prove it.

She rejoined Gretchen and Caleb, and they ate dinner together in the living room like they never had. She told stories of the past, ones she knew would bring a smile to Gretchen's face. Caleb laughed along at every story he was in and cared way more about his Legos when Jax told a tale without him. She was shocked by how little effort it took to keep the mood happy. She told Gretchen to stay put while she cleaned up and got Caleb ready for bed. When she walked back into the room, Gretchen was snoring on the couch.

Jax looked over Gretchen's peaceful face, noting the lines around her eyes and the tightness at the corners of her mouth. She grabbed a nearby blanket and covered Gretchen. She leaned forward and kissed her forehead. Gretchen let out a small, contented sigh. Jax hoped that somewhere in her slumber, Gretchen knew she was still there.

She shut off the lights and started up the stairs. On her way to her room, Jax stopped in front of her old art studio. She felt frozen in place, like she had to go in or never move forward again. Jax knew exactly where to find her watercolors and the paper she'd need for a quick painting. All she would need was a cup of water. Before she could question herself, Jax grabbed the supplies and sat at her drafting table. She wet her brush, touched it to the most vibrant pink she had, and put it to the paper. The color spread hypnotically. Jax kept building upon one simple shape. Eyes, a small nose, and full cheeks came to life before her eyes. Her hand moved as if possessed with inspiration, a feeling she had missed almost as much as Gretchen's love.

"Is that her?"

She jumped at Gretchen's voice and turned to find her looking over her shoulder. She never heard Gretchen walk in the room. Jax turned back and looked at the child's face staring back at her.

"That's her." She'd never forget Aurora's face, no matter how small and heartbreaking. Her eyes filled with tears, and for the first time, Jax felt a little less pain. "She was so small, but still kinda chubby." She heard Gretchen sniffle and knew better than to turn around. "What made you come up here?" she said as she started to wash out her brush, studying the way the water turned a darker shade of pink.

"I just wanted to say good night and thank you."

"For what?"

"Tonight, for bringing dinner and for just, I don't know." Jax could hear the shyness in Gretchen's voice. "Tonight felt really good."

She finally turned around. Even in simple sweats, Gretchen was her muse. "It really did." They looked at one another for a moment that dragged on, and Jax soaked up every detail of the silence, sentiment, and small smile on Gretchen's gorgeous face.

"Okay," Gretchen said, looking at the floor before turning to the door. "Good night, Jax."

"Good night, Gretchen." Jax felt her hard edges soften as she watched Gretchen leave.

She looked back at her painting of Aurora, and she felt different somehow, like she understood life a little better now—not the loss or the accident, but the connection. She lost her inspiration the day she lost Gretchen, and she stayed in her job to punish herself. She should've never walked away from Gretchen because when she did, she walked away from the greatest joy in her life, her family.

Jax tucked the painting into a box, careful not to crease it, and closed up the room for the night. When she finally went to bed, fatigue was slow to hit. Jax shifted to her side. Her mind was going a million miles a minute with thoughts of Gretchen and whether she really did come upstairs just to say good night. Was she expecting more? Did she *want* more? All these questions led Jax to wonder how they ended up having sex last time. She laughed into the quiet room. Jax didn't believe there was actually a last time, but Gretchen believed it. Jax knew her job was to prove Gretchen's predictions wrong, but did that mean she have to prove *all* of them wrong?

CHAPTER THIRTY-FIVE

33 days, 7 hours, 11 minutes

Jax jumped when Gretchen opened the bedroom door before she even knocked. "Holy shit," she said, grasping her chest, "you can predict the future."

Gretchen rubbed her eyes. "No, I just heard you out here and thought you were Caleb. What are you doing?" Gretchen looked back into the room. "It's almost four in the morning."

"I couldn't sleep." Her explanation was too simplistic but said it all. "Can I sleep with you?"

Gretchen shot her a sleepy smirk. "Are you sure you're not Caleb?"

"Yes, but I did teach him a lot of his tricks."

They climbed into bed and minutes passed. Jax figured Gretchen was already asleep, but then Gretchen rolled on her side and moved the covers around. She looked at the back of Gretchen's head.

Jax collected her courage and said, "Can I hold you?" She waited and waited in the agonizing silence. Just when she figured Gretchen really was asleep, she heard the quietest *yes*. Eagerly but slowly, she moved closer to Gretchen and wrapped her arm around her waist. The feeling of coming home blossomed in her heart. She smiled. "I want to try again," she said, needing Gretchen to know her desires before the sun rose on a new day. She didn't want to waste another moment. "I want to move back in, and I want us to be a family."

Gretchen covered Jax's hand with hers and laced their fingers together. "I'm scared."

"So am I, which means we'll have to work together to beat our fears."

"You're going to leave again."

"No, I'm not."

"What about Meredith?"

"We broke up last night." Jax burrowed her nose into Gretchen's hair just to inhale her scent. "I realized I could never love anyone the way I love you."

Gretchen turned around. "You still love me?"

"I do," she said with such conviction that she felt the words through and through.

"Say it again."

"I love you."

Gretchen blinked slowly. "You never said it last time."

She couldn't believe that in any version of her life she wouldn't tell Gretchen she loved her. She touched Gretchen's cheek delicately. "Maybe that's why we got this second chance, to get it right." A tear fell down the side of Gretchen's face.

"I want to believe that, I want to believe you so badly, but what happens tomorrow? What if you leave again? What if everything goes black, and I wake up in the same place, and what if I have to do this again and again?"

She could feel Gretchen shake, so she pulled her against her chest and held her tightly. "Shh…" She rubbed circles over the plane of Gretchen's back, the material of her thermal sleep shirt warming beneath her touch. Gretchen's concerns sounded so much like her own. She turned again to the advice she'd never forget and always need. "Don't think about *what if*—focus on what *is* happening right now. I'm not going anywhere. I love you and Caleb, and the only thing happening tomorrow is another day of the same old same old, but now we'll be together for it."

"Do you promise?"

"I do," she said with certainty. "You should get some sleep."

"I don't want to sleep."

"Everything will be fine tomorrow, but you will be really tired if you don't sleep."

"I'm not tired right now, and since I can't stop the inevitable, I might as well enjoy it." Gretchen dipped her hand beneath the hem of Jax's thin T-shirt.

Jax sucked in a breath, her mouth covered by Gretchen's. The kiss brought with it every ounce of happiness she had been missing, a feeling of belonging and completion. She traced the bow of Gretchen's full upper lip with her tongue and breathed in her soft moan. When Gretchen opened up for her, Jax tasted her mouth and lost herself to the way they fit so perfectly together.

Gretchen palmed Jax's bare breast. "I missed you." She scratched her short nails along Jax's defined abdomen. "All of you."

She stopped Gretchen's wandering hand. "Wait. Are you okay? With this? Do you feel okay?" She could see Gretchen's vibrant smile in the darkness.

"I am sure about this, about us. It's what I wanted since I woke up in the hospital the first time." Gretchen moved to place her hand over Jax's heart. "And physically, I'm okay. I just shouldn't put too much weight on my shoulder."

"Easy fix," she said, moving to position Gretchen on her back and hover above her. She settled between Gretchen's legs. "Does this work for you?"

Gretchen canted her hips. "Very much."

Jax removed her shirt quickly, and Gretchen nodded when Jax looked at her for permission to take hers off, too. Jax smirked at the way Gretchen stared at her naked torso. "See something you like?"

"Your tattoo?"

Jax looked down at her bare, blank skin. "I've been thinking about getting one but never pulled the trigger."

"You should," Gretchen said immediately, reaching out to run her finger below her breast. "Right here."

Jax didn't want to talk anymore. She grabbed Gretchen's hand and kissed the inside of her wrist. She looked at the rest of her body and couldn't decide which dark nipple deserved her attention first. She must have hesitated too long, because Gretchen grabbed her head and drew her mouth down to her breast.

Jax lavished attention on her puckered skin until the nipple couldn't get any harder. She drew it between her teeth and bit down hard enough to draw a whimper from Gretchen. Jax kissed her way up to Gretchen's throat and licked along her pulse point. She started a steady roll of her hips, just enough to press into Gretchen's center on and off and drive her completely crazy.

"Do not tease me," Gretchen growled. She reached into Jax's boxers and grabbed her ass roughly.

Jax brought her lips to Gretchen's ear. "I want you to touch me," she whispered, then took Gretchen's earlobe between her teeth. Jax jumped at the first touch of Gretchen's fingers. Gretchen wasted no time before exploring her folds. "This is what teasing you does to me." She reached beneath the covers and slid her hand into the front of Gretchen's shorts, pleased to find she wasn't wearing underwear. Beyond a thick patch of curls, Jax sank into Gretchen's drenched pussy.

"Oh my God," Gretchen said, panting. "You feel so good, fuck."

She pumped her fingers in and out, in time with Gretchen's hips. She moved her own hips in search of Gretchen's touch, which had become unfocused and erratic. She didn't care, though—she'd get her pleasure eventually. All she cared about now was reconnecting with Gretchen. "Are you still okay?"

"Mm...Even better. Just don't stop."

She pulled out of Gretchen and started working her clit, knowing what Gretchen wanted and when. "Can I taste you?" Gretchen spread her legs in an enthusiastic invitation. Jax made her way down Gretchen's body, kissing various spots along the way and taking time to tease Gretchen's sensitive nipples some more. Out of the corner of her eye, she watched Gretchen lick her fingers clean.

She pulled Gretchen's shorts down and dived right in, burying her mouth between Gretchen's thighs. She missed Gretchen's flavor—so uniquely sweet and salty, with a hint of earthiness that made her taste like she had been picked fresh from the garden. She was greedy with her tongue, lapping up Gretchen's juices and savoring each drop.

"I'm gonna come, don't stop." Gretchen grabbed her hair with a painful grip, turning Jax on even more. "Don't you fucking stop."

Jax ran her tongue around Gretchen's clit in tight circles and entered her swiftly with two fingers. Gretchen's back bowed off the mattress. Jax knew exactly what Gretchen needed to reach an explosive orgasm. Jax dipped her other hand lower between Gretchen's ass cheeks. She pressed her fingertip into the tight ring, the muscle contracting against her touch.

Gretchen covered her mouth, but her moan was still loud.

Jax didn't stop, she couldn't stop, and no fear of an embarrassing moment could make her. She knew the moment Gretchen started to climax. Her thighs tightened around Jax's head and her inner muscles convulsed, milking Jax's fingers for all the pleasure they could give.

Gretchen fell back on the bed a sweaty mess. She twitched as Jax continued working her tongue. Gretchen pushed her head away and started giggling. "Take it easy on me. I'm a seizure risk."

She traced her way back up to Gretchen's lips and kissed her. "Don't joke like that." She kissed her again, more deeply, to share the flavor between them.

"I'm sorry." Gretchen bit at Jax's lower lip and reached down to toy with her entrance. "Forgive me?" She dipped into Jax just enough to ignite her sensitive entrance, but not fully. Just the way Jax liked it. Gretchen spread her wetness up and started to rub her clit.

"*Yesss…*" she hissed. Her arms went weak and she fell atop Gretchen. She buried her face into the crook of Gretchen's neck and breathed heavily. She sank her teeth into the damp skin of Gretchen's shoulder. "I'm already so close. How do you do that?"

"It helps that I love your body."

She lost herself to the feel of Gretchen's hands, one working the most sensitive skin between her legs and the other caressing as much as it could reach. She wanted this moment to last forever, for it to wash away every painful memory. That was exactly how Gretchen's touch felt—like a baptism, cleaning them of their sins.

"Make me come," she said between clenched teeth. Her command was met with the quickening of Gretchen's fingers. She came quietly, riding out the pleasurable waves against Gretchen's hand. Her whole body went slack. It took her a while to come back to her senses, and she realized how she must've been crushing Gretchen. "Am I hurting you?"

Gretchen wrapped her arms around her body. "Don't move. This feels nice. I want to keep you here forever."

"You have me forever." She kissed the tip of Gretchen's nose. "You always have." She kissed her eyelids. "I love you," she said, kissing her cheeks next. "I love you, I love you." She finally kissed Gretchen's waiting lips. She noticed Gretchen's tears and panicked. "Are you sure I'm not hurting you?"

"I'm fine. I'm happy." Gretchen pressed her forehead to hers. "I feel like me again, thanks to you."

Jax's happiness was quickly quelled by fear and insecurity. She rolled off to the side of Gretchen and looked up at the shadows across the ceiling. She saw many shapes and faces, and none of them made her feel better.

"What just happened?" Gretchen said.

She almost lied, not wanting to add to Gretchen's already mounting stress, but she needed to do things right this time. No more hiding, no more lying, and no more keeping quiet. "I guess I'm the scared one now."

"What are you afraid of?"

"You remembering." Jax felt silly once she admitted it. Gretchen stayed silent. "I know it's selfish, but what if you remember why you didn't stop me? What if you had a great reason, and once you remember it, you don't want to be with me anymore?"

"Oh, sweetheart," Gretchen said, taking Jax's hand once more. "I thought we were focusing on what *is*, not what *if*."

"I know, I know." She traced the lines of Gretchen's palm in the darkness. She knew Gretchen's skin so well. She didn't need light to know she was touching the faint gray dot caused by a graphite pencil in elementary school—one of her favorite spots to focus on when she needed to calm her racing mind. "Our life changed when you fell and forgot so much. I'm just worried it'll change again if you remember."

"I'll remember this moment still, and I'll remember all the fighting I did to get here. I'll remember the good times in the past four years, too. Caleb's first steps and our best moments. Don't assume the bad memories will outweigh the good. Don't think four bad years erase thirteen great ones."

Jax tried her best to swallow back her fear and put on a brave face. She nearly laughed at how quickly the tables turned, and now she was being comforted. "Okay."

"Okay?"

"Yes."

"We'll be okay."

She heard the certainty in Gretchen's voice, and it immediately transported her back to their engagement, their wedding day, and the moment they found out they were pregnant. Gretchen believed in them, and she did, too.

"We will be."

Chapter Thirty-six

33 days, 11 hours, 33 minutes

Jax was determined, even in her sleepy haze, to call out of work. She didn't care if Randy would be mad—she didn't even care if Randy fired her. She was too happy and too content. She pulled Gretchen closer, molding her front to Gretchen's back. The feel of skin on skin brought a sense of euphoria. Jax could easily lie there all day and forget about the outside world.

"Bug?"

She sat up so quickly her brain spun. How did she not hear the door open? She turned to Caleb, who was standing beside the bed, and then down to her bare chest. She covered herself and smiled. "What's up, Cricket? Are you okay?" She felt Gretchen moving next to her and next thing she knew her shirt was in her hand.

Caleb hugged his stuffed triceratops and buried his face into its plush horns. "I wanna cuddle."

"Okay. Get in here." She quickly pulled on her shirt before lifting the covers for him. Caleb climbed over her, and his sharp little knees hit her in all her soft spots. He fell into the small space between Jax and Gretchen. She sighed. So much for a little extra time to herself with Gretchen, but she wouldn't have it any other way. She settled back in and closed her eyes.

Caleb said he wanted to cuddle, but he must've meant squirm. He did not stay still, which made the early morning relaxation disappear.

"What's the matter?" Gretchen said, mumbling with her sleepy voice.

"I have to poop."

Jax opened her eyes and raised her eyebrows at Gretchen, who was smiling. "And people think family life is all sunshine and rainbows."

"I'd like to meet one person who believes that." Gretchen got out of bed and stretched. Jax watched her long limbs glowing in the morning light. "Go ahead." Gretchen motioned for Caleb to go to the bathroom. He rolled, dramatically, out of bed and scampered to the bathroom. He didn't shut the door. "At what age will he start wanting privacy?"

"If spending a lot of time with Wyatt has taught me anything, never. Men wouldn't even notice if all the bathroom doors in the world disappeared."

Gretchen smirked and crawled back on the mattress. She looked positively seductive. "When was the last time we had a morning to ourselves?"

"It's been a very long time."

"Maybe we can get Amanda to take Caleb for the night. We can talk, get reacquainted, and enjoy a lazy morning together."

Jax could feel the excitement building inside. "I like the sound of that a lot, but I feel like we've passed him off to Amanda too much recently."

"One more night, and then we'll pick him up tomorrow afternoon and do something fun. Like take him to the aquarium."

She did know for a fact that taking Caleb to the aquarium would mean more to him than anything else they did or didn't do. "Fine. You convinced me."

"Sorry to twist your arm." Gretchen started to lean in, her hair falling and ticking Jax's face.

"Mama!" Caleb's voice shattered the moment. "I need help."

Gretchen sat back on her heels and slapped her thighs. "Duty calls."

"Literally."

"Just try to forget about this when you imagine all the things you plan on doing to me later." Gretchen winked and disappeared into the bathroom.

Jax's mind was flooded with images of Gretchen bent over, ready to be taken roughly. Gretchen always looked delectable on top, riding Jax and taking control of her pleasure. She needed this to happen, and she knew where to find their favorite toy. She rolled over and opened the bottom drawer of the nightstand. Papers were piled up. It seemed their toy drawer had become Gretchen's junk drawer. She sifted through the papers in hopes of finding at least one of their many favorites accumulated over the years.

"She couldn't have thrown them away," Jax said to herself.

"What?" Gretchen's voice barely carried from the bathroom. She sounded strained, which was not a good sign.

Jax spotted an envelope with her name on it, unmistakably written by Gretchen. "Nothing," she said distractedly. The envelope was taped to a larger manila envelope, which had the return address of Gretchen's lawyer in the top corner. She took the documents, shut the drawer quietly, and got out of bed. "I'm going to get ready for work."

"So early?"

"Early in, early out. That's what I'm hoping for." Jax left the bedroom and rushed up the stairs. She threw the envelopes on the bed and stared at them. She started to pace, dread building heavily in her gut like a boulder. She wanted to tear into them and read every word, but they weren't hers, not technically anyway. She considered her options carefully as she pulled clothes from the closet. She could open the envelopes with Gretchen, but there was the slight chance that Gretchen already knew about them. Despite the anxiety she felt, she knew she didn't have to open them right away. She could think this through and consider what the smartest move would be. She checked the time on her phone and saw several messages from Wyatt.

Carly's water broke! What do I do?

Dude, where are you?

We're heading to the hospital.

She won't stop yelling at me.

We're at the hospital. Please respond ASAP.

Jax could feel his panic through the phone. She felt for Wyatt, but she still laughed a little. *Stay calm. She's going to do a lot of yelling, but you'll be okay. The doctors and nurses will take over, and all you'll have to do is help Carly.* She sent her reply and started getting ready for the day. When she came back from the bathroom, she had a new message.

Good to know. Also, where the hell have you been?

She tilted her back in thought, unsure of how to answer. Her possible reconciliation with Gretchen was pretty big news, but a baby was even bigger. Jax decided to split the difference and sent an underwhelming answer. *Gretchen and I spent some time talking last night. Sorry I missed all this. I'm here now, so please keep me updated.*

You're not coming here?!?

Trust me when I say Carly does not want any company right now. I will be there the moment the baby's born. Promise. Jax picked up the envelopes and stuffed them into her work bag. She didn't need to tell Wyatt how she had more than enough on her plate as it was. She pulled on a sweater and her favorite pair of Timberlands. She normally dressed more professionally, with at least a collar or oxfords, but today Jax really didn't care.

The door creaked open and Gretchen poked her head in. "Our child is demanding chicken nuggets for breakfast. He is now crying because I told him no."

Jax chortled. "Sounds like his teacher's problem to me. What did he eat?"

"A waffle with peanut butter."

"Good," she said, zipping up her bag.

"I'm going to ask Amanda to pick him up later, so this way if you do get off early, *we* can get off early." Gretchen wrapped her arms around Jax from behind.

She loved the feeling of Gretchen's warmth and affection, but she couldn't stop thinking about the envelopes. "I'll try my best."

Before she could get out the door, Gretchen called to her. "Is everything okay?"

She held up her phone. "Carly went into labor. I'm waiting on updates from Wyatt." The concern in Gretchen's eyes did not fade, but she smiled genuinely. After their earlier shared fears, she knew Gretchen needed a little more reassurance. Jax leaned in and kissed Gretchen. When she pulled back, Gretchen's eyes were bright once again. "I'll see you later."

Jax wrangled Caleb into her truck and drove him to preschool. She answered a million questions about their future trip to the aquarium, and she wished Gretchen hadn't told him about their plans just yet.

"Will the penguins be happy to see me?"

"I bet they will be."

"What about the gator?"

"I don't think he's happy to see anyone," Jax said seriously as she pulled up into the designated drop-off lane. "Be good for your aunt, and maybe we'll get you a stuffed gator."

"I want a stuffed shark."

Jax got out of the truck and opened the back door. "We'll get you the biggest shark." She had never seen his eyes get so big. She walked him up to the school entrance and watched as he ran inside eagerly. The kid didn't get his love for school from her. She said a quick good-bye and left.

She had little traffic on the drive to the office, so she pulled into the parking lot with ten minutes to spare. She cast a glance at her messenger bag and decided that moment was as good as any to read the contents of the envelopes. She opened the small one first, instantly recognizing it as a letter.

Jax,

I'm sorry our story had to end this way. It's hard to imagine that after so many years together we chose to go our separate ways. I honestly don't even know what to say. I wanted to write you one last letter to let you know I wish you nothing but happiness, and I hope you find that with Meredith. You're probably surprised right now, but even though I may not have seen the end coming for us, I did see the way she looks at you.

Jax looked out her windshield. She tried to process what she had just read, but her head was spinning. She continued reading.

I knew you were going to leave me eventually. I know you want another baby, but I don't think I'll ever be ready again after losing Aurora. I watched you pull away, and I just waited for the moment when you realized you deserved more. I won't fight with you. I want you to have the life you deserve, while giving Caleb the best childhood possible. I'm sorry for all your pain. I truly am.

Love,
Gretchen

Her stomach rolled as she slid her finger beneath the thick flap of the manila envelope. She pulled out the papers, unmistakably divorce papers. She knew they existed, so why was she filled with so much horror as she read them? *Irreconcilable differences* caught her eye immediately. She scanned the rest of the legal mumbo jumbo and felt the color drain from her face. Gretchen wanted full custody of Caleb. She knew Gretchen was fucked up for even saying it once, but to go and actually file for it? Jax felt sick. She crumpled the papers into a ball and put the truck in drive. She sped the entire way home and pulled into her driveway at an angle. She slammed the truck door and marched into the house. Gretchen was on the couch reading.

"Hey," Gretchen said. "Why—what are you doing home?" She looked frightened.

Jax threw the balled-up papers at Gretchen. "I found the divorce papers," she said, struggling to keep her voice even. "You were going to take Caleb from me."

"What?" Gretchen smoothed out the papers and read them. "There must be a mistake."

"It's all spelled out right there. You wanted full custody. I know we were both hurting, but Jesus, Gretchen, what kind of monster are you?" She wanted to cry, but she was so angry her body couldn't work properly. Like she was experiencing a traffic jam of emotion.

"I don't understand why I would do this."

"Try!"

Gretchen looked at her with tear-filled eyes. "I don't know," she said, her voice shaking.

"You're going to pretend you had no idea about this?"

"I didn't."

"You knew we were going to fuck but had no idea that was in your nightstand drawer? You expect me to believe this magical power you woke up with only predicts things that are beneficial for you, but everything else was just plucked from your memory?"

"Jax, please believe me when I say I didn't know." Gretchen stood and took cautious steps toward her. "I don't want any of what's in these papers."

"We've done some fucked-up things to each other," she said, her fury dissipating to unrestrained sadness. This was their story, and it was destined to end unhappily. "And I do believe you now, but if you were capable of doing this once, I can't trust that you wouldn't do it again."

"I won't."

"What happens when we hit another rough patch, and then another, like we always do?"

"We figure it out together."

"I can't believe that. Not anymore." She turned for the door, but Gretchen grabbed her wrist to stop her.

"You said you wouldn't leave me." Gretchen's face was red.

All Jax could muster was a shrug. She pulled her hand free and walked out the front door. She heard Gretchen's shrill cries through the door as she called for her. She climbed in her truck, and that's when her rigid posture finally fell. She felt tears come to life as she pulled out of the driveway. She checked over her shoulder for traffic and noticed

Caleb's dinosaur in her back seat. Jax knew she didn't have time for another detour. She was already late as it was, and she didn't need to add groveling for her job to the list of things to do today. She threw the truck in park and reached back to grab the stuffed animal with a death grip.

She walked back into the house. "I have to get to work, and Caleb forgot his dinosaur in the car." She looked around for Gretchen before raising her voice to make sure she could be heard anywhere in the house. "See if Amanda can bring it to him. His teachers will not be able to handle his—" Her words died in her throat. "Gretchen?"

All she could see were Gretchen's feet sticking out from behind the couch.

No...The darkness is here again, and I can't, I won't...

I hear you, Jax. I hear you calling my name, but I'm too tired. I can't follow you this time. I'm sorry, my love, I tried. I really tried. It'll be okay.

CHAPTER THIRTY-SEVEN

00:00:00

Everything was still and quiet. Gretchen struggled to open her eyes. They felt so heavy and sticky. Every time she got them to open for more than a second, she'd shut them against the bright lights in the room. She knew it couldn't be sunlight. It was too white to be natural. Once she finally fought against the painful urge to squint, she looked at the ceiling, a ceiling she immediately recognized. It had happened again.

"No…" Her throat and her head hurt. She was scared to move for fear of feeling that sharp pain in her ribs again. "Not again." She clamped her eyes shut and started to cry.

"Hey," Jax said. "Stay with me—you're okay."

"I can't do this," she said through her hysterics. "Not again. Please, not again."

"I'm getting Dr. Melendez."

"There's no point." She hiccupped. "No one can help me."

"Gretchen." Jax took her hand. She wanted to pull away, but she was so weak. "Listen to me."

She rolled her head to the side and looked at Jax. Her mind must've been playing another trick because Jax looked the same. "I'm sorry, I'm so sorry. I know I did some messed-up, unforgivable things, but I don't deserve this. No one deserves this."

"Shh…" Jax wiped a tear from her cheek and held her face gently. "Try to calm down and listen to me. It's February sixteenth."

Her shock stopped her tears. "What?"

"We fought this morning. It was ugly, and I stormed out. I came back in and found you on the floor. You've been unconscious for over an hour. I was terrified."

"February sixteenth," she said in wonderment.

"Do you remember any of that?"

Gretchen looked at Jax in a daze, unable to believe her life was really moving forward.

"I have to get the doctor."

"Wait." She watched Jax turn back to her slowly. Jax looked defeated with her eyes slightly downcast. One sleeve of her sweater was rolled up, and she wouldn't look at Gretchen. Gretchen struggled to sit up. She pressed her fingertips into the center of her forehead. She felt like she had the worst hangover of her life. A wave of nausea kept her from speaking again. She sucked in a deep breath, but she couldn't stop the bile from rising. She grabbed a nearby basin and heaved until her stomach burned and throat felt raw.

Jax rubbed her back as she coughed. "Gross."

Gretchen laughed even though she felt atrocious. "My head is killing me."

"They did a scan when you first came in because we were afraid you hit your head in the fall. Again. But everything came back clear. All the previous damage has healed." Jax cringed as she took the dirty basin from her and moved it to the farthest corner of the room. "We were worried this latest seizure would set you back. Do you feel any different?"

Gretchen shook her head and regretted it immediately. "I remember everything, even not remembering everything." She blinked hard a few times. "Was that English? Am I speaking English?"

"You are." Jax picked up her jacket. "I'll make sure someone comes in to check on you."

"You're leaving?" she said, knowing she sounded desperate, and she didn't care. Jax leaving never led to anything good.

"Carly's on the floor above us. She had the baby, so I'm going to check on Wyatt."

"But you'll come back?"

"There's no reason for me to stay."

Gretchen struggled to get her body to move, but she used all her energy to get out of bed. She walked up to Jax on wobbly legs. "Stay because I need you to." She wouldn't accept this ending. She didn't live and relive a nightmare just to lose all over again. "Stay because you promised."

"You're going to hurt yourself. Get back in bed."

She grabbed Jax's hand as she reached out to steady her. "You promised to always love me the way you did when we got married."

Jax pulled her hand away. "Things changed."

"*We* changed, both of us," she said, waving her hand between them, "and I lost my mind when I lost you. I have no explanation for what I did, but I am sorry."

Jax bunched her jacket in her hands and still wouldn't look at her. "I don't think I can forgive you."

"Then hate me until I prove to you I would never do anything like that again. I didn't try to stop you from leaving the first time, and I refuse to make that mistake again."

"Just let me go."

Gretchen flinched at Jax's loud voice. "I can't."

"Please," Jax cried. She took a deep breath. "I do hate you. I hate you for destroying our marriage, and I hate you for making me believe we could fix it. I hate you for making me believe in you again." Jax wiped her nose. "You know why you let me go before?" She didn't wait for Gretchen to answer. "Because you knew I was going to leave you anyway. How fucked-up is that? You knew I was going to go, so instead of talking to me, you said *see ya later* and kicked me on my way out."

Tears made Gretchen's eyes hurt, but she was powerless to stop them. "Well, I don't hate you—I never could. And you can chalk that up to me not remembering all the bullshit built up between us, but I refuse to believe that." She squared her shoulders. "Because when I look at you, I see the same woman from that first day in the library. I see the person who vowed forever, and I see the woman who held our newborn son like he was the most precious thing on earth."

"Gretchen—"

"Who I *don't* see is the woman who left or the woman who moved on with the nanny. So no, I don't hate you. And even if you leave this hospital room, I will not stop fighting for us." Suddenly, she was overwhelmed with an odd calm from either knowing how strong emotion could hurt her, or from believing so deeply in the love she felt. She didn't know which, and she didn't care.

Jax looked contemplative, but she only let out a long breath. Turning, she bumped into Dr. Melendez.

"Gretchen, what are you doing out of bed?" Dr. Melendez pushed Jax aside gently to get to her. She held her elbow gently and looked at her in concern. "You should know better by now."

Gretchen didn't care what Dr. Melendez was saying. She watched Jax leave, and then went back to bed with a heavy, sad sigh. She missed the days where a proclamation of love could solve everything, when it *was* everything.

"How are you feeling?" Dr. Melendez shined a penlight in her eyes, and she quickly decided that was the worst part of having a head injury.

She barely resisted the urge to swat away Dr. Melendez's hand. "I'm fine. I have a slight headache and I puked once," she said, pointing to the basin across the room. "You may want to have someone come and take that."

"Are you still nauseous?"

"No."

"Has the headache worsened or lessened?"

"It's about the same since I woke up."

"What's the last thing you remember before your seizure?"

She stared at the empty doorway. "Jax leaving."

"Were you emotional?"

"Yes."

Dr. Melendez let out a heavy sigh, clearly disappointed. "I'm going to adjust your meds a bit and prescribe you something to help keep you calm."

"I don't want it," Gretchen said firmly. "I'll be fine without it."

Dr. Melendez looked at her sympathetically. "There's nothing wrong with taking medication for help."

"I have nothing against medication, I'll even take the prescription and fill it if necessary. But I'm going to focus on fixing the things that are upsetting me instead."

Dr. Melendez pulled her notepad and a prescription pad from her jacket pocket. She scribbled on both before handing a small blue slip to Gretchen. "Fill it and keep it handy."

"I will." Gretchen noticed a sparkle on Dr. Melendez's left hand. "You're engaged."

Dr. Melendez peeked at her own ring. "I am," she said with a blissful smile. "My boyfriend proposed over the weekend. I was completely surprised."

Boyfriend. Gretchen shook her head and laughed. "Congratulations." Dr. Melendez continued taking notes and checking Gretchen's vitals. "Can I ask you a question?"

"Sure." Dr. Melendez wrapped her stethoscope around her neck and held both ends.

"Have you ever considered using an iPad?"

Dr. Melendez looked at her oddly. "For what?"

"Your notes."

"I've been handwriting my notes since my first year in med school. You know the saying," Dr. Melendez said, putting the pads back in her pocket, "if it ain't broke, don't fix it."

"Yeah."

"I'll have an orderly come in to clean that up. You can get changed back into your clothes. I'm sending you home shortly."

Gretchen spotted her bag of belongings on a chair. "That's it?"

"Do you miss your usual lengthy stay?" Dr. Melendez said with a smirk. "Your tests came back fine, and I don't see any reason to keep you. Our work here is done for now. You should arrange for a ride, or is Jax coming back for you?"

"She's not," Gretchen said sullenly. "I'll call Amanda."

"I guess I'll see you at your follow-up, then, as long as you stay out of here. Tell your sister hello for me." Dr. Melendez offered a friendly smile before leaving the room.

Gretchen was then alone. Alone in the silence with her thoughts, fake memories, and a hundred different outcomes for tomorrow. But all she could really focus on was taking a nap when she got home. She was so tired from everything. Getting dressed was slow going, and her tight jeans were a struggle she wasn't prepared for. By the time Gretchen was done, she sat winded on the edge of the hospital bed. She messaged Amanda to come pick her up and made pleasant small talk with the nurse who stopped in with her discharge papers. Her head still ached slightly and buzzed with an odd sense of fatigue, a feeling she would never be able to describe. Amanda walked through the door no more than five minutes after Gretchen hit *Send*, a nurse hot on her heels.

"Are you here to take Ms. Mills home?" the nurse said.

Amanda looked like she wanted to ignore him but nodded instead. He left after getting confirmation.

"How did you get here so fast?"

"I was already on my way. What the hell happened? You can't keep scaring me like this."

The nurse returned with a wheelchair and motioned for Gretchen.

"I'm fine," Gretchen said to both of them, already making her way to the door. She just wanted to be home.

"Hospital rules," he said, staring her down until she sat in the chair.

"I had a seizure, but I'm fine. They adjusted my meds, and hopefully I won't have another episode."

Amanda walked quickly to beat Gretchen and her chauffeur to the elevators. She pressed the button and turned back. "What caused this one?"

Gretchen bit the inside of her cheek and refused to meet Amanda's eye. "Jax and I fought."

"Jesus Christ," Amanda said under her breath. "I'm going to have to keep you two apart until you get the doctor's okay."

"That won't be a problem."

Amanda looked at her in shocked confusion. "What do you mean?" They stepped into the empty elevator.

"She left for good this time." She looked at Amanda, tears blurring her face. "I won't stop fighting for our marriage, but she won't come around anytime soon."

Amanda placed her hand on Gretchen's shoulder. "I'm sorry, sis."

"Don't be, because nothing's over. Not yet." Gretchen's voice came out surprisingly strong in spite of her fatigue. "The divorce papers were never signed. Jax found them this morning after we woke up together."

"Oh…"

"Oh." The deep male voice sounded out of place. Gretchen shot a glare over her shoulder.

No one said another word until Gretchen was at the front of the hospital and Amanda was helping her into her car.

"Isn't that a good thing, though? The waking up together part?"

Gretchen rolled her eyes. "It was until she read the papers and saw the part where I wanted full custody of Caleb." She pulled on her seat belt forcefully. Amanda had yet to put the car in drive—she just stared at Gretchen, agape.

"Yeah, I know. Can you please take me home? I need to lie down."

"If Mom was alive, she'd tell me to pray for you."

"If Mom was alive, you wouldn't be here."

"Very true."

"And she'd probably say my seizures and amnesia are punishment for whatever sins I've committed."

"That's terrible."

Gretchen watched an ambulance pull in, its flashing lights bright to her tired eyes. "It's true, though." And then she wondered, could this be a higher power's punishment?

Chapter Thirty-eight

Gretchen bounced her leg up and down, and the receptionist gave her a dirty look. She didn't care. She was nervous. Her lawyer held the key to everything—he could tell her what exactly she was thinking when she decided to fight for full custody. She had messaged Jax seven times, asking her to come to the appointment with her, and then another four times just to beg for her to answer her. No messages came through, and Gretchen was starting to lose hope.

"Gretchen," a man said from a nearby doorway. "It's good to see you."

She didn't recognize him. "Are you Mark Goldmann?" He looked at her curiously and nodded. She realized her error as she stood and followed him into his office. "I'm sorry. I was in an accident and lost four years of my memories." She said it so evenly that she felt proud of herself.

"Wow. I'm sorry to hear that. Was it an auto accident?" He held his burgundy tie as he took a seat. He motioned for Gretchen to sit as well. "Is that why you're here?"

Gretchen shook her head. She probably looked like a walking, talking dollar sign to him. "I'm here because I have some questions for you." She reached into her purse and pulled out the wrinkled paperwork. "Can you explain to me what happened with these?"

Mark took the papers and put on his glasses. He was silent for a moment while he read. "These are your divorce papers."

"That I asked for?"

"Yes."

"I asked for everything in there?"

"Yes." He sat back. "You explained your situation to me, and I advised you."

"Can you tell me what my situation was?"

His glasses hung on the tip of his long nose as he stared at Gretchen over the rims. "Let me get my notes."

Gretchen looked around his small office as she waited. He didn't seem overly impressive or even well established. She wondered what made her choose him to represent her in the divorce, or at all, for that matter. "Did I come to you by referral?"

"You were my aunt's therapist." He dropped a thin folder on the desktop. "She's eighty-four and had surgery to repair some tendons in her hand." He flipped open the folder and licked the tip of his index finger before filing through the pages. "Okay, Gretchen Mills." He ran his fingertips down the page as he read. "Shared home that was purchased by your mother, one child, and a hefty savings account you wanted no one to know about."

"Savings account?"

"Yeah. You didn't ask for much, just for everything to be done as easily and as quickly as possible, while keeping your child's best interests in mind."

"Is that why I wanted full custody?"

"I urged you to fight for that." His smile was too proud given the circumstances.

"You did? Why?"

"You were very upset after your ex-wife made a comment about taking your child with her if she chose to move away. I explained that your child—"

"Caleb."

"Caleb would have more stability with you. I directed you to go for the custody clause, and then amend it as necessary as your ex-wife's plans changed. We needed to beat her to the punch."

"Beat her to the punch?" Gretchen sat back in disbelief. She and Jax had turned into an angry, tit-for-tat couple. She understood the rationale behind the lawyer's suggestion, but she couldn't apply it to the people she knew they really were. "That's disgusting."

"That's exactly what you said the first time, but I kept it in the papers, figuring we would work it out if your ex had a bad reaction." He placed his glasses down and sat back. "You hired me to make everything work out for the best, not to take emotions into account. And that's what I did."

"Did I seem sad? Like I didn't really want any of this?"

"I'm not sure I follow."

"Was I unhappy about divorcing my wife and using my child?" she said bluntly.

Mark nodded.

Gretchen closed her eyes. She took a calming breath to quell the faint throbbing between her eyes. "Cancel everything. We're not getting divorced." She got ready to leave, not really caring if Mark had any thoughts on the matter.

"I'll save your file."

"Please don't." Gretchen walked out of the office feeling heavier than she had before. She had let a lawyer, a stranger, talk her into the most hurtful action she had ever done, even if she was driven by a sick form of retaliation. But at least she learned some of the truth, and she had more of an explanation for Jax. If Jax ever spoke to her again. She checked her phone and wasn't at all surprised to see only one message from Amanda, checking in. She called an Uber and hoped the bank would be able to give her some good news.

"Gretchen!" Virginia, the head bank teller, came out from behind the counter to greet her. "I'm so happy to see you. We all heard about what had happened. How are you feeling?" She urged Gretchen to take a seat.

"Fine. A little off from time to time, but I'm getting there." Gretchen soaked up the comfort of recognizing every one of the staff members. Small-town banks were a blessing. "Is Joanne here today? I was hoping to talk about some of my accounts."

"She ran across the street for a coffee. Do you want anything? I can shoot her a quick text."

She waved Virginia off. "No, thank you. I'll just wait here." She took off her knit hat and held it on her lap with her purse. Her wool coat was cumbersome as she sat, but the outside temperatures were so low, she still felt a chill.

Joanne's grin was broad and open as she approached Gretchen. She put down her coffee and opened her arms. "I'm so happy to see you."

Gretchen hugged her back and knew this type of closeness was odd between bank personnel and customers, but she had been using this very bank since they had moved to the area. "It's good to see you, too." She sat again and waited for Joanne to get settled before asking her questions. "I'm curious about my accounts. I'm not sure if you've heard, but I had an accident and lost some of my memory."

"Oh, dear. I heard about the accident, but I had no idea."

"I'm doing much better and I'm working on getting my life back together. Which is why I'm here. I'd like to see all of my account balances and, if possible, statements from the last six months."

As Joanne typed away, Gretchen looked around and marveled at the bank's unchanged interior. The only difference was the winter decorations. She distinctly remembered summer decorations the last time she was in. Joanne's loud printer tore her from the memory of American flags and sand pails.

"Here's for one account," Joanne said, placing a small stack in front of Gretchen on the desk.

She looked through each page. "This is only two months."

"You closed that account."

Gretchen looked at the heading. The statement was for the joint account she had with Jax. These little evidences of separation would never get easier to stomach. "What's next?"

"Your checking account and the savings account you have set up for Caleb. How is he, by the way? Still a spitfire?"

"And then some." Looking through the paperwork, Gretchen was pleased to see their son had a good start to a college or house fund, and she had enough of a cushion to go back to work part-time at first. She noticed the printer was still going. "There's more?"

"Your personal savings." Joanne handed her the last stack of papers.

Her eyes widened the moment she saw the balance. "This is mine?"

Joanne nodded and smiled. "You've been working very hard to build it up."

"Did I ever tell you what for?"

"No, but you always wore a smile and said you hoped it all worked out."

"Wow," she said while folding up the statements. "Thank you, Joanne. This will be a huge help."

"I'm really happy you're okay. We were worried when we hadn't seen you around."

Gretchen forced a smile, just a small tug at the corners of her mouth. "I'll see you soon." She waved to everyone as she left.

By the time she got home, Amanda was already there with Caleb. "Hey, sorry I'm late."

"Late for what?" Amanda said. She placed a plate of dino chicken nuggets in front of Caleb, who was clearly too excited by his snack to care about the adults in the room. "We haven't been home long, and judging by your tone on the phone, you had a busy day planned. I didn't expect you home for hours."

"I went looking for answers." Gretchen dropped her purse on the table and took off her coat. "I needed to know what my life was like. This whole time I've been so focused on Jax and stopping all that bad stuff from happening that I never learned about me." She knew she must've sounded crazy because Amanda's eyebrows rose nearly to her hairline.

"*Okay.*" Amanda drew out the one word for too long.

"I have a hefty savings account I knew nothing about."

"Yeah."

She tilted her head. "You knew?"

"Of course I did. After Mom died, I felt guilty she didn't—"

"I'm not talking about the money for Caleb."

"Wait." Amanda raised her hands and waved them from side to side. "You remember that?"

"Yes and no, but that's not important."

"You remembering *anything* is important."

"It's crazy to get into all of that right now."

Amanda crossed her arms. "Try me." Caleb started a gladiator-like battle between two nuggets.

Gretchen sighed in frustration. Suddenly now people wanted to listen to her. "After my first seizure, I woke up, but not for real." She waited for a sarcastic comment, but Amanda stayed silent with a surprisingly open expression. "I remember the account for Caleb—"

"What?" Caleb looked at her with curious eyes.

"Nothing, Cricket. We're just talking about boring adult stuff."

"Okay." A T. rex took a dive into a puddle of ketchup.

"I knew where my letters were, when Jax and I were going to fight, and I knew I was going to have that seizure yesterday. None of that had to do with my memory. It's because I lived it all already."

Amanda was visibly working through in her mind everything Gretchen said. "That's what's been going on with you."

"I know it sounds crazy, but I'm telling you it happened to me."

"How come you couldn't prevent the seizure?"

"I don't know," she said. "I tried to keep everything from playing out the way it did, but it didn't make a difference. Even if the reason for the fight changed, we'd still fight. Everything was inevitable."

"What do you think that means?"

Gretchen watched Caleb play with his food, pure happiness on his face as he massacred dinosaurs and devoured them. "I don't know, Amanda, but I'm terrified it means Jax and I are done for good. And maybe that's what's meant to be." Silence stretched on after her final word. She never took her eyes off Caleb.

"What were you going to say about the other account?"

Gretchen snapped back to attention. "Oh. I've been saving, a *lot*, and I don't really know what for."

"Maybe the split?"

Amanda's suggestion disgusted her. "No. I started well before that, and my lawyer told me the account was a secret."

"Still sounds to me like you knew you were splitting up."

She shook her head forcefully. "No way." She thought of Jax's parting words. "Shit."

"That's a bad word!" Caleb said angrily.

"I'm sorry." She felt silly for apologizing to a four-year-old and looked back to Amanda. "Jax told me the reason why I let her go was because I always knew she was going to leave. I wrote that to her in a letter." She hated Amanda's smug look. "It doesn't add up, though. None of it feels right in here," she said, pointing to her heart. "I started working more and saving money like my life depended on it, and I just let my wife leave. I haven't done a thing with or about the money since, and I just kept working. No. I refuse to believe it."

"I wish I could help you figure it out, but you never mentioned a thing to me."

"Who would I have told? I wouldn't have told Wyatt or Carly, and the only other person I talked to regularly was—" Gretchen grabbed her phone from her purse and started dialing.

Amanda held her arms up in question. "Thanks for the suspense."

Gretchen held up her index finger as she waited for an answer.

"Shore Health Occupational Therapy. How may I direct your call?"

"This is Gretchen Mills. May I please speak with Omar Runge?" She gave Amanda a thumbs-up.

"Gretchen, hi, it's Sharon. How are you feeling?"

"I'm doing okay." Gretchen had no idea who Sharon was. "May I speak with Omar? It's important."

"I hope you're calling to tell him you're coming back. It's not the same without you around here."

Her patience was waning. "I am actually. Can I speak with him? Now, please?"

"Sure thing. Hang on."

The hold music filled the phone and Gretchen turned to Amanda. She just blinked until the music stopped. She perked up.

"It's so good to hear from you, Gretchen. How are you?"

"I'm fine. I want—"

"Are you ready to come back to work already?"

"Yes. I just need clearance from my doctor, which should be soon," she said, not wanting to commit to work before she'd untangled her life. "Then I'll be cleared for part-time. Look—"

"That's great to hear."

"Omar," she said firmly. "I lost four years of my memories, and I need you to help me." She decided to cut to the chase. "Why did I start working like I wanted to live my life at the office?"

His laugh was deep in the phone. "That's a bit of a long story."

"I've got time."

Chapter Thirty-nine

"I can't get over how perfect she is," Jax said, touching the baby's feet for what must've been the hundredth time. Wyatt and Carly had arrived home with little Bethany the day before, and Wyatt begged Jax to come over after work. The newborn wiggled before falling back into a sound slumber. "Enjoy these early days when all she does is sleep and gurgle."

"And poop. Don't forget all the poop." Carly sat on the couch, looking exhausted.

She snickered. "And you're just getting started." She flicked the plush stars hanging above the baby on her swing and took a seat across from Carly.

Wyatt walked into the room with two bottles of beer. He handed one to Jax before sitting next to Carly. His eyes stayed on his daughter. "I can't believe she's here."

"I can't believe you managed to put her down for more than a minute." Jax smiled around the bottle. She couldn't get over how attached Wyatt had become in an instant, and she planned on teasing him about it for years to come.

"I yelled at him for it. The kid will never sleep. I'd like to try for healthy sleep habits early on."

Good luck. "I'd be worried she'd get lost in that beard of yours." She expected a snappy retort, but Wyatt blurted the unexpected.

"We wanted to talk to you about the baby's name."

She sipped her beer. "Why? I think Bethany is a great name. Are you doubting your choice? Because it's completely normal if you are. For the first few weeks, I called Caleb all kinds of names just to check."

"It's her middle name." Wyatt shrugged at Carly, who elbowed him and shook her head. Clearly, he was discussing something Carly didn't want to talk about.

"Gretchen isn't here," Carly said.

Wyatt's shoulders fell. "We don't know if or when we'll be able to get them together."

Jax held up her hand. "Guys. I'm right here." Wyatt winced, and Carly covered her face with her hands. Jax racked her brain for Bethany's middle name, but she couldn't recall. Her birthday hadn't exactly been the calmest day for Jax. "What's up?"

Wyatt cleared his throat and watched the baby swing back and forth for a moment before speaking again. "You and Gretchen both came up a lot in our conversations about her name. The both of you have been there for us so much over the years, and we wouldn't even be together if it wasn't for you."

Jax felt her cheeks warm. For a split second, she felt honored that they'd name their baby after her, but then their odd behavior made her think. "Look, Gretchen and I may be splitting for real, but I can't blame you for picking the name. It's a great name and fitting for a beautiful, strong female."

Wyatt sat back on the couch and let out a long breath. He smiled. "Good. We were worried it would be too hard for you, especially now after everything. But we wanted to honor both of you, and this felt right." They looked at their baby, who snoozed peacefully.

"Bethany Aurora," Carly said with awe.

Jax's stomach clenched. She looked at Bethany. She was alive and well and moving, along with her little baby dreams. She had the same chubby cheeks as Aurora, but her head was full of dark hair instead of the peach fuzz Jax had felt for such a short amount of time. "Bethany Aurora," she said, reaching out to touch the small set of feet one more time. She felt a rush of sadness and stood. "I'm gonna head out. I have to stop at the grocery store."

"Are you sure?" Wyatt followed after her as she collected her coat and knit hat. He grabbed his jacket, too.

"Yeah. I've put off all my errands lately. I haven't even gotten my mail in days." She leaned over and kissed the top of Carly's head. "You're doing great. *She's* great."

Wyatt had his hand on the front doorknob already. "I'll walk you out."

She stole one last glance at Bethany before following Wyatt out into the cold. "You don't have to walk me a whole twenty-five feet. It's freezing out here."

"Are you okay?" Wyatt said the moment the door closed behind them.

Jax had flashbacks of the past few months and chuckled. "I've been better—that's for sure."

"With the name."

She looked him in the eyes. Wyatt had always been her one constant, and she was lucky to still have him in her life. "I can't think of a better way to honor Aurora." She patted his arm.

"Do you think Gretchen will be okay with it?"

"Without a doubt. I'll tell her the next time I see her. It'll give us something to talk about instead of fighting."

"So you two are really over?"

Jax didn't want to give verbal confirmation of a truth she hated so much. She nodded. "Thanks for the beer—I owe you one." She started to walk away.

"I'm holding you to it."

"I'll be back soon to snatch up that baby."

"I'm holding you to that, too."

Jax got in her truck and started the ignition. Her heart was heavy, but her smile was genuine.

❖

Jax carried seven grocery bags in her hands, refusing to make two trips out to her truck. Her refrigerator was empty, and she needed to fill it up again. She struggled to get her key in the lock of the main building door and grunted as she pushed it open. Just inside the small entryway was a wall of mailboxes. She glanced at her box twice, debating putting the effort into checking for mail. She looked down at her shaking fists, each fingertip a different shade of purple or white. She walked slowly to the elevator and used her elbow to hit every button near her floor.

After three unnecessary stops, she made it to her floor and into her own apartment. She raced to her couch to set the bags down and yelped in pain as she released her fists. "Son of a bitch." She shook her hands out and kicked the door shut. She barely paid any attention as she put the food away, acting more robotically with each step back and forth in her small kitchen.

Jax had done very little since leaving Gretchen in the hospital the week before. She went to work and came home to emptiness. Every night in bed, she analyzed their final conversation, wondering if she had made the right choice. She almost called Meredith one night just to see how she was doing, but Jax knew reaching out wouldn't be fair, and she would only be doing it to soothe her wound.

Her apartment only felt like her home when Caleb was staying with her. She looked at her couch and television, deciding against watching anything. The bedroom off in the distance was the only room that called to her. She could sleep off her melancholy and tackle tomorrow with new energy. But more than likely she'd wake up in worse shape than before. That seemed to be her every day.

Maybe a trip down to her mailbox would do her good. She grabbed her keys and headed down to the main floor. She decided to take the stairs, figuring there was no real point in rushing. She smiled at an elderly lady next to her. Her mailbox was packed, and she struggled to get all the envelopes and magazines out in one piece. She looked back to the woman, who was now grimacing at her. Jax shrugged and said, "That'll teach me to skip a few days."

"What if someone sent you something important?" The old woman's face was twisted with unabashed confusion and judgment.

Jax gave the question real consideration. "That's not very likely." She held up her mail and nodded her good-bye. She fingered through the catalogs, bills, and advertisements as the elevator crawled to the twelfth floor. The elevator doors opened just as she came to the last letter in the pile. The handwriting on the envelope was Gretchen's. She hadn't heard from her in a week, since her onslaught of texts abruptly stopped, and now she felt overwhelmingly naive to have believed they'd finally find peace. The doors slid closed.

Jax hit the button to open them again and marched to her apartment, frustration fueling her as she paced. She didn't want Gretchen to reach out, not like this. A letter between them was never simple. Her hands shook as she held the paper. The rustling sounded loud in her silent apartment.

Jax,

    I know you asked me to let you go, but I couldn't do that without knowing I did everything in my power to put together the pieces we had broken into. You're everything to me and I do believe, deep down and regardless of everything, you still care for me, too. So here it is, my final plea in the form of a letter. You and I have done some of our most significant communicating like this, so putting my thoughts and feelings to paper only seemed fitting. There are truths I've learned recently about the custody clause and why I threw myself into my work that I think you need to know.

I would love to tell you more about it, maybe over coffee?

If we're really over I think we both deserve the chance to say our final words. But I won't lie, I hope we still have a chance. I love you too much. If you're willing, I'll be at Café Devon this Thursday at eight o'clock.

Love always,
Gretchen

Jax checked her watch. Thanks to her delay in getting the mail, she had ten minutes to make a decision. Times like this were when she envied Gretchen's strength and hardheadedness. She wanted to tear up the letter and move on, really move on, and focus on giving Caleb a good childhood and figuring out how to start healing. But her heart... that part of Jax was as stubborn as Gretchen. After seeing Bethany and hearing Aurora's name, she felt jolted and dizzy, and her first instinct was to talk to Gretchen, to cry with Gretchen. Was this a habit she'd have to learn to break, or was it a sign of how connected they'd always be? She felt silly for thinking in terms of signs, but if Gretchen had lived the past few weeks according to a premonition or nightmare or whatever she called it, maybe believing in signs wasn't so foolish after all.

CHAPTER FORTY

Gretchen spun her coffee cup three times clockwise and once counter. Remnants of foam still clung to the rim even after she drank half her cappuccino. She knew it was past eight o'clock, but she wasn't surprised. Throwing the invitation out to Jax was risky and her chances of a good outcome were slim, but Gretchen didn't care. She'd wait and wait until the café shut down if that's what it took. She looked around the small space again, probably for the fifteenth or sixteenth time, and checked to see if anyone was watching her. She didn't want a stranger's pity, yet she was seeking it out. Her phone whistled. She turned off the sound before checking the message from Amanda.

Still a no show?

Gretchen sighed. *Yes.*

When are you coming home?

I'm not. Gretchen wished phones were capable of bold lettering for texts. *I can't. Not yet.*

She's obviously not coming. Stop torturing yourself and come home. We'll have ice cream and curse the day Jax was born. It'll be therapeutic.

She shook her head like Amanda could see her. She couldn't explain her feelings. Gretchen just couldn't leave. *Keep the ice cream in the freezer.* She stashed her phone away and took a sip of her cold cappuccino. The bitterness clung to the back of her tongue. She heard the door open, and she turned, her last bit of hopefulness hanging on the new visitor. She made awkward eye contact with the old man walking in. In her slight discomfort, she felt an energy from the far wall of the café.

Jax sat motionless, no more than twenty feet away, with her eyes on Gretchen.

Gretchen stared, unable to move or think or speak beyond wondering how long she had been there. Gretchen's heart started to pound. She felt so much hope and fear in that moment, but her body was paralyzed, too afraid to get up and find out what Jax's intentions were. Instead, Gretchen raised her hand and offered a sheepish wave. When Jax didn't wave back, she pointed to the empty chair across from her. Again, Jax remained motionless.

"Not making this easy, are you?" Gretchen said under her breath. She gathered her purse, jacket, and chilled cappuccino and walked slowly to the other table, trying to gauge Jax's feelings with each step. She used to be able to read Jax better than any other person in the room, but not this time. She placed her cup down gingerly, less worried about spilling than she was of startling Jax. "Is this seat taken?"

Jax barely looked at her when she shook her head.

Gretchen settled in and waited for Jax to talk, but words never came even as the minutes ticked away. She started to worry the café would close before they acknowledged the elephant standing right between them. She looked over at Jax, who sat in her thick leather jacket and sweater beneath. She wondered if Jax was hot or if she even cared about being comfortable. Gretchen tugged at the cuff of her own thermal Henley.

"So..." Gretchen said, hoping the simple starter would open the floodgates of conversation, but all she got was a drip. "How long have you been here?"

"Since a little after eight fifteen."

"I'm happy you came."

Jax's eyes seemed more focused now when they met hers. "I don't know why I did."

"I hope you came because you wanted to."

"I just read your letter today." Jax shifted. She appeared more uncomfortable than Gretchen had ever seen her.

"I sent it days ago."

Jax shrugged. "If I had read it days ago, I probably would've never shown up tonight."

"Oh." She looked away, taking a break from Jax's cheerless face. "What about reading it today brought you here?"

"Aurora."

Gretchen looked at Jax as if seeing her would help things make sense. "Aurora?"

"I went to go see Wyatt and Carly's baby. She's cute, lots of hair."

Jax smiled and Gretchen couldn't help but join. "They named her Bethany," Jax said. "Bethany Aurora."

Gretchen pushed herself back from the table and knocked her mug on the floor. The sound echoed through the café, and patrons turned toward the clatter. A young waitress rushed over and pulled a towel from her waist and started cleaning up the mess.

"I am so sorry," she said quickly.

"It's okay." The waitress waved her off and held up the mug. "Not even a chip." When the young woman looked at Gretchen, she seemed puzzled. "It's really okay. I can get you another, no charge. No point in crying over spilled cappuccino."

She became aware of the tears streaming down her face. She touched them and flushed with embarrassment. "Thank you—I mean, no, thank you. I'm fine." Gretchen turned away and hid her face. She waited until she heard her walk away before looking at Jax, who wore a small smirk.

"I had the same reaction, but I didn't throw anything on the floor."

Gretchen closed her eyes and let out a small laugh. She felt her hot tears and the warmth of familiarity in her heart. Jax always had a way of making her feel better. "Bethany Aurora," she said. Oddly, the name now carried peace instead of pain. "I like it."

Jax folded her hands on the tabletop and tapped her thumbs together. "After that, I just couldn't stop thinking about her, and then I read your letter." Jax swallowed hard and bit the inside of her cheek, but she couldn't control the quivering of her chin. "You were right. We should each be able to say our piece."

Gretchen's hopes sank, but she always knew this was the more likely outcome. "I'll let you go first. You're really doing me the favor by being here."

"You know, I sat watching you check the door and drink your coffee, and I still don't know what to say."

"Anything. You can say anything to me." She felt awash with nerves when Jax pinned her with an intense stare.

"I missed you." Jax held up her hand when Gretchen tried to speak. "I'm not talking about recently. I'm talking about when we lived in the same house. When you were always working, and I was always waiting for you to come home."

"It won't be like that anymore."

"Please. I'm here to say my piece. I believe you when you say you've changed—I can see it in the way you look at me and Caleb—but

I'm still so fucking hurt. I don't know what to do with this darkness in my chest."

"I am so sorry, for everything." Gretchen placed her hand, palm up, on the table. Jax didn't take it, but she'd leave it there and wait. "I'm mostly sorry for running to a lawyer and letting him talk me into fighting for custody when I should've talked to you. You threatened to take Caleb and I panicked, but that's no excuse for doing what I did."

Jax looked at her with shame-filled eyes. "I wouldn't have done it."

"I think we both spiraled out of control, and I was desperate to make it stop, to do something to make things better. Even if that meant getting a divorce."

Jax snorted. "All you had to do was come home more."

"I was trying," she said quickly, jumping on the opportunity presented. "I was working a lot for the money and for a promotion. There was a management position I had my eye on that would guarantee a raise and no more than nine-to-five. No weekends, no after-hours."

"You didn't have to kill yourself for money. We were fine."

"Except you weren't." Gretchen reached into her purse and pulled out a bank statement. She unfolded the paper and handed it to Jax. "I was saving for you. You can quit your job and find something that makes you feel good again." She watched Jax's eyes widen as she read the paper. "I figured it all out—between these savings and me going back to work part-time, you can take at least six months off to take care of yourself."

Jax looked between the paper and Gretchen. "I don't know what to say."

"You don't have to say anything. Just believe that we could've been okay—that we *can be* okay."

"I know I sound like a broken record," Jax said, folding up the paper, "but it's not that simple."

"Nothing is simple. If this was simple, we would've known to talk to each other more when shit got hard, but we didn't. If this was simple, I wouldn't have had to live through a nightmare twice to see the difference between hate and love. But you know what? I'm better because of it and I think we can be, too."

"What exactly are you proposing?"

A light bulb went off, and even as Gretchen felt more and more sets of eyes on her, she couldn't help herself. She got down on one knee right beside their small café table and took Jax's hand. "Jacqueline Shay Levine—"

"What are you doing?" Jax said, and her expression was somewhere between amused and panicked. Quiet gasps could be heard around them. Several patrons raised their phones.

"Would you make me the happiest woman in the world and not divorce me?"

"What did she say?" a woman beside them whispered to another stranger.

Jax looked around before standing. "Come on," she said, pulling Gretchen up to her feet. "We're leaving now."

Gretchen grabbed her stuff as quickly as she could while being nudged by Jax to hurry up. Once they were out in the cold night, she turned back to Jax and held her in place. "Answer me."

"You're crazy."

"I know."

"Why would you want to stay married? After everything we've been through and all the fighting—"

"Because I'm crazy."

"I don't know if we can make it work."

"No one ever knows," she said, shivering. "We didn't even know for sure when we got married, but we loved each other so damn much we chose to believe it. I still believe it."

Jax took Gretchen's coat and wrapped it around her. "What if we're just not meant to have our happily ever after?"

She held Jax's face in her hands, feeling the chill of her cheeks and warmth of her own love. "I would rather a *realistically* ever after with you than any version of a fairy tale with someone else."

Jax rested her forehead on Gretchen's. "I keep coming up with reasons why I should say no, because I'm scared."

"Do you love me?" She felt Jax's cheeks spread with a smile barely visible in the glow of the streetlight. "Can you forgive me?"

"I think we can both forgive each other."

"So is that a yes?"

"This is the strangest proposal ever."

"Stranger than getting down on one knee after eating chili dogs at the Windmill?"

"You were so happy when you finished. It was the perfect moment."

Gretchen pinched Jax's cheeks. "I'm not moving from this spot until you give me an answer, and I'm starting to get really cold."

"Okay, okay. Yes, I will make you the happiest woman on earth and not divorce you."

She wrapped her arms around Jax and held her. Her jacket fell on the sidewalk, but she didn't care. All that mattered was how tightly Jax was holding her back. She pulled away just enough to kiss Jax. For the first time since waking up, Gretchen felt confident and happy in her reality.

Jax pulled back. "As much as I love kissing you, your face is like ice. Let's go home."

Gretchen practically raced Jax to her truck, even though she wasn't entirely sure where Jax parked. Gretchen was almost to the truck when she slipped on a small patch of ice, but Jax's arms were around her before she fell to the ground. She didn't move or say a word, paralyzed by the terror of a fall she couldn't remember.

"You're okay," Jax said. "I got you."

Gretchen looked into Jax's eyes and saw fear, but she also saw safety and love. Jax steadied her and opened the passenger door. Once she was inside and all the vents were pointing at her, she smiled at Jax. "Make me two promises."

"Why am I not surprised you're already making demands of me?"

"Shush," she said, raising one finger. "Promise me we'll face any memories that come back together, no matter how bad it is."

"I promise."

Gretchen raised a second finger. "And promise me you'll never, ever let me give up coffee again."

Jax's laughter carried over the music on the radio and the hum of tires against asphalt. "I promise."

Gretchen laid her head back against the seat and listened to a woman sing about love. She considered her past and the future she was finally excited to live. Without forgetting, she never would've remembered what mattered most.

1,460 days, 11 hours, 12 minutes

Gretchen awoke with a start. "I had a dream Caleb rode an elephant. Did that really happen?"

Jax poked out from the mound of pillows. "What?" she said with one eye cracked open.

Gretchen sat up on one elbow. "He was about three. We were at a zoo, maybe, and he rode an elephant. Did that really happen?" Dreams like this were a common occurrence, and Gretchen believed they could be memories trying to return. She refused to give up hope that those four years would eventually return to her. And Jax, with all her patience, humored her every time.

"No. He never rode an elephant. Now, go back to sleep. It's Sunday, and Sundays are made for sleeping late."

"I can't go back to sleep now," she said, sitting up. She hugged a pillow to her chest. "It felt so real. I thought I finally got one back."

Jax wrapped her arm around Gretchen's waist and laid her head against her hip. "I know, baby. I'm sorry."

Gretchen looked down at Jax, who appeared to be falling back asleep against her. Jax's breath tickled the exposed skin of her hipbone, and her pink hair looked vibrant against their white pillowcases. "You could always help me fall back asleep."

Jax stirred and kissed Gretchen's skin. "Wish I could, too tired."

"Jax Levine, choosing sleep over sex. We're officially old."

Jax ran her hand up Gretchen's thigh and into her shorts. "It's not about age. It's about exhaustion and not wanting to get caught again."

"The kids are sleeping."

"Nuh-uh. Serena is sneaky," Jax said.

"And soon to be ours forever."

Jax jumped up and covered Gretchen's mouth. "Don't jinx it!" They had filed the adoption papers after being Serena's foster parents for over six months. Serena's caseworker had promised to contact them soon.

Gretchen kissed Jax's palm. "You're very cute, but there's no such thing as jinxing."

"That's exactly what people say before they get jinxed."

She framed Jax's face with her hands and looked in her eyes. She examined the lines surrounding the sparkling blue. Jax's graceful aging and constant wisdom continued to amaze her. "I love you so much." She kissed Jax sweetly. "Even if you're crazy."

"Crazy for you," Jax said, wiggling her eyebrows. She kissed Gretchen again.

Gretchen kept her lips within a breath of Jax's mouth. "Promise me something."

"Anything."

"Be mine forever?"

Jax smirked. "You always make these promises so easy."

"Promise me."

"I promise."

"And promise me you'll get rid of those awful cargo shorts."

"I love those shorts."

"They're dad shorts," Gretchen said, breaking out into a grin. "If we're going to have a daughter now, she needs proper fashion influences."

"And what about Caleb?"

"I will keep him from wearing similar cargo shorts."

Jax poked her sides, giggling as she pinned her to the mattress. "You're so mean. You make fun of my shorts like you never went through an olive drab phase."

"We agreed to never speak of that again."

"Let me keep one pair of shorts, and I'll keep your secret."

She loved these playful moments—the ones where Jax would smile down at her with mischief in her eyes. These were some of her favorite memories. "You sure do drive a hard bargain."

A faint knock sounded at the bedroom door. Jax moved off Gretchen but allowed no distance between their bodies.

"Come in."

The door opened slowly and Caleb poked his head in. "Hey,

Moms, I know it's early, but can I play Nintendo in the living room? I don't want to wake Serena."

Gretchen's heart melted into a puddle of pure happiness. "Of course you can—just keep it down. Bug and I want to relax for a little bit longer."

He nodded and left just as quickly as he came.

"He needs to stop growing," Jax said through a big yawn.

"Please." Gretchen fell back into her pillows and stretched her arms over her head. "If he stops growing, maybe I'll stop getting old. Every time I look in the mirror, I find another wrinkle."

Jax propped herself up on her elbow. She traced the lines of Gretchen's face with a delicate touch. "Funny, every time I look at you, I find another reason why you're the most beautiful woman I've ever seen."

She grinned and patted Jax's cheek. "You're smooth, but you missed your chance to get laid today. Caleb's already up, and I promised Serena you'd teach her how to paint a giraffe after I make chocolate chip *and* blueberry pancakes, which means I have to get up really soon."

"Just a quick lightning round."

"You could've had all the rounds last night, but you stayed at the studio." She ran her hands across Jax's broad shoulders, silently encouraging her to continue.

"*Mmmm*…" Jax dipped her hands under Gretchen's shirt. "But my installation is almost done, which means I'll be yours all day and all night soon. You can have me whenever you want me."

Gretchen sucked in a breath when Jax touched her nipples. "Guess I'll be taking a few days off to play catch-up."

"That's what I like to hear." Jax kissed her as she trailed her hand lower at a painfully slow pace.

Gretchen clamped her thighs closed. "You made me wait—now I make you wait."

"That's not fair," Jax whined. "I was working."

She got out of bed and smiled at Jax over her shoulder. "And I have to go be a doting mother to our children." She grabbed her phone from the nightstand and turned to Jax.

Jax covered her face with her hand. "You really don't have to do that every morning."

Gretchen took one picture. "Yes, I do," she said, taking another. "Now smile." She took one more picture of Jax, then put her phone down. "I don't want to risk fully forgetting anything ever again. Especially any little thing about you or our family."

"The map layout for the kitchen cabinets was a bit much," Jax said, throwing the covers aside and standing. She stretched her arms and back.

"That only lasted a week after we moved."

"A very long week."

Gretchen pulled her unruly hair up and secured it atop her head. "Stop complaining and get moving."

"You're so bossy." Jax wrapped her arms around Gretchen's waist and held her close. "I love it."

"I love you." She leaned in and kissed Jax. They had always been mushy and affectionate with one another, but since her accident and the near death of their marriage, Gretchen didn't want to let one moment slip away without making sure Jax knew how she felt.

Jax's hands started to wander again, clearly in search of another attempt at morning love, but an unkempt and sleepy Serena swung the door open.

"Hungry," she said, her voice firm and full of three-year-old attitude. Serena rubbed her eyes.

Gretchen looked at the little girl, her heart swelling at how perfectly her spicy personality fit into the family. Her blue eyes nearly matched Jax's in depth and sparkle. Pure mischief. "Blueberry and chocolate chip pancakes, coming right up."

"I want gapes."

"Grapes?"

"Gapes."

"Okay."

"Gape pancakes." Serena started to giggle. Jax's chortle was loud in Gretchen's ear.

"Sweetheart," Gretchen said, kneeling to look Serena in the eye. "People don't put grapes in pancakes."

Serena's frown grew so deep, everything angelic about her small face disappeared. "Gape pancakes." The words left her mouth on a shriek.

Gretchen stood quickly. "I can make grape pancakes."

"And they'll be delicious," Jax said, not helping matters, but the small kiss she placed on Gretchen's cheek did. Jax lifted Serena over her shoulder. "Let's go, kiddo. We need to clean you up before you get any gapes."

Her cheeks hurt from grinning as she watched Jax carry their almost-daughter away. She took a deep breath, closed her eyes, and listened carefully. She heard the faint sound of Caleb's video game and Jax's footsteps thumping down the hallway. The birds were chirping outside, and summer bugs were buzzing, hinting that the day would be hot. Gretchen cherished every detail of every day because she knew it could be stolen at any moment. But what she also knew, without a doubt, was that the heart remembered so much more than the brain ever could.

The heart remembered love, and that's all Gretchen ever really needed.

About the Author

M. Ullrich has always called New Jersey home and currently resides by the beach with her wife and boisterous feline children. After many years of regarding her writing as just a hobby, the gentle yet persistent words of encouragement from her wife pushed M. Ullrich to take a leap into the world of publishing. Much to her delight and amazement, that world embraced her back.

Although M. Ullrich may work full-time in the optical field, her favorite hours are the ones she spends writing and eating ridiculously large portions of breakfast foods for every meal. When her pen isn't furiously trying to capture her imagination (a rare occasion), she enjoys being a complete entertainer. Whether she's telling an elaborate story or a joke, or getting up in front of a crowd to sing and dance her way through her latest karaoke selection, M. Ullrich will do just about anything to make others smile. She also happens to be fluent in three languages: English, sarcasm, and TV/movie quotes.

Books Available From Bold Strokes Books

Face the Music by Ali Vali. Sweet music is the last thing that happens when Nashville music producer Mason Liner and daughter of country royalty Victoria Roddy are thrown together in an effort to save country star Sophie Roddy's career. (978-1-63555-532-5)

Flavor of the Month by Georgia Beers. What happens when baker Charlie and chef Emma realize their differing paths have led them right back to each other? (978-1-63555-616-2)

Mending Fences by Angie Williams. Rancher Bobbie Del Rey and veterinarian Grace Hammond are about to discover if heartbreaks of the past can ever truly be mended. (978-1-63555-708-4)

Silk and Leather: Lesbian Erotica with an Edge, edited by Victoria Villaseñor. This collection of stories by award-winning authors offers fantasies as soft as silk and tough as leather. The only question is: How far will you go to make your deepest desires come true? (978-1-63555-587-5)

The Last Place You Look by Aurora Rey. Dumped by her wife and looking for anything but love, Julia Pierce retreats to her hometown only to rediscover high school friend Taylor Winslow, who's secretly crushed on her for years. (978-1-63555-574-5)

The Mortician's Daughter by Nan Higgins. A singer on the verge of stardom discovers she must give up her dreams to live a life in service to ghosts. (978-1-63555-594-3)

The Real Thing by Laney Webber. When passion flares between actress Virginia Green and masseuse Allison McDonald, can they be sure it's the real thing? (978-1-63555-478-6)

What the Heart Remembers Most by M. Ullrich. For college sweethearts Jax Levine and Gretchen Mills, could an accident be the second chance neither knew they wanted? (978-1-63555-401-4)

White Horse Point by Andrews & Austin. Mystery writer Taylor James finds herself falling for the mysterious woman on White Horse Point who lives alone, protecting a secret she can't share about a murderer who walks among them. (978-1-63555-695-7)

Femme Tales by Anne Shade. Six women find themselves in their own real-life fairy tales when true love finds them in the most unexpected ways. (978-1-63555-657-5)

Jellicle Girl by Stevie Mikayne. One dark summer night, Beth and Jackie go out to the canoe dock. Two years later, Beth is still carrying the weight of what happened to Jackie. (978-1-63555-691-9)

My Date with a Wendigo by Genevieve McCluer. Elizabeth Rosseau finds her long-lost love and the secret community of fiends she's now a part of. (978-1-63555-679-7)

On the Run by Charlotte Greene. Even when they're cute blondes, it's stupid to pick up hitchhikers, especially when they've just broken out of prison, but doing so is about to change Gwen's life forever. (978-1-63555-682-7)

Perfect Timing by Dena Blake. The choice between love and family has never been so difficult, and Lynn's and Maggie's different visions of the future may end their romance before it's begun. (978-1-63555-466-3)

The Mail Order Bride by R. Kent. When a mail order bride is thrust on Austin, he must choose between the bride he never wanted or the dream he lives for. (978-1-63555-678-0)

Through Love's Eyes by C.A. Popovich. When fate reunites Brittany Yardin and Amy Jansons, can they move beyond the pain of their past to find love? (978-1-63555-629-2)

To the Moon and Back by Melissa Brayden. Film actress Carly Daniel thinks that stage work is boring and unexciting, but when she accepts a lead role in a new play, stage manager Lauren Prescott tests both her heart and her ability to share the limelight. (978-1-63555-618-6)

Tokyo Love by Diana Jean. When Kathleen Schmitt is given the opportunity to be on the cutting edge of AI technology, she never thought a failed robotic love companion would bring her closer to her neighbor, Yuriko Velucci, and finding love in unexpected places. (978-1-63555-681-0)